the weight we carry

LOGAN MEREDITH

Riptide Publishing
PO Box 1537
Burnsville, NC 28714
www.riptidepublishing.com

This is a work of fiction. Names, characters, places, and incidents are either the product of the author's imagination or are used fictitiously. Any resemblance to actual persons living or dead, business establishments, events, or locales is entirely coincidental. All person(s) depicted on the cover are model(s) used for illustrative purposes only.

The Weight We Carry
Copyright © 2021 by Logan Meredith

Cover art: L.C. Chase, lcchase.com
Editors: Veronica Vega, Carole-ann Galloway
Layout: L.C. Chase, lcchase.com

All rights reserved. No part of this book may be reproduced or transmitted in any form or by any means, electronic or mechanical, including photocopying, recording, or by any information storage and retrieval system without the written permission of the publisher, and where permitted by law. Reviewers may quote brief passages in a review. To request permission and all other inquiries, contact Riptide Publishing at the mailing address above, at Riptidepublishing.com, or at marketing@riptidepublishing.com.

ISBN: 978-1-62649-943-0

First edition
April, 2021

Also available in ebook:
ISBN: 978-1-62649-944-7

LOGAN MEREDITH

This book is dedicated to Walt, who loved me and my fuck-ton of extra baggage.

Table of Contents

Chapter 1 1
Chapter 2 19
Chapter 3 31
Chapter 4 51
Chapter 5 65
Chapter 6 83
Chapter 7 97
Chapter 8 109
Chapter 9 119
Chapter 10 133
Chapter 11 151
Chapter 12 163
Chapter 13 181
Chapter 14 191
Chapter 15 201
Chapter 16 215
Chapter 17 229
Chapter 18 235
Chapter 19 241
Chapter 20 249
Chapter 21 257
Chapter 22 261
Chapter 23 269

Chapter One
Brady

Josh's fingertips dug into my shoulder as he marched me to my execution. The manner of my death—a painstakingly selected stack of denim and "fun but not too flashy" XXL shirts.

"Would you stop making that face?"

The corners of my mouth lost all structure at Josh's chastising tone. When he wasn't plotting death blows to my fledgling self-esteem, Josh Meyer doubled as my roommate and best friend.

"You're going to look amazing."

On the surface, Josh had the terminal optimism that rivaled most motivational speakers. After six years, I knew better. Don't get me wrong: Josh was the best. He was generous, intelligent, and hardworking . . . but complicated. I liked to think we'd gotten past the need for him to mat talk me through this shopping trip, but here we were.

His perpetually sunny disposition didn't bother me unless I thought he was forcing it, which he did occasionally, or I was irritable. And since I'd spent yet another month wasting my hard-earned degree as a glorified receptionist–slash–administrative assistant, irritable had been my default setting.

In the competition for things that annoyed me, Josh's enthusiasm met its match at the back of a platinum-blonde woman in a skirt so short I wondered how she sat. She sorted through clothes, bobbed her head, and swayed to the in-store music. Her long ponytail oscillated back and forth like a pendulum ticking away moments of her obliviousness. I exchanged an amused acknowledgment with Josh, and when I rolled my eyes, Josh cleared his throat to cover my snicker.

She turned, and her eyes flew past me to focus on Josh. *Typical.*

"Oh. Hey." She dropped her shoulder and pushed it forward, gaping her v-shaped neckline and expanding our view of her ample cleavage. Unashamed, I looked. Josh didn't. He still carried some PTSD-like reactions to boobs. Not for the first time, I wondered why, but he hated talking about his straight-high-school-football-star days, and I respected that.

On the other hand, I liked them. I didn't want to grope them or anything, but they sort of mesmerized me, and sometimes I fought the urge to bat them like a cat with a piece of string.

"He has twelve items." Josh flashed his toothy smile standing right next to the sign that declared the limit was six.

She swooned, and I involuntarily scoffed, which might have been joined by a muttered, "For fuck's sake," or something equally inappropriate. I'd tired of Josh's "too pretty for rules" nonsense, and honestly, I had zero control over my mouth. Not what came out of it and certainly not what went into it.

Two glares—one confused (Blondie) and one irritated (Josh)—turned my direction. I shifted the clothes to my left hand, taking a second to wiggle my fingers and restore the blood flow to my right. Fat jeans weighed a fuck-ton. Rolling my eyes, I pointed to the sign.

"Oh," Josh drawled, then smiled again, his eyes wide and innocent, before dragging his lower lip between his irritatingly straight and white teeth. "What's your name?"

"Misty." She giggled, and the sharp jab of Josh's elbow landed into my ribs, cutting off my annoyed huff midexhale. I coughed, and a little phlegm flew out of my mouth and landed on one of the shirts I surprisingly didn't loathe. Totally worth ruining the last one like that in my size to see how far apart Misty's eyes would go. *Impressive.*

"My friend has a big date in less than twelve hours. Do you think you might help us out and let us take these back to the dressing room?"

She glanced at me briefly with an ambiguous wave of her hand, like she didn't care what I did, as long as I removed myself from her presence. Which, I would've happily obliged were it not for the fact that Josh's eyeballs were warning me not to leave him alone with her.

"What about you? Do you have a date tonight?" Her eyes locked on Josh and I knew I couldn't abandon him. When Josh flirted with girls, he wasn't interested in bending anything but the rules, but Misty clearly hadn't picked up on that.

Man or woman, young or old—Josh flirted. They always flirted back. The earth revolved around the sun. So on and so on. The only one spared from his charm offensive seemed to be me.

My stomach gurgled, and Misty scowled in my direction. I hadn't eaten in preparation for this little self-flagellation, and a belly like mine tended to get a bit pissy when deprived of regular meals.

Her sardonic expression blossomed. *Ugh.* Of all the ways I'd been put down over the years, that look of revulsion still cut. If Josh's stomach growled, she'd rub his belly and offer to make him a sandwich, but my stomach she treated like an IED about to explode.

"I just need a new shirt. I have jeans." I launched the jeans at Misty, but Josh's ninja reflexes snatched them back and pushed them against my chest.

"You cannot wear your jeans tonight. They are way too baggy. He won't be able to see your ass." Josh's voice gained an octave and the sheer horror he displayed at my fashion choices sent out red flares of gay.

"Oh," Misty breathed, and her expression landed somewhere between hard-ass professional and bona fide mean girl. "He's right. The limit is six."

Josh pouted, more at me than at Misty, but Josh's puppy-dog eyes were gender neutral in their effectiveness.

Misty's stance softened. "But there are two of you..." she hedged. *Don't give in, Misty.* "So, I guess you could each take back six items." She freed two plastic door hangers that bore a large number six on them. "Let me know if you need anything."

I snatched the tags from her hand and beelined for the last dressing room—the accessible stall, which I know, I know... However, mild claustrophobia *is* a disability. Besides, none of the other rooms had a place to sit, and we'd been walking and standing for hours. I tossed the jeans on the floor and hung the shirts on one of the three hooks opposite the mirror. As I sat, Josh's feet appeared under the stall door accompanied by a firm knock. "Brady, let me in."

"No way," I insisted. "If I'm doing this, I'm doing it alone."

"Fine. But show me each pair. Your ass is thick. You need to show it off."

Sighing, I stood and turned to check out my backside in the mirror. In most circles, *thick* implied muscular. Josh's perky cheeks, for example, were firm and round and probably had sexy dimples on them when he flexed. My ass dimples were courtesy of cellulite. I unbuckled my belt, removed my shirt, and lowered my pants and, in an afterthought, my boxers. My task had zero use for bulky underwear. I tugged at and stretched my skin, but a Shar-Pei puppy had a better chance of pulling off a tight body.

What a ridiculous way to waste an afternoon. The jeans wouldn't fit. My ass hadn't been squeezed into a size forty-two in well over a year. The last time I'd tried, it required a prolonged fast, a thorough cleanse, and a warped sort of gymnastics to get them on. There remained one lonely pair in the *someday* pile in the back of my closet. Josh had always complimented me when I wore them, and I'd paid a small fortune for them, so I saved them in case I was lucky enough to contract a tapeworm or some tropical disease like dysentery. *Is dysentery a tropical disease?* I wasn't sure. Regardless, forty-two was solidly in the "need a life-threatening illness to fit" category now.

I picked up the first pair and held them to my body, lifted my left leg, and slid it into the pants. The fabric pulled tight at my calf, and I inserted my right leg, then yanked at the denim. About midthigh, my legs bore an uncanny resemblance to sausages, and flab overflowed from the top. The blood flow cut off as I wiggled the fabric over my ass, and the zipper teeth bit into my skin while I struggled to protect the essential parts of my anatomy. Inhaling deeply, I tugged as hard as I could to bring the button to its hole. Within seconds, I was sweating profusely and still inches from my goal. I squatted to stretch the fabric, and an ominous ripping sound stole the last vestiges of my dignity.

No. No. NOOO.

I braced my hand on the wall and hovered midsquat, mouthing curse words. My thighs burned, and I tried to straighten my legs to minimize the damage, praying there was some defect in the fabric to blame.

One glance down and the herniated fat pushing through the inner thigh of the heavy denim gave me my answer. I closed my eyes, lost my balance, and collapsed onto the small triangular seat with a thud. Another prolonged ripping noise pierced my soul like a knife.

I stared at the pale, fleshy blob sandwiched between jagged denim edges with disgust. How had I let this happen? I didn't have some trauma in my life I could point to and say, *That! That's why I have no willpower. That's why I don't take care of myself.*

My previous go-to excuse had also expired. I'd mostly grown out of the childhood asthma that had put the kibosh on sports, and I'd ceased the daily steroid breathing treatments before high school. *Face it. You're lazy and have a weak character.*

Slouching my five-foot-ten frame, I forced my abdominal rolls into tangible evidence to justify my self-loathing and jiggled it, wondering how much longer I had before I'd be one of those poor saps who couldn't reach his own dick to jerk off.

A knock at the door startled me— "C'mon. I want to see. I know you have the first pair on." *Ugh. Josh.*

"Almost," I lied and rolled the denim down. I folded the jeans to hide the rip and yanked on my own jeans.

Josh huffed an inpatient sigh. "Christ, Brady. I can see your legs."

I flung open the door. Josh's face flashed irritation, then melted into concern. He opened his mouth, probably to say something encouraging, but I held up my hand.

"This is pointless. They aren't gonna fit, Josh. I need a forty-four." Actually, a forty-six because I preferred baggy clothes these days, but why quibble over semantics? The shredded jeans had become a metaphor for his fantasy of me walking out of the mall with a date-perfect outfit.

"Why didn't you say so?" Josh's face brightened. Too brightly. That was his *I can fix this* look. "I'll go grab them." Before I could object, he scurried away. *Surely, he . . . Well, no. I guess he wouldn't have any experience with a store not having his size.* I debated letting him figure it out on his own, but after considering the likelihood that Misty would be involved in sorting it out, decided against it.

"Josh, wait."

Josh rotated toward me. "Why?"

My humiliation rose to the surface, choking off my words. Josh's carefree smile dimmed, and the second he realized I wasn't okay he stepped toward me. "What's wrong?"

I glanced around the empty dressing room and jerked my arm in a come-here motion. Josh returned to me, the usual bounce in his step noticeably absent. I tugged him inside the dressing room, and the momentum sent him stumbling into me. When he reached out to steady himself, a surprised breath sweetened by the fruit smoothie Josh had earlier mingled with my own.

"Sorry." Josh's hands slipped lower on my hips. Our eyes met, and a little spark of awareness sent a shiver up my spine. For a brief moment his expression changed, almost like he . . .

I shook my head to remove the thoughts. The lack of food was making me hallucinate. "No problem." Josh released me, and I took a step back as my brain returned from fantasyland to real life.

Josh cleared his throat, shifting uncomfortably. "What's up?"

"They don't have a forty-four, Josh. This is the largest size they carry in this store."

Admirably resisting his urge to be optimistic, Josh accepted my declaration with a furrowed brow and pursed lips. "Since when?"

I guffawed. "Since forever. Most stores in the mall don't carry my size, which is why I'm gonna wear what I usually do. It won't matter anyway. This guy isn't going to be interested in me. I'm not good at dating. We're going to dinner, so I'll spend money I don't have to eat a salad with kale or some shit like that and talk about the gym, so he'll think maybe I'm trying to do something about myself." Shame burned my cheeks as I detailed my inevitable humiliation. Josh's eyes bugged out at my rambling, but I kept going, frustrated that he didn't understand how hard dating was for me.

"Meanwhile, I'll spill something on my new shirt like a total slob. Then this guy is going to make an excuse for why he needs to call it an early night, and I'll never hear from him again. And that's if I'm lucky and he doesn't bolt before we get to dinner."

Josh's big hands closed on my head and massaged my temples. "I wish you wouldn't get so down on yourself. You're a great guy. Any man would be lucky to have you."

Josh tugged me into his arms and squeezed. He didn't understand. He had no idea how much he took for granted. I tried not to fault him. Guys *like* him? Sure. With rare exception, I begrudged anyone who sported a sculpted body. Never had that been in the cards for me. I came out of the womb weighing twelve pounds—double the average newborn. Even my baby clothes were too small.

"I'm sweaty," I said, freeing a hand to wipe my nose and sniffled.

"I don't care." Josh laced a hand through my hair and petted me. The tension in my neck and shoulders eased at his touch, despite desperately wanting my shirt on and dreading the wet spot my chest would leave. To say I was "not a hugger" would be an understatement, but with Josh, I'd learned it was best to go with it.

I owed the gods a sacrifice for our roommate match. After being outed in his close-minded small town, Josh needed new friends and as his roommate, I was convenient, but through the years we became inseparable. Now, Josh's hugs were some of the few I tolerated.

When my emotions threatened to turn liquid, I broke away and grabbed my shirt. "I'm starving," I declared. "Let's go to McDonald's."

Josh laughed and tussled my hair. Although I was older by two months, sometimes he treated me like a little brother. I never figured out how to process the affection he sent my way, and I was sure he didn't realize how easily a guy like me could read something more into it, but I liked it enough that I didn't say anything that might discourage him.

"How about we go home? I'll make those turkey-stuffed peppers you like."

A half smile crept onto my face. I did like Josh's peppers. "Fine, but don't skimp on the cheese this time, and I'll know if you use that low-fat bullshit."

"Deal." Josh laughed. "But I'm making mine without cheese."

"Whatever," I muttered as I replaced my shirt and slipped on my shoes.

"What? I've put on weight too." Josh lifted his shirt, and I nearly swallowed my tongue.

"Yeah. You should really increase the gym trips to seven times a week. Five clearly isn't cutting it."

Josh swatted the back of my head.

"Ouch," I cried, before he smoothed my hair. He led me out of the dressing room, then the store.

A pang of nostalgia hit me. "This was nice," I said suddenly. "Seems like it's been forever since we hung out just the two of us."

Josh's face tensed like he thought I was blaming him instead of my empty wallet, so I added, "I wouldn't want to deal with my grumpy ass either. I know you're busy. You charge me next to nothing to live in your house, and I practically have the whole place to myself."

Josh flashed a brief contrite smile. "It's our house. And work should slow down for me." When I gave him a questioning look, he sighed. "Ken reassigned the Peterson Furniture account to Larry."

Larry was Josh's work nemesis. Their boss, Ken, had been pitting them against each other since they were both interns and were told they were competing for the same job. I'd never met the guy, but I was duty-bound to hate him too. It pissed me off that anyone would try to get ahead by making Josh look bad. "You're kidding? What did Ken say this time? You worked your ass off on that one."

Josh shrugged. "It is what it is."

I debated letting his nonanswer go. Josh struggled with anything he perceived as a failure, and the last thing I wanted to do was send him down a shame spiral. "I'm sure you'll get the next one."

"And I'm sure you'll get a better job soon."

"I hope so. If not, I'm going to have to sell a kidney."

Josh shook his head. "Quit it with that."

"I mean it, Josh. If it weren't for you letting me live—"

"Brady, it's fine. Stop, okay?"

Tension followed us to the car. His lower lip was tucked between his teeth as he walked. *Ah, hell.* He was working up the courage to say something else. Josh had two big problems: he had ridiculously high expectations of himself, and he hated disappointing people. Which basically guaranteed he'd put up with far more than most before complaining about anything. It was the main reason I'd been sweating the bills so much. I hated that money, or my lack of it, had become a factor in our friendship. I'd watched my mom struggle long enough that I wasn't about to run up credit card debt trying to keep up. Every time I told him I couldn't go out, he looked so hurt, but when I let him pay, I felt like I was taking advantage of him. All the stress was doing a number on my waistline, which in turn made me a cranky bastard.

We slid into the leather interior of my car, recently cleaned for my upcoming date. The air freshener Josh had picked tickled my nose. My airway bitched up a storm around certain chemicals and smells. I started the car and cracked the windows to air it out, then twisted to buckle my seat belt. Josh had his focus set on me, and his lip tucked between his teeth again.

Oh, boy. Here it comes.

"Come workout with me tomorrow."

I couldn't help the laugh that escaped. "I'm not going to your gym."

"Why not?" His hand rested over mine on the gearshift, preventing us from going anywhere until I answered. "Look. I know you're frustrated about the job hunt, but you have to find ways to relax. Exercise is great for stress relief. We can invite Adam if you want to."

I rolled my eyes. Adam was our friend and my former obsession. Like being the fat guy at a gym wasn't bad enough, I sure as hell didn't want to be standing next to the two most attractive men in the room. "Canal Street Gym is a meat market, and I can't afford it."

Josh thought on that for a beat with a pensive expression. Great. I'd activated the problem-solving wheels in his brain. Should have just said no.

"Fine. Let's go running, then. We can start slow."

I glared at Josh as though he'd proposed climbing Mt. Everest. He laughed, breaking the tension momentarily, and making me laugh too.

"What? It's something people do, Brady. It's not as hard as you think."

"No, thanks," I deadpanned.

"Brady. Please. I hate seeing you so down on yourself. If you don't like the way you feel, please do one thing to change it. You know you can talk to me, right?"

I hated the hesitation in Josh's voice. I knew he'd always support me, but I'd been less than forthcoming about everything I was going through in the last few months. More for my sanity than anything. I couldn't handle his disappointment along with my own. Interview after interview, I'd walk away thinking I'd nailed it only to find out I didn't get the job. "I know. Can we please go eat? My blood sugar is dropping, and I'm getting cranky."

"Fine." Josh released an exasperated sigh and lifted his hand. I took advantage of the reprieve and put the car in reverse. After living together for six years, Josh and I were both clear on the location of each other's red lines. However, as quickly as Josh retreated if I stepped near his, my date tonight was proof that he had no issues about kicking rocks over mine.

At six that evening, Josh's persistent throat clearing risked causing him permanent damage. Yes, I needed to start getting ready. No, I didn't want to stop playing the game I had used to distract myself thank you very much. I completed the mission I'd been stuck on for three days moments before Josh took matters into his own hands and switched off the television.

"Hey!" I objected.

"Brady. If you don't get in the shower in the next thirty seconds, I'll drag you in there myself. You haven't dated in months."

Technically, I'd reached the one-year mark three weeks before, but the clarification seemed unnecessary. With a sigh, I tossed my controller on the couch seat next to me. "Fine."

I trudged to our shared bathroom and ignored the looming figure behind me. Twisting to conceal the stretch marks on my left love handle, I peeled off my shirt and held it over me for cover.

I turned on the water, sat on the edge of the tub, and toed off my shoes and socks. Josh hadn't moved. "Am I in prison now? Gotta have a guard to watch me shower?" And now I was being an asshole. Great. "Sorry," I grumbled.

Josh pouted and shook off my apology. "Just making sure you don't flee out the window."

I glanced above the tub at the small square window and huffed. "Like my ass would fit through that," I mumbled. Steam began to fill the room, and I reached for the faucet.

"Brady. Enough." The harshness of Josh's tone was reminiscent of my stepfather's tough-love voice.

I nudged the dial to adjust the water temperature then turned toward him. "Jesus, now what?"

A sheepish expression replaced his resting smile. "Sorry," Josh muttered. "I thought you were going to turn it off."

"Was that an option?"

"Please trust me. You need to do this. It's one dinner." Josh didn't have to keep repeating the mantra. He was right. I was in a rut, and all a rut ever got me was a bigger clothing size. "I thought you liked him?"

"Yeah. He's all right, I guess." So far, chats with Matt had shown promise. He wasn't anywhere close to as perfect as Josh, but then that was the point. Matt was obtainable.

I eyed Josh, allowing a moment to appreciate his physical attributes. It was hard to pinpoint exactly what made Josh so damn attractive. He was above-average height, his body rivaled Hollywood's leading men, and he was blessed with skin that tanned easily, but lots of men had those things. His face though—that was the real draw. It was so symmetrical that even a small freckle on the right side of his angular jaw had a perfect match on the left.

Josh heaved an impatient sigh. "Is this still about Adam?"

"No." Adam had been my excuse to not try to meet someone far longer than he'd been my reason for it. He'd made it abundantly clear he wasn't interested in me, but my go-to move in college had been to pine wordlessly and fall on my mattress with angsty sighs, so I'd stuck with what I knew. It had sucked, but the idea of putting myself out there for real sucked ten times harder.

Josh's skepticism was delivered with a pointed stare and a single arched eyebrow. "Great, then there is nothing keeping you from having a good time tonight."

I sighed acquiescence. I would go on this date. Josh had the best of intentions. He always had the best intentions. He was near perfect in that way. I sort of owed it to him after the months of attitude I'd given him. Josh went through a lot of trouble to set up a dating profile for me and even managed to take some halfway decent photos. Not that I thought I was ugly. I had big blue eyes and a full head of mahogany-brown hair that was easy to style, straight teeth, and clear skin. Like the rest of my body, my face was too round, and only one of my chins was strong, but with a proper angle and lighting, I pulled off a decent headshot. Nothing was going to make me sexy—no Instagram filter was *that* good, but neck up wasn't awful.

"Brady." Josh's plea drew me out of my contemplations.

"What?"

"Shower."

I nodded and pulled the curtain back. "All right. Fine. You win. I'll date Matt. I'll fuck him. We'll fall in love and get married and tell our future children how their Uncle Josh forced me to go on our first date. Happy now?"

Josh nodded with an expression that registered a far cry from happy, but before I could apologize for my outburst, he left and shut the door behind him. Not long after while brushing my teeth, I heard the garage door open and close, and came out of the bathroom to find an empty house and a note from Josh.

Good luck tonight. Have fun.

At seven on the nose, I entered Campriani's Italian Restaurant still puzzled by Josh's disappearing act. It's not like I expected him to hand-hold me through getting ready, but he hadn't mentioned having plans earlier. When I texted to see where he'd gone, he didn't answer. Not even when I threatened to stay home. I considered that it might be Josh's way of helping me not be nervous. Like maybe if he racked me with enough guilt for snapping at him, there'd be no room left for anxiety.

He wasn't really pissed because, well, Josh never got mad at me. Frustrated? Sure. Exasperated? Often. Disappointed? More than I liked. But never angry. Plus, he left the note on one of my more flattering shirts, freshly ironed, on my bed with my jeans and his favorite Cole Haan loafers. Josh had an extensive shoe collection that had tripled since we'd left college. If I ever gained so much that we wore different shoe sizes... I shivered, unable to contemplate such a cruel world. I doubted I had worn one of the five pairs I owned in over a year. He'd also left his favorite cologne on my dresser. I hadn't worn it. On the odd chance things between Matt and me turned toward sexy town, it would be hella-weird to smell Josh.

I made my way through the weekend-night crowd to the hostess stand. My phone vibrated with an incoming text. Across the room, Matt sat at the row of tables for two against the wall, alone, phone in hand. He glanced up and waved, and I bypassed the hostess and weaved my way toward him.

"Hey, Brady." Matt stood and greeted me with a loose side hug. The forced intimacy sent my stomach acid racing up my throat. He motioned to my seat, which backed up to an occupied chair at the next table. I sized up the easement and froze. Even if I pulled the chair all the way back, I'd be eating with my gut heaved on the table or the table digging into my stomach. Neither sounded appetizing.

Matt smiled acknowledgment. "Will you be more comfortable over here?"

"Do you mind?"

"Of course not. I took this seat so I would see you walk in." Matt placed his hands on my shoulders and squeezed affectionately. He slid past me and took the seat I'd rejected. Inwardly, I sighed relief, and a fleeting moment of optimism tickled my brain. Maybe my date wasn't going to be a flaming pile of dog shit. I smiled, knowing Josh would be proud of me for that.

Once we were settled and had ordered our drinks, Matt kicked off the first-date conversation by exploring the menu options with me. He'd already decided on a dish from the specials list, but that menu had no prices. He highly recommended their Fettuccine Campriani.

I found the description and paused at the cream-based sauce. "Um. I'm trying to avoid white sauce. Anything else you'd suggest?"

Matt frowned as though I'd rejected him and not his suggestion.

"Or did you want to share?" I offered.

"No. I have some food restrictions to deal with and don't want to limit you. Please get whatever you want. If you're aiming for something on the lighter side, their chopped salad is pretty good, or you can get any of their penne options with whole wheat pasta. The arrabiata sauce is amazing, but I'll warn you it is very spicy."

I perused the menu on my own for a minute. By the time I eliminated the red sauce items for stain prevention and the white sauce options for fat-shaming prevention, I was down to the chopped salad and Chicken Caesar, which in a happy coincidence were the least-expensive items on the menu. The server arrived, and Matt ordered the shrimp special. The server seemed a little too surprised at my choice of the chopped salad with a light dressing. *Yes, the fat man ordered a salad. Alert the media.*

Matt and I had already discovered a shared interest in the Mission to Mars video game series, so we burned most of the conversation time before our meals arrived discussing the latest release. "Have you found the glitch on the Isidis basin mission?" I'd spent three weeks figuring out how best to exploit it.

"Not yet. I bought it last week but haven't had much time to play."

"It's kind of complicated, but when you go into the room where you get the mission briefing, there's a door on the right. If you go through it before the briefing is over, you can score an unlimited oxygen tank and everything you need to survive the Tharsis volcano eruption. If you wait until it's over, you get a regular six-hour tank, and you have to upgrade your heat shield at least three times to survive."

Matt flashed an amused smile and nodded. "Cool. Maybe when I get there, you can come over and talk me through it."

"Sure," I agreed, before his offer fully translated into a potential second date. As I considered the ramifications of that, our meals arrived.

I managed to contribute a few witty stories and some thoughtful questions, but Matt carried most of the conversation for the remainder of our meal. He was interesting and friendly. I liked him enough that I gave myself a moment to consider if I found him attractive. Matt reminded me of the men in the J.C. Penney's catalogs my mom used to get—handsome, yet kind of *meh* about it too. For a guy like me, that should be #goals.

Matt's body-type fell into the black hole of descriptions the app used: he lacked muscle tone, so *athletic* didn't seem correct, but neither *slender* nor *a few extra pounds* would have been more accurate, so I didn't fault him for his choice. I wagered he didn't own a gym membership, but did something physical on the weekends, like playing golf. The app listed his eyes as green, but in the dim lighting, they appeared brown. His front teeth had a slight gap, which explained all the closed-mouth smiles in his profile pictures. Still, I liked that he was taller than me. And the way he regularly ran his fingers through his full head of product-free, silky brown hair. He laughed generously at my jokes and showed far more interest in what I said than what I ate.

At the end of the meal, the server cleared our plates and offered us dessert. Matt raised a questioning eyebrow at me but followed suit when I politely declined. About five minutes later, the server brought our check. Matt ignored the leather folder and continued his story unbothered. Usually, I could set my watch to a date ending the evening immediately following my last bite. My fingers twitched, and I suppressed the urge to reach for my . . . *Oh, shit!*

With a sudden jerk, I checked my pocket. *Nothing.*

"You okay?" Matt asked. My face heated and my deodorant failed. Matt and I had agreed in advance to split the bill. I glanced at the door, then back to Matt. The only dignified exit strategy was the truth.

"Um. So, this is super embarrassing, and I'm going to sound like a total tool, but I think I left my wallet at home. Maybe it's in the car, but I kind of don't remember leaving the house with it."

Matt wiped his mouth and shifted. "Oh, that's okay. I can get this one." He picked up the folder.

"No," I insisted too strongly and picked up my phone, noticing the low battery warning over the navigation app I'd used to find the restaurant "Damn. Stupid GPS kills my battery. What's your Paypal? I'll transfer it to you." Trying not to panic, I raced to find the app. The screen froze and went black. "Fuck. It died. You wouldn't happen to have a charger, would you?"

Matt shook his head and held up his phone. "I don't have an iPhone. Sorry."

"Then would you mind paying, then following me back to my house? I have the cash to pay you back. I'm so sorry about this."

"It's fine," Matt said graciously, pulled out his wallet, and slipped his credit card into the folder. "You don't have to pay me back, but I wouldn't mind coming home with you if you want to continue this date somewhere more private."

My heart entered my throat. *Continue? In private?* I swallowed hard. "I have a roommate."

Matt stiffened. "Would he mind?"

"No," I said. "I don't think so. I've never actually brought a date home before."

"How long have you lived together?"

"Let's see. Freshman and sophomore year at Loman Hall, two and a half years in an apartment off-campus, and almost two in our house. Well, his house."

"Ah. College roomies, huh? Must like each other to keep it going after graduation."

"Yeah. Josh is great."

"You've never discussed having dates over in six years, though? No boyfriends or... girlfriends?"

"Boyfriends," I clarified. "And it hasn't come up. Josh doesn't want a relationship."

"I see. And you?"

"It hasn't come up," I repeated. What could I say? I always fell for unobtainable guys? I was a glutton for rejection?

Matt nodded understanding and smiled. "So... Where does that leave us tonight?"

My heartbeat against my chest while the offer hung in the air between us. Matt reached for my hand and squeezed. "No pressure," he said softly. "But I vote we go for it."

Josh would kill me if I let the opportunity pass me by. He would also be a smug son of a bitch if he learned my date ended horizontally. I exhaled the breath I didn't realize I was holding. What the hell. I was overdue for a win of some sort, right?

"Well, I should pay you back for picking up the check."

Matt smiled from his pretty eyes, which now that he was closer, did appear to be, in fact, green. "I'm sure we can find something that will do the trick."

I laughed it off, although my nerves and body responded with interest. My knee drifted over, and even through two layers of denim, the touch of our legs unleashed a wave of tingles under my skin.

The server returned Matt's credit card, and with a hurried scribble, Matt added the tip and his signature to the sales slip and shoved the card into his wallet. "You ready?" he asked with a flirty wink.

I had no idea what I had committed to, but lacking any real desire to back out, I nodded, followed Matt out of the restaurant, and hoped like hell Josh wasn't home.

Chapter Two
Josh

I drove aimlessly, but the guilt and regrets swarmed around my brain like a colony of angry bees. Another text from Brady came in wondering why I'd left, but I didn't answer him. I couldn't. Not when the truth was that watching him leave for his date would probably lead to me confessing things I had no business thinking, let alone saying out loud. What had I done? It seemed like such a great plan a month ago.

The idea for the dating profile for Brady came to me from, of all things, a movie. The lead character, down on his luck, remarked that he didn't feel like a total loser because of his hot girlfriend. Maybe I couldn't help Brady land his perfect job, but he was such an amazing, thoughtful, funny guy. How hard could it be to find him a man to tell him that? Especially since he didn't seem to take my word for it. Brady would feel better, our equilibrium would be restored, and all this tension from his crappy mood and bickering over money would go away.

I hadn't considered the downside of my plan until Brady spelled out the natural consequences. My focus had been how meeting someone special would improve his self-esteem, usher back his fun-loving personality, and give him a much-needed confidence boost. Perhaps enough to be the edge he needed to score his dream job. However, the rest of it—love, marriage, kids—had never occurred to me.

This was such a mess.

Stopping for gas, I found myself across the street from a leather bar I'd learned about from a guy on Jack'd or Grindr, I didn't recall which. I'd only been there the once, and we hadn't stayed long, but

Grizzlies had been less intimidating than other bars and clubs I'd explored in the area.

When a spot opened up on the busy street, I took it as a sign. A quick flash of my ID and I was inside.

Grizzlies wasn't a dance club. The small interior consisted of a U-shaped bar and a handful of wobbly tables and chairs that had seen better days. The patrons had a "regulars" vibe to them, which tilted the bar's ambiance away from pickup spot toward a social club. I drew a lot of curious, borderline-surprised stares on my way to order a drink.

Half of a Jack and Coke later, an older guy—early fifties, at least—hovered on the other side of the bar in my line of sight too long to be unintentional. He had a smooth head and bearded face and wore jeans with a black leather vest opened to reveal a shirtless paunch, hairy chest, and nicely muscled arms and pecs. His tongue made a small trace of his top lip as he started his approach.

"Hi there. Get you another?" He saddled up to the barstool next to mine and angled himself toward me.

"Sure, but I'm not interested in anything beyond conversation."

He laughed. "That so?" He motioned to the bartender. "Get this young man another of whatever he's having, and I'll have another of that IPA."

The bartender nodded and moved down the bar to fill our order.

"What's your name?" he asked.

"Josh." I offered my hand.

His palm was warm and his face friendly. "Nice to meet you, Josh. Name's Barrett, but most folks call me Bare." He lifted his nearly empty bottle to his mouth and drained it.

"A bear named Bare?" I laughed, and his smile reached his eyes. "Cute."

"So, what brings you to our fine establishment? Usually a sweet, young thing like you comes in, they're on the hunt for men or trouble." Bare winked, and I couldn't help another amused laugh that only encouraged him. Flirting was a reflex. I'd always put extra effort into my appearance and social interactions because, as my father would remind me, "Appearances matter, son." Not that flirting with half-naked men was what he'd had in mind.

The bartender delivered our drinks and moved on. I lifted my glass as an answer and took a sip. "No trouble. Just this."

"Never search for solutions at the bottom of a glass, young Josh."

I huffed, because maintaining control was a constant struggle in my life already. I couldn't imagine what a disaster I'd be with a drinking problem. "Nah. Have a lot on my mind and driving wasn't working, so thought a drink might help."

"I see." Bare nodded. "Boy troubles?"

"Yep," I answered hastily. "Wait. No." My cheeks heated, but I met his questioning look head-on. "It's not like that."

Bare laughed boisterously and slapped the bar hard enough to rattle my glass. "Well, now we're getting somewhere. Tell me what it *is* like and maybe old Bare can help you out."

"It's not boy troubles like you mean them."

"Ahh. Well, get on with it. I love untangling a good mess."

"He's a friend," I said, "and roommate."

"Go on."

"We're sort of drifting apart."

Bare smiled at me, a sympathetic quirk of his mouth. "That happens."

"I did something to try to stop it, but I think it might backfire."

"Did you fuck him?"

"No," I blurted and bit my lip to keep the nervous laughter from escaping.

"Why not? You're not attracted to him?"

That was the thing. I *liked* stocky guys, and as far as my physical preferences were concerned, Brady checked all the boxes. "That's not a problem," I said. My heart sped up. I'd never admitted my attraction to Brady to anyone before. I slammed back my drink to distract myself with the burn. I couldn't let myself think of Brady like that. I wasn't a total masochist. Shaking my head cleared the thoughts that never entirely went away, not even after years of witnessing Brady's tortured, unrequited crush on our friend Adam. He was my best friend. Family. That was enough. More than enough. "No. It's not that. It's, um . . . We're friends."

"Oh, so you're both bottoms?" Bare nudged my shoulder with his own.

A surge of anxiety spiked through me. I mean, I was, but I didn't like it when guys assumed. "How do you know I'm a bottom?"

Bare laughed, rolled his eyes, and quirked his eyebrow as if challenging me to deny it. Instead, I huffed. "That's not the issue. We've always been friends. I don't want more than that."

"You're awful young to be so cynical. Burned out on love at what . . ." He sized me up. "Twenty-two?"

"Twenty-four. It's not so much burned out. I just . . . My ex ruined me for that."

Bare sat back, and a protective veneer swept over his expression. "I'm sorry some asshole hurt you, baby. But don't let that scare you off of love. Lots of good men out there. Give yourself time to heal."

"You really think I'd allow some dude to hit me?" I scoffed and cracked my knuckles.

Bare frowned. "I didn't mean physically, but victims of domestic abuse hardly *allow* it to happen to them."

My face heated. "It wasn't like . . . My ex was a girl. She did something . . . Look, it's . . ." *And now I sounded like a basket case. Fantastic.* "Not something I want to talk about."

Bare's face screwed up tight, and a bemused grin overtook his earlier concern. "'Girlfriend'? You bisexual, sugar?"

I pinched the bridge of my nose. Ugh. Would I ever say the words without getting anxious? "No. I'm gay." There was a reason I didn't go to gay bars often and always managed to have some work-related crisis when Pride rolled around. I wasn't out at work and too embarrassed to admit that to my friends. Needless to say self-acceptance remained a struggle.

"Ahh. I see. Your beard outed you. I'm guessing she didn't know she was a beard and was none too pleased to find out. That sucks, my young Josh, but it also means you've never had a boyfriend and that's a shame."

I wished I could explain the depths of Anna's betrayal in a few pithy sentences, but it was the convoluted nature of her scheme that made it so evil. No one understood how far I'd been willing to go to keep my secret. Not even Brady.

"Look, Brady is a friend. I don't even know why we're talking about him. If I had a boyfriend, I wouldn't be in here letting you buy me a drink. Now would I?"

Bare welcomed my subject change with a feral grin. "No, I guess you wouldn't. Probably wouldn't let me do this either." He leaned in and brushed a thumb over my cheek, stroking me. A flush warmed my body. "I like the way you blush. It's pretty."

Bare continued to warm me up with sweet words. When I responded with smiles, his meaty hands took liberties, gentle touches I liked. He hit all my turn-ons like he'd been given a checklist of how to get me on my knees, but there was something about his energy that made it impossible to relax. I usually did all the back-and-forth banter on a chat screen so the live-action parts could stay safely within my razor-thin strike zone. I loved feeling sexy and desired but not used. Being on my knees, but not pushed there. If someone looked or acted like they might want to hold me down, it was game over. Something about Bare's dominating vibe was throwing me off and making my stomach sour.

"Can I ask you something?"

"Sure," Bare said, running a hand over my thigh, "you can ask me anything." My lips flattened, and I forced a smile before shifting my leg away.

"How would you react if you had a friend you thought was trying to do something nice for you, but then you realized they only did it for a completely selfish reason?"

Bare's blue eyes drifted up, and he took a sip of his drink before responding with too much alacrity. "I had a brother who used to watch my dog for me. Sweet little thing—the dog, not my brother." He chuckled at his own joke, and I smiled reflexively. "Anyway, Beau used to take that dog out to pick up women. I only found out when the young woman who worked at my vet's office told me after she'd recognized the old girl and gave Beau a good what for."

I took a sip of my drink to avoid cringing. My attempt to be vague had landed me an unrelatable response and left me desperate for an exit strategy. It was a good reminder of why I didn't go to bars much. There really should be a human interaction equivalent to the block feature. Bare stroked the outside of my bicep with one finger. I sighed.

"Not what you meant, huh?" Bare asked.

I closed my eyes, swallowed the lump in my throat. How could I explain what I'd almost done when I'd gone to Brady's room to lay out his clothes?

His phone was right there, on his bed, charging. My heart was aching from Brady's words.

"*We'll fall in love and get married...*"

I keyed in my birthday and my thumb hovered over the small numeral one in the upper-right-hand corner of the app icon. Brady had an unread message. An idea tickled my brain. What if I canceled their date? Brady wouldn't have to know.

I couldn't believe I had almost violated Brady's privacy like that. Brady trusted me, and I'd gone on his phone plenty of times, but for an expressed purpose and with his permission. Never to read his private messages and absolutely never to make a decision that wasn't mine to make. After what Anna had done to me. How could I think of doing such a thing? What was wrong with me?

"No. Sorry. But thanks anyway."

Bare dropped his hand to take a sip from his bottle and shifted uncomfortably, adding rigidity to his spine. "Maybe this will help. After I asked Beau to stop, he still offered to watch the dog. So perhaps the better question to ask isn't what this friend of yours got out of the deal, but what would happen if that math changed? If you took away their part of the equation, what would they do? That should tell you where your friend's motives truly lie."

My pulse quickened. Would I still want Brady to meet someone special, someone that might make him happy, even if it meant things didn't improve between us?

I tossed back the rest of my drink, thanked Bare, and said my goodbye.

On the drive home, I reexamined the evening's events with my new understanding. It didn't matter why I had done what I'd done, as long as I stayed clear on the objective. I'd nearly convinced myself I had it all figured out. I would encourage Brady to be happy, in whatever form that took. I *was* a nice guy. A good friend. A *worthy* friend. Yes. Everything fit together neatly in my head.

Right up until I was confronted by an unfamiliar car in my driveway.

You have got to be kidding me.

I had mentally prepared for Brady to not come home that night. As long as I'd known him, I'd suspected Brady had gotten physical with about five guys, which averaged to about one new guy a year. So, mathematically, the odds were in Matt's favor. Brady was overdue for his annual one-night stand. So, I half expected him to go home with his date. Just not to *our home*. We never hosted our hookups. It was basically an unspoken rule.

Brady deserves to be happy.

"Good for him," I said aloud and stiffened my upper lip. With renewed determination, I exited my car, prepared to greet them with stories of my fun night with a bear named Bare.

I tossed open the door between the garage and the house with a flourish, only to be greeted by a dark, empty kitchen. Maybe they'd taken an Uber somewhere. I collapsed on the couch and grabbed the remote, searching for a mindless comedy to clear my brain, but Brady's rhythmically creaking bedframe sent a stray bullet directly into my plan.

Scanning the guide, I selected a movie title that promised gunfire and action sequences, then upped the volume. When the sounds of muffled laughter, followed by an unmistakable moan of pleasure drifted through the wall, I abandoned the movie for my bedroom and noise-canceling headphones, then willed myself to sleep.

I woke in the morning to the muffled sounds of Brady singing, "My, My, My," in the shower. Although he had a fantastic voice, outside of the bathroom, Brady hummed, he never sang. Troye Sivan was his go-to for shower karaoke, but this song was new in the rotation. He probably danced in there as well. He was too self-conscious in public, but I'd caught him dancing when he thought he was alone enough times that I knew Brady had rhythm. Suddenly I had an image of a naked, wet Brady washing his hairy chest to the sexy track and . . . *Oh, God. What if he wasn't alone?* Matt could be in there with him, running his hands over him. Brady could ask him to stay all weekend. Or what if Brady wanted to go to Matt's place so they could be alone... *Nope. Not going there.*

I grabbed my laptop from my desk and returned to bed, answering emails to keep my mind from going any further down the anxiety rabbit hole. When a single set of footsteps emerged from the bathroom and walked down the hall, relief chased away enough of the what-ifs so I could try to get some more sleep.

By the time I got out of bed, Brady was on the couch alone, eating a bowl of cereal and playing Mission to Mars. I went directly to the coffeepot and filled my favorite mug.

He paused his game as I came into view. "Rough night?" Brady asked. I scratched my messy hair and adjusted the waistband of my boxer briefs that were askew from tossing and turning.

"Mauled by a bear," I lied, with a wink.

Brady laughed. "You slept in late. I had to fix my own breakfast." He held up his bowl. "It's that Kashi cinnamon stuff you bought and almond milk. You're right. It's pretty good."

Brady took another bite, then a sip of his coffee while I added almond milk to my own. "You need a warmup?"

Brady shook his head. "I poured this about ten minutes ago. I was surprised I slept so late. I figured you'd wake me up at the crack of dawn to ask me about my date."

I offered him a blank stare while I took a sip of coffee. He was right. The last time he'd been on a date, I'd done a much better job pretending to want the details. "Didn't need to. I heard how your date went."

Brady, to his credit, blushed furiously. "Oh? Sorry about that." He held up the controller. "You want to play?"

I shook my head. I didn't share Brady's affinity for video games. While we gamed together frequently, I had mostly played as a way to spend time with him or to clear the air about something that was bothering me. It was easier for me to talk with no one staring at me. Even with his focus on killing aliens, Brady had gleaned some fairly deep insights out of my rambling chatter. But lately, all he wanted to do was play. Now that I spent so much time at a desk, the last thing I wanted to do was sit around all weekend.

"It's a nice day. I'm going to change and go for a run. Then I have some errands." I started down the hall and paused at the bathroom to brush the scum out of my mouth. When I'd finished, I found Brady lurking in the hallway.

Our house was originally a one-bedroom, one-bath bungalow that the former owners had extended to a two-bedroom. Brady had to walk through the family room to access the bathroom next to my room. We loved the neighborhood so much, we'd been willing to overlook the wonky room configuration and the single bathroom. "Did you need to get in?" I asked.

Brady shook his head and shifted. "What's wrong with you?"

"Nothing."

Brady released a relieved breath. "So, we're cool? About yesterday? Matt?"

"Yeah, Brady. We're cool. I'm fine." I slapped him on the shoulder.

"Okay. Good. Um . . . So, I thought about what you said, and maybe I would like to try it. Do you still want to help?"

I ended the standoff I had going with the Almighty and prayed for strength. *Desperate times called for desperate measures.* "You swipe right on the guys who you like. Left if you don't. I think you can manage."

To my relief, a glimmer of bewilderment crossed his face. "Um. Not that. I meant what you said at the mall. I don't feel good about myself, and I should do something to change that. Will you help me? Maybe jogging at first, at least for now."

"Really? Yes, Brady. That's awesome." My facial muscles stretched to accommodate my enormous grin, and I threw my arms around him for a quick hug. "Go get changed. I'm so proud of you. You're going to feel amazing." I wanted to wrap up every endorphin exercise had ever given me and infuse them into him. I wanted this for him so much, and I loved that he was coming to me for help. The residual anxiety from the previous day vanished. My plan had worked even better and faster than expected.

Brady's expression soured, so I tamped down my enthusiasm. "It's going to be fun," I said. "You'll see. Like old times. Go change. I'll get us some waters."

"Josh," he warned. "Don't set your expectations too high."

Undeterred, I changed quickly into workout clothes and waited for Brady in the family room with an eager smile and two S'well bottles full of ice water. He would come around once he got into it. I was sure of it.

Brady emerged from his room wearing knee-length basketball shorts and an old *Twilight* T-shirt he'd gotten as a gag gift from our friend Sid. The sleeves pulled tightly around his biceps and over his chest. Brady rarely wore shorts, so his hairy legs were easily four shades lighter than his arms. I was about to crack a joke when he beat me to it.

"I know what you're thinking. It's a real challenge to pull off Jacob's werewolf and Edward's vampire at the same time." He placed his hands behind his head, revealing a sliver of his belly and did a showgirl kick of his legs. "But try to control yourself."

I laughed at first, but quickly sobered. If I didn't know him so well, I might have missed the flicker of pure dread in his eyes. How could going for a little jog on a sunny day make anyone that miserable? "Aw, Brady. Come here."

He grumbled something as he walked toward me. When he was within touching distance, I tugged him to me and squeezed hard. "I'm so proud of you. And you are a sexy beast, don't forget it."

"Don't—" He tried to pull back, but I held him tighter.

"I know. My only expectation about this Brady is for you to feel better."

"Look better," Brady mumbled and shifted uncomfortably.

I released him to see his face. "Don't say that."

"Why?" Brady sniffled and fussed with his shirt, then as if sensing he'd been too defensive, forced a smile. I hoped my acting skills were better than his, because it was painful to watch. "I'm fat, Josh. It's not a state secret."

"I don't like it when you put my best friend down."

He slowly exhaled through his nose. "Can we not make this an Afterschool Special moment? It's not an insult. It's an adjective. A truthful one."

"You are amazing, Brady. You're handsome and smart. Not to mention incredibly talented. I love listening to you sing." Brady's voice was one of the things I loved most about him. If only there were a way to listen to him without being weird about it.

He snorted. "You have to say that. It's like when my mother says it. It doesn't count."

I swallowed hard. "Well, that guy Matt must have thought so too. 'Cause it didn't sound like you were playing Mission to Mars to me." I waited for Brady's inevitable joke about alien probing or exploring a dark hole, but he didn't take the bait. He didn't react at all. Brady passing up a chance to banter with me didn't sit right.

"I don't understand. It's like you refuse to believe anything good about yourself these days. It's exhausting."

Brady's shoulders slumped. "Look, I'm sorry, but I'm not trying to get into a philosophical debate with you. I want to lose weight. That is my motivation. We can say it's so I'll be healthier too if you want, but I'm doing it because I'm tired of being fat. I'm tired of having guys say, 'You're amazing, but . . .' all the time. I'm tired of my clothes not fitting. I'm so tired of being me. So, are we doing this or what?"

Shocked by his outburst, I stepped back from him. The Brady I knew could be diffident, self-deprecating, and occasionally hangry, but never this . . . dejected. Anxiety sent my heart into my throat, but I swallowed my frustration and focused the whole of my mind on helping my disconsolate friend.

I scrutinized his body language, mentally comparing the present version of Brady to the man I'd come to admire. The light in his eyes wasn't dim, it was gone. And while Brady had been a stocky, broad-shouldered man, he had always taken pride in trying to look his best—shiny hair, tweezed eyebrows, clean-shaven, buffed nails, and hydrated skin. When he went out, he dressed fashionably and to emphasize his best features. This version of Brady reeked of someone who didn't care anymore. I didn't know how I'd failed to appreciate the totality of the change, except I'd been too focused on me, and on building my career, to notice.

"Yeah, Brady. We're doing this." I wouldn't let him down again.

Chapter Three
Brady

It was nearly noon on an unseasonably crisp August day. Stanwell Park was crowded with people taking advantage of the first break in the hot weather. I had to admit, if you were prone to enjoying the great outdoors, it was a perfect day for it.

Watching Josh stretch before our run, his muscles flexing as he reached down to touch his toes, was almost enough to make me call the whole thing off.

Then, I noticed his expression.

I smiled at the serenity on his face. I'd forgotten how exercise changed his whole demeanor. Even a glimpse might have made my looming humiliation worth it. I swallowed hard, ignoring my accelerated pulse the way I usually did when I checked him out.

A rogue impulse made me wish I could stroke a hand over his cheek. To tell him how happy it made me to see him like this. I shook my head, chastising myself for my random weirdness.

"You okay? Want some suggestions for stretching?"

I startled and met his curious eyes. "I'm good," I stuttered, then pretended to know what I was doing and mimicked his movements. His face glowed from my effort, so I pushed harder, pulling my quad up until my knee groaned in protest.

A group of men walked by carrying a basketball, headed toward the courts on the far side of the park.

"How's it going, boys?" one of the men said, glancing back with a smile and observing Josh's clinic on flexibility with far more interest than his friends.

Josh smiled, waved, and moved into downward dog, then walked his hands back until his arms hooked around his ankles and relaxed into the stretch. I rolled my eyes as his gorgeous admirer walked straight into a trash container. Even guys that looked like *that* didn't stand a chance for anything serious with Josh.

"You about ready?" Josh pulled out of his pose.

"For what?"

Josh's face fell like a child who'd dropped their ice cream cone. I couldn't hold back my smile. His unbridled enthusiasm for exercise was adorable when it wasn't directed at me.

"I mean, the way you were stretching, I was wondering if this was a walk or you want to get gangbanged on the basketball court?"

He laughed but didn't deny it. Other than exercise, Josh's go-to stress relief activity was random sex.

"Come on. We'll start slow. Jog for a lap, then walk for a lap. Think you can manage four laps? It's a mile."

A mile... I suppressed a groan. The walk to the park had already exceeded my plans for the first day. I nodded, ready to get it over with so I could go finish the game I'd left paused. "Fine."

I took off at a slow jog. My breaths came sharp and heavy before we were halfway around the track. Everything about the motion felt wrong. My knees wobbled, my ankles clicked, and my thighs were generating enough friction to start a brush fire. Still, Josh jogged next to me, his arms swaying and his sandy-blond hair ruffling in the breeze, his blissful expression resembling that of a Golden Retriever, head cast out a car window on a Sunday drive.

When I was almost at a breaking point, Josh cheered, "One lap down, Brady. You want to walk this one?"

I pulled up to a stop. "Water?" I gasped, clutching my sides and breathing hard. Josh ran over to the bench where we'd started and grabbed the bottles he'd left.

"Here." He offered. "You're doing great." He opened his water and took a quick sip. He didn't look the least bit winded and hadn't broken a sweat. Me? I had enough moisture pooled for each new drop to have its own Slip 'N Slide.

"It's one lap, Josh." His smile dimmed, so I threw him a bone. "But it's a start."

"It's a start," Josh echoed, beaming.

"Okay, let's keep going." I handed him my bottle, and he returned them to the bench. We took off at a brisk walk. Josh was taller than me, but my legs were longer, so our strides were evenly matched. The reduced pace allowed the burn in my lungs to ease, but not the stitch in my side. The cramp was an unwelcome reminder of my abysmal physical fitness level and my night with Matt.

The kissing had been hot. I liked kissing more than most guys. It was the one sexual activity you could do wholly clothed, so it was the only one I relaxed enough to truly enjoy. Matt had been into it as well. The press of his hard length on my thigh as he moaned into my mouth let me know he was enjoying himself. I liked that a lot.

"You ready to pick it back up?" Josh asked.

I glanced over, surprised we'd completed the second lap already. *Damn.* A half mile under my belt. Maybe this wouldn't be so terrible.

Josh set our pace, and the third lap started closer to a run than a jog. About a quarter of the way around the track, I groaned and slowed my stride, but Josh went full cheerleader. "Come on, Brady. You got this." My desire to not disappoint him kept my legs moving until I could scarcely exhale between gasps. I squeezed my eyes closed and pumped my arms. No matter what I did, my nylon shorts rode up, fueling the itchy brush burn between my thighs. If one flame so much as licked at my balls, I'd abort this mission so fast... *No. Don't quit. Refocus, Brady.*

I conjured a mental image to remind myself why I was doing this. Seeing Matt's body had been jarring in a way I hadn't planned.

"I need to warn you about something," Matt said as I reached for his shirt. I recognized his anxious tone, and my heart instantly opened to him.

"Do you not want..." I shifted onto my back, and he followed, settling at my side, but avoiding eye contact.

"No. Not that. I, um... Last year, I had weight-loss surgery, so there are scars... and, um, skin."

I chuckled gently. "Yeah, the skin part was what I was hoping for."

Matt smiled and met my gaze, clearly grateful for the levity. "It's kind of disgusting. I'll understand if you change your mind." He went on, making fun of himself, but underneath all the laughs was a pain I understood well.

"Matt, it's fine. I'm not exactly Ryan Gosling here either, but I like you, and I want this if you do."

With a nervous smile, Matt lifted and straddled my hips. He ran his hands over my bare chest, dropped a gentle kiss on my lips, and reached over to turn out the lamp.

"Owww. Shit. Calf. Cramp!" I stopped and reached down to massage my leg, but quickly realized I couldn't breathe bent like that. "Can't. Do. This." I hobbled over to the bleachers and held on to the railing, attempting to force my heel down to the track.

Josh jogged back to me and placed a supportive hand to my lower back. "Yes, you can, Brady. You're almost there. We're on the last lap."

My eyes flew open, and I oriented myself to our location on the track. Not only had I run all of lap three, but I'd also run about half of lap four. I resumed walking, the back of my left calf aching, my legs spread wide enough to keep my thighs from combusting, and my chest on the verge of collapse. "Fucking sadist," I barked at Josh.

"You were in the zone. Brady, you were going hard. I'm so proud of you."

My gasping made it difficult to express my irritation. I worked to slow my breaths, stopped again, and clutched at the pain in my side. Josh patted my back. "Keep walking," he encouraged. "Stretch your arms up if you have a cramp. We're almost there."

I shook his advice off, not because it wouldn't help, but because my shirt was too small to lift my arms without my gut flopping out. I concentrated on getting my breathing under control, resisting the urge to reach for my inhaler. Having had asthma as a kid, not being able to breathe triggered some severe panic. But I wasn't wheezing, only short of breath from exertion. I couldn't talk as I worked through it, so Josh kept a hand on my back and rubbed in soothing circles. By the time we approached the bench, every muscle in my body had turned to jelly, but at least my airway functioned.

"I'm so pro—"

"Proud. Yep. Got it the first twenty times."

"Sorry," Josh mumbled. He picked up the water bottles, handed mine over, and headed back toward the house. I could handle "dropped ice cream cone" sad, but his expression was more "bully knocked it out of my hands" sad and ugh . . . that face did not belong on Josh at all. I was such a jerk.

I accelerated to catch up with him. We'd gone our whole friendship never having to apologize to each other. Now, it was a near-daily occurrence. "I'm sorry, Josh."

"I'm only trying to help. You don't have to be so . . ." He flailed a hand in my direction.

"I know. I'm tired and grouchy. And I'm gonna be walking bowlegged for all the wrong reasons." I lifted the hem of my shorts so Josh could see the irritated skin.

Josh grimaced. "I should have thought about the chafing."

"I appreciate the help. It wasn't so bad. Really. If I'm not too sore, let's do it again tomorrow."

Josh gave me a hopeful smile, but it was pretty clear from his lack of enthusiasm he didn't necessarily believe me. He was quiet as we walked side by side toward the house.

"You have errands to run?" I asked as we neared our street.

Josh nodded. "Yeah. I need to shower, pick up my dry cleaning, and run to the grocery. Do you have plans?"

"I thought maybe I'd call Matt and see if he wants to hang and play MtM."

Josh's mouth gaped. "You're going to see him again?"

"Yeah. I think so. Why not? He's a good guy."

"Oh."

"What's the matter?"

"I'm surprised is all. Usually, you don't."

I huffed before mumbling, "Usually I don't have an opportunity to."

"What does that mean?"

I turned to face Josh, who'd stopped without me noticing and stared incredulously. *Did he really not understand why I didn't have second dates?* "Did you think I enjoy having sex and never hearing from the guy again? Jesus, Josh. Is it sunny all the time in the world that you live in?"

Josh bristled, which he did less often than I dated. Guilt niggled at me. Of course he didn't know. I'd always kept my pitiful sex life closely guarded. I was usually relieved that he'd never pushed to hear details, so I had no clue why it suddenly annoyed me.

"Brady, there are entire companies built around the concept that people want to have one-time, meaningless sex with near strangers. Don't act like what I do is depraved."

"That wasn't what I— It's not . . ." I sighed. His face was a ball of tension again, and we hadn't even made it home. *Great job, Brady.* "You know I wouldn't think that. I don't care if you hook up or whatever. But I want to get to know someone, and when I think I've made a connection . . ." My voice choked up and damn it, I did not like explaining how pathetic I was, especially not to him. I blew out a breath and gave him the honesty he deserved. "Look, most times when I give a blowjob, all I get in return is blown off."

Josh's expression bordered on shock, but quickly leveled up to pity, and finally settled on empathy. I waited to make sure he wouldn't challenge me until I breathed again.

"But you always made it seem like you didn't want . . ." Josh's dismay faded with a long exhale. "I thought it was because of your feelings for Adam. Why didn't you tell me?"

"Because it's humiliating." I tossed my hands in the air, equal parts frustrated that I had to explain this and grateful he hadn't already assumed. Josh recoiled with my confession. "Don't you understand why I wouldn't want anyone to know about that? Why I wouldn't want *you* to know about that? Maybe it was about Adam in the beginning, but now . . . I know it's not your thing, but I'd like to have a real relationship. Even get married someday." I rubbed my hands on my shorts, trying to distract myself from the mortification twisting my chest. It wasn't Josh's fault I'd resigned myself to rejection. I reminded myself he only wanted me to be happy. "You were right about the dating. If I want to change, I need to do something different. Try to meet someone who wants what I want. I think it'll be good for me."

"I didn't . . . I'm sorry. Matt's different, then?" Josh's voice hardened, and he pulled his arm across his chest, first right, then left, before cracking his knuckles.

"Yeah. I think so. He mentioned hanging out more when he left last night. He's going through some health problems. Not sure he's in the market for a boyfriend or anything, but I don't know, seems like we fit."

"That's . . . great, Brady. I *only* want you to be happy. You *know* that, right?"

I nodded, a little taken aback by how pained he sounded. "Of course."

Josh resumed walking, and I trailed after him into the house, begrudgingly accepting the abrupt end of our discussion . . . at least while we were standing in the middle of the sidewalk. By the time I removed my shoes and returned the water bottle to the kitchen, Josh was already in the shower, which was Josh's way of saying he was done talking. Period.

I texted Matt, who was at his nephew's birthday party, but he invited me over to his place that evening. I waited for the bathroom door to open and met Josh in the hallway. He was still wrapped in a towel, and I couldn't help a glance at his smooth chest.

"What's up?"

I cleared my throat and lifted my eyes. If Josh noticed my bold stare, he didn't let on. "Matt and I are gonna hang out tonight, so I can go to the store with you if you still want."

Josh shook his head. "Actually, I think I'll go into the office and get some work done first. I'll stop on my way home. Do you need anything? I have meals planned for the week already."

"No. I'm good. I'll leave fifty in the envelope. Maybe I can push it to sixty this week."

Josh's lips pursed, and I braced myself for yet another uncomfortable conversation about money. "Don't leave yourself short."

When we had moved into the house, Josh started buying organic and hormone-free ingredients I couldn't afford, but when I balked, he insisted it was too much trouble to cook for one and suggested I pay him a set amount. I had peeked at the receipt once and lost my mind with how much he'd spent, but there wasn't much I could do. I couldn't afford to contribute more. Buying my own was dumb because I was useless in the kitchen and it seemed unfair to limit him. So instead, I paid him back in other ways. Which reminded me. "Did you ever change your oil?"

Josh's eyes crinkled at the corner. "No, but I can—"

"Take my car. I'll change yours while you're at the office."

"Really?"

"Yeah," I said. "I still have the stuff I bought last winter. You're way overdue. Sorry. I spaced it."

"Thanks."

"No problem. Want me to swing by and pick up your dry cleaning? It's next to the place I drop off the old oil anyway."

"Sure. Thanks. It's already paid; the slip's in my car console."

"Okay. I got it. You finished in the bathroom? I reek."

"Oh." Josh smiled and shifted out of my way into the hall. He looked back, a little tentative. "You did good today, Brady. Were you serious about going again tomorrow morning?"

Sunday mornings used to be reserved for Bloody Marys and brunch with Adam, plus Cade and Sid, other former floor mates from our college dorm, but no one had taken over when Josh resigned as our unofficial organizer, and the weekly gathering had been hit or miss at best. "Sounds like a plan."

His face split into a grin, and I smiled back. In the privacy of the bathroom, I permitted Josh's pride to infuse me with a dash of optimism. After peeling off my sweaty clothes, I turned on the shower and bent to pick up items from the floor that Josh had let accumulate before dumping everything into the hamper. I caught a whiff of something distinctly Josh in the process—his aftershave mixed with sweat from his workout clothes. My senses were alive, heightened by the awareness of overworked muscles and sexual energy only attributable to the potential of orgasms on the horizon. I stepped into the hot water. My body buzzed as I poured the soap onto my loofah and tuned into the beat of "My, My, My," singing softly to myself.

I swayed my hips and ran the loofah over my body. When I got to the chorus, I raised the loofah handle to my mouth and belted it out.

Fully dressed and pleasantly sore, I set about my afternoon tasks with a noticeable pep in my step. I hummed along to the radio while working on Josh's Honda Accord and, in under an hour, was on my way to dispose of the old oil and pick up Josh's suits.

I couldn't be sure if it was from the sex, the exercise, or just feeling like I wasn't a complete leech on Josh for a change, but somehow, I'd tapped into an energy that had eluded me for months. There was this little tickle in the back of my mind I couldn't quite identify, but if I had to name it, I'd call it hope.

Whatever it was, it led me to the nail salon next to the dry cleaners. Even in a foreign language, I could hear the judgment as the nail technician cleaned up my severely neglected cuticles, but the price was right and my hands no longer resembled an auto mechanic's.

On a whim, I called Rafi, my hairstylist, whose delight at working me in for a trim told me I'd gone too long between cuts as well. Before I could consider the toll all this "me-time" would take on my bank account, he'd finished the cut and was working some amazing-smelling styling product through my hair.

"It looks great, Rafi. Thank you for working me in at the last minute," I said as I removed the smock and handed it to him.

"No worries. Let's book your next appointment before you leave this time." He winked at me, and I followed him to the reception desk to check out, wondering if I could push my next appointment out three paychecks instead of two so I could give Josh the extra ten bucks a week for groceries.

While I waited for Rafi to make my appointment, the door to the salon opened behind me.

"Brady?" a familiar voice said. "I thought I recognized Josh's car out front."

I swallowed hard and turned on my heels. "Hey."

Adam approached, his shoulder blading toward me, but arms extending. I tried to anticipate his contact, shuffling forward in the first eight counts of a "do we hug or shake hands" dance. When it seemed he'd settled on a handshake, I extended my arm only to have my hand land on his waist.

Okay, awkward side hug with two bro pats to the shoulder it was.

I pulled back, slightly mortified there were witnesses to that encounter. I swear we did fine in the group. Adam and I actually had a lot in common, but when we were alone, it was like he was terrified of giving me any sign that there was hope for something more, and I acted as though mere contact with his body would give me wood. Which, granted, might have been an actual problem when we'd first met, but my loins had chilled quite a bit since.

"So, um, how have you been?" I asked.

"Good. You know, busy. How are you? Any luck with the job search?"

"Nope. Nothing yet," I said succinctly, doing my best to keep my bitterness under control. There was a long pause before Adam spoke again.

"Where's Josh?"

"Oh. We just switched cars so I could change his oil. He's working today."

Adam nodded, his head bobbing as through I'd unleashed some fascinating new information. "That sucks."

I was about to offer additional confirmation of the suckage that was Josh's work life when Rafi interrupted to hand me an appointment card. "Bye, Brady. Good luck on your date tonight."

"You have a date?" Adam seemed a little too thrilled by the possibility. But then again, hurray for a new topic of conversation. "That's great, Brady."

"Your card, sir." I turned back to the counter and scribbled my name on the slip the receptionist handed me while she checked in Adam. His stylist appeared like an angel of mercy to end our conversation.

"Hey, so we should get together soon," I said trying to bring to a close this delightful case study in why you should never develop crushes on uninterested friends.

"Sure," Adam said with more enthusiasm than I'd expected. "Yeah, Cade and I were just talking about how much we miss seeing you guys. Maybe we can do Sunday brunch, so we can meet your new guy."

"Sure. Take care, Adam."

"You too, Brady. Have fun tonight."

I was going to make it home with time to take a quick rinse before my date. Seeing Adam fully reinforced my decision to put some actual effort into trying to find someone. Matt was sweet and funny and, most importantly, interested. If I could convince Adam he didn't need to walk on eggshells around me anymore, while getting some regular sex with a nice guy . . . Well, dating Matt was starting to look better and better.

My phone rang as I pulled into the drive.

"Hey. It's Matt."

My heart sunk at his tone. He was canceling. I never should have gotten my hopes up. No sense in beating around the bush. "Hey. We still on for tonight?"

"Yeah. That's why I'm calling. I ate something at my brother's I shouldn't have, and my stomach . . . I'm feeling better, but I thought I'd warn you. I'd still like you to come over, but literally it will be to hang out and game."

"That's what I thought we were doing anyway." I smiled, hoping he'd detect the feigned naivety in my voice.

"Oh," Matt said, clearly disappointed. He stuttered a few times, so I put him out of his misery.

"Matt, I'm joking. 'Hang out and game' is second only to 'Netflix and chill' in subtlety, but it's cool. Should I bring my controller, or have you got a spare?"

"I have an extra," Matt said. The eagerness in his voice sent little flutters to my stomach. The butterflies felt good. Really good, actually. Maybe I'd finally outgrown my tendency to crush on men completely out of my league. I was disappointed his stomach wasn't cooperating, but he had explained he was still figuring out his food tolerances postsurgery. Would losing over a hundred pounds in eight months be worth the constant guessing game? I didn't think so. Sometimes Josh put stuff on my plate I couldn't even identify, but I counted on three things—it would be healthy, it would be delicious, and my iron-clad stomach would welcome it home.

Josh pulled into the drive as I was removing the dry cleaning from his back seat. I waved at him and gestured so he would know I was on the phone. "Hey, Matt. I've got to help bring in groceries. I'll see you in about an hour."

After hanging up, I rushed to help Josh at my car. "Hey," I greeted him with a butler's bow. "Your dry cleaning and car keys, sir."

Josh flashed an amused smile, slipped the keys into his pocket, and accepted the bundle of hangers. "Thanks again."

I gathered as many cloth Whole Foods bags as I could carry, cheering when I spied the bag of banana chips on top. "Awesome. I love these things."

"I got you the peanut butter too. I know you like to dip them." Josh laughed, grabbed the remainder of the bags, and followed me into the house.

Josh was fussy when it came to his kitchen, so I fought the urge to rush and made sure I stored things in their proper places—commingling cans with boxes or baking shit was one of the few ways to get Josh aggravated. While Josh organized yogurt by expiration date, I pulled the colander down, rinsed the grapes, and plucked them from the stems so they'd be ready to eat.

The refrigerator door shut, and I glanced up, intending to ask for the fresh fruit containers and found him staring at me. "What?" I mumbled due to the grape between my lips.

"You got your hair cut."

"Yeah." I swallowed the grape with a lump of guilt. I knew I shouldn't have spent so much on myself. "I left you sixty. I'll do seventy on my next paycheck."

Josh shook his head. "No. That's not what I meant." He waved his hand dismissively. "Fifty is fine. Getting ready for your big date?"

"Yeah. Well, we're just gaming tonight. Matt's under the weather, but why? Is it okay?"

"Yeah." Josh cleared his throat. "I like it shorter on the sides."

"Thanks. I've got to hustle, or I'm gonna be late. Your oil is changed. I noted the mileage and date in my phone, so I'll remember to do it on schedule next time. You all good here? Oh, can I borrow your blue Adidas tonight?"

He nodded but said nothing as I popped a few stray grapes in my mouth and stashed the rest in the fridge. "Thanks for the groceries. You're the best husband a man could ask for." I kissed his cheek and spanked his ass playfully. Granted, it had been a while since I'd been in such a good mood, but Josh gawked at me like I'd suddenly grown an extra head. I didn't know why. It wasn't anything I hadn't said or done before, but I didn't have time to ask.

Matt's place was pretty swank, and, for a minute, I regretted paying him back for my dinner. I could have used the extra twenty bucks, and the seventy-seven-inch OLED television told me he could afford to buy a boy a chopped salad. He had mentioned he worked for a security firm, but it turned out his company was less the rent-a-cop I'd envisioned and more of the "protect your network from international hackers" variety. Matt greeted me with a nervous kiss, and I couldn't erase the smile he'd put on my face, while he powered on his Xbox.

"Damn, this is some setup." I marveled at the entertainment system in his den. *A freaking badass den.* Everything from the surround sound to the gaming chairs was top of the line. "My ass may never leave this spot." I sighed as the soft leather seat cradled me in ergonomic love.

"That's a shame. I'd rather hoped to see your ass again."

I blushed and let go of a full-belly laugh, quickly adjusting my shirt to keep it from clinging to my fat rolls. Man, it was a head trip to be flirted with. "Don't start with that if you can't deliver." I sucked at flirting, but Matt seemed unbothered as he handed me my controller with a bemused smile.

"Before we start, I need to run to the restroom. Can I get you a drink—soda, beer, water?"

"Water is good. Thanks."

Several minutes later, Matt returned with a Fiji bottle, and I burst into laughter.

"What's so funny?" he asked.

"Josh gets so mad when I drink bottled water."

"Why?" Matt looked offended, so I got my laughter under control to recite Josh's whole diatribe on bottled water. ". . . So, when you consider the nonbiodegradable plastic that's poisoning the ocean and the hazardous chemicals leaking out of the bottle, it really does sort of make you feel stupid for buying it when it's no better than tap in most cases."

Matt sighed. "Do you want me to get you tap?"

"Oh, no. Shit. I'm sorry. It's fine. Most of my friends are also friends with Josh, and he's sort of beaten us into submission about it.

It'll be fun, actually. Like a little rebellion." I reached for my bottle and took a sip. "If you two ever meet, we will never speak of this."

Matt cocked his head as though uncertain if I was kidding.

"I'm joking," I clarified. It was going to be a long night if I had to keep explaining my sense of humor to him.

Initial awkwardness aside, playing MtM with Matt was a blast. We were a good match skill-level wise, and our conversation fell back into the same comfortable rhythm as our first date when we focused on the game. As the night wore on, however, I couldn't help but notice something was missing. Maybe it was our six-year age gap, which felt much wider now that I had a sense of how Matt lived, or the few uneasy, borderline uptight looks he'd given me that made me feel immature. They were all small moments, but I could practically feel the kaleidoscope of butterflies that had danced around my belly on my way over to his house take off one-by-one until there was no flutter of anticipation left at all.

By the end of the mission, Matt seemed to be recovered from whatever he'd eaten and had loosened up. I wondered if we might make out a little after all. I looked at him, searching for interest, but I dunno... Matt kind of gave me an "I guess if you really want to" vibe, which about summed up my opinion on the matter.

"You want to do another one?" I asked as Matt yawned. I checked my watch and was surprised it was nearly midnight.

"Sorry," he said. "I went hard with my nephews at one of those trampoline places. It wore me out. I'm still building up stamina."

"That's okay. I'm tired too. I went running today with Josh. First time in a long time."

Matt studied me for a minute. "What made you decide to start running?"

I stammered for an answer and ultimately decided to go with the truth or at least a modified version of it. Matt didn't need to know all the ways he'd shown me a future I didn't want. "You, actually. I guess seeing all you're going through opened my eyes a bit. I need to get some of this weight off. I've been heavy since I was a kid, but now? I don't know. It's like I was always gay fat, but now I'm *fat* fat. It's... I need to do something. It's starting to impact my life."

"Is Josh heavy too?"

I screwed up my face, unable to even comprehend a fat version of Josh. "Ah. No. Josh looks like Captain America."

Matt's lip quirked, and he chuckled. "So, he's helping you lose weight?"

"I mean, he already had me eating healthy, but the exercise is new."

"He cooks for you?"

I nodded, smiling fondly with the thought. "I told you he's awesome. Well, he is good in the kitchen at least. Me? Not so much. But I help too—clean the bathroom, laundry, car maintenance, take care of the yard. Stuff like that."

"Sounds like a good roommate arrangement."

"The best," I said. "You'd like him. Why don't you come over next weekend? We can all hang out." *And I could get Josh's opinion on Matt.* "Josh would dig helping you with your diet. I didn't tell him, by the way, I wasn't sure if you cared, but it seemed personal."

"I'd like that, but work is hectic right now. I'm trying to get everything done before I go out again on surgery leave."

He'd mentioned the possibility previously but hadn't offered any details. I didn't want to pry, but it seemed wrong not to acknowledge it. "Nothing serious, I hope."

Matt's face split into a wide grin. "I got the insurance approval today. I'm having a body lift to remove all the extra skin."

His excitement at the prospect of going under the knife caught me off guard. "Can I ask you what it's like?"

"The surgery or looking like a deflated balloon?"

"I guess to have such a dramatic change in your life. I don't think I qualify for weight-loss surgery, but I'm curious. Other than some mild asthma, I don't have serious medical issues, but sometimes it feels like it'd be easier to binge my way into qualifying than to work hard enough to lose the weight."

Matt nodded. "I actually did gain a few pounds to qualify."

I laughed, but he didn't. "You're serious?"

Matt cringed. "Yeah. When I was diagnosed with diabetes, I was less than ten pounds away from hitting the BMI criteria. And to answer your earlier question, the surgery is pure hell. Don't get me wrong, the weight loss is incredible. I know for sure I couldn't have done it on my own, but you've seen the after picture. I thought when I got below two hundred all my problems would be solved. I had visions of wearing a speedo on the beach and hitting the bars. I planned to live out every fantasy I thought the weight had robbed me of, but you know what? The scale reads one hundred and seventy-two pounds, the diabetes is gone, and I can play with my nephews again, but there is no magic cure for everything else. It's work. Every damn day is a struggle. You'd be much better off to lose the weight at a reasonable pace. You're not nearly as heavy as I was."

"Well that's good since my insurance is crap." I laughed, and Matt stroked my arm sympathetically.

"Where do you work again?"

"Stanford Mortgage," I said.

"You'd think they'd have decent benefits."

My cheeks warmed. "They do if you're willing to pay for them. I'm on my stepfather's insurance plan. It sucks, but I can't afford to pay the premiums myself until I get a real job." If Matt didn't already think I was a loser, that should do it.

Matt quirked his eyebrow. "Your job isn't a real job?"

"I'm an admin assistant, so yeah, it's a full-time job, but it's not what I went to college for."

"What's your degree in?"

"Business administration. I should've done finance like Josh."

"Why did you choose your major?"

"I liked the organizational management aspects and thought maybe I'd go into human resources with it. Outside an internship with this small software company, my work experience is all in the mortgage industry, and even that is limited to front desk help. I did learn this software package called HRworks at my internship, though. I was hoping that it would make me more marketable, but so far, no luck. I should have been more strategic with my internships. That's how Josh got his job. He was hired our senior year. The place I interned wasn't hiring."

Matt thought quietly for long minutes that stretched my comfort with the silence. He stood, walked to his desk, grabbed something, and exhaled. "Brady, can I ask you something?"

"Sure."

He turned to face me. "Do you think there is something between us? Like on a scale of one to ten, would you say we have a connection that is worth pursuing?"

My doubts aside, his question seemed way out of place for a second date. "I thought you wanted something casual?"

Matt laughed. "Okay. Good. Judging by your expression, we're on the same page."

"I like you," I explained, awash with guilt. I'd slept with Matt because I believed there was something between us beyond mutual horniness, but less than twenty-four hours later, we'd lost whatever connection we'd shared. The "I'm not feeling it" conversation wasn't foreign to me, but being on the other side of it indeed was.

"No. It's fine. I like you too. A great deal, which is why I'm going to tell you that my company has an opening in HR. It's entry-level, but we've had trouble filling it because we want people with HRworks exposure. No guarantees, but I could send your résumé to the hiring manager."

"Really? That's awesome, man. I'd appreciate that so much."

"But the thing is, it's my company, so . . ." He handed over a business card. *Weston Security. Matthew Weston, Owner and CEO.*

"You own it?" I asked, my eyes wide. "I thought you were thirty."

"I am." His eyes shined with amusement.

I glanced down at the card and back to him.

"You own your own company at thirty? Holy shit. Dude, you should lead with that on dates. It's impressive."

Matt chuckled. "I'll keep that in mind, but, um . . . I guess what I'm saying is we can keep dating, or I can send your résumé to the hiring manager. I'm not comfortable doing both."

Oh, I mouthed, quickly sobering to reality. It would be rude to say yes to the job. I was nearly sure of it. "I see. Well, in that case, I guess I should ask where you fall on this scale of one to ten."

Matt sat next to me and leaned in to grab my hand. "Listen, last night I would have said an eight or nine, easily, but I think maybe the chances of you getting this job are better than the prospect of you and me becoming us. When I said I wanted casual, it's because I know I'm really not in a great place. But the truth is I'm still holding on to this fantasy that after my body lift, I'll look... Well, to be frank, I hope I'll be hot enough to be a total man-whore for a while."

I laughed because I got what he was saying on an emotional level. It sucked to be heavy, but I couldn't help thinking it sucked twice as much to be heavy and gay. Men and women were supposed to have different body types, but gay men—when we got naked, it was hard not to compare what you had with your lover. If I ever experienced that Freaky Friday body-swap thing with Josh, the first thing I'd do is open his Grindr account. "I guess I'll send you my résumé, then."

"One more thing..." Matt waffled.

"Yeah?"

"I hope I'm not way out of line here, but since I do like you and I think you'd be an amazing boyfriend for someone, I have to tell you the other thing that's holding me back."

"Is it my humor? I'm not everyone's cup of tea."

"No." He huffed a laugh. "It's Josh."

"Josh?" I gritted my teeth. "You don't even know him."

"I know but, Brady, the thing is you talk about him. A lot. I'm saying that because I'm a bit intimidated by how close you two are, particularly if he's as good-looking as you described."

"We're friends," I repeated.

"Okay, but... Never mind. It's none of my business."

I sighed, then reined in my exasperation. Matt barely knew me, and while it would be easy enough to dismiss him, the guy had the potential to be my boss or my friend. Maybe both. And I didn't want him to think I'd slept with him thinking about another guy. He'd say his piece and I'd clear up the misunderstanding. "Say it."

"You've lived together six years, and neither of you had even discussed bringing home dates? That's just... That says more than you think. Have you never considered what would happen if you or Josh had a significant other someday?"

I stared at him, and for a second, I pictured Josh living with another man. My heart rate sped up, and my breaths came too fast. "We've never even kissed. Seriously."

"I believe you, but maybe before you go on another date, you should ask yourself something. Besides the fact that you don't kiss, what distinguishes your current relationship with Josh from the one you're looking for?"

I sputtered and made a few attempts to answer. I'd lost enough time pining after Adam. My first instinct was to explain that I wanted a boyfriend who made me feel good about myself, not someone who had settled. Whenever I tried to explain it, I realized that Josh would never—could never—make me feel like he was too good for me, so I stopped trying to find the words and left it at "There's no way that would ever happen. Josh doesn't date. He doesn't even like to talk about relationships." I didn't mention that I wasn't naïve enough to think someone like me would be the one to change his mind.

Matt patted my shoulder and kissed me gently. The kiss was different from the others we shared, and I could tell by Matt's face full of friendly affection that he'd only meant to be helpful.

"Send me your résumé, Brady, and think about what I said."

Chapter Four
Josh

The first time Brady jogged an uninterrupted two miles, my heart exploded in an amalgamated blend of pride, euphoria, and awe. When Brady started his workouts, I wasn't confident we'd get to this point. Certainly not in such a short time. "You did amazing," I cheered. "I'm so—"

"Proud of me." Brady smiled patiently. "Yeah. I know." He wiped his brow and took a gulp of his water.

I'd stopped apologizing. I *was* proud of Brady for keeping with the program and for his slight, but noticeable, improvement in attitude. I placed my hands on my hips and stretched while basking in the glow of his swagger. "You want to add more distance?"

Brady shook his head. "Let's do something else."

In the few weeks that Brady and I had been running, I'd suggested we mix it up. Brady didn't even enjoy playing the video game version of sports, so I'd proposed hiking, swimming, and rock climbing at various points. He'd dismissed all my suggestions, even the no-cost ones. "I have a guest pass. Do you want to try the gym?"

"No," Brady said firmly. He sat in the grass and stretched his legs out in front of him, reaching for his toes. He still hovered around his lower calf, but near-daily runs were starting to pay dividends. His energy level was up, and his clothes fit better.

"So . . . what were you thinking?"

Brady straightened his spine, crossed his bent right leg over his left, twisting to stretch his piriformis. "I don't know, but Matt warned me that doing the same thing for too long might cause me to plateau, plus it's getting colder out. Maybe something indoors."

The mention of Matt's name ignited an overpowering level of irritation. I turned my face to hide my scowl until I regained control, but by the way Brady's jaw dropped, it was too late. Brady's moods had returned to normal, and most days I was happy enough to have my friend back that I could ignore the way Brady raved about Matt. He still had his crappy job, but judging by the shoes he borrowed, he'd had at least two interviews in the last few weeks. He was losing weight, and I knew he felt better about his appearance. Most importantly, he laughed like Brady again. Matt's role in all that couldn't be dismissed. So why couldn't I be happy about it?

"Why the face?"

"What face?" I picked up my bottle and took a big gulp. When I lowered it, Brady was gawking at me. "What?"

"You're acting weird."

"No, I'm not," I challenged with all the maturity of a five-year-old. Spearing my fingers into my hair, I forced my voice to a less defensive tone. "What does Matt suggest we do?"

"Josh . . ."

The wary look on Brady's face shifted my brain into overdrive, desperate for some plausible explanation for the sneer he'd clearly seen. Since there was none, I soldiered on. "It's fine. There's this work thing on my mind," I lied. I reached out a hand and helped Brady to his feet. "Listen, I think I'm going to run home, okay?"

"I can run with you. Let me rest a bit more."

"It's fine." I needed to run. I got it. Matt played MtM like a badass, was some business genius with mad hacking skills, and fucked like a God. Okay, that last one I might have inferred, but Matt must have had something special in his pants to have earned Brady's unchecked admiration. I could work through this if I could just run hard enough to get the images of Brady and Matt out of my head. The jealousy had to burn off eventually, right?

Brady's face demanded justification. Damn, why was this so hard? Why should I care if Matt wanted to help Brady with his workouts? Maybe because Matt was full of shit. His fancy tailored shirts were obviously not concealing the body of a gym rat, so what did he know about working out? I had no idea why Brady cared what Matt thought about his training. "Listen, if Matt wants—" I swallowed my words, but it was too late to peel back the bitter edge in my voice.

Brady turned rounded eyes on me. "Holy shit. You're mad at me. You're never mad at me."

"No," I insisted. And it was the truth. I loved running with Brady. It wasn't anger I was feeling, it was... frustration. I didn't understand how I had kept all my bullshit insecurity controlled for years when Brady mooned over Adam, who we socialized with all the time, but with Matt... Ugh. Why that guy?

Maybe because deep down I knew Adam was never the man for Brady. But Matt? Matt *could* be the guy. *The one I lose him to.*

Except I was the one there every morning. I smiled through all his complaining and encouraged him even when he snapped at me. Matt didn't wake up an hour early every day. He didn't make him special protein shakes. He didn't teach him to lean from his ankles and not his hips. A flare of possessiveness surged in my blood. I wanted Brady to be mine. Only mine. But *fuck*, how selfish was that? It was clear Brady wanted things I'd never be able to give him. I wanted him to be happy, and as much as it killed me to admit, Brady had been happier since he'd met Matt.

I exhaled a long breath and plastered a smile to my face. "Maybe you would prefer to work out with Matt."

"Well—"

"I mean, I'm sure he's an expert on weight loss and fitness. And you have so much in common." I'd aimed for levity, but the words even tasted resentful.

"Josh." My name came out of Brady's mouth like an apology. Great. Matt practically cured his depression, and I was making him feel guilty about liking the guy.

Damn it. "Forget it, I'm going to run home. I'll see you there." I took off at a sprint before Brady objected. I was halfway home before I realized I'd left my S'well bottle along with my dignity at the park. *That was bad. So, so bad.*

Brady was wrapped up in his whatever-they-were-calling-it thing with Matt, but he wasn't an idiot. The countdown to our next serious heart-to-heart had begun.

I made it to the house, breathing hard from my efforts, and proceeded to the bathroom. I stripped off my clothes and heard the front door open. *Did he run home?*

"Josh," Brady yelled, and the front door slammed shut.

I scrambled to turn on the shower and jumped directly into the ice-cold water. "Shit," I chanted over and over and not because my balls retracted into my body from the icy jolt. How was I going to explain myself to Brady?

Brady is happy. Do not mess this up for him.

I hovered in the corner until the water heated, then washed quickly. After turning off the water, I reached for the towel bar. The *empty* towel bar. In my rush to avoid Brady, I'd forgotten to grab one. I peered in the hamper, but it was empty too. My running shorts were lying in a pool of water next to the tub. Sweaty T-shirt it was.

With my shirt clutched over my crotch, I tip-toed toward the hall linen closet. About midway down the hall was the entrance to the family room, and I paused to peek before zipping past to the closet on the other side.

The sound of my name proceeded Brady's hurried footsteps across the hardwood. In a frenzy, I dropped my shirt and yanked a towel from the overstuffed closet.

Brady rounded the corner and froze, his mouth gaped. Our eyes locked long enough to fuck with my pulse.

"Brady," I stuttered and frantically struggled to secure the towel. I used the moments Brady averted his eyes to take a sharp inhale and summon a convincing smile. "Sorry. You surprised me. I forgot a towel."

Brady turned his searching stare back on me. "We need to talk."

I surveyed my wet, naked skin and the puddle pooling at my feet and glanced back up. "Now?"

"Get dressed." Brady had that *I'm disappointed* look my father used to give me when we'd lost a game. I nodded slowly and walked past him toward my room. When I reached my bedroom door, I glanced back, but Brady was no longer there.

In the sanctuary of my room, I pushed out a long breath through my nose. I sat on my bed and grabbed my phone, needing a distraction. Ken McConnell had emailed me twice while I was at the park. I was sorting through files to find what he'd asked for when Larry, another junior account manager and all-around ass kisser, sent Ken the files he'd asked for and two additional attachments, noting that since it appeared I hadn't had a chance to convert my clients into the new pricing tool yet, he'd taken the liberty.

If brownnosing was a sport, Larry was LeBron James. Ken's message even said it could wait until Monday, and the pricing tool conversion deadline was two weeks away. I grumbled as I typed out a response to say thank you, making sure to copy Ken so he would know that I, too, was working on the weekend, even if Larry beat me to the response.

A hard knock at the door announced that I'd overplayed my procrastination hand.

"Josh," Brady called. "Can I come in?"

"One sec." I grabbed my sweatpants from my dresser and slipped them on. As nonchalantly as possible, I opened the door. Brady's unamused face greeted me. "Hey. What's up?" I rubbed the excess water from my hair with the towel draped over my shoulder.

"What's going on with you?"

"Nothing. It's just—"

"Stop saying it's work. You took off on me at the park. Why?"

"I told you. I wanted to run, and you were tired."

"No. I said I needed more rest."

"Oh. Well, sorry. I misunderstood." I forced the corners of my mouth as high as they would go. "You did great today. First nonstop two miles. I'm so—"

"If you say you're proud of me, I might waterboard you with bottled water."

I pursed my lips together to keep the unkind thoughts from escaping. My mouth twitched, desperate to lay out all the reasons Matt could never be good enough for Brady that I'd come up with over the past few weeks. He wouldn't know how to switch Brady's brain from frustrated at himself to motivated to do something about it. He wouldn't appreciate the subtle difference between Brady's self-deprecating humor and actual hurt. He didn't know yellow mustard made him gag, or that he liked his coffee the color of gingerbread, or that you had to put the toppings in the cup first, then add strawberry frozen yogurt because he insisted it was easier to mix it up that way.

"Sorry." I left Brady at the doorway to sit on my bed. Brady stared at me and sighed when I switched on the television.

"You know that Matt is a friend. I think you'd like him. His company actually just got this big award for their LGBT policies. Cool, right?"

Brady's enthusiasm only added to my agony. I shrugged.

"Josh," Brady pleaded. When I ignored him, he sat on the bed next to me and stretched his legs. After a few seconds of silence, Brady nudged my foot with his own. "Josh," he repeated. "What's wrong?"

I sniffled and changed the channel. Brady made a move for the remote and with a pointed stare, dared me to not let go. I relaxed my hand and said nothing as Brady muted the television.

His troubled eyes wore me down. I had to tell him something. "Brady, I don't know what you want me to say. I'm sorry that I'm proud of you."

"Why are you acting so weird?"

"I'm not."

"Are you tired of helping me with all this? I never realized I'd last so long, and you know, I don't expect you to make all my food too. I know you'd rather go to the gym, but I'm not ready for that. I can run by myself. I'm starting to feel like I'm taking advantage of your generosity again. You have to promise me you'll say no if it's too much or I'm holding you back."

Great. The last thing I wanted was for Brady to start pulling away again. I was being a selfish asshole. If Matt was who Brady wanted, I needed to try harder. "You know I love our runs, and you eat what I eat; it's not like I make special food for you." *Much.*

"But then why—"

I affixed a crowbar-proof smile to my face. "Listen, I'm your best friend, that's why. I know how down you were feeling. If this is making a difference, then I'm happy to help. Speaking of which, do you have plans tonight? I was thinking of inviting the guys over to try out this new vegetarian lasagna. You should invite Matt."

Brady eyed me skeptically. "Which guys?"

"The Loman guys," I said, referring to our dorm building. "Cade and Sid, maybe Adam if he isn't busy."

"Are Cade and Adam back together?"

I shrugged. "Seems like it. They were cozy when we had lunch last week." I wasn't sure if the disappointment on his face had to do with Adam's on-again, off-again relationship with Cade being back on or me not inviting him to lunch, which I'd have happily done if he hadn't already been doing something with Matt. Whichever it was, Brady seemed to be willing to let the topic of "what the hell was going on with me" die, so I ran with it. "Sid got his visa issue all worked out finally. He texted Cade when we were at the restaurant."

"We need to reinstitute brunch," Brady said. "I hate to think we'd lose touch with them."

"Like I said, I'll go if someone else plans it, but that last time was the final straw. Adam and Cade can't show up with one rando after another to make each other jealous. I know you live for their drama, but I'll only do it if there's a no-boyfriend rule."

Brady rolled his eyes. "I wish they would either get back together for real or break up. This will-they-or-won't-they business is getting old."

I nodded.

"You sure you don't care if I invite Matt tonight? He's still recuperating from his surgery, but I think he's going stir-crazy."

"Why should I care if you invite your boyfriend?"

"Josh, we're really not dating; we're hanging out. I'm sure he'd love to meet the guys, but I won't invite him if you don't want me to."

"Whatever makes you happy, Brady." I tried to mean it this time. "Just remember we share a wall if he stays."

Brady blushed, and my stomach rolled with thoughts of Brady waking up in Matt's arms.

"What time?"

"Let's say seven."

Brady stood, and I shooed him from my room before he realized I'd completely hijacked the conversation.

I paced my room trying to summon the courage to put my dinner party plan in motion, but I couldn't stop picturing Brady's face when he mentioned Matt's name. Brady might have lusted after Adam, but arguably he checked me out just as much. With Matt, it was different—it was like he admired the guy for his accomplishments. He was so out and proud that he'd won awards for it. Nothing I did could compete with that. My coworkers didn't even know I was gay. Not that Brady, or really anyone, knew that small detail.

I had no choice but to power through with this fucking dinner and figure out how to deal with my crushing jealousy without arousing Brady's suspicions. Since I had no idea how to do that, I committed myself fully to faking it.

My first call was to Cade, and while I was prepared to arm-twist him into the last-minute dinner party, luckily, he needed only mild guilt-tripping.

"Please, Cade. How many guys did you make Brady and I meet? This is the first guy he's excited about. We need to vet him. It's your duty as his friend."

Cade's deep rumbling laugh sounded like it belonged to someone twice his size. "Fine, Josh. So, Brady finally found himself a man, and you sound happy about it. That's probably worth a night of vegan food."

My brain stumbled, deciding which of Cade's assertions to correct first. "It's not completely vegan." Something stopped me from addressing the other statement. "Can you call Adam?"

"Adam's coming?"

"I hope so. Why?"

"No reason. How about I call Siddharth?"

"What happened with you and Adam? On Wednesday, you were fine."

"Look, it's, um . . . We've been sort of hooking up again lately, but Adam wants to try again for real."

"Really?"

"Yeah. I'm taking time to think about it."

"Oh, shit. Is it going to be weird?"

"No. Don't sweat it. Adam will come for Brady, you know how he feels about him." The truth was Adam would go to the moon if Cade asked him to, which is why I'd started with Cade in the first place. Adam had a deep affection for Brady too, always had, but he could also be aloof. I thought it was his way of not encouraging Brady's crush.

"He'll be thrilled to meet the guy Brady is in love with." Great. Now Cade was baiting me. This wouldn't bode well for the evening.

"'Love?' I swallowed hard. "I said they were dating. Not in love. Brady won't even admit they're dating yet."

Cade laughed again. "Watch it, Josh. If I didn't know you better, I'd think you were a pessimist. Leave Adam to me. Want me to call Siddharth too?"

I checked my watch. "No, I can call him."

"What time?"

"Seven okay?"

"Yep. Sounds good. Can I bring anything? Is this BYOC?"

I laughed with the memory of our first few months in the house. We'd only had a small table and two chairs from our apartment, so we supplemented entertainment seating with camping chairs. "No. We have a full set of furniture now. No need to bring your own."

"Damn, Josh. Dinner parties and actual dining furniture? You and Brady are slaying this adulting thing."

When I finished my call with Cade, I dialed Sid—only Cade got away with calling him Siddharth. Sid had initially been assigned to live with the other international students across campus, but he'd hit it off with Cade so much that they'd roomed together the next semester until graduation.

"Hello," Sid greeted me with heavy breathing.

"Hi," I answered with a laugh. "You busy?"

"I'm leaving the gym."

"You sure you're not still on the treadmill?"

"Ha ha. Shut up. I missed Canal Street. I'm so out of shape."

"Are you glad to be back?"

"So much. I loved being home but, you know, India isn't the easiest place to be . . ." His voice trailed off, and I heard mumbling in the background, then Sid's laugh.

"Sid," I called to get his attention.

"Sorry, Josh. I got, um, distracted." I laughed and pictured what exactly had distracted him. My guess was tall, salt-and-pepper hair, and glasses. Brady and I had met Sid when he'd overheard us making sexual references about our accounting professor. Brady had noticed his interest and, without missing a beat, had invited him into our conversation. Sid's type hadn't evolved much from Dr. Sullivan, and every guy he dated had the intellectual look on lock.

"Well, we're thrilled to have you back in the land of the free-to-be-a-raging-homosexual."

Sid sighed. "India might be getting better, but my parents—"

"Yeah. I know." Sid and I had similar experiences in that regard, but he stayed closeted around his family. Unfortunately, that meant he'd spent the better part of the last year hiding who he was every day while back in India.

My stomach flip-flopped, and I got that lump-swallowing feeling in the back of my throat. The same sharp, breath-stealing ball of raw emotion I'd choked on every day in high school. When pretending hadn't been good enough. I'd convinced myself that anything less than authentic disgust at all things remotely gay would give me away. Now we were both in the half-out, half-closeted world, the only difference being that Sid's situation was entirely understandable. I considered what I'd do in Sid's position. What if Anna hadn't outed me? Would I have come out to my parents? Countless family wars had been waged over my salvation. While Sid's choice meant he could go home and be the celebrated son of proud parents, Anna's scheme had made me a source of shame and worry to mine. I came to my answer quickly—the only family I needed was Brady.

"Listen, so I'm calling to invite you over for dinner tonight."

"Oh. Cool. Is Brady going to be home?"

"Yeah. Plus, Cade and Adam. And Brady is bringing his new boyfriend."

"Brady has a boyfriend?" Sid laughed. "When did that happen?"

"Yeah. They only recently started dating."

"Hmm."

"What?"

"Nothing. I guess I figured you guys . . ."

"Us guys, what?"

"Never mind. That's awesome for Brady. You like him?"

"This is the first time I'm meeting him too."

Sid snorted.

"What?"

"Nothing. Sounds fun. I'll be there."

Cooking relaxed me, so I shifted to preparing for the dinner party. I decided to make the lasagna noodles from scratch and mapped out a schedule, so I'd be sure everything came together at the right time. When Cade texted to confirm Adam was in, I sent Brady to the store for wine and kale for the Caesar salad I wanted to make.

As soon as Brady left, another email from Ken arrived. He needed some slides prepped for a potential new client, something he and the other partner, Mike Kennedy, were working on. He'd copied Larry again. I wasn't surprised since he'd always stoked our rivalry. Unfortunately, it changed exactly nothing about my Pavlovian response. No matter how far away the next promotion was for both of us, I still couldn't let Larry get the jump on me. I punched out a quick response to let Ken know I was working on it.

I hauled my laptop out and manipulated a few spreadsheets. When I'd finished drafting the materials, I reviewed all the numbers and sliced and diced them in every imaginable combination, making sure each graph was as visually pleasing as it was accurate. Ken was known to be both picky and impulsive, so the key was to ensure he had options. It could be tedious, but it was a good job, and I had been lucky to land a position with who was widely considered to be the better partner. Ken was a shark, and my job was to throw the chum, but he had a strong reputation in the field and a work ethic to match. He was shrewd, a little ruthless, but mostly fair. Mike Kennedy, on the other hand, had come up the ranks in record time to make senior partner despite his reputation for being an arrogant prick.

I glanced back to the email to confirm the name of the company was correct on all the slides—Freedom Athletics. It sounded familiar, but I couldn't place it. Search results revealed it to be your run-of-the-mill women's athletic line. I spent a few minutes poking around the website, scrunching my face at the leggings' wild prints. "Blue camo?" I asked out loud. *Who thought that was a good idea?*

I surfed some more, hoping Ken would respond that he had what he needed so I could log off. Thirty more minutes went by before I noticed the time. *Shit. I'm behind schedule.*

With a frustrated huff, I snapped my laptop closed and tossed it onto the couch. I knew Larry was combing through my spreadsheets, looking for an error to point out to Ken, so I grabbed my phone to keep my eye on my email.

I pulled out the stand mixer from the cabinet and smiled at the sunny yellow color that always reminded me of Joy, Brady's mom. It took me a few tries to use the pasta attachment, but soon I had several picture-perfect sheets of dough. I stood back and admired my work.

I was filling a pot of water when Brady called.

"Hey. I got your organic kale. They were out at Target, but I found it at Whole Foods."

"Oh, good. And the wine?" I added salt to the pot of water and turned on the burner.

"Matt wanted to bring something, so I told him he could bring a few bottles from his collection."

Of course, Matt had a wine collection.

"Cool, so are you on your way?"

"That's why I called. Matt's not too far from Whole Foods, and he can't drive yet, so I can either pick him up early, and we can hang at the house, or I can kill time at his place. I didn't want to leave you high and dry, but I didn't know how you'd feel if he came early?" I hated the dilemma in Brady's voice and the fact that he knew he needed to check with me on something so trivial. Matt was probably a go-with-the-flow type like Brady.

I glanced at the oven clock and mentally recalculated the schedule for the lasagna assembly and bake time. It would need at least forty minutes to cook. I'd lost most of my buffer, but I could still make it work. If Brady and Matt came home now, that pretty much maximized my stint as a third wheel, but if they came later, I'd need to set the table and put out appetizers on my own, which wasn't accounted for in my schedule. I summoned all the cheer I could muster before answering. "No worries. I got it."

We said our goodbyes, but the phone rang again just as I was slipping the noodles into the pot.

Figuring it was Brady to double-check me, I answered without looking at the screen. "I swear I can handle it," I laughed.

"Since when do you password protect your spreadsheets, Meyer?"

My shoulders tensed. Fucking Larry. "Since someone tampered with my macros on the Peterson Furniture account. Never can be too careful."

"Whatever. Ken needs me to fix something, so I need the password."

I switched on the speaker so I could navigate to my email. Fuck. Ken had sent the request twenty minutes ago. "I'll fix it," I said, already halfway to my laptop.

"You're clearly busy."

"I'm doing it now."

"Whatever, Meyer. I was only trying to help." The phone went dead, and a loud sizzling noise sounded from the kitchen.

I ran toward the stove and yanked the overflowing pot from the burner. "Damn it," I yelped as some water splashed on my skin. When I saw the pasta-turned-ball-of-mush, a familiar panic roiled in my chest.

I finished making the changes for Ken, then left the mess on the counter and ran to the store to buy replacements. I tried to let the stress of the last hour go, but the unplanned trip was sending jolts of thunder through my nerves.

When I returned, Brady and Matt were clutching four bottles of wine between them and standing dumbfounded in the messy kitchen.

"There you are," Brady said. "Where did you go?"

"Sorry. Noodle emergency." I held up the cloth bag containing the no-bake lasagna noodles and set it on the counter. Having resolved the look of concern on Brady's face, I turned my attention to Matt.

Matt was taller than me by an inch or two, which made him a head taller than Brady. He had mousy, overgrown brown hair and a gap between his front teeth. His pallid skin bordered on unhealthy. I hoped it was from his recent surgery and that he wasn't on one of those fad diets where you only eat one food group. It wasn't my place to say anything, but Brady had really been doing great with eating healthy, and I didn't want that derailed. Matt wasn't exactly ugly, but Brady was infinitely more attractive. I summoned my best grin. "You must be the famous Matt."

Matt appraised me skeptically, and I felt his judgment before I heard it in his voice. "And you must be the world's best roommate."

Roommate? You shady bastard. My competitive side ignited. "Among other things..." I sauntered up to Brady and pressed a kiss to his cheek. When I pulled back, Brady's eyes were wide and confused. Granted, I wasn't usually so coy about the nature of our relationship. "Brady and I are best friends as well," I clarified to lower the raised eyebrows in the room.

"Of course." Matt nodded and took a step closer to Brady. He set his wine down on the counter and took Brady's from him. "I brought these from my collection. Brady said you liked white wine, but since you were making lasagna, I thought Italian reds paired best. I also brought you a Riesling, in case you were serious about the white. It's from my last trip to Germany." He flashed a Cheshire cat smile and surveyed the noodle disaster. "But maybe the dinner menu has changed?"

Game on, motherfucker.

Brady's gaze darted between Matt and me. I forced myself into my well-practiced work stance—spine tall, shoulders back, and corners of my mouth turned up. Projecting confidence was all about posture.

Brady shook his head at the opening act of our evening and grabbed a bottle from the counter. "All right, well, I'm going to open this one." He pulled down a single wineglass and filled it with one of the reds. "Matt, you want anything?"

"Just water, thanks." Brady nodded and began to fill a cup with ice when Matt added, "Oh. Do you have bottled?"

Brady choked on his laughter, but his head whipped toward me. The apparent joke at my expense knocked me out of my fighting stance, and I lost control of my facial muscles. Before I recovered, the doorbell rang.

"We'll get it," Brady said, shoving a still-smirking Matt toward the front door. On his way out of the kitchen, Brady squeezed my shoulder. Coupled with his remorseful expression, it might have been his way of calling it a draw, but it felt like a knockout blow to me.

Chapter Five
Brady

Adam's blue eyes used to make my insides swim, but less than an hour into the evening, it was crystal clear that Adam was now the one underwater. The way he looked at Cade... *Damn.* I would kill to have a man look at me like that. I didn't know how Cade kept up his constant silly banter with Adam's eyes fixated on him.

"Brady—" Cade laughed "—do you remember?"

"I'm sorry. What?"

Matt flashed an amused expression and patted my thigh. "Cade was telling us about your speech at the freshman dorm 'safe sex' lecture. He couldn't remember the name of the RA you scandalized."

"Oh." I smiled at the memory. I could see the kid's face clearly. An absolute stunner until he opened his mouth. Blond hair, California tan...

"Oliver," Josh's voice called from the kitchen. "Oliver Torball," he added as he emerged, clutching the pan of lasagna with potholders. "Dinner is ready," he declared proudly and placed the lasagna dish in the center of the table. Josh fussed over the table's aesthetics and filled wineglasses—with red wine.

"That's right," Cade said as we situated ourselves at the table. "Oliver had finished instructing us on how to tell the nice girls from the disease-ridden sluts when Brady got up and asked to see his disease-ridden dick."

"I did not," I said mostly to Matt, who was the only one who hadn't heard this story a million times. I dared a glance toward Josh, gauging the level of stress he hid behind perfectly formed lasagna slices.

"I still can't believe I made it through the year without punching that guy," Adam said. "You should've heard the bullshit he spouted after Josh asked about guys who wouldn't wear condoms."

"Yeah, but then Brady suggested that he put up a picture of himself, so he'd know how to avoid fucking an insufferable, misogynistic, homophobic dude-bro," Cade continued.

The table laughed, and I zeroed in on Josh's reaction. He'd settled in his chair across from me and between Sid and Cade. The dimple on his right cheek, coupled with the little lines around his eyes, was inconclusive.

Pre-college, the toxic masculinity in Josh's world had been thicker than the odor of Axe body spray in a middle school locker room. Oliver's mocking had set Josh's progress back months, but Adam's response that if a guy refused to wear a condom "you tell him to fuck right off" had sparked our friendship, so the memory wasn't all bad.

Josh laughed a little too loudly as he shared another of our well-told encounters-with-Oliver stories with the group, and the hairs on the back of my neck stood up. No one else noticed, but I knew Josh's laughs. That one was a red flag. I definitely shouldn't have left him alone to get the party together.

"Brady should have been an RA," Sid said and took a sip of his wine. He lifted his glass. "This is fantastic, Josh."

Josh cleared his throat. "Oh. Thank Matt. He brought the wine."

Sid raised his glass in Matt's direction, and Matt nodded his acknowledgment to the chorus of agreement from the table.

"Should we toast?" Matt stood with his glass in hand.

I swallowed hard. Other than Josh's occasional sentimental gush, we weren't a formal-toast kind of crowd, and I had no idea what to expect. Josh shot me a perplexed look, but before I could tug Matt back into his chair, he spoke.

"I want to say thanks to Josh and Brady for including me tonight. It's been kind of a rough couple of weeks for me. It's nice to get out of the house for a home-cooked meal and to laugh. I didn't have many friends growing up, so being included in an evening like this means a lot. I also want to make a toast to Brady." He gazed down at me and smiled with a huge teeth-baring grin. "Earlier today, I officially signed off on your offer to join our company. Angela will be calling you to discuss specifics, but she told me I could let you know tonight. Congratulations! You got the job."

I didn't care that it was wildly inappropriate, I jumped up from the table and hugged Matt so hard he had to remind me of his incisions. "Sorry," I said, stepping back. Tears were streaming down my cheeks. Cade, Adam, and Sid rose to shake my hand and pat me on the back.

"Oh my god. This is ridiculous." I wiped at my eyes. "I'm so happy right now." I thanked Matt again profusely, and a sense of profound relief settled over me. For so long, I'd watched my friends start their adult lives while I fell further and further behind. I exhaled, fanned my face, and worked on gathering all my emotions when I caught sight of Josh. His forkful of lasagna was frozen midway to his gaping mouth like someone had hit the Pause button.

"Josh," I prompted.

He blinked hard, then dropped his fork. "This calls for bubbly. We have that bottle left over from New Year's Eve. I'll go get it." His eyes welled red, and he shot up from the table.

Everyone stiffened at Josh's reaction, and when he left, all the eyes turned to me for an explanation I didn't have. "Um . . . excuse me for a minute." On my way out, I flashed a look to Sid. He kicked off another conversation to drown out whatever was about to happen in the kitchen.

I found Josh bent over, peering into the open refrigerator. "Um . . . Josh." I tapped his back.

He sniffled. "Just a minute," he said in a stilted voice that did little to hide his emotions. "Where is that bottle?"

Josh cleaned the fridge out every week. There was no way he thought that it contained a mysterious bottle of ten-month-old champagne hidden among obsessively organized bins and shelves. "Unless you've found a new access point to Narnia, I'm prepared to stand here until you look at me."

Josh sighed heavily. "Are you alone?"

I glanced over my shoulder, although no one had followed me. "Yes."

Josh straightened slowly and shut the fridge. His neck and cheeks were splotchy red.

"I'm an idiot. I'm sorry."

Josh's puppy-dog eyes weren't enough this time. "Tell me why." I locked the full weight of my confused expression onto him and touched his arm.

He flinched as though I'd hurt him. "Brady." He sighed. "Can we . . . later." He nodded to the room full of guests. Josh was a master at distraction. He thought I didn't notice when he procrastinated and dodged conversations, but I did. I debated forcing the issue, but no matter what he put out to the world, deep down, Josh was a private guy. Getting to the truth mattered to me, and that wouldn't happen until we were alone. "Later. You promise? No more bullshit."

Josh turned an alarming shade of white and held my stare for a beat. A swell of Cade's laughter and Adam's answering snort bellowed from the dining room, and we exchanged a smile at the tension breaker. Josh nodded, and since apparently a job offer and two glasses of wine turned me into a hugging fool, I tugged him into my arms. Josh burrowed into me and squeezed my waist while wiping his cheek on the shoulder of my black shirt.

When he pulled back, the emotion in his eyes had waned. "I'm thrilled for you, Brady. You absolutely deserve this job, and you're going to be amazing at it." He used the back of his hand to wipe his cheeks, then used his jeans to dry his hands. When he glanced up, I laughed. The word he was trying not to say was practically written on his face.

"You can say it." I rolled my eyes and returned his smile. "Just this once."

He exhaled a breath of laughter, and his face lit up. He placed his hands on either side of my cheeks and pressed a lip-smacking smooch to my forehead. "I'm so freaking proud of you."

"I'm sorry I didn't tell you about the interviews. I was trying to keep my expectations really low, and I was worried talking about it might get my hopes up."

Now I could finally stop keeping this secret from him and pay him back for everything he'd done for me. Miraculously, that freed me of more weight than the twenty-five pounds I'd shed in the previous two months. With Josh's wholehearted approval, my mind accepted

Matt's offer as a reality. "You're the only one who always believes in me. I mean it, Josh. I would have given up if it weren't for you."

I'd done it. Four years of college, countless job applications, endless rejections, and three rounds of grueling interviews, but finally I could quit my job and start a career.

Josh kept his arm draped over my shoulder, grabbed another bottle from Matt's contribution, and walked with me to the dining room. When the group turned to acknowledge our presence, Josh held up the bottle.

"Brady drank the champagne, boys. So, we'll have to make do with Matt's wine." Everyone laughed as Josh topped off glasses and raised his to the center. He placed his free hand over his heart and smiled. "To Brady," he declared, and a series of clinks ushered in a new round of congratulations.

When we took our seats, Matt patted my thigh and leaned into me, asking quietly if I was okay.

With my eyes trained on a smiling Josh, I nodded, and Adam clapped a congratulatory pat to my shoulder. He beamed at me with the brother-like affection I used to overanalyze to the point of insanity.

"I'm happy for you, Brady," Adam said and gave me a friendly kiss on the cheek.

"*We* are so proud of you," Cade clarified with his arm hoisted around Sid's shoulder.

I nodded my appreciation and exchanged a look with Adam. When he nodded, I felt his understanding with a profound sense of relief—a final confirmation that the feelings I had once held for Adam were well and truly dead. I wanted nothing more than to move past the drama of our college days.

"Thanks," I said solemnly. These guys were the best friends a guy could ask for.

"To Brady!" Cade offered and his toast sealed the moment. I caught the heat flashing between Adam and Cade, and for the first time, I genuinely hoped they figured it out. They were kind of perfect together.

Soon the conversation returned to catching up, gentle ribbing, and explaining our inside jokes to Matt. While everyone was helping with dishes, Matt asked to speak to me, so I led him to my bedroom.

"You seem happy," he said and shut the door behind us.

"I'm doing great. I can't thank you enough, Matt. Really. This is amazing, I won't let you down."

"This was all you, Brady. Guys like Josh have a tendency to make everything about them, but you worked hard for this."

My mouth gaped as I struggled to find the context for his comment. I stammered a few times before finally getting out what I wanted to say. "Josh is happy for me. Really. That was about something else. We're good."

"If you say so," Matt quipped. "I wanted to say thanks again for including me. You seem to have really genuine friends. People who *will* root for you."

I wondered if he included Josh, arguably my biggest cheerleader, in that comment. I didn't think so, but now that he was my boss, it wasn't worth getting into it.

"I should probably go help with clean up."

Matt nodded and followed me to the kitchen, where the guys had already done the bulk of the work. Josh's eyes traced from Matt to me and grew wider as Matt wiped his mouth with the back of his hand as though there had been some exchange of fluids during our little confab. Josh's jaw opened, but I gave him an almost imperceptible shake of my head asking him to not engage. I needed both of them to cool it.

We talked, laughed, and—since I'd forgotten I was Matt's ride—drank into the early-morning hours. Before I confessed to my new boss that if he valued his safety, he should stay the night, Sid offered to drive Matt home. When Sid excused himself to grab his coat off my bed, I followed him and hugged him from behind as a thank-you. "You're the best," I slurred.

Sid tapped my arm and wiggled free, laughing. He steadied me with hands to my shoulders. "Easy there." He glanced at the doorway. "Brady, how drunk are you?"

I shrugged. "Too drunk to drive."

"So if I asked you what was *really* going on between you and Matt, you could tell me?"

"Nothing's going on. We're friends. He's gonna be my boss, so yeah . . . friends."

"But do you have feelings for him at all?" Sid bit his lip.

It took me about three times longer than a sober person to connect the dots. "Oh, shit. You and Matt?"

Sid looked guilty. "Um . . . say the word, and we can pretend I didn't ask. Josh said he was your boyfriend, and if that's true, we're cool. It's just . . . Matt made a point to say you and he were friends, and you didn't seem too bothered by that. Did I misread this situation?"

"No," I said loud enough for Sid to glance nervously toward the family room.

He held up his arms, palms out, in a surrender gesture. "Okay. It's fine. I'm sorry. I'm totally hands-off."

"No. I meant you didn't misread. Full disclosure, we did sleep together, but only the once. We're on the same page. There is no reason for you to not . . . make a move . . . if you want."

Sid's bottom lip slipped from his teeth's hold, and he smiled. "You're sure?"

"Yeah. Matt's loaded. One of us should snag a sugar daddy." I laughed too loudly, and Sid cringed. "Kidding," I said, swaying slightly as the room spun. "I need to lay down." My face hit the mattress.

I opened my eyes to a sunny morning, a killer headache, an upset stomach, and a message from Angela asking me to call her to review my offer.

Two ibuprofen and a handful of antacids mostly fixed me right up. And as a bonus, the scale dropped another two pounds. I took a long, hot shower and worked out a plan for the day. I'd apologize to Josh for how much I'd let my prolonged job search and financial strain impact our friendship. He'd tell me whatever was bothering him. We'd hug it out and spend the day celebrating my new job.

My good mood minimized the effects of my hangover, and I exited the bathroom, singing to myself and feeling better than I had in ages.

Until I stopped suddenly and turned, staring at Josh's empty bed. *Damn it.*

"Josh," I yelled, then flinched at the loud noise. Expecting the silence didn't diminish its impact. My heart sunk. I should have pushed Josh for an explanation the night before. It was a good thing my endurance had improved. Getting a real answer from him was gonna be a marathon, not a sprint.

I waited for Josh to come home for a while, then texted. When he didn't respond to any of my messages, I figured my plan to clear the air with Josh was going to have to wait.

After I spoke to Angela and accepted my offer, Josh still wasn't home, but the prospect of earning real money was burning a hole in my pocket. It was rare I had the desire to splurge on my wardrobe, but my take-home pay was about to double and I needed work clothes, so it felt like the perfect distraction.

Since Josh was AWOL and I admired Adam's style, I figured why not build on our breakthrough from last night? Adam needed to meet the new-and-improved adulting Brady, untethered from petty jealousy, painful awkwardness, and hopeless crushes.

"Hello," Adam answered the phone cheerfully.

"Hey, it's Brady."

"Whoa. You're alive. Thought you'd be nursing a serious hangover today."

I chuckled, pleasantly surprised by how well this was going. You'd have thought I called Adam all the time. Feeling braver, I proceeded full speed ahead. "The headache I woke up with wasn't pleasant, that's for sure. You and Cade doing okay?"

There was a brief pause before Adam responded earnestly. "Yeah. We're good. Real good. Cade's just getting ready to head over to Sid's."

"Oh, were you . . . I don't mean to interrupt."

"No, it's fine. They're going to a movie that I have no desire to see. It's based on a book they like."

"Ask him if he and Brady want to go," Cade hollered in the background.

"It *is* Brady," Adam hollered back.

"Really?" Even whispered, the question in Cade's voice punctuated how far out on the limb I was.

"Cade wants to know if you want to join them. You don't. I practically fell asleep during the trailer. Seemed depressing as shit."

"Josh had to go out, but, um, I was calling to see if you maybe wanted to go shopping with me today?"

"Really?"

I heard the limb crack, but there was no turning back now. "Yeah. I need to spruce up my work wardrobe. It's, um, just a thought. If you're busy, it's fine."

"Hold on." The phone went mute long enough for me to determine I'd overestimated our progress. Maybe Adam still felt uncomfortable hanging out one-on-one with me. I probably needed to tell him that I was over him. That'd be the adult way to handle this, but since I'd never actually admitted to having feelings for him, it wasn't a conversation I was eager to have. Maybe I should wait for Josh to go shopping...

"Sorry about that, Brady," Adam said. "You still there?"

"Never mind, it's okay, I'll let you go."

"No! I'd love to go with you. I know a great place too. It's where I get my suits. I'll text you the address. Give me an hour or so?"

As soon as Adam disconnected, I exhaled a deep breath. This was gonna be interesting.

The piano music and the wide gaps between hangers told me I should have mentioned my budget before agreeing to Adam's suggestion.

"Hey, Brady." Adam waved to me from a plush leather chair and rose as I approached.

I ambled toward him and glanced around. "Hey. So, listen. This place..." I gestured to the sparse racks.

"Too expensive?" He raised an eyebrow.

"Yeah," I breathed, grateful he understood.

"Don't sweat it. I brought you here because they'll take your measurements and give you a ton of style advice. When we're done, you can take that knowledge and bargain shop. I'll hook you up with my tailor; he can make an off-the-rack suit look custom for a fraction of the price." Adam winked at me, and his reassuring smile set me at ease. "You ready?"

"Yeah, let's do this."

I followed Adam to the service counter and nodded as he explained what we needed. Before I knew it, I was in a mirrored dressing room while a lovely man named Santiago ran his fabric measuring tape all over me. Adam distracted me with funny tweets.

"Now, your waist," Santiago said.

I glanced down at the lithe man and frowned. Slowly, I lifted my arms and squeezed my eyes closed. He wrapped the measuring tape around me.

"Forty-two," he said as he jotted it down.

I shrieked.

"What's wrong?" Adam's head whipped up from his phone screen, eyes full of concern.

"Nothing," I said, forcefully containing my smile. *Two months*, I screamed internally. *I was down to a forty-two in two months.* Which meant the suit I'd bought for my interviews was officially too big already. "Adam, can you text me the name of your tailor?"

He eyed me suspiciously but smiled. "Sure thing."

After an hour of advice about which colors and style best flattered me, I found a suit I'd buy in every color if ever I won the lottery. I stared at myself, turning to admire my profile.

"Wow," Adam said when Santiago returned with a few ties.

Santiago scrutinized me and held up a series of ties to my chest before declaring, "I think purple is better." He tossed the yellow and red one on the chair, then slid the tie around my neck and secured it. I eyed myself as Santiago did a three-sixty, tugging on fabric and smoothing out imaginary lines. With an approving smile, he angled me toward Adam and winked. "Now you can give that wow."

Adam's blue eyes danced over me. His face split into a grin. "Wow."

"Really?"

"Oh, yeah. Total stud. I can really tell you've lost weight."

The bill for the shirt and tie was more than my car payment but entirely worth it. The suit would have required a black-market organ donation, but Adam ended up with a sweater and some new shoes, so at least Santiago got some commission for his time.

"That was fun," I declared.

"It was." Adam smiled, his tone sort of sentimental. "I'm happy you invited me. You want to grab a bite? I know you're trying to eat light, but..." He glanced across the expansive parking lot to a row of popular chain restaurants that circled the mall. "I could go for a steak right now. What do you say? My treat."

I shook off his offer to pay but accepted his invitation. "A steak sounds good. Want to walk it?"

We stashed our packages in our cars and strolled toward the steakhouse.

As soon as we had ordered, Adam coughed and cleared his throat. "So, Cade said I should clear the air today." He laughed, probably at the unnatural circumference of my eyes.

"Damn, here I thought we were doing so well at ignoring the elephant in the room."

Adam chuckled. "I guess I wanted to say that I hope we can put the past aside. I don't want there to be any hard feelings."

"Adam." I sighed. "It's fine. I always understood it. I know I wasn't your type, and you didn't need a guy like me lusting after you. I'm sorry I made it so weird, especially when you and Cade first got together."

He cocked his head and gave me a twisted smile. "What are you talking about?"

I froze. "Um, what are *you* talking about?"

Adam took a long drink of his water and coughed again. Shaking his head, he gritted his teeth. "I'm going to kill Cade."

I stared. "Wait. What?"

"Listen, Brady. I don't know what you mean by 'my type.' The only reason—and I do mean the only reason—that I kept my distance was out of respect for Josh."

"Josh? What does Josh have to do with this?"

Adam's face turned crimson, and he shook his head, apparently working through what to say. "I knew Josh wasn't okay. Damn it, Cade," he muttered, dropping his gaze to the table. He peered up and met my dumbstruck expression. "So, you *are* dating Matt?"

"No, I'm not, but I'm honestly so confused right now. You like guys like Cade. I get it. It's not your fault. Most guys don't find someone like me attractive. There is no reason to bring Josh into this."

Adam's jaw fell, and he stammered a few times. "You should know that Cade and I are going to have an earnest discussion about meddling. But in the interest of acknowledging the elephant and the hippo and any other number of wild animals you seem to be oblivious to . . . I'm going to say this as plainly as I can. The reason I went out of my way to avoid encouraging your crush, the reason I never once considered dating you—" Adam grabbed my hand and squeezed it "—is because Josh was so obviously, painfully, over-the-moon in love with you, and I could never bring myself to hurt him."

I ripped my hand out of Adam's grasp and knocked over my water glass in the process. "Shit." I sat the cup upright and used my napkin to push the ice cubes from my lap to the floor.

"Brady, I'm sorry." Adam handed over his napkin and shuttled cups and silverware out of my way. "Josh was so fragile. It didn't seem right to move in while he was figuring his shit out. Then when we met Cade . . ." He swallowed hard. "Please tell me you understand. I couldn't even entertain it."

"Stop," I cried. "Just Adam. Please stop." *What was happening?*

Adam stood and snagged another napkin from an empty table. "Here," he said meekly.

I soaked up the excess water from my jeans and closed my eyes. I took a few deep breaths and finally braved a look at Adam, who, from his body language, appeared mortified by his confession. "What did Cade tell you?"

Adam shook his head. "Cade and I are rocky right now. I have a lot to make up for, and I . . . Please don't ask me to throw him under the bus."

My jaw clicked. The sound of enamel being worn off my teeth resonated in my ears. Damn it. First Matt, now Adam. Everyone needed to stop tossing out accusations and refusing to explain themselves. "There's no bus. We're adults. Please tell me."

Adam opened his mouth as if to protest, but he seemed to change his mind. "When Cade called to invite me to dinner last night, he said you and Matt were dating. Which you had pretty much told me yourself. We all thought including Matt in the party meant Josh had finally moved on. Then Matt kept calling you a friend, but he also tried to make Josh jealous, so we were all confused. Sid told Cade you gave him your blessing if he wanted to ask Matt out. And somehow Cade became convinced you were talking about Josh when you told me you had a date, and maybe that was the reason Josh was so weird last night. My working theory is Cade's 'clear the air' was code to find out what the hell is going on with you two."

Okay, maybe some of his confusion made sense. "Look, Matt and I were dating, but when the job thing came up, we decided we'd be better friends. Josh and I are friends, we've always been friends. No dating. I'll admit things are a little off between us now; he's definitely not happy I didn't tell him about my interview. We were supposed to talk about it this morning, actually, but you know Josh—he hates conflict."

I didn't think Adam needed to know how far Josh and I had drifted apart during the last year, particularly because it would inevitably lead to me explaining how a lot of that drifting stemmed from how much money Josh had fronted me. Adam grew up rich. He wouldn't understand how uncomfortable it made me. How much I worried I was taking advantage of Josh's endless generosity.

"I don't know, Brady. It seemed like jealousy to me, but you and Josh are hard to read sometimes, and I guess I wanted to believe Cade was right." He paused, seeming a little disappointed. "You honestly didn't notice Josh trying to one-up Matt in the 'who knows Brady best' contest all night?"

It hadn't escaped my attention that Matt enjoyed needling Josh, but he'd been pretty confident something was going on with Josh and me, so I'd attributed that to him testing his theory. And I kind of liked his ability to elicit real emotion from Josh. There was clearly something about Matt that got under Josh's skin. I figured most of that had to do with his reaction to Matt's fitness advice. Josh knew his stuff, and I understood his not appreciating me questioning it.

"Josh has been weird lately. I don't know what is going on with him." Now Adam had me worried, and Josh and I were severely overdue for that talk.

I took a long drink of ice water before I realized it was from Adam's cup. I wiped the liquid—more sweat than condensation—off my palms onto my pants leg. "You think he's mad about having to workout with me instead of going to the gym? You know how he is about exercise—It's like Prozac to him. I'm probably taking advantage of him."

Adam rolled his eyes. "Brady. Oh my god. I'm telling you he's jealous."

I thought through the night before—what I remembered of it anyway. There'd been an unmistakable memory-lane theme in Josh's stories. He had made some vague comment that we were more than roommates, and he'd been a little over-the-top with affectionate touches. So maybe he was flirtier than usual. But Josh was flirty with everyone; he didn't mean anything by it.

I knew Josh, and he knew me—better than anyone. I'd told him what I wanted. He knew how tough this last year had been for me. Why would he listen to me talk about wanting a relationship, know how lonely I was, and not say anything if he was even remotely interested? That couldn't be it. If he was jealous, it was because Matt and I had gotten close. Maybe I'd been neglecting our friendship more than I realized.

"I'm not sure where the misunderstanding was, but nothing is happening with Josh and me. He flirts with literally everyone. If he had feelings for me, why would he create a dating profile for me? It's ridiculous." I shook my head. "I hope this doesn't change your mind about us hanging out now. I'm over my crush and have been for a while. For what it's worth, I'm rooting for you and Cade. Your virtue is safe with me."

"Brady." Adam sighed, and I knew my attempt to change the subject had failed. "C'mon."

"But why?" With an incredulous huff, I flung my hands in the air, narrowly missing the other water glass this time.

Adam swiftly moved the cup out of my way. His eyes narrowed. "What do you mean *why*? The man has idolized you forever."

I *tsk*ed and waved my hand dismissively. *Idolized*? "Now I know you're wrong. What in the world would Josh idolize about me? My killer body? My winning personality? My rousing business success?"

Adam gave me a look that seemed to say he'd *seriously* underestimated my low self-esteem. "Fine. I said what I had to say." Adam turned his attention to the server who approached with our meals, and we paused our conversation while she situated our plates.

After she left us to it, I glowered at him. His eyes really were breathtaking, but the only thing shining through them at that moment was sympathy, so I ate.

A few bites in, Adam broke our standoff. "Let me ask you something. Of the five of us, which two do you think are the closest?"

His question gave me pause. Cade and Adam had dated hot and heavy for years, but since Adam had cheated, there was a distance between them. Sid and Cade had been roommates, and those two shared a comradery the rest of us hadn't even tried to understand. I made my way through each of the combinations, but the answer was obvious.

"Josh and me. But that doesn't mean he's in love with me. We've lived together for years, Adam, and never even kissed."

"Brady, I'm not talking about physical contact. The other three of us have had sex with each other"

"Wait. What? Who did Sid sleep with?"

He waved me off. "Both of us. It involved alcohol. Don't change the subject. My point is that sex doesn't make you close. I've fucked Cade so many times I've lost count—I know what makes him come. I know what makes him laugh. I know what makes him throw shit across the room and grind his teeth at night. But you know what I don't know?"

"What?"

"I don't know how to fix him when he's upset. When I tell him things are going to be all right, he doesn't believe me. When he looks at me like I ripped his heart out for a mediocre blowjob after too many margaritas, I don't know how to fix that either. And when he insists I'm not ready for a commitment even though I'd marry that boy tomorrow, I don't know how to prove it. I've tried everything."

Adam sniffled.

"Adam, I'm sorry."

"Don't be. I'll figure it out. I will. If it takes me the rest of my life. But this is about Josh. Do you know how many times I've watched you put him back together? You just have to be there, and he's calmer. Less anxious. Happier. It's like he needs you to chase all the bad stuff away. You know the bullshit his parents filled his head with. Sometimes you can see in his eyes how hard he fights against those voices.

He might be smiling and giving pep talks and making sure the table is set correctly, but inside that perfectly wrapped package are a whole lot of dark thoughts."

I shook my head, refusing to allow the idea to take root. "We're friends, Adam. Josh doesn't want a relationship."

"And normally I would be the first to say you have to respect that, except Josh and you are already in a relationship. Josh and I are friends too, Brady. We've known each other almost as long as you two have. I know how Josh looks at his friends, and trust me, that's not how he looks at you. The fact that you two haven't labeled it doesn't make it any less true."

I was officially in a twilight zone. He wasn't wrong exactly. Josh and I would probably fail a "just roommates" test on paper, but Josh had practically forced me to go out with Matt. Why would he do that if he wanted something more? It made no sense. "I don't know what to say. You're crazy if you think Josh is interested in me like that."

"It's not only about what Josh wants. You don't know how many times I wanted to tell you to quit wasting time on me and see what was right in front of you. Maybe I should have. I underestimated how clueless you are."

I huffed. "Adam, I'm glad we cleared the air, but Josh and I? We make as much sense as you and I would have."

Adam raised an eyebrow. "There you go again. What does that mean?"

"It means, there's you and Josh. Then there is me." I slouched my back and framed my protruding belly roll with jazz hands. "Some of us have six-packs, and some of us have two liters."

"Hold on." Adam sat back from the table, his expression hardening. "How shallow do you think I am?"

"Huh?"

"You think I wasn't interested in you because of your body? You know that's messed up."

I guffawed. "Fine, call me out for having fat shame, but you forget I've seen your Sunday Parade of Twinks. You and Josh have bodies that say 'I just came from the gym' and my body says 'I just came from a bowling alley.' No one attracted to a guy like Cade is going to settle for a guy like me."

He rolled his eyes like he did when Cade was dramatic. "Now you're insulting Cade?"

"What? No, I'm not."

"You're basically saying all Cade has to offer me is his body. That I wouldn't be interested in Cade if he was your size."

"That's not what I'm saying at all. I'm saying that initial attraction is mostly physical, and most guys have a type that attracts them. Plenty of guys are attracted to bigger men, but you're not one of them. Take Sid—his type is nerdy professors. Cade's is tall, athletic guys with blue eyes. Yours is cute elfin twinks."

"And Josh's is?" he prompted, his smile blossoming so rapidly I instantly grew defensive.

"How would I know? When I'm around, he doesn't—" *Oh, shit.* Had I ever actually seen Josh go home with someone? I knew he met guys off the apps, but could I remember one instance where Josh pursued another guy in front of me? Surely, he had... *Damn it.*

Adam gave me a cocky grin and took a big bite of his steak. He moaned as he chewed, leaving me to process my revelation in the prolonged silence. Josh never hit on other guys around me because a good friend didn't ditch his pathetic fat friend. Right?

Adam swallowed and gestured with his fork as he spoke. "For the record, Josh's type is hairy guys with dad-bods. As for your type . . ." He tucked his hand under his chin and batted his eyelashes.

I rolled my eyes. "Maybe I liked it better when we didn't really talk."

Adam laughed. "Unfortunately, I'm taken. However, you might be interested to know Josh and I wear the same size, are about the same height, and work out at the same gym where we often get asked if we're brothers."

"Are you done?"

"Not quite. You should go to Canal Street Gym with Josh. He always wears a black jockstrap when he works out. It's worth the price of admission." He wagged his eyebrows.

A flash of Josh's round perky ass framed by black straps . . . Maybe the red-striped ones with . . . *Nope.* "I do his laundry. I've seen his underwear."

"You do his laundry? Jesus. You two." Adam shook his head.

"So? He cooks and shops for me."

"The fact that you don't realize how much that doesn't help your 'We're not in a relationship' case is profoundly concerning."

"Can you be done now?"

"No." He smirked and took another bite. "And I won't tell Cade you called him an elf. You're welcome."

I sat silently while Adam mowed his way through a rib eye. I'd also been given a lot to chew on, but I'd completely lost my appetite.

Chapter Six
Josh

Canal Street Gym was too expensive, too far away, and too crowded, but for a fit, gay man in his early twenties, you couldn't find a more stimulating environment. There was a reason Adam and I had no qualms about forgoing our work discounts at other gyms, and it had nothing to do with the abundance of first-rate *exercise* equipment.

I stopped at the front desk to scan my membership card.

"Joshie," Trevor, the front desk clerk, greeted me. His full, pouty lips curved into a smile, and he batted his unnaturally long lashes. Today he wore a face full of makeup and pink booty shorts. "Long time, no see. I thought maybe we lost you."

"Hey," I said, eyeing the single open treadmill in the front row. "Nope. Can I have a towel?"

He glanced down at the empty rack where they stored fresh towels and sulked. "Morning rush drained me dry," he purred and winked unnecessarily. "Should have a fresh warm load ready soon. Where should I deliver it to you?"

Thank God the scanner turned green before I turned red. I pointed to the row of treadmills and gave a quick wave to Trevor, but without a towel to claim the machine, I was screwed.

I changed in record time and emerged from the locker room to see some Muscle Mary step onto my treadmill.

The adjacent stretching area was more commonly used as the waiting room for an open machine, so I detoured. I stretched and waited, but I couldn't stop my racing thoughts. *Matt was who Brady deserved.*

My childish response to Matt the night before needed a plausible explanation. I couldn't out and out deny my jealousy, but even the thought of confessing my feelings of inadequacy sent me into a tailspin. I really needed someone to get off a damn treadmill.

My patience waned, and my frayed nerves threatened to unravel if I didn't get on a run soon. I sought out the location of the fire alarm. *Could I?*

Suddenly, a blond head broke the synchronous lines of movement and dipped behind the crowd. My pulse jumped. I out-glared my competition to claim the dated, too-noisy machine they hid in the back row behind all the newer, fancier models.

I secured my headphones and pushed Start. I felt the rhythm of my run, my heartbeat, and the music in my ears. *One mile, two, three . . .* I waited for it. Whether I ran ten miles or thirty, something magical always kicked in at mile six.

My heart pounded against my chest and a lump formed in my throat. Like always, my fears over losing Brady chased me, and I knew from experience, there was no way to outrun them completely.

The replay of all my mistakes from the previous night continued, so I ran faster, hoping to close the door on my messy head for a minute of peace.

Five miles, six . . . He was so happy last night. Because of Matt. What if he moves out now? I'll be all alone. Alone. Like before.

My mind fought me to go back to Hobart. Flashes of Anna clutching dozens of intensely personal emails I'd written to a man who didn't exist—a man she'd made up and tricked me into falling in love with. Her cruel smile as she held me hostage with a weapon she'd fashioned out of my own words.

I pushed harder, upping both the speed and the incline. Sweat poured off me. *Brady, Anna, Dad, work, Brady . . . seven, eight . . .*

I found a glimpse of what I'd been looking for. My past, my parents, my job, everything gone. I floated out of my body, all discomfort disappeared, and running became easier than stopping.

By mile twelve, the euphoria had already faded. The throb in my left knee had intensified, my lungs burned, and instead of my music, my ears kept finding the annoying, uneven rumble of the tread flowing through the archaic machine. I got that odd prickly sensation of being watched, and when I glanced up, Trevor was in front of me. He lobbed a clean, but worn-thin towel, over the top of my monitor and made a show of adjusting himself in his tiny shorts. I lost my rhythm, and awareness chased away what little endorphin high I had left. My body demanded to stop, so reluctantly, I did.

I sopped up the sweat and wiped down the machine, then retreated to the locker room. Annoyed at myself for my unproductive run, I sat on the bench, chugged some water, and peeled off my drenched shirt. While considering my plan for the rest of my day, an imposing figure stepped into my personal space.

"Hey," the voice said. "You looked good out there." A hand came to rest on my shoulder, and I inclined my head. The machine thief's sweaty bulging pectorals and oversized nipples were far too close to my face, his body angled into my space.

"Thanks," I said, and jumped to my feet. The drumbeat of alarm eased. "Excuse me." I gestured to my locker.

His lips quirked, but when I didn't blink, he took the hint and walked away.

A familiar laugh bellowed from the other end of the row of lockers, and I turned to locate the source. I wasn't surprised to see Bare staring back at me; nearly every gay man in the city belonged to Canal Street.

"Well, if it isn't young Joshua," Bare said. He removed his weightlifter's belt and tucked it into his gym bag. "Fancy meeting you here."

I smiled in a way I wished said *Fuck off* but didn't, and Bare's resounding chuckle echoed in my head all the way to the showers.

I pressed my hands against the shower wall and closed my eyes as the hot water cascaded over my crawling skin. What was I going to do? I couldn't avoid Brady forever, and I'd promised him an explanation. But what could I say? *Matt seems super sweet and cares about you enough to give you your dream job, but sorry, I can't handle it when I'm not the center of your world. Oh, and I sometimes have sex dreams about you and fantasize about sucking your dick while you play Mission to Mars, but I'm too messed up to be in a relationship, so let's agree to be single forever. Deal?*

I scoffed. Brady would run from the house screaming. As well he should. Brady deserved whatever future he dreamed of, and he didn't need my baggage holding him back.

No closer to an answer, I dawdled my way through washing and getting dressed. Finally, I checked my phone and read the string of text messages. All from Brady.

Where are you?
Seriously, we are supposed to talk today. Did you go to work?
I got my offer letter. The salary is amazing. Call me when you can.
Let's go shopping. When will you be home?
Okay. I'm going shopping without you.
Adam is coming.
Do you want to go?
When will you be home?
Text me back, please.
Fine. I guess call me if you want to join us.

He was shopping? With Adam? Fuck. Lately, I had to drag Brady shopping, but apparently, if Adam was going, it was a gay ole time. Even after a decent workout, I didn't think I could handle seeing Brady with Adam, especially if he was going to be fawning over what a fantastic guy Matt was—and I'd just had a seriously shitty run. On days like this, my insecurities had insecurities.

Gah. I needed to get a grip.

My friendship with Brady was special—there were only so many people in your life you thought hung the moon even when they were calling you out on your shit. Nothing had changed about that.

As I debated how to respond to Brady, another message arrived. It was from an unidentified number in a very familiar area code. *Hobart, freaking Texas.*

They prayed for you at service today.

I stared at the message and the unfamiliar string of numbers. Maybe it was from a family member or the handful of former friends I hadn't bothered to block after Anna unleashed her treasure trove of emails to the entire three hundred and twenty-two members of Hobart High School. Just because a handful of my so-called friends hadn't sent me vile comments, didn't mean I owed them a response, so I ignored it. A rally full of red-hat-wearing MAGA chanters wished they could secure a border as tight as the one I had erected between my hometown and my new life.

Profound fatigue settled into my muscles as I stepped outside the locker room. My phone dinged again, this time with a link to the announcement pages of my parents' church. Before the page even loaded, I regretted clicking it. My name was in the small square labeled *Prayer Request*, but it was the larger box to the left that made me gasp.

Anna Young to marry Martin Walker.

Anna, appearing pretty much the same as I remembered, posed gazing down at her diamond-clad finger, her palm supported in the much-larger hand of a man I didn't recognize. She seemed happy, like karma hadn't even managed a slap on the wrist.

My heart hurt with the memory of every confession I'd carelessly handed her. Every second I'd wasted agonizing over each word, painstakingly detailing what I wanted in life, my dreams, my deepest fears, how I touched myself, what turned me on . . .

My eyes stung. Tears of anger, pain, betrayal—too many emotions rushed in, overrunning the small peaceful space my run had managed to create.

I pushed past the front desk to the parking lot. I wanted to punch something or be punched, anything to dull the edges. I wanted Brady, but that wasn't an option. I paced by my car, not knowing what to do. I was in no shape to drive, and there was no one to call. Why did this always happen to me? Why couldn't I just get my shit together?

Bare approached. He paused about five feet from me and cocked his head. "Are you okay?"

"You busy?"

Bare smiled, clearly intrigued, and shook his head. "Nope."

"You want to fuck me?"

His eyes widened, and he opened and closed his mouth a few times. "Well—" he chuckled "—it's been a good while since I've had such a tempting offer."

I frowned. "I'm serious, but it has to be now."

"You sure you're okay?" He motioned to my hot mess of a face.

I wiped away the dampness from my cheeks. "I don't want to talk about it. You want to or not?"

"Boy." He flared a wicked smile. "I don't care how tight your hole is, you sass me like that again, and I'll put you over my knee."

I rolled my eyes. "I didn't ask to be your boy, and I don't like being spanked. I need someone to fuck me until..." Humiliation and anger bubbled up to the surface again. Bare stepped toward me, and I backed up toward my car. As soon as I hit the metal, fear stole my breath. "Don't," I said, and Bare froze in place with his hands up.

And goddamn it, I was crying. "Never mind." I ducked away from him, my fingers already searching out my Grindr app. From the parking lot of *this* gym, it'd be like shooting fish in a barrel.

"Josh." Bare reached for my shoulder. "Wait."

I stopped, only on the odd chance he might have changed his mind and could save me the trouble of finding someone else. When I turned to face him, the paternal vibe killed my interest. "What?"

"Instead of fucking some random, maybe we could talk? I can buy you a drink."

My phone dinged. *Brady.*
Please come home. We need to talk.

My skin felt three sizes too small, and I never could think clearly when it got that bad. The gym door opened, and a couple of men spilled out. My eyes met Bare's. His eyebrow peaked, and he challenged me with a gesture toward them. "I'd avoid the blond. Contrary to popular belief, steroids do not do a body good. Nor a personality. You sure you want to risk it?"

I knew what he was insinuating. I needed something specific. Asking a stranger to deliver it was a little like taking a random party drug—the risk-reward calculation wasn't exactly in my favor.

Damn it. "Fine. One drink," I said, sticking my phone into my pocket and cracking my knuckles.

Bare laughed. "You are something else, boy. Get your ass in my car."

I didn't bother to correct him. By the way he looked at me, we weren't ever going to fuck.

I'd never been to a bar in the middle of the day, and I had to say, Grizzlies didn't really appear all that different. There were a handful of guys, mostly in pairs, scattered throughout. Bare pulled out a chair for me at an empty corner table and excused himself to get drinks from the bar. I fidgeted as I waited, blocked the Hobart number that had texted me again, and switched my phone to vibrate.

Bare returned, carrying a glass and a bottle of beer. "Jack and Coke, right?" He set it on the cardboard coaster and took the seat across from me. "You hungry? I ordered some fries."

"Those are loaded with fat and cholesterol."

"Yep." Bare wet his lips. "But since I still have twentysomethings asking me to fuck 'em, I guess I can afford it." I groaned, but he ignored me. "So, tell old Bare all about your boy troubles."

I shook my head and took a sip of my drink. All I tasted was bitterness.

"Come on. Don't make me coax it out of you. I've never seen someone who needed to talk more."

My second sip tasted sweeter, and the alcohol that washed over my tongue promised me relief if I kept going. I should have ordered a shot or twenty. "You do this often?"

"You could say that. I'm a therapist."

I unloaded a mouthful of Jack and Coke.

Bare laughed, wiped the spray from his skin, and handed me a few napkins. "Careful now."

"Are you serious?" I dabbed at the table. Wow. I had not seen that coming.

"You sound surprised."

"To be honest, I pictured you as some kind of dungeon master."

"What's to say I'm not both?" Bare chuckled at my expression, and then grew more serious. "You want to see my degrees, or will a business card suffice?" He reached for his wallet and started pulling out random cards. "I think I have one in here somewhere."

"I believe you. Shouldn't I be lying on a couch or something?"

"Let me guess. You've only seen therapy in the movies?"

I nodded, and his gentle smile set me at ease. "Let's consider this a friendly chat, but if you ever do see someone professionally, you should know couch-lying is entirely optional. Now come on. Get it out. You can start with that boy trouble you mentioned the other day or, if you prefer, whatever set you off in the parking lot."

"My ex, um, the girl I told you about . . . she's getting married."

Bare leaned back and exaggeratingly stroked his bearded chin, making me laugh. He encouraged me to continue. I explained about the catfishing scheme, mostly so that he'd understand why I was so messed up without having to get into everything Anna had done. Even with the vaguest of details, Bare's expression reflected genuine sympathy.

"Wow, Josh. It's terrible enough that she would make up a fake persona to confirm her suspicions about your sexuality, but then to distribute your letters and out you to your friends and family is downright cruel. I'm so sorry she put you through that. I can understand why finding out she's engaged feels very unfair."

I nodded. "Pretty much. But life isn't fair, right? Whatever. I'm doing all right for myself and I have a good job." I mustered up as much enthusiasm as I could, but it wasn't enough to pull off "my life is great."

"Tell me about your job. Do you like what you do?"

"I'm a junior account manager at McConnell & Kennedy."

Bare made a hand motion for me to continue, so I kept on. "I guess I like it. I'm actually the youngest person to be promoted to my position. It wasn't like my dream job or anything, but I'm good at it and it pays well. So, I guess that was one thing my father may have been right about. A lot of my friends really struggled to find jobs after graduation, but I got hired during my internship."

"Does that include your friend, the one you mentioned you were drifting apart from?"

"Brady. Yeah. He got a job actually. He didn't even tell me he was interviewing. I found out last night."

"You don't sound happy about that."

I pursed my lips, summoning enthusiasm with little success. "No, I am. I'm thrilled. And it's going to be great to have him pitch in more with the bills."

If Bare's face was any clue, my feigned sentiment was coming across about as inauthentic as it sounded to my own ears. I paused and gave myself a moment to breathe. This was my one chance to get it all off my chest with virtually no risk of Brady finding out.

"Actually, I'm kind of pissed off about it. Brady was dating Matt—his new boss—or I guess they were . . . Brady insists they're friends now, but whatever. So last night, Matt told Brady about the job in front of all of our friends. I know he did it on purpose to remind me that he can give Brady everything he wants. They've known each other for a couple months, and I didn't even know he was interviewing. I was caught entirely off guard . . ."

The further I got without Bare stopping me to ask questions, the more tension eased out of my shoulders. Then something unexpected happened. Somewhere along the way, I hit mile six, and it became easier to keep going than to stop. I explained more about the dinner party and how jealous and competitive I'd been, which somehow led to explaining how being blindsided by Brady's job offer had rocketed me back to the day I'd learned Anna had shared my emails. How both events felt like having the rug pulled out from me.

Bare eventually did ask me questions, probing a little deeper about my relationship with Brady and my parents until finally, I told him about the day everything changed. Another rug-pulling moment in my life, the one that finally yanked away my entire family.

"It was my second year of school. The first year, I didn't go home at all, but that year my mom made this big gesture. Said they would pay for my trip. Told me they missed me." I took a deep breath, remembering the hot, white pain in my throat I had during that phone call with my mother. I'd spent days agonizing over the decision. Brady and I had made arrangements to stay in the dorm since Brady couldn't afford the time off work to go home, but he insisted that if I had a shot at repairing my relationship with my parents, I should take it. "I knew something was wrong, but you know . . . it was my mom, and she'd barely spoken to me, so I went."

"That's understandable, Josh. We all want to believe our parents wouldn't hurt us, but it's too often not the case. What happened when you went home?"

"It was okay at first. Tense. I tried to stay out of the house when my dad was there, but I didn't really want to see people, and it's a small town. I'd run or just drive around for hours. My mom had stopped wanting to be in public with me, but Christmas morning, she insisted we go to church as a family. I thought maybe things were getting better, but during the service, our pastor made this big speech. He mentioned my parents and how they needed prayers because of me.

I was humiliated, everyone was staring and praying for my soul. Putting hands on me. I tried to run out, but my dad held me there . . . he couldn't be seen to be disrespected like that. He said if I left, I was dead to him . . ." I paused to take a deep breath, letting the memory ricochet through me like a bullet, splitting open old wounds that refused to heal completely. I sniffled, sealing in tears.

My breath stuttered as I looked at Bare. There was a hint of reassurance in his expression that I clung to like a lifeline. Like he was saying it was perfectly okay to still be as angry as I was sad that they'd written me off.

"My whole life I tried to make my parents proud of me, but none of that counted—years of straight A's, trophies, perfect attendance, volunteer work, and charity projects—worthless to them coming from a gay son, so I left." I still wasn't sure if that decision was my biggest accomplishment or my biggest failure; sometimes it felt like both.

"Luckily, my ticket was exchangeable," I said, with a wry laugh that didn't garner a response. Bare was still there, listening quietly with the same sympathetic expression.

"That must have been incredibly difficult. How did Brady react to what happened?"

I closed my eyes, recalling the memory of walking in on Brady singing. Troye Sivan's *Blue Neighborhood* had dropped earlier that month, and Brady and I had spent finals week studying to the album on repeat. One specific track, "Heaven," had resonated with me from the second I'd heard it. Before I'd taken the time to learn the lyrics, it had stirred bubbles of awareness inside like the first fizzy, sweet-bitter sip of a carbonated beverage. When I heard Brady singing over Troye's vocals, it was as though Brady's powerful, low tenor had taken years' worth of bottled-up emotional bubbles and shaken them violently until they had nowhere to go but out. I'd never cried so hard in my life, and not one time had Brady judged me for it. That moment felt too precious to share, so I skipped ahead to later that weekend.

"He was so angry for me. Outraged Brady is like the Hulk if the Hulk was gay and at a slumber party with his superhero friends. He helped burn the 'Find your way back to the Lord' books my parents gave me for Christmas, then stayed up the entire night with me ranting, listening to music, and stuffing me full of ice cream. He took me to a drag show where a nun queen named Anita Amin baptized me with a sprinkle of her Cosmo and serenaded me to 'Born This Way.'"

Bare laughed, and I smiled reflexively.

"Sounds like an amazing guy."

"He is." My face trembled, straining to hold back the floodgates. Brady's family wasn't religious like mine, but after that weekend, Brady understood me on a level that no one else ever would. It was a good reminder we were meant to be family and *only* family. Asking for something more would be inviting trouble.

When I was done, we'd eaten two plates of French fries, a heap of nachos, and I was too drunk to drive, but there it was—an emotional vacuum.

Bare blinked hard at me. "Josh, can I ask you a question?"

I hated messing with my high, but he'd let me vomit my past all over him, so I figured I owed him something.

He leaned toward me and lowered his voice. "Let's say you go home today and tell Brady the truth. You tell him everything Anna did. Except you don't sugarcoat it. You give him all the gory details. Then you tell him you're not sure what you want yet but that your feelings have evolved beyond friendship and you are having a hard time seeing him with another man."

I swallowed the lump in my throat, and Bare gave me a reassuring smile. If only he knew *everything* Anna had done. What she'd demanded in exchange for keeping my secret.

"What's the worst thing that would happen?"

"I could never—"

"Hypothetically. Play it out. What would happen?"

"I don't know," I said. "He'd move out."

Bare raised an eyebrow. "Why?"

"Because . . ." I paused. Brady wouldn't really move out. At least not because I told him I might sort of want to be more than friends. "He'd probably let me down gently, and things would be weird between us until he couldn't stand it anymore and he'd start looking for his own place as soon as he had the money."

"Okay, but if he moved out, would you still be friends?"

I thought about it. Acutely aware that Brady and Adam, who had the world's most awkward friendship, had gone shopping together this very day. "Yeah," I admitted.

"So, the worst-case scenario is he isn't interested in more, moves out, but you stay friends. That could eventually happen even if you don't tell him what's going on too. At some point, he might meet someone or move out because he can afford his own place, but you'd stay friends."

"That's not the worst-case," I admitted. "What if Brady *is* interested, and I'm the worst boyfriend in the world? He'll hate me."

Bare nodded sympathetically. "Why do you think you'd be a bad boyfriend?"

"Because... Look, I didn't ask for therapy."

"Okay, Josh." Bare raised his hands in surrender. "Let me give you one thing to think about. Sometimes how we feel about something isn't true. You said your experience with Anna has made you not trust other people, but maybe it's your own judgment that you don't trust. You said you've never had a boyfriend." I nodded. "So what evidence do you have that you'd be bad? And what evidence do you have that you'd be good? From what you've described, you and Brady already have a harmonious, mutually beneficial living arrangement. You clearly enjoy caring for him, which I suspect is your default setting."

"I tried to get you to do me in a parking lot."

"Sure, but we both know that wasn't really about sex. If you had a commitment with Brady, would you have been looking for someone else to fuck you stupid?"

I took the question as rhetorical and didn't answer. Talking exhausted me, and I hated it. So many easier ways to reach oblivion. "I can't tell him until I'm sure. It's not right to put that on him. I don't want..." My heart ached. "I don't want to hurt him. What if he wants to try, and I change my mind? He'll never forgive me."

Bare acknowledged my thought without agreeing. "You have to tell Brady something sooner or later, don't you think? You don't seem like a guy who would lie to a good friend."

"I'll think of something truth adjacent. I always do."

"I'm sure." Bare nodded and fished out some cash and a business card. "Listen, if you want to talk more . . . maybe at my office next time. Or I have a business partner if you'd be more comfortable . . ."

I took his card with a noncommittal noise and tucked it into my wallet. "Thanks, Bare. I really appreciate earlier. Most guys would have taken advantage of . . . you know."

"No worries. I'm glad I didn't take you up on your offer. You are way too headstrong for me anyway. I like my boys kinky and malleable."

I blushed. "I'm . . . yeah. I'm not into that." His belly shook from laughter, and I blatantly admired his muscular arms. "I mean, I like you, but not . . . not really too rough unless I want to get out of my head." We'd need a whole other session to get into my sex hang-ups.

Bare's face split into a grin, and he gazed at me in the same paternal way he had in the parking lot earlier. "Josh, I do hope you come to see me. What a pleasure it would be to see you grow."

I breathed in deeply and slowly exhaled, considering his offer while waiting for Bare to pay the bill. It felt like the conversation had eased something that had been coiled tightly in my chest for years. When he returned, he offered me a lift home or back to the gym to get my car. "No, thanks. I'll call an Uber," I said and pulled out my phone. I'd missed another text from Brady.

Worried. Let me know you're okay.

I sighed happily. No matter how crazy I acted, Brady never gave up on me.

"Mighty big smile that boy puts on your face." Bare gave me a hug and wished me well. "Maybe you ought to spend some time thinking about the best-case scenario. I think he might be worth the risk."

After Bare left, I let myself consider the possibility that I could maybe be a somewhat decent boyfriend to Brady. He needed someone to care for him, which I already did. And I'd long ago figured out how to navigate his moods. Warm feelings marinated me. What was the best thing that could happen? Would he sing for me? Would he want to cuddle on the couch during movie nights? Brady was made for cuddling. I closed my eyes and pictured Brady's reaction to every single confession I'd made to Anna. Brady already knew my dreams and fears—well most of them. But the rest. *Oh, God.* I wanted it.

I wanted it so bad I couldn't breathe. Before I sobered up and lost my nerve, I texted Brady back.

I'm sorry for worrying you. I'm okay. Heading home now.

There. Done.

Two minutes later, I panicked and canceled my ride.

But ten minutes after that, when my app alerted me that my second Uber driver had arrived, I hesitated a measly four minutes and thirty seconds before going outside and getting in the car.

Chapter Seven
Brady

I tossed my controller on the couch and checked my phone. Forty minutes. Where the hell had Josh gone? His office was less than five miles. The gym maybe thirty minutes in traffic, but on a Sunday? Twenty max. *Unless there was an accident?* I rechecked the volume of my phone and rested it on my thigh to keep my leg from bouncing.

I refused to text him again. I didn't need to be worried about Josh and what might or might not be delaying him.

Since my conversation with Adam, my mind had been stuck playing a highlight reel of my friendship with Josh. From the earliest days when I'd worried about my attraction to my mysterious new roommate. I'd been surprised how timid he was at first. I remembered teaching him how to play Mission to Mars and the cute little noises and funny faces he'd made when he'd make a mistake. Always such a perfectionist. So many of our earliest heart-to-hearts had been while playing games in our dorm room.

I really loved Josh, loved him in my life, loved sharing and laughing with him. There were so many times where we'd lean on each other for support, for comfort, to be cheered up, to make an important decision . . . but that's what best friends did, right?

As time passed with still no Josh, thoughts of potato chips invaded my brain. Not the baked cardboard kind either. The salty, greasy ones, with melted cheddar cheese and drowning in a pool of ranch dressing. My mouth watered. Ugh. Hopeless.

I needed to do something or I was gonna grab my keys and hit up McDonald's for a milkshake or fries. I could mow down a double quarter pounder right now, maybe even two. I scoffed and made my way to my closet.

I found the jeans easily enough. They were folded and stashed in the bottom of a box of summer clothes. I shook them out and held them to my body. I still remembered the day I bought them. They were a relaxed fit, which was my usual, but Josh had said the low rise and pocket placement would do good things for my ass. He wasn't wrong.

With a deep breath, I changed into them. They were snug, but when the button slipped through the hole, I could still breathe normally. They fit. I did a celebratory dance and held my arms up to the sky in victory. Turning in the mirror, I cataloged the results of my hard work. I ran my hand down my flatter belly. My hips were finally narrower than my shoulders. I'd lost my third chin.

My stomach growled, and I accepted it as a sign that my hunger was real. Nothing in the kitchen would blow my diet. Josh's shopping habits ensured if I ate at home, I would be fine. I changed out of my jeans and made my way toward the kitchen.

The silhouette of a man standing on the other side of the frosted front door stopped me. I stared motionless for a minute, but he made no attempt to knock or ring the bell. Suddenly, the figure shifted in front of the sidelight. *Josh?*

I probably should have made him start talking the second I opened the door, but he seemed spooked, so I treaded carefully.

"What are you doing?" I stood aside so he could enter. "Did you lose your key?"

That didn't make sense. Josh parked in the garage and came through the kitchen entrance we never locked. I scanned the driveway. "Where's your car?"

"At the gym," he said, as though that were a perfectly complete explanation.

"Did something happen? Are you okay?"

"Yep. Fine."

The way he wouldn't meet my eyes unnerved me. He stood in the entryway and glanced around like he wasn't sure what to do or where to go.

"You hungry?" I asked. "I was getting ready to make a snack."

Nothing.

"Josh," I said sharply.

"Let me cook you something," he said, blinking once. Then twice. But his expression was otherwise unchanged. The flatness of his voice was enough to grow my concern into alarm.

He listed forward when he tried to toe off his shoes, and my face twisted up. The overwhelming odor of whiskey explained his unsteadiness. His Stepford wife smile freaked me out. "No," I said slowly and cocked my head, surveying him for clues. "I can manage."

"Okay," Josh said, about ten levels north of cheerful, then walked toward his bedroom. "There's edamame in the fridge if you need protein," he called behind him.

Baffled, but still hungry, I went to the kitchen and settled for carrot chips and low-fat ranch dressing. I sliced some apples and measured two tablespoons of almond butter to head off any critiques about my lack of protein.

Vvvvvrrrrr.

I dropped my head, shaking it in consternation as the vacuum swept over the hardwood floor. A sudden cleaning frenzy was never a good sign. I added a second scoop of almond butter. I'd need extra energy if I had to deprogram Josh in addition to cajoling answers from him.

An hour later, my patience had worn thin. "Josh, can you put that down so we can talk?" I asked for the third time.

He spun away from the entertainment center, ridiculous rubber gloves still protecting his manicured fingernails, a dust rag in one hand, and wood polish in the other. "Sorry. Let me finish dusting the tables. Then we can talk." He sprayed his rag.

When he set the polish down, I braved a cloud of lemon-scented cleaner and dust particles to move the can out of his reach. My lungs did not appreciate my efforts, and I debated grabbing my inhaler before the irritation worsened.

He chewed his lip as he wiped down the wood and zeroed in on offensive streaks with the precision of a bomb technician. Was his poker face always this terrible? "Do you honestly think this is gonna work? Sit down. You've been cleaning for an hour." I coughed to clear the tickle from my throat.

Josh's forehead creased, and he seemed to realize the flaws in his incredibly shaky avoidance plan all at once. Nevertheless, he persisted. He kneeled on the floor and started organizing clutter from the table. "Let me—"

"What? You gonna alphabetize the magazines? Jesus, Josh. Sit down."

Josh pushed a strand of hair out of his face and made a put-upon sigh as he snapped the rubber gloves from his hands and collapsed dramatically into the chair we never sat in across the room. "Fine. We'll live in filth."

It might have been funny if his smile didn't stop at his mouth. I could practically hear the drumbeat of "Don't make me talk" coming through his expression growing louder and louder. "Your acting skills suck." I coughed again to clear my raspy voice, more annoyed by it than concerned. "Will you tell me what's going on with you? Where did you go this morning?"

He dropped his gaze, and a sudden lump in my throat made it difficult to swallow. He looked skittish. My mind went to a dark place. "Josh, come on. You're freaking me out."

"I went to the gym."

Okay. Not a crisis, then. So why had Josh dodged me to get drunk? Why lie? I exhaled, before searching his face for an explanation that wasn't there. "Why?"

He shrugged.

"No bullshit. You promised."

"I owe you an apology for last night."

I shifted back on the couch and arched an eyebrow. That wasn't where I expected to start, but whatever. As long as he talked. "Okay," I said.

"I didn't react well to your news."

That was an understatement. Josh met my stare as though waiting for me to call him out on that. Curiosity got the best of me, though, so I nodded for him to continue.

"Listen, I was a jealous little bitch, and I'm sorry. So that's what that was all about. I'm over it now and completely happy for you. In fact, we should celebrate tonight. Just the two of us. We can have a cheat night. My treat."

I exhaled, surprised by the sharp pang of disappointment in my chest that Adam had been wrong. A little insecurity about my new friendship with Matt was a lot more plausible than his being in love with me. "You don't have to pay for me all the time anymore. It'll be easier for me to keep up. Maybe we should take a road trip as soon as I've earned some vacation time. I'll get four weeks paid the same as you."

"Brady, I don't care about how much money . . ." Josh swallowed nervously, and his eyes welled red with emotion. He gazed out of the window to the single immature tree in our back yard. I'd planted it the summer we moved in, partly to shade my bedroom, but mostly for Josh, because it bothered him that the former owners had been so injudicious when clearing the lot for the expansion. I left him to his quiet contemplations.

He chewed on his bottom lip. Then finally, a small smile. Like he was relieved that he'd reached an answer but wasn't sure if he was happy about it yet. His pensive expression announced his decision held meaning, to him, for us. I straightened my spine and prepared for real communication to begin.

"Do you feel like things are kind of changing between us lately?"

His loaded question lacked the frankness I'd hoped for. *Yes, because you won't talk to me.* I huffed out of frustration, then thought better of it. If Josh insisted on speaking in cryptograms, at some point, I needed to decipher the code. We'd never get to the bottom of this tension if I didn't dig deeper. Like a feral cat, Josh couldn't be forced. He wouldn't tell me anything if he wasn't ready. I knew that better than anyone. "Is it Matt? You insisted I go."

"I know," Josh said in a pained voice. "I thought you were in a funk."

"I *was* in a funk. The running has helped. You helped. I'm down a size." I debated assuring him he was still my best friend, but how could he not know that?

Josh shot me a grateful smile with a look that roughly translated to a plea to end the conversation.

"What else?" I asked instead. "Please talk to me."

He twisted in the chair and cast another wistful glance out of the window. He turned back toward me, his eyes timid, but resolute. Slowly, he rose, and a facade fell away.

The first step he took toward me set my heart into an erratic rhythm. Suddenly I wanted to hold him. Wanted the ability to be something more than whatever time had decided we were. *This is how it happens. This is the moment that changes everything.*

"Brady." His voice barely carried the distance between us. He lowered himself to the couch, took my hand, and peeked at me through uncertain eyes.

My body knew what was happening. Heat flushed through me preemptively. Then it got very hard to breathe.

"Lately . . . I guess for the last few months, I've been a little confused—"

I inhaled, and a loud wheeze cut off his words. *Ah. Shit.* The whistling noise accelerated when my airway constricted to the size of a coffee stirrer. My cough sent pain through my chest, and I yanked my hand back to cover my mouth out of reflex.

Josh panicked for a second, then sprang into action. He took off toward the bathroom, and I could hear him tossing drawers and cursing. He ran back to me triumphantly, inhaler in hand, and I took a hit, still coughing and wheezing through watery eyes.

The medicine worked its magic, and my airway relaxed enough that I could worry about Josh. Damn, he looked terrified. "Sorry," I rasped as my wheezing yielded to the medication.

"Take your time." He soothed his hand over my back, but as my lungs fought to expel the irritants I'd inadvertently inhaled, his touch crept up. Soon, he was caressing the little hairs on the back of my neck. I couldn't speak, so I tried to tell him with my mind. I needed him to know how much I liked his hands on me, but when he met my eyes, he pulled back like my skin was fire.

"Josh," I said, suppressing a need to cough that forced my eyes closed. My heart raced. I placed a hand on his thigh to keep him from running, but it was too late. He was slipping through my fingers.

"Are you all right?"

I held my hand up to ask for a minute, then cleared my throat again. "What are you confused by?"

"Oh." The determination in his eyes had been replaced by something far less. "It's not important." At that, Josh walked into the kitchen.

My chest hurt, and I wasn't entirely sure my dysfunctional respiratory system was to blame. I leaned my head on the couch and tested my ability to take a deep breath.

"No ice, right?" Josh extended his hand with a glass of water. I stared at him in amazement before accepting the glass and taking a sip. The water soothed my throat, and I took another hit of my inhaler to stamp out the last of the attack.

Josh sat next to me, wringing his hands, but otherwise waiting patiently. When my breathing seemed back to normal, he handed me my game controller. "Want to play?"

Something about the expression on his face took me back to Loman Hall. He'd never enjoyed video games the way I did, but when he had something important to say, he'd take the initiative to start a game. I think he found it easier to say the hard stuff when he had an excuse not to look at me. I reached over to the drawer, pulled out the second controller, and connected it for him.

After thirty minutes of silence, my hopes for another heart-to-heart had faded. Josh had gone back to twitchy, and I remembered why pushing him to talk always took patience. I glanced at him as he channeled his energy into the game. His eyes were on the screen, narrowed in concentration. When I'd watched Josh in the past, I'd mostly been concerned with what he was thinking. I'd admired his physique, sure, but with envy, not lust. Now that Adam had cracked that door, my body seemed hell-bent on pushing it open.

Josh cocked his head when he was thinking hard about something. But now all I could see was how that small tilt expanded the highly kissable expanse of flesh below his ear. He bit his lips when he was nervous, but I'd never noticed how full those lips were. How fun they'd be to suck and nibble if we ever really kissed. Jesus. Adam was right: Josh was exactly my type. I shifted to find a more comfortable position to ogle him, too far gone with the possibility.

My movement sent Josh's heavy-lidded brown eyes in my direction. He flashed a concerned smile. "You feeling better?"

"Yeah. Thanks. You still want to help me celebrate my new job?"

"Sure. Anything you want."

I suppressed a groan. *If only.* Josh couldn't have handled my *anything.* I wanted the type of honesty that came with drunken confessions, and I wanted touches that had only one meaning. I wanted to KonMari our relationship until I knew every part that sparked joy in him, and I wanted those parts folded neatly and labeled. And damn it, I wanted to hear what he needed without a goddamn decoder ring all the time. But that wasn't Josh.

There was something about him, though. A possibility I'd never fully considered. At least not after Josh swore off relationships. Now all I could do is consider it. What if a future with him was possible?

He might show me what he wanted eventually, but time was not my friend here. If this was all in my head, I needed to quash my fantasy right the hell now. But how?

When I liked a guy, I tended to work in subtle touches until he either pulled away or leaned in. That wouldn't work with Josh. I'd have to push enough to know if there was a chance without ruining our friendship, embarrassing myself, or scaring Josh away.

Great. No pressure or anything.

"Actually, it's been kind of a long day. Want to stay in and watch a movie tonight?"

He nodded enthusiastically. "Sure. Your choice. But don't you want to celebrate?" On the screen, Josh's avatar died when he ran out of oxygen, and he set the controller down. I turned off the game.

"We can celebrate next weekend. Saturday night? Maybe even get a little dressed up." *A date by any other name.* I smiled.

"Sure. Where do you want to go?"

"What about that place Cade mentioned? The one that got a Michelin star." Josh's eyes widened. I'd heard him gushing to Cade the night before about how he'd been dying to go to the new seafood place downtown. "My treat."

"Lotus," he gasped the restaurant's name. "Are you sure? It's so expensive."

"Yeah. Consider it a thank-you for all you do for me. I figure I owe you like a million dinners for all the meals you've cooked me over the years. Not to mention the grocery bill."

Josh smiled, and I knew I had him.

"If you're sure. I've been *dying* to go there."

"Absolutely. It's a special occasion."

Since Josh and I weren't winning any communication awards, I knew I was going to need some help to turn my celebratory dinner into a date. As soon as Josh excused himself to take a nap, I phoned Adam.

"I need to know everything Cade did to make you look at him like you do."

"Brady?" Adam laughed. "I take it that you finally talked to Josh?"

"Not exactly. But we're, um... I don't know what we're doing, but I don't have a lot of experience with this, and every guy you date seems to fall hopelessly in love with you, so spill it."

"He does this thing with his tongue—"

I guffawed. "Be serious. You know what I mean. Not the sexual stuff." I couldn't even begin to process having that with Josh.

"How do I look at Cade?"

I hesitated for a minute but ultimately decided to tell him the truth. "Like you're watching him dance the can-can."

Adam choked. "What?"

"The night of the Loman talent show freshman year. When we met Cade. He was in that Moulin Rouge routine, dancing the can-can with the guys from the fourth floor. I was staring at you, but you couldn't take your eyes off him." I didn't blame Adam. Cade was undeniably attractive. Before we learned his name, Josh and I referred to him as Tinkerbell, because he was tiny and mischievous. "It's like you still see him up on stage dancing the can-can and laughing his head off and you'd give anything to reset to that night and do things differently." Adam's breath hitched. "I'm sorry, Adam. I shouldn't have said that."

Adam sniffled. "No. It's fine. I deserve it."

"You made a mistake."

"Yeah, I did."

"Cade is no angel, Adam. He's a horrible gossip, and he's flaky. Sometimes he uses your mistake to get his way, which is shitty and manipulative."

"I know," Adam admitted sadly.

"But the point is you don't stare at Cade like you want to fuck him—"

Adam snorted.

"Fine. I guess you don't *only* stare at him like that. Sorry to go all mushy, but you, like, yearn for him, or something."

"I don't yearn." Adam laughed.

"You do. And it's very nineteenth-century-English-lit level yearning too. So much yearning. My point is you look at Cade like he's perfect, and I want to know how you get someone to see past all your flaws like that."

"Brady," Adam groaned, clearly exasperated.

I could picture him shaking his head. I had to be more convincing than every neuron screaming at him not to get involved. So, I flat-out begged. "Please, Adam."

"Josh already thinks you're perfect."

"Then why doesn't he do something about it?" I flailed my hand. "I've been thinking about it all afternoon. I can be moody. Josh acts like it doesn't bother him, but I can get really shitty with him, and I know it upsets him. Hell, you should hear what I say to him on our runs. If we're in a relationship, then we jumped over all the flirty, sexy, best-behavior stuff, and landed in a twenty-year sexless marriage. I need to woo him without scaring him off. But how do I do that when we already live together?"

"Wow. You're serious, aren't you? Okay. I'm so down for this. We need to bring the romance. Let me think . . ." He paused. "When Cade and I first got together, he used to put a flower in this vase in his room. It was a new one each week. When I finally commented that I liked one, he bought me a dozen on our date."

I sighed heavily. "It's not like I can pretend I don't know Josh loves lilies. Not that he brings them into the house because he knows they set off my asthma. The man knows what foods give me gas, Adam. Think bigger."

Adam laughed. "Jesus. The pressure." Adam was silent for a minute. "Holy shit. I have it."

"What?"

"Your voice," he said.

"Huh?"

"Josh loves your voice. He's always bragging about it. He thinks you sound like Ed Sheeran."

I shook my head. *Josh and his Ed Sheeran obsession. How many times did I have to listen to "Thinking Out Loud"?* "I really don't."

"Whatever. You want to woo him? I'm thinking candlelight dinner and serenade."

"I can't do that. You know Josh; you can't force it or he'll freak out. I need something subtle."

"I don't think subtle is going to get the job done, my man." He laughed. "We've had six years of subtle. What you need is a full-court press."

"I'm terrible with sports metaphors."

"In basketball, when the defense—"

"Don't explain basketball to me, Adam. Just tell me what to do," I said with exasperation.

"Aggressive defense, Brady. You've got to get in his face. Make sure he can't avoid you. From now on, no sitting on the bench. He goes to the gym; you go to the gym. He wants to run; you want to run. He cooks, you're in the kitchen helping. Better yet, stop letting him cook every meal for you like a child. Show up at his office in the middle of the day to take him on a picnic. Or buy him lunch." Adam laughed, clearly pleased with himself. "What are you two doing tonight?"

"We talked about watching a movie."

"Awesome. Find something romantic. Better yet, make it a friends-to-lovers flick."

Rom-coms were really more Josh's thing. "I was thinking more action—"

"Romance, Brady. Arms up. In his face at all times."

"Seriously. Sports metaphors are—"

"Cade's here. I've got to go."

"Wait," I said before he could hang up. "Can you maybe keep this between us?"

"Sure," he said. "But remember to keep your arms up, Brady."

Cade's unmistakable deep laugh rumbled in the background as Adam hung up the phone. Shortly after, I heard Josh stirring in his bedroom. I still wasn't quite sure what *aggressive defense* meant, but I was reasonably certain it didn't involve the almond butter stain on my T-shirt and bed hair. So, I guessed it was time for kickoff, or whatever—I hated sports.

Chapter Eight
Josh

I stretched and rubbed the gunk from my eyes before rolling out of bed with a clear head. Luckily, my nap had erased the impact of my day-drinking and restored my self-control. Thank goodness for Brady's asthma attack. Well, not really. I hated seeing him like that, but Brady's distress was precisely the wake-up call I had needed.

My throat thickened with thoughts of what I'd almost done. I could have ruined everything. With completely sober eyes, I was more determined than ever to stay in the friend lane.

I had to arrange to get my car, but first things first. Between the fried food, my workout, and the alcohol, I desperately needed to hydrate. Then I needed to do some serious damage control.

In the living room, I passed Brady leaning in his bedroom doorway, his brown hair artfully messy like he'd recently styled it. He'd changed his clothes. His aqua-blue shirt made his eyes pop, and his jeans... *My God*. Those were not lying-around-the-house jeans.

I tamped down my disappointment and put on a happy face. "You going out?"

Brady frowned. "I thought we were gonna stay in and watch a movie?"

"Yeah, me too." I laughed off his look of confusion and gestured to the television. "Find something, and I'll get us some dinner together." I continued to the kitchen and chugged a big cup of water.

"How can I help?"

Brady's voice startled me midgulp. I spun around, losing some water out of my mouth in the process. Brady laughed and handed me a kitchen towel. I wiped my face. "What? Why?"

"Because I plan to eat too. I can help."

"Just pick a movie. I got this." I pulled out the bag of raw chicken I had already marinated and some veggies for a salad. When I turned toward the counter, Brady was lurking behind the fridge door. "Jesus. You scared me."

"Are you making a salad? Let me dice the veggies." He pulled the cucumber and tomatoes from my arms, and I had to let them go or risk dropping everything else. I set the chicken and the remaining vegetables down.

Brady opened and closed a few cabinets. *What in the world was he doing?*

"Where's the blue plastic thingy you use?"

"It's in there." I pointed to the cabinet next to the sink where I kept the cutting board. The kitchen felt a third of the size it normally did, way too small for me and Brady in those jeans.

Brady swooped to retrieve it, proving in the process exactly how well his jeans fit him. I swallowed and bit my fist to keep from saying anything. *Friend zone*, I reminded myself.

"Thanks," he said.

"Here you go." I handed him a knife and a bowl.

He nodded and sized up the stack of veggies. "All these?"

I made a move toward the cutting board. "I'll do it."

"No." Brady shooed me away. "I can manage raw veggies. Are you grilling the chicken or, um, braising it?"

Braising? I cocked an eyebrow, amused by his new fascination with cooking. "Baking," I said. We didn't own a grill, but I could have said I was poaching the chicken and I doubted he knew the difference.

Brady nodded with a determined expression, and turned toward the counter, knife in hand. He crooned what sounded like a children's song about chopping vegetables, his eyes twinkling. It was kind of adorable, and the awkward *thwack*s of the knife weren't even enough to sever my need to stand there, mooning at him and wishing. Wishing so goddamn hard that I could have him.

Brady glanced up, a curious half smile playing over his face like he wondered if I was going to take over. "I got it," he said, chuckling, and motioned for me to quit hovering, so I focused on heating the oven and coating the chicken in panko.

I was sliding the cooking sheet into the oven when I heard an ominous splat. "Fuck," Brady cried. I turned to see Brady holding the top of a tomato and gawking at the mess the other half created on the floor.

I shook my head, laughing. "You're hopeless."

Brady's face matched the color of the vegetable. "I'm sorry."

We squatted at the same time, our eyes met over the mess, and the smell of him engaged my already battered senses. He lowered his head and attempted to scoop up the tomato guts with his hands, which as when I noticed they were shaking.

"Brady," I said gently and stilled his hand. "You okay?"

He cleared his throat. "Yeah. Sorry. That inhaler gives me the shakes sometimes."

"Why don't you let me do this?" I patted his shoulder, and his eyes instantly flew to where I'd touched him. *Damage control*, I reminded myself and stood. I grabbed a towel from the drawer. "You hate those jeans. Why don't you go change?" *Please change. For the love of God.*

Brady peered up through his long lashes. "Not now that they finally fit me again."

Damn right they do. "It's just us, so get comfy." I wet the rag, and Brady rose to his feet to grab the kitchen cleaner. He stood, fixed his shirt, and sucked in his gut. His body really had started to change, and he moved differently. More confidently. I had missed confident Brady, but I'd forgotten how sexy he was when he was feeling himself. "I love that color on you."

His eyes sparked with something I couldn't identify, and he straightened a bit taller. The smile he gave me was so gooey, it reminded me of melted chocolate. All very un-Brady like. "I don't mind helping."

"I know. But I kind of like doing it myself." I glanced toward the pile of mutilated cucumbers and cringed. "If not for me, do it for the vegetables."

The corners of Brady's eyes crinkled, and his tongue traced a path over his upper lip. "Fine, I surrender to your perfectionist ways." He picked up the knife and presented it to me with a flourish and a bow, then exchanged the knife for the dishrag.

I assumed the spot Brady had occupied and tried to salvage the cucumber into uniform quarters while Brady kneeled to scrub the tomato juice off the white tile. If my eyes didn't stop drifting toward him, I was going to lose a finger. It was a good reminder I'd made the right decision. I should have told Bare my worst-case scenario meant not making Brady dinner anymore. He'd starve to death.

Brady chose that moment to peer up at me with dilated eyes, and his fast blush caused me to reevaluate the distance between my crotch and his mouth. Startled, I scrambled backward against the edge of the sink. Brady used the open cabinet door next to my leg as leverage, rising so close to me that I could smell the mint from his mouthwash.

Time slowed as I tracked his movements. Brady's hand came to rest on the counter, and the tip of his pinky stroked over my hip, sparking awareness in my body. My hips came off the ledge as if magnetically drawn to his. I clenched my hands around the counter to keep from touching him. Sweat beaded on my skin, and my breath hitched in anticipation.

His shoulder brushed my bicep, as he reached behind me to drop the dirty towel into the sink. "Sorry." The word released on a sexy low breath that sent a shiver reverberating through me and my heart racing. He stepped back, and his touch slid from my body in a torturous glide. It was all too much, and I averted my eyes to avoid Brady's open stare.

"I'll go pick a movie." Brady stepped back, leaving me gripping the counter as he strutted out of the kitchen like he'd been privy to my every thought. *Had he?*

I channeled my confusion into salvaging dinner. I'd witnessed Brady flirt before when he liked a guy. His main move, if you could call it that, was to get touchy-feely. Brady didn't really seek contact casually, so when he did, it didn't come off in a subtle, maybe-it-was-accidental way. There'd been times, like when he pulled me into the dressing room, where his touch sparked a flicker of hope, but those moments were quickly extinguished by ambiguity. Never had we shared a moment as electric as that one, but the mere presence of doubt meant it had to be the residual alcohol and my overactive imagination.

When dinner was ready, I made up two plates and carried them to the family room. Thankfully, Brady never cared about the presentation, because it was far from my finest effort.

I stopped, surveying the oversized throw pillows on the floor and placemats arranged on the coffee table and smiled in approval.

"You okay with eating in here? I found a movie."

"Sure."

I set the plates down and sent Brady for napkins and silverware. He did as I asked and also brought Matt's bottle of Riesling and two glasses before settling next to me. I placed the utensils and napkins next to our plates. "What are we watching?"

"You said my choice, right?"

Brady and I both liked action movies, but other than that, our genre preferences didn't overlap much. "Yeah. Please tell me it's not a slasher flick."

"No. It's, um, *Love, Simon*."

I guffawed. "Seriously?"

"Yeah. I know it's like a cheesy teen movie, but how cool is it that a gay romance did so well? I wanted to see it in the theaters, but I was kind of worried about losing my shit in public. Is it okay?"

"Yeah, it's fine." I had wanted to see what the buzz was about when the movie first released but hadn't found the time.

Brady poured me wine, but I sipped it carefully, determined to stay clear-headed. The movie started out sweetly, but I found I was far more interested in Brady's reactions and longing sighs than the plot.

The main character and his band of friends lived in huge houses, and except for the gay stuff, the director had embraced every Hollywood teen movie cliché there was. The plot was simple enough. Closeted gay boy exchanges sweet pen pal letters with an unknown closeted gay boy. My mind drifted to the persona Anna had created. The excitement and anticipation of each new communication. Sharing the *real* me for the first time. I couldn't help but wonder how different things would be if the persona had been real. What if there had been a boy—just as lonely and scared as I was—on the other side of those emails? What if my first experience with falling in love had been sweet? What if it had been Brady? I let my imagination play out that scenario. I hadn't known Brady in high school, but he'd come out at fifteen, and while he hadn't had many close friends, he seemed to be adept at finding a crowd to hang out with. In a more perfect world, he would have been my Simon.

During a poignant scene, Brady brushed his fingers against mine, and I stopped breathing for a moment to concentrate on the touch of our little fingers. My pinky twitched. Brady responded by hooking his over mine and leaning into me until our shoulders were overlapping. We stayed like that, breathing a little heavier than usual, but not really moving. The vagueness of his intentions were enough to let me relax and indulge. I shifted my back against the side of his chest, and he rested his arm around my shoulder.

When I dared a glance at him, I expected a sarcastic comment, not a sweet-almost-shy smile. My heart jumped in my chest—the energy between us was too charged. I tried shifting away, but Brady squeezed me tighter, holding me close to him, so I closed my eyes and continued mentally rewriting my own story to be more like Simon's.

Everything was fine until my brain tuned back into the movie's plot and I realized Simon was being blackmailed. I tensed, and Brady must have noticed because he squeezed my hand. Determined to enjoy this moment with him, I gritted my teeth and forced myself to relax. It almost worked, until . . .

"Oh shit," Brady cried. He dived for the remote as Simon realized that his secret emails had been uploaded to a school gossip website, but instead of pausing or muting the movie, he changed the channel on the television. Static blasted from the speakers, and I didn't move as Brady scrambled to lower the volume. "I'm so sorry. I didn't know that part of the plot."

"It's fine," I said, face forward, fantasy eviscerated. "But maybe 'guy gets maliciously outed to entire high school' hits a little *too* close to home for me."

"I didn't know. I thought it was a happy gay rom-com." He touched my face. My eyeballs were dry. Too dry. Why? Oh, yeah. *Blink, idiot.*

"Shit. Come here." Brady pulled me into him. He rarely initiated hugs. Not like this. He held me like he needed to touch me, hauling me up to the couch with him when he couldn't get his arms around me at a good angle.

My already weak defenses washed away. I leaned against his broad chest and buried my face into his T-shirt. He was hard and comfy in all the right places. I freaking reveled in it.

I nuzzled against him, and Brady sort of rocked me gently and rubbed my hair. When I tried to sit up, he loosened his grip to let me.

"I'm sorry," I said, rubbing my thumb under my eyes. They were still dry.

"No. I'm sorry. I feel terrible."

What was I doing? This wasn't a scene from a romantic comedy. I didn't know how the movie ended, but I was pretty sure Simon wouldn't lose his best friend like I could. My chest clenched as I fought to return my mind to real life.

"Brady, you don't have to research the plots of movies we watch in advance like I'm a little kid. It's fine." I shifted away. "It probably wouldn't have hit me so hard, but I found out Anna's getting married, and it's just like . . ." A tremble swept over my skin, a vague reminder that being this vulnerable with Brady was dangerous, but I couldn't hold it in. ". . . she gets to ruin my life, turn my family against me—friends I'd known since I was in kindergarten wouldn't speak to me. But she gets to be happy . . ." My voice cracked. I met Brady's gaze. The air between us crackled alive again.

"Josh," Brady whispered. "I wish I knew what to say to make it better."

"I appreciate the sentiment, but honestly, I'm fine." I stood and Brady joined me, his quick breaths warming my skin. I turned away from him, fighting to rebuild the dam that had crumbled with Brady's embrace.

"Josh . . ." Brady warned and grabbed my hand. "Don't . . ."

I shook my head, begging him with my eyes to stop pushing. As much as Brady wanted to shoulder this burden for me, he couldn't fix it. He couldn't fix me. Yet, the way he held me made it impossible to pretend and, selfishly, I wanted to let him try. "I've been trying to forget about it all damn day. It's why I didn't drive home. When I left the gym, I went to a bar and got wasted."

"You should've called me. You can't get drunk alone."

"I, um, wasn't alone. I went with this guy. He kind of saved me from doing some stupid shit."

"Oh," Brady said in a breath full of judgment. He stared at me, blinking rapidly.

"It's not like—"

"No. It's fine. I mean, I'm glad you had someone."

Except he wasn't glad. He was disappointed, and I needed to explain. But how? How did I tell him that I needed him . . . that I wanted him to be the one who made it better? Who quieted all those voices . . . ? My chest tightened from what I wanted to say.

"It's late," Brady mumbled, dropped my hand, and stepped back.

"I wanted it to be you," I blurted, clenching his arm to prevent him from leaving me.

All the air left the room.

His mouth snapped shut, and his eyes pined for an explanation that would probably take an entire summit to resolve. So much for damage control.

"Shit." I dropped my gaze to the floor. When I glanced up, Brady's heated expression stopped me cold.

"Josh," he whispered and stepped toward me, his hand settling behind my neck.

"I didn't fuck him," I said. The light sweeps of Brady's fingers over my skin sent a shiver down my spine.

"It's okay if you did." There was no disappointment in his eyes any longer. There was only hunger, and maybe a hint of hopefulness as he scrutinized my movements. I didn't know what to do, so I patted my shaking hands on my thighs and broke free of his hold.

"Josh," Brady said, his voice husky and not at all uncertain. "C'mere."

And I went—somehow, I went. Brady's gentle lips ghosted over my skin, then lingered. The kiss started out slow, and my mind fought me every second. I was scared shitless. But I wanted it. I wanted my best-case scenario. I wanted my happy ending. And I was tired of being afraid. I placed a trembling hand on his cheek, pushing us past any possibility that this was something less than it was. This was everything. This was the moment I knew every other kiss in my life had been wrong.

A faint gasp parted the seam of his lips, and I seized the opportunity to take what I wanted. A subtle tilt of my head and we rolled into something deeper and hungrier. His tongue slipped over mine, and he scraped my bottom lip between his teeth before moving over my jaw. He pressed his nose against my neck, breathing me in, and sucked on the patch of skin under my ear. I released a groan he caught with a kiss. He squeezed my ass, drawing me closer, and pressing his tongue against mine. I was too far gone to censor myself. I rutted against him, rolling my hips and running my hands under his shirt in a frantic quest for skin-on-skin contact.

Brady stiffened against me, and a breathy sigh formed my name. He shifted back and braced his hands on my hips to prevent my body from following.

"What's wrong?" I asked breathlessly, craving his swollen lips on me.

His breath stuttered. "We should stop."

"Why?"

"Because you've had an emotional day and I'm . . ." He dropped his head, leaving me to fill in the blanks.

"Brady." I stepped toward him, but he recoiled. Panic shot through me. I could fix this. Explain it somehow. "Maybe you're right." Fuck Bare. Fuck best-case scenarios. "I'm sorry I got carried away. It was a rough day." I turned toward my room, fighting the hot well of tears behind my eyes.

Brady rushed forward and grabbed my shoulder. He spun me, and slowly, surely, brought his lips to mine again. "I wanted you to get carried away. This . . . this wasn't only you, okay."

"Then why are we stopping?"

"You've had a lot to deal with today . . . with Anna and the movie and you've been drinking." He kissed me again, smiling against my lips. "This is huge and, I mean, it's you and me. Please. I can't . . . then go back."

I wrapped my arms around his waist, and he squeezed me tight. "I don't want things to change." *I can't lose you.*

Brady's warm breath was at my ear, and he pressed his lips to my neck. "I think they already have."

I held on to him, considering the weight of his words. It was hard to say who let go first, but we came apart in a different place than we'd come together.

"So now what?" I asked. Did I go to my room like nothing had happened? I didn't have the capacity to put any of it into words. Words Brady would want to hear from me.

"Now? I think we see how things feel in the morning." Brady rubbed the back of his neck.

I nodded. "You still want to run?"

"Yeah, I still want to run. I need to get in early so I can give my notice."

"Six okay?"

He nodded.

"I'm so proud of you."

Brady brought our foreheads together and took a satisfied breath. "You know what? I'm kind of proud of me too."

Chapter Nine
Brady

Before she married my stepfather, my mother worked the breakfast shift at a twenty-four-hour diner a few blocks from our house. Each morning, she would coax me out of bed with promises of pancakes and bacon. I'd sit in an empty booth, waiting for sunrise, knowing that the school bus arrived shortly after daybreak. I swore when I grew up, I would never voluntarily get up before the sun. When my alarm went off at five thirty the next morning, I hadn't yet managed a minute of sleep, so I figured it didn't really count.

I slid out of bed and into my running gear. The inventor of spandex should get a Nobel prize. What a difference a little synthetic fiber made under my running shorts. I brushed my hair and applied deodorant in an attempt to make myself somewhat presentable. Adam hadn't made allowances for coffee before the aggressive defense commenced. My hand paused at the doorknob. One small twist of my wrist separated me from Josh. I counted to three, breathing slowly to stop my heart from beating right out of my chest.

I followed the sound of running water to the kitchen, equally unprepared for an impromptu make-out session as I was for supreme awkwardness. Unfortunately, I found neither.

Standing at the sink, Josh filled reusable water bottles and swayed his hips to whatever streamed through his earbuds. My first thought was to press him against the counter like I had the day before, only this time I'd be brave enough to kiss him senseless. I smacked my mouth, wrinkling my nose at the scummy feeling, and decided to wait. Instead, I stood in the doorway and watched him.

Energy level—higher than usual.

Cheerfulness level—maxed out.

Hotness level—off the charts.

He turned and ripped the earbud from his ear. "Hey. I didn't hear you get up."

I checked the Fitbit Josh had given me when he'd upgraded to his Apple Watch. "We said six, right? We were going to try three miles today, and I assume I still need to take you to the gym to pick up your car."

"About that . . ." Josh said, mouth forming into a cringe.

"Why do I think you're gonna suggest a terrible idea?"

"Because you have eyes . . ." He gestured toward the kitchen window. The rain passed in front of the back-porch lights. "It's been pouring all night. The track will be a muddy mess."

Fuck.

"I have a guest pass. We can try it. If you hate it, I won't ever mention it again. I swear on my entire shoe collection." Josh crossed his pinky over his chest and smiled.

Adam's voice screamed at me to put my hands up, so I let my protest lay on the bench, or whatever. Now I was thinking in sports metaphors. *Great.* "All right," I grumbled.

"You can bring your work clothes if you want and change there."

I laughed. "Yeah. No." I would come back and shower at the house.

We were halfway to the gym before it dawned on me that except for my sudden willingness to sacrifice my dignity, the morning had been unremarkable. Josh had acted like it was a typical day instead of the first day in a universe where I had kissed him.

"You okay?"

Josh nodded.

Apparently, we weren't going to talk about or deal with or even acknowledge our kiss. I looked at him frequently during the drive, waiting for anything. A single goddamn word about what he was thinking. No *Yes, Brady. I'd like our penises to get to know each other.* No *I think we made a mistake.* Not a single goddamn clue. "You sure?"

"I'm fine." Josh shrugged, diverting his gaze to the passenger-side window. He stared quietly out of the window at the rain, chewing on his bottom lip. The wiper blades ticked off the silence until I sighed in surrender.

I was pissed. At the person who decided to put mirrors across from the treadmills. At the jock next to me who smirked when I had to walk my third mile. At the trainer who grabbed my arm when I lost my balance stepping off the treadmill and told me to "be careful" in the most condescending tone imaginable. I was pissed at pretty much everyone in the entire gym.

Even Josh.

There was no hint of that carefree Golden Retriever smile. His pace had been the final straw... if Josh hadn't been on a treadmill, he'd be in another State by now. His robotic intensity made me wonder if he wished he were.

I wiped off my machine, grabbed my belongings, and made my way to the parking lot. I tried to be patient with Josh when he was like this. I knew avoidance was the way he dealt with anxiety. But, damn it, my entire world had been flipped upside down by that kiss. I felt vulnerable, and so damn scared things would never be the same. No matter how many times Josh's asshole father told him men shouldn't acknowledge emotions, I needed him to be in this with me. To be scared and vulnerable *with* me.

"Brady," Josh yelled at me from the entrance, but I continued, power walking my way through the horizontal rain. "Damn it, Brady. Stop."

"What?" I turned to find Josh an arm's reach from me, not in the least bothered by how hard the rain fell.

He stopped and shook the wet strands of hair from his face. "You were going to leave without saying anything?"

"Um. Yeah. I was."

Josh shifted uncomfortably. He tossed a glance over his shoulder like he planned to go right back into the gym. Just a totally normal day, right, Josh? Sharp stabbing pain in my chest stole my breath. Grateful for the rain, I inclined my head, trying to conceal the drops sliding down my cheeks that hadn't come from the sky.

When his gaze swung back to me, there was the smallest fracture of his hardened visage. I looked into his eyes, and for a second, my heart soared with hope.

"Okay. Have a good day." He moved toward me, and I stayed rigid while he hugged me. He stepped back, fake smile in place, but clearly disappointed that I hadn't responded. Like he expected me to play along with his game.

What the...? "Is this a joke to you? We fucking kissed last night."

Josh gasped and stared at me with his eyes wide enough to make me think maybe I'd dreamed the entire thing.

Then he laughed.

And laughed some more.

Until he sounded slightly hysterical and started to hyperventilate, his eyes issuing an urgent cry for help.

I rushed toward him. "Jesus," I cried. "Slow down. Take a deep breath. That's it. Calm down." I rubbed his back and focused on the problem instead of the massive hit my ego had taken by his reaction. "Breathe," I reminded him and guided him through some deep cleansing breaths. When he regained control, his back muscles relaxed under my palm, and he turned to meet my gaze. He leaned toward me, the heat flaring between us.

Our eyes stayed locked until Josh looked away. *Goddamn it.*

"This was supposed to be a great day, Josh. I get to quit my job today. And it's ruined. I didn't want to come here. I don't want to keep my hands up. I thought..." Emotion choked off my words. "When I said we'd see how things felt in the morning, I wasn't prepared for you to act like nothing... for you to feel nothing."

"How can you say that? I feel. I don't know what I'm doing, Brady, but I feel... all the— I can't stop..." His voice quivered, and he trembled.

"What?" I yelled. "I can't do this, Josh. Not after Adam. Don't let me hope for something that isn't possible. Just tell me what you want. Please."

"You," he screamed and clamped his hand over his mouth.

As if God himself recognized the miracle behind the statement, He punctuated Josh's declaration with a crack of thunder. My pulse shot up to somewhere around the rate that heart monitors started smoking. I'd heard him wrong. Somehow my sleep-deprived, pissed-off, overactive-imagination mind had conjured the whole thing. I blinked back the rain crashing into my face. "You—" I cleared my throat.

Josh's lips parted, and his eyes unleashed a head-to-toe warmth that chased away the chill from the October rain. My vision tunneled, and the world fell away as he launched himself against me. My back hit a random SUV, setting off a series of whoops and whistles and flashing lights. The howling rain. The thunder. The damn car alarm. Josh either didn't notice or didn't care. For every word he couldn't bring himself to say, for every conversation he'd avoided, he kissed me. And it was so, so good, except . . . it wasn't enough.

I didn't push Josh away. I held him and kissed him back until the moment ended naturally. When he stepped away, I grabbed his hand and squeezed. We were drenched. I was pretty sure the guy hovering nearby with an umbrella in one hand and his key fob in the other wanted us to find a new place to make out. But I smiled at Josh gently, afraid of saying something that might hurt him or, worse, failed to recognize the magnitude of his declaration.

The man approached with an apologetic smile, and the door I was pinned against clicked. Josh flinched and dropped my hand. Before he could bolt, I moved aside and pulled Josh with me. To my surprise, he came easily and knotted his fists in my wet shirt, shivering. He whimpered softly, low in his throat, like a frightened animal.

My arms closed around him, gathering him to me. "You're shaking," I said, rubbing him to warm him up.

"It's freezing."

"Hey, Josh," I whispered against his ear.

"Yeah," he breathed.

"What you said . . ." He stirred, but I held him tighter. "We'll figure this out, okay? It's gonna be fine."

An almost imperceptible change on Josh's unreadable face told me I'd found the words to chase his dark thoughts away. Adam had been right, Josh believed me. And that was enough for now.

It figured the first time I had ever been late to work was the day I handed in my resignation. I'd left Josh to finish his workout, which I suspected would involve many more miles than I would ever run.

Amelia, my boss, tapped her long, painted fingernails on her desk and smiled. "I knew this day would come eventually, yet I'm still aggravated."

I struggled to keep my smile under control. I hated my job, but Amelia and I had enjoyed a productive relationship over the years.

"Who is going to keep the loan processors from storming in here to complain about the office being too cold? You are such a great problem solver. It will be bedlam without you."

"Thanks, Amelia. I'm sure you'll manage. The space heaters are in the storage closet. Just bring them out when it gets cold again."

She tucked my letter into the inbox on her desk. I debated pointing out that she could have slid it into the personnel files I'd organized for her but decided against it. It seemed fitting that my last act as a glorified receptionist would be to file my own resignation letter and archive my employee file.

Word of my resignation spread quickly through our small office. It was bittersweet to say goodbye. Stanford Mortgage was the first place I'd worked outside fast-food stints in high school. As I looked around, a wave of nostalgia dampened my enthusiasm. I remembered the excitement that came with landing a job that didn't require a uniform. I'd grown up here, really, and the same staff who'd thrown me a graduation party seemed eager to throw me a farewell.

"We can have it at that bar over by the FedEx office," Erica, one of the underwriters, said.

"Chester's?" I guessed.

"Yeah. How's Saturday?"

Josh's face popped into my brain. *Shit. Our dinner plans.* We were doing this whole relationship thing so ass-backward. A romantic date to kick-start another conversation? It could be a good idea . . . *or a recipe for another panic attack.* "Oh. I sort of have plans this Saturday. How about next weekend?"

"Okay. Where are you going anyway? Is it nearby? I know you're on your health kick, but I want to have our Margarita Mondays occasionally."

"Weston Security," I said.

"Never heard of them. Good bennies?"

I checked over my shoulder to make sure Amelia wasn't lurking. "Amazing—six percent retirement match, four weeks paid vacation, and medical, dental, and vision for half the price of our medical."

"Nice. Let me see what I can arrange for your farewell and twist Amelia's arm into paying for it." She winked at me and headed back to her desk.

I busied myself making a list of all the little things that had become my job over the years for Amelia to assign to my replacement. I made it until eleven, when I couldn't stand it anymore. I needed to know how Josh was doing. I typed out and deleted a few versions of the same message. All attempts to boil down the scope of what he meant to me into a few benign words. Nothing felt right, so I spent the day willing him to do the work for me and planning our sort-of-probably first date.

A cheerful voice answered the phone with "Lotus. This is Karen. How may I help you?"

"Hi, Karen. I'd like to make a reservation, please."

"It's Kara. Certainly. My next availability is on November twenty-fifth."

"I'm sorry, Kara. Can you repeat that?"

"Yes, we are currently booking for November twenty-fifth."

"I'd hoped for Saturday. Is there any—"

"Next Saturday is October ninth, sir."

"Yes, I'm aware. This is for a really important—"

"Sir, October ninth is not available."

"But—"

"Sir, can I book you a table for November twenty-fifth?"

"Listen . . . I really need October ninth. It's a matter of life and death, Kara."

Click.

"Son of a bitch," I said, holding the phone from me as Erica approached.

"What happened?" She plopped a bunch of files on my desk. "These are ready for Amelia's review."

"I tried to make dinner reservations for a, um, date and they're booked a month out."

"Awe. You have a date, Brady? That's sweet. Where were you going to take him?"

"Lotus."

Amelia gasped from her office and came flying around the corner to join us. "Oh my god. I went there last week. Their shrimp scampi is to die for. It's a perfect date place. Romantic, not too loud. The food is amazing."

"Well if I can't get in—"

"We were so lucky. Apparently, they only use half their slots for public reservations. They save the rest for VIP and businesses to give away. It's all this elaborate scheme to build buzz. Create the illusion that they are very hard to get into," Amelia said.

"They are hard to get—"

"We're too small, of course. But if you have any connections, you might want to use them. It really was a great night."

Amelia thumbed through the files Erica had placed on my desk and frowned. "Brady, can you please organize them the way I like?"

I sighed. *Didn't I always?* "Sure thing."

Amelia pivoted on her heel and retreated to her office, leaving Erica and me to finish our conversation. I picked her brain for date options, but she laughed.

"I haven't eaten in a place without a kid's menu in ten years."

In between answering phone calls and buzzing people into our secure office, I googled other date-friendly places that I thought Josh might like. We didn't get many outside visitors, most of the clients were dealt with on the phone, but we had regular package deliveries that had to be signed for. In desperation, I began asking each delivery person their favorite place to eat. I kept getting stupid answers like Chili's that made me want to throw things. It had to be special. Nothing measured up. I had the stack of files ready for Amelia when her earlier comment floated back to my consciousness.

I bit my lip. Damn, I didn't want to do it, but Josh really wanted to go to Lotus, and I really wanted to be the one to take him there. So, to hell with it.

Matt answered with a succinct, "Matt Weston."

"Hey, Matt. It's me. Brady."

"Oh. Hi, Brady. What's up?"

"Sorry to bother you. I was wondering if you've got any pull with this place called Lotus downtown. I've heard they sometimes save reservations for certain businesses."

"Um . . . hold on." Matt called out to someone else and posed my question. "Hey, Brady. Yeah, good news. Apparently, Tessa says we've got a person we can call for recruitment and client dinners."

"Oh, so would you be able to book a table for me?"

"Sure. Um . . . wait. You haven't started yet, right? Is this for work?"

Ah. I froze. Maybe this was what Matt had meant when he said he wanted to make sure our personal relationship didn't get muddied with our professional one. The pause stretched the limits of normal response time. I cleared my throat. "No. Just, um, celebrating my new job. Sorry, is this . . . Should I not have asked?"

A long pause. "Oh. Nice. Okay. Well, I guess that is sort of job related, so we can make the case this is a business request. Call my office number and speak to Tessa. I've got to run."

I let Matt go, and Tessa worked her magic. With a reservation confirmation firmly in hand, I made it through the remainder of my day, barely even obsessively checking my phone for texts from Josh. The first arrived as I shut down my computer for the day.

Are you home for dinner?

I could scroll through two years of my messages with Josh and see that phrase hundreds of times. Before I could answer, another appeared.

Or we could meet somewhere.

This is so weird.

I exhaled. Finally, something to acknowledge that things were different. I took it as a good sign.

I wanted to text you all day, but I didn't know what to say.

I laughed and my fingers flew over the keyboard. *Me too.*

I'm sorry.

Don't be.

He texted me the grimacing face emoji. He was nervous, which was at least an actual human emotion, so that was something. I typed

the kissy-face, then changed my mind, settling on the smiling face with heart eyes. *Josh, it's gonna be okay.*
Do you want chicken enchiladas tonight?
I laughed. Okay, Josh. I got it. *Real cheese?*
An eye roll face. *Whatever you want, baby.*
Then a second later: *Oh god. Ducking autocorrect. BRADY, not baby* and an embarrassed emoji. Then *fucking**
I typed a response. Deleted it. Typed it again. Deleted it. Took a deep breath and said, "Fuck it" out loud. *I think I like you calling me baby.*
Josh: *Green sauce or red sauce?*
Brady: *Green.*
Josh: *See you at home.*
Brady: *Yep. C u soon.*
Halfway home, his response came. With a flutter of anticipation, I checked my messages.
Can't wait, baby. Kissing face. Heart eyes. Winky face.
My face heated. Josh was flirting with me. This was so weird.
A traffic snarl gave enough time for my healthy uncertainty to dissolve into crippling doubts. By the time I pulled into the driveway, I'd bounced back to cautious optimism. Pragmatic to a fault, that's me. I reasoned one of us had to keep a level head and drive this thing. Clearly, Josh had the drama queen role staked out.

The opening garage door unveiled Josh's car parked on the right instead of the left—Josh's way of reminding me about trash day without having to remind me. I exited my car and lugged the recycling and trash containers to the curb, smiling all the way. Adam would give me so much shit if he knew, but I liked it. One benefit of having Josh as a roommate—he had a system for everything, and it pretty much ensured zero conflicts on mundane stuff. He never nagged. Would that be a good trait for a boyfriend? Hell if I knew, I'd never had one.

"Honey, I'm home," I yelled as soon as I stepped into the house from the garage. Josh stood at the stove, stirring something with a wooden spoon. He still had on his suit pants and a white collared shirt, top button undone, tie off. The smell of enchiladas permeated the air. My mouth watered, and I couldn't be sure of the reason. "How was your day, dear? Were the children good?"

Josh turned to me, and his face turned down briefly. I'd joked about Josh being a good househusband back in the dorms. Any time he'd do something nice like bring me food from the cafeteria or move my car on game days, but for the first time he'd reacted as though I wasn't joking. It seemed to take him a minute for that realization to catch up to him. "Ha ha," Josh deadpanned. My stomach did a little flip.

He looked at me expectantly. Should I kiss him? Should I offer to help? I had no idea, but my face had started to hurt from smiling at him. "So..."

Josh blushed and returned his attention to the stove. "How did Amelia react to your notice?"

Oh no. I'd been fighting off fantasies left and right all day; we weren't skipping over the good part. I willed my feet to move and stood behind him. It was better than face to face, my belly didn't feel quite so in the way. He startled, but I slid my hands over his hips and nuzzled my mouth into the crook of his neck. I breathed him in, and he let out a surprised sound, which withered into a low groan that my dick really liked. He tilted his head to give me better access. I kissed his neck, smiling at the goose bumps that formed under my lips. "Hi," I said, as sexy as my voice allowed.

"Hi," Josh breathed. He dropped his spoon on the stove and cupped the back of my head to keep my lips on his neck. His ass pushed back into my body and, oh yeah... that's more like it.

Josh turned in my arms. His pupils almost eclipsed the brown of his eyes, and he appeared more aroused than terrified—a good sign. Josh brought his lips to mine, and we began a thoroughly slow kiss. I slipped my tongue over his. He tasted like cilantro and Josh, and now that I'd kissed him, I deciphered it as a combination of Extra peppermint gum, his whitening toothpaste, and Kind bars.

The kitchen timer started beeping, and we groaned into each other's mouths. Damn. Thwarted by another alarm. "Dinner smells good."

"You smell good," Josh said, seemingly surprised by his quick retort. "Um... I need to get the enchiladas."

I stepped aside, and Josh pulled the pan from the oven. "It's ready," he declared. He searched around, and it took me a minute to figure out why. Oh yeah, I'd been too distracted kissing him to set the table.

"Oh, sorry," I said and opened the cabinet where we kept the plates. "Dining room?"

Josh smiled. "Yeah. That'd be nice."

We sat in our regular seats, and besides the level of sexual tension and my semierect penis, dinner felt normal. I filled Josh in on my day, and he did the same. It was comfortable and familiar and not at all what I wanted to be talking about.

"So," I said after Josh finished his story about a work presentation. "Funny thing . . . this morning, my roommate sort of told me he wanted me, but I had to go to work, and we didn't get to talk about that."

Josh turned crimson. "Um . . . wow, that must have been so embarrassing for you. Your roommate clearly has issues."

"Yeah. He does this weird thing where he doesn't tell me what's going on, and things get really bottled up and the next thing you know, we have this super-hot make-out session. But when I try to talk to him, he had a panic attack."

"That sounds awful."

I grinned. "It kind of was, because I'm kind of liking it, but I'm also flummoxed. I had no idea, and I'd really like to know some basic things, like how long he's felt this way. And I need to stop having the conversation like this and just talk, so can we?"

Josh dropped his fork, and for a second, I worried I'd pushed too hard.

"A long time," Josh said, voice barely above a whisper.

"What?"

"Um, I've been feeling this way . . . a long time. I didn't really understand what it was until recently."

"How? What changed?"

"Brady, I don't know. I'm sorry."

"Why are you apologizing?"

"Because I feel like I called an audible. This play is all on me, and it's risky."

"Called a . . . Is that a damn sports metaphor?" I cried, slapping the table harder than I'd meant to.

"Yeah, in football, when the quarterback—"

"Josh," I said through barely constrained laughter. "Do not give me a football lesson. Jesus, Adam was right. You two are so much alike. How did I miss that?"

"What?"

"Never mind." I laughed again. "Just something Adam said the other day. It's not important." Josh ran his fingers through his hair, and his pained expression quieted my laughter. "It's not risky. A lot of relationships start as friends."

Josh challenged me with his disbelieving look. We did live together. That could get messy.

"Okay . . . so it's a little risky, but not being honest about this is adding to the risk, don't you think? Tell me what's going on. If you were feeling that way, why push me to go out with Matt?"

"Matt was a mistake."

"How so?"

"I thought you needed to get laid, so you'd be yourself again. I, um, I didn't . . ." Josh's cheeks pinked, and he seemed almost bashful as he fidgeted with his clothes. "I thought when you said you wanted to date, it meant you liked to talk and have dinner before you hooked up. Then you said that shit about getting married and having kids with him, and I don't know . . . it pissed me off. I don't think about wanting stuff like that."

"Do you . . . Did you change your mind? What are you . . .?" I inhaled sharply and closed my eyelids tight. *Jesus Christ. Take the wheel, you coward.* I opened my eyes. "Josh, are you wanting more than a hookup with me?"

Josh's eyes skimmed past me to somewhere in the family room before I could get a read on his face. My stomach lurched. I placed my hand on my knee to keep my leg from bouncing while I waited for his response. "I've never tried to have more," he said quietly.

"I know, but do you want to? Is that what we are talking about, because if this is just some jealousy over me going out with Matt, I wasn't lying. We agreed to be friends after our first date. You don't have to do this."

Josh mumbled something that sounded like yes, and my vision blurred a little. Holy shit. This was happening.

"You want to maybe look at me for this part?" I asked, and Josh turned. The fear in his eyes didn't stop me. "I want that too."

Josh smiled half-heartedly. There were still so many unanswered questions between us, but Josh's expression told me he'd reached his tolerance level. There was only one thing more I had to clear up, because it had the potential to keep me awake at night.

I loved the kissing, but Josh wasn't really the kind of guy who would want to stop at first base all the time. There was no way I had lost enough weight to let him see me naked. Not yet. I needed time, and I didn't think I could handle competition while I worked up the courage.

"So, we already live together, and there's not a whole lot about each other we don't know." *Although that assumption might have been shot all to hell.* "I think we should maybe take it one step at a time."

Josh nodded. "I'm . . . Yeah . . . that's good."

I cleared my throat. "While we do that, um, I'd like it if we didn't have distractions." *Good job, Brady. Clear as mud.* Josh's brows furrowed so I continued. "Um, I mean, if you didn't. I'm not. Except for that one time with Matt, I don't really . . . So . . ."

Josh smiled and he placed his hand over mine. "Brady, I deleted Grindr last night after you kissed me."

"Oh, thank fuck." I crashed my head to the table in relief.

When I peeked up, Josh beamed at me with a smile that screamed sex, and I leaned into him so he could kiss me. When he did, that kaleidoscope of butterflies returned with a vengeance.

Chapter Ten
Josh

I had work clothes, gym clothes, "lying around the house" clothes, and "fuck me" clothes. What I didn't have—and didn't discover until thirty minutes before I was supposed to be ready—was "first date with my best friend" clothes.

"Josh," Brady yelled from the front door. "I'm home." He'd gone to wash his car like he did most Saturdays. His footsteps traipsed to my door, and he knocked seconds before entering.

"I'm gonna grab a quick..." Brady's face crinkled with amusement. "What the hell happened in here?"

"I have nothing to wear."

Brady chuckled, surveying the mountain of clothing piled on my bed. "I think we need to work on your definition of *nothing*." He eyed me lustfully. It'd only been a week, but damn did I like how he watched me with naked...

"Shit." *I'm naked.* I yanked on sweatpants and let the towel tied around my waist fall to the floor. Brady tracked my movements with interest. "Quit looking at me like that."

"Like what?" Brady batted his eyes, which seemed a little irritated. He better not be getting sick, not after I'd spent serious time preparing for what I hoped would be the night our physical relationship got off the ground.

"Like you want to get lucky *before* you take me to Lotus."

Brady smacked his lips but didn't acknowledge the underlying offer. "I'm gonna take a shower. Reservations are in an hour. You have about twenty minutes to decide."

"Do we have five minutes for you to come make out a little?"

Brady laughed, but his feet were moving. His cheeks pink and neck flushed, he leaned in and paused for a second before he pressed his lips to mine. I loved that little pause. Like he wanted to savor the anticipation.

I lost myself in the rhythms of his kiss—full lips, soft sighs, and little flutters of his long lashes—and clutched on to the new feelings I discovered I could find there. Cherished. Needed. Maybe even loved.

I lifted my hands to his waist, sliding them under his T-shirt and moaned my enjoyment as I contacted his warm skin.

Brady rocked back, and my throat made an involuntarily whining noise as he straightened his shirt.

"That's all you get. We have dinner." He cupped the back of my neck and squeezed.

I had interpreted Brady's one-step-at-a-time request to mean we'd go slow, and even though I was getting sort of frustrated by whatever we were using as a benchmark on those steps, Brady only had to train his baby blues on me and I knew I could survive on nothing but the affection in his gaze for as long as he needed.

"Wait. What are you wearing?" I called as he stepped into the hallway.

He turned back toward me and frowned. "You'll see."

"You need me to iron something for you?"

Brady laughed. "I got it."

"But I always—"

"That was before."

I opened my mouth to protest, but Brady's determined chin warned me off. "Fine," I said. "But you better step up. If it weren't for me, you'd still be wearing cargo shorts and gamer tees."

Brady guffawed. "Contrary to popular belief, I'm capable of dressing myself. And I gave up cargo shorts in college. Remember Cade and Sid staged an intervention. I'll look good for you."

"You always look good, baby."

Brady's forehead creased in disapproval. *Damn it.* I had to get my mindless flirting under control.

"Whatever you say, Josh." Brady shook his head and turned away. Shortly after, the shower ran. I strained to listen to Brady sing, but his voice was too muffled, so I returned to getting ready and adjusting my expectations for after dinner.

I'd been assuming Brady's pumping the brakes was because he wanted our first time to be special and not something we did on a random weekday. The way he pulled back whenever I tried to touch him anywhere below the chest was making me doubt that assumption. What else could it be? He'd had sex before—hell, he got naked and fucked Matt on their first date, so if nothing had changed for him, I had to wonder if it was me?

I had been with a lot of guys, but I'd used condoms religiously. Brady knew that. Every time he recoiled under my touch, it made me feel like an asshole. After my experience with Anna, the last thing I would ever do is push him. I had no idea what I was doing wrong, and my obvious ineptitude triggered a steady churn of worries about my ability to do this whole boyfriend thing. It was like my brain had a contest going to see if I could keep upping Bare's "worst-case scenario."

My confusion extended to figuring out what to wear. I settled on some dark jeans and a long-sleeve white button-down shirt with a lightweight sports coat. I ditched the sports coat for an olive-green sweater. Then ditched the jeans for black pants. Then ditched the white shirt and sweater for a gray shirt and maroon sweater. Then went back to the dark jeans.

"Josh, are you ready?" Brady called from behind my door, then started coughing.

"Are you all ri—" I opened my door, and Brady thrust an arrangement of stargazer lilies at me. "Oh my god."

"These need to stay in your bedroom."

I laughed and took the vase to the opposite side of the room.

"Hold on," Brady said and went to the bathroom to wash his hands. When he reappeared, his eyes were still bloodshot like he'd recently smoked a lot of pot, but he'd stopped coughing.

"You didn't have to."

Brady waved me off. "I wanted to."

"Thanks. I've never gotten flowers before." Brady's grin and the gleam in his eye made me think he already knew that. It made sense. Grindr hookups weren't known to bring floral arrangements.

"You look amazing." He kissed me on the cheek.

I did another quick glance in the mirror before realizing I'd been so distracted by the flowers, I'd failed to notice Brady. "I'm underdressed."

"No, you're not."

"Yes. Purple is a great color on you. When did you get that tie? And that shirt? I've never seen that—"

"Josh, calm down. It's new. I bought them with Adam the other day for work, but I wanted to wear them tonight. The pants are old, but I had a tailor take them in a few inches. You, on the other hand..." He shook his head, admiring me. "It's almost obscene how handsome you are. Let's go, we're gonna be late."

"Let me change back into the black slacks. I can't wear jeans if you're wearing a tie."

Brady smirked. "If you keep taking off your pants around me, we're really gonna be late."

Although I was ninety-nine percent sure he was teasing, hearing those flirty lines of his about killed me with temptation. One percent meant there was a chance... "I'd be okay with that..." I swished my hips, prepared to do a full striptease when the response I'd anticipated came.

Brady flushed bright red. "Josh," he whined.

"Then stop teasing," I said, laughing as I shoved Brady into the hall. I quickly changed back into the black pants, then selected a slightly dressier belt and shoes. Then I switched from my casual watch to my dress watch. I headed for the family room and found Brady playing Mission to Mars.

"What are you doing? Let's go." I checked my watch. "We'll be late."

"*Now* he's worried." He rolled his eyes, but I could hear the affection in his voice, so I hammed it up with a chop-chop clap. He took his time turning off the television and slipping on my black loafers, which I'd mainly bought for him anyway.

We exited the house, and both of us headed for our own cars. "I'm driving," Brady said.

"You drive like my mom."

"If you mean with a driving record free of speeding tickets or accidents, then yes, I do." Brady hovered near his car door and shot me a knowing smile. Geez. You get two speeding tickets and run over a mailbox, and suddenly you're a terrible driver.

We were going to be late. I cracked my knuckles, trying to decide what to do. "Fine," I said, aware of a newly formed thickness in my throat. When Brady rushed to open his passenger-side door for me, I heard my father's mocking tone. *"You call yourself a football player, Joshalyn."* His barbed words—sarcastic, demeaning sneers—had left their scars every time we'd battled. I could only imagine what he'd say if he knew how much I loved getting flowers. I climbed into the passenger seat of Brady's car and did my best to not let the doubts win. Not this time. *There was nothing wrong with letting Brady drive. It didn't make me the girl.*

I shook my head, attempting to remove all the poisonous thoughts. Brady kept his hand on my thigh as we drove, which seemed to have the effect of turning me on enough I didn't care so much that my father's voice was apparently tagging along on our date.

When we pulled up to the valet stand, the valet opened my door first, and I beat Brady to the tip, which helped settle some of my anxieties. He frowned as I climbed the stairs to the revolving door. I took his hand, and he squeezed it, so that took care of that.

Brady stepped past me to the host stand and gave his name. The tuxedo-clad man searched his screen and told us to follow him.

Lotus was gorgeous. The restaurant was laid out like a flower: the center of the space had a trickling water feature with lotus flowers floating in a stocked pond and the pattern of the floor marked the shape of petals in a pale-pink hue extending toward curved walls. Tables draped in crisp white linens and highlighted by small, stylish lights were arranged throughout. The host led us through the restaurant to the back of the petal-shaped room, where I stopped cold.

Brady ran into me, knocking me forward a step and into an empty chair. "What's wrong— Matt?"

"Brady. Josh." Sid stood and greeted us with a big hug. I hugged him back, shooting a death glare at Matt, who rose to his feet on the other side of the four-top table.

"Hi," Brady said, his eyes as wide as I'd ever seen them. He let go of Sid to shake Matt's hand. "What a... surprise." He gulped.

Matt extended his hand to me, but it took an elbow from Brady to relax my scowl to shake it. Matt flashed a concerned expression to Brady. "Didn't you get my email?"

Brady gaped, bouncing his gaze between Matt and me, then to Sid who, by the mortified expression he wore, noticed how surprised we were. "No," Brady answered while staring directly at me. "No email. No idea you were gonna be here."

"Oh no," Sid breathed. "Maybe we should—"

"Is something wrong with your table, gentlemen?"

"Yes," Sid and I said right as Matt said, "No."

The host scanned our expressions, clearly concerned. "We need separate tables," Sid explained.

"But I sent you an email," Matt said to Brady. He pulled out his phone to show him, touching his arm in the process. I might have fallen into a rage-induced blackout. The next thing I knew, the manager was apologizing to Sid that there were no other tables and Matt was apologizing to Brady for using his new work email he didn't have access to yet instead of texting like a normal human. But absolutely no one apologized to me for ruining the story I'd planned to tell when people asked me about the most romantic night of my life.

"I'm so sorry for crashing your da— um, night, Brady," Sid said, seemingly more mortified than sorry. Brady tugged me to my chair next to him.

"Be right back." I stood so abruptly Brady had to reach out to keep my chair from tipping backward. Still a little dazed, I made my way back to the garish center and got lost hunting for the petal with the stupid men's room. When I found it, I ran the water and studied my reflection in the mirror, debating the best way to handle the situation, and wishing Brady had followed so we could strategize our escape together. When the door opened, I startled. *Brady.* My breath caught with the possibility I'd summoned him with that thought.

"Oh. Hey, Sid." I forced the disappointment off my face.

"Josh, there you are. I'm so sorry," Sid said. "This is all my fault. Matt said something about making a reservation to celebrate Brady's job, and I said I wanted to try this place. He made it sound like it was a group thing. I didn't realize it was the four of us until we got here. I'm so embarrassed. This was a date, right? Like your face was, oh, it killed me."

"It's fine," I said. "Matt made the reservation?"

Sid nodded.

"Of course he did," I muttered under my breath. Sid's eyebrow raised, so I clarified, "I was sort of . . . I don't know. Maybe—" I cut myself off. Whatever Brady and I were doing was way too new to bring our friends into it. "It's a thank-you dinner. I didn't know you and Matt were joining us." I forced a smile. "But it's great. So great. It's good to see you. How are you and Matt doing anyway?" I met his eyes, begging him to let it go.

Sid frowned and surveyed me. "We've been texting and met for coffee once. He's been busy. This is the first time we've actually gone out. It's good so far. I like him, but do you think Matt would rather be with Brady?"

"No," I said harshly. I knew he wanted more of an explanation, but I couldn't . . . not when I realized I'd left Matt and Brady alone. "They're friends, but, um, we should get back to the table."

Sid grimaced as I led him by the arm toward the door.

I could read Brady's body language from across the room. A pinched face and slumped shoulders I wanted to rub the tension out of was all it took for my irritation to give way to compassion. I decided on the fly to make the best of a bad situation. Despite what I'd told Sid, I wasn't convinced Matt hadn't concocted some scheme to use Sid to sabotage my date with Brady. But after Anna, I could be paranoid about things like that. There was no doubt in my mind, however, that Brady wasn't in on Matt's plan.

I retook my seat and rested my hand on the back of Brady's chair. His concerned gaze sought an answer, which I gave with a gentle squeeze to his shoulder. "Sorry about that. What is everyone looking at for dinner?" I perused the one-page menu.

"We ordered a bottle of white wine," Brady said. "Riesling."

"Thanks." I smiled.

"German Rieslings had a great year in 2015. Nearly perfect growing season. The grapes retained their acidity," Matt said.

Oh, for Christ's sake. "Aren't you a wealth of wine knowledge?"
Sid laughed nervously. "Matt's family owns a vineyard."
Brady's jaw dropped, and he shook his head in mock disapproval. "You started your own company and your family owns a vineyard. Dude, we talked about video games for an hour. You've got to learn how to market yourself on dates."
I meant to kick Brady silently, but his knee jumped and the whole table rattled. "Sorry," I mumbled.
"I don't usually like to talk about my family's money or mine, for that matter," Matt said directly to me.
Before I could clap back, I caught sight of Sid. He had hearts in his eyes, so I forced my smile instead. I guess there was *one* thing Matt had in common with a sweetheart like Sid.
"Josh, I don't think I ever asked what you do for a living?"
I made a show of unfolding my napkin and laid it across my lap. The dinner knife was right there. I straightened it, making sure to run my thumb over the blade. *Too dull. Wouldn't work.* I sat up straighter. "I'm a junior account manager at McConnell & Kennedy."
Matt sat up even straighter than I had. "Oh. Are you in the business strategy practice?"
I took a slow sip of my water to find the trap. Matt didn't care what I did. "No. I'm in business intelligence. I mostly help corporations use the data from our business analytics tool to maximize their operations."
"Yes. I've seen it. It's quite impressive. But I have to confess I'm not a fan of letting metrics and graphs replace people. I'm sure Brady as a human resource professional would agree."
And there it is.
My eyes assessed Brady, who rightfully looked slightly nauseated. Did Matt expect him to have developed deeply entrenched philosophical positions before his first job in HR? Of course not. Matt wanted Brady to take his side over mine. Part of human resources was letting people go when their salary wasn't adding value to the company. It wasn't personal. Numbers don't lie.
I patted Brady's leg. I had this. Brady wouldn't fall victim to Matt's game. "I'm sure we'd all agree that sometimes businesses have to make decisions that can impact their workforce adversely."

Matt huffed. "Clearly, you've never had to lay someone off before."

"Well, you know how it is when some cocky asshole starts a company and makes promises he can't keep. We help make sure they can get right financially instead of laying off their entire workforce." *Check and mate, asshole.*

Sid took a drink of his water. "I think I'll have the risotto. Brady, what are you going to have?"

"The scallops sound good, but not sure about that sauce, probably all butter. Maybe the Swordfish. What do you think, Josh? If I get it grilled, that's not too bad, right?"

"Oh. Yes, I forgot Josh is also an expert dietitian," Matt mocked.

"What is your problem?" I slammed my fist down, upending my empty wineglass as the sommelier approached with our wine.

"Who would like to taste?"

Sid powered through the standoff Matt and I were having and pointed to Matt's glass. Brady reached under the table and squeezed my thigh while Matt tasted the wine and the sommelier poured our drinks.

When the silence dragged on for several second after he'd left, I cleared my throat. "I'm here to celebrate Brady, so allow me to offer a toast." I raised my glass. "To the most amazing man I know. Congrats on reaching the next stepping-stone in a wonderful career. Well deserved."

"Cheers," Sid said and brought his glass to mine. Matt hesitated, then clinked with Sid and Brady. I thought we'd managed to overcome the awkwardness, but nope. Brady sighed, and my heart dropped when he raised his glass and thanked Matt for giving him the opportunity. Matt's smug expression grew as Brady went out of his way to say how he hoped to have a long career at Weston Security.

Brady and I spent dinner listening to Sid and Matt have a date. We didn't touch. We didn't flirt. I sat there and plastered a smile on my face, nodding and blinking at random intervals and died a little inside every time Brady seemed slightly less miserable than me. But I didn't speak, and no one attempted to ask me questions. At first, I thought it went unnoticed by everyone at the table, but at some point, Brady started moving the sharper knives out of my reach, so maybe not.

The dessert tray came, and my eyes issued a death warrant to anyone who dared prolong the evening. Of course, Matt ordered eight-dollar black coffee and called the server back to ask where the beans came from. Our server didn't know, but instead of lying like any decent waitstaff would, she had to go find someone and ask. When the answer revealed the coffee wasn't from a fair-trade source, Matt declined. Even though agriculture was a major contributor to deforestation and fair-trade had a significant impact on environmental practices, I didn't respect Matt's decision because he'd been a colossal, pretentious douche about it.

I wasn't even sorry Matt paid forty-five dollars for my untouched meal. *Screw him. Screw them.*

After we said goodbye to Sid and Matt, Brady handed the valet our claim ticket. "I'm sorry," he said solemnly to me. "I'll make it up to you."

I did my best, but I'd run out of fake smiles. When the car came, I snatched Brady's keys from the valet and announced, "I'm driving." I needed something I could control. Matt shouldn't have been able to get under my skin. What was my problem? I dealt with assholes like him all day at work without losing my shit. It was the only good lesson my father taught me—how to compete. How could I have allowed myself to be so blindsided?

Brady didn't argue. I pulled out of the parking lot, not even bothering to adjust the mirrors or seat. When I did slide the seat back, the resulting jerk and click was a satisfyingly angry sound. I gripped the steering wheel so hard my hands cramped, weaving in and out of traffic, my foot heavy on the accelerator.

We were halfway home when I dared a glance toward Brady. His eyes wide, white knuckles wrapped tightly around the handle. *Shit!* I eased off the accelerator and willed myself to take some breaths. My pulse settled, and guilt absorbed the adrenaline coursing through my veins. What in the world made me think I could do this? I couldn't even make it through one lousy dinner.

"Josh," Brady pleaded. "I don't know what to say. Are you—"

I pulled into the driveway and threw his car into park, jumped out, and made a beeline for the bathroom. If this was dating, no thanks.

Count me out. I scrubbed my face and peeled off my sweater. My skin buzzed, and I dug my vibrating phone out of my pocket. It was Cade.

"I can't talk right now."

"Oh, Josh. What's wrong?"

"Nothing. Just in the middle of something. Come over for brunch. Next Sunday." I hung up and opened the door to find Brady on the other side of it.

"Was that Sid?"

"Cade."

"Did you tell him?"

"Tell him what, Brady?"

"About us ... dating." He swallowed.

I stared at him incredulously, biting my lip to keep from saying that dinner with his ex was hardly a date. Luckily, he read my comment in my expression.

"I asked Matt to make us a reservation because I couldn't get one without him and I wanted you to get to eat there. He wasn't supposed to be there. I have zero interest in Matt."

"Fine," I said glibly.

"I want a do-over."

"I think tonight proved this was too damn risky. Nothing has happened yet besides a few flirty texts and some kissing. We should throw in the towel before we do real damage."

Brady shook his head. "First, we should stop using sports metaphors. And second, we shouldn't do any of that. This was a shitshow, but I wanted to take you out as an appreciation for what you do for me and to show you how much you mean to me, and I didn't get to do that. So, I want a milligan."

I laughed. *God, I needed that.* What a shitty night. "A mulligan?"

"Yeah. That. I want another chance."

"It's—"

Brady grabbed my hand. "Josh, please. This was so bad, and I get that, but I was looking forward to tonight. I'm disappointed too. Nothing has changed. I still want what we talked about."

I glanced at where our hands were connected, then returned to Brady's face. His expressions were easy to read. He scowled when grumpy, smiled when happy, laughed when amused, but the emotion

143

in his eyes staring back at me now, I hadn't seen in a few years. Not since he first laid eyes on Adam at that safe sex lecture our freshman year. Unadulterated desire. How did he do that? Just trust me with what he wanted like it was nothing.

"I need more control," I blurted.

"Huh?"

"You can't involve Matt without telling me. You can't take his side over mine."

"But I didn't know he was going to be there! And I didn't take his side, I was only trying to keep things civil."

"I know. It's . . . Sid already told me he made the reservation, but he . . . Look, I know I reacted childishly, and you didn't mean for him to show up, but I can't feel like this."

"What do you mean by control? You're the least bossy person I know."

"I don't know. I want to know the plan and have a say. And drive and pay or do something. I don't know. This feeling isn't good. I'm not the girl." My heart pounded in my chest with my slip. I usually managed to keep that particular insecurity inside. I winced, knowing what was coming.

"Josh! Me taking you on a date does not make you a girl. You know that. I know you know that."

"Ugh. I know! It's like I can hear my dad quoting Ephesians 5:22 to my mom when I say things like that. It's not even what I mean. It's not like I think girls have no control." *After Anna, I know exactly how much control girls can have.* "I'm not explaining it right . . . You tell me I need to be honest. This is me being honest. I don't like how this feels."

"Ephesians? I don't know what any of that means. Um, is it the flowers?"

"It's a Bible verse about wives submitting to their husbands. Not surprisingly, one of my dad's favorites . . ." I could see from Brady's face that I wasn't making sense. I stopped to take a deep breath and gather myself. My issues with the start of the evening had me in a bad headspace for the night, but that wasn't what I needed to explain, so I parked my femmephobia and took my control issues out for a spin.

"You know when we were in school, how I'd transfer every syllabus to a wall planner so I could see the entire semester all at once?" I had every class color-coded—test, papers, projects—all laid out, blocks of time shaded to ensure I left enough prep time. The system had served me well, except once. My professor had left abruptly, and another instructor had taken over, then rearranged the entire class to match their other sections.

Brady's brow furrowed. "Yeah," he said slowly.

"Tonight felt like Private Equity all over again." Brady's confusion yielded to clear eyes, and finally, we were getting somewhere. I wasn't asking for guarantees, just the ability to rely on the information I had to make decisions and plan—simple probabilities. Maybe there was no way to map out my future with Brady like a class schedule, but I couldn't face the inherent and unavoidable uncertainty of our future without some assurances that this wasn't going to blow up in my face.

"I'm sorry. I didn't... Don't give up on this. Please, we can figure it out."

"Fine, but I can't do it right now. I can't even think straight. I'm... I really need to go run."

"Do you want me to come with you?"

"You can, but I'm going to run as long and as hard as it takes to forget tonight or I puke, whichever happens first."

Brady grimaced. "I don't want to hold you back."

Same, Brady. Same. "Okay."

"Will you maybe come watch a movie when you get done, maybe cuddle? You didn't eat anything. Want me to make you a snack? Popcorn?"

"If you're still awake when I get home, we can talk more." He had no idea what it took to clear space in my head but explaining it would only prolong the time it took to get to mile six.

The skin-crawling sensation from dinner subsided about mile fifteen, so I headed toward home. I knew Brady would be waiting for me when I got in, wanting to talk. I worked though my speech—carefully mapping out my logic for why we should stay friends.

The entire night had sent a pretty clear warning that this was a bad idea. My anxiety was off the charts. I refused to risk him when I didn't have the first idea of how to be in a relationship. *Fuck!*

My stomach lurched, and my hand shot over my mouth, before leaving what little dinner I'd eaten all over it and Mr. Santino's bushes.

I walked the remainder of the way and slumped to the curb in front of our house. My conversation with Bare kept floating back to me. This *was* my goddamn worst-case scenario.

The porch light came on, and Brady stepped outside. "Josh," he said, his voice wary.

I glanced in his direction and, upon seeing the hesitation on his face, returned my attention to the ground.

Brady sat next to me, wrapped his arm around me, and pulled me against his shoulder. "Feel better?"

"Yeah," I said, lifting the hem of my shirt to wipe my forehead.

"Good. Want to come inside?" He squeezed my shoulder.

I met his concerned gaze. "Can we sit here for a minute?"

"Sure." Brady extended his legs and leaned back, waiting quietly. I knew he'd wait all night for me to be ready. We'd done this dance too many times. He was so patient with me.

I closed my eyes, sorting out my feelings. Bare had said some of my feelings might not be correct. What if this was one of those times? *What evidence did I have that this would work?*

I opened my eyes and twisted to see Brady. He returned my hesitant smile with a tender one that reached into my soul and quieted my fears. I could be honest with Brady. He wouldn't judge me.

"I didn't like it when you wouldn't let me drive."

Brady tipped his chin up. "Your dad again?"

I bit my lip and nodded. "He never let my mom drive when he was in the car. I know it's stupid, but 'men are always in control' was a pretty major theme of my dad's bullshit. It didn't matter if it's behind the wheel or in life in general."

"Your childhood was so fucked up," Brady said.

"Yeah, I know. It put me in a weird headspace."

"That's everything?"

"Matt," I confessed. "It was beyond immature to put you in that uncomfortable situation with your boss. I'm sorry."

"I wanted you to think I pulled off a perfect first date by myself. You have nothing to worry about with him."

But I was worried. Very worried. Because a guy like Matt would be better for Brady, and all of this was me being selfish. "I'm not sure I can be your boyfriend, Brady."

Brady recoiled. "Because you don't want to or because you're afraid?"

"Are you really asking me that?"

Our eyes stayed locked together until he shook his head and sat straighter. "I was thinking about sophomore year while I was washing my car. You remember we snuck that fresh Christmas tree into our dorm room?"

Of course. I should've stayed with you instead of going home."

"That day we went to pick it up. I remember thinking... maybe this could be us in the future. Then when you got home from Texas, and your parents had pulled that shit with your church. We cuddled a lot that weekend, and I don't know. It felt right, but I wanted to make you feel better and protect you from what they'd done. You needed me to be your best friend, so I was. I'll always be that for you, Josh." He cupped a hand to my nape, thumb caressing some magical pressure point that sent tingles down my spine, I sighed contentedly, pressing against his touch. "But I want to be more than your best friend. It feels right to be more than friends."

I nodded. "For me too."

Brady scrambled to his feet. He reached for my hands, yanked me up until my chest bumped his, and pressed his lips to mine. When he pulled back with a sharp grimace, his eyes watering, I laughed.

"Damn..." Brady pushed his palm over my mouth as my laughter breathed more stench into his face. "What the hell died in your mouth?"

"Sorry. I puked a few minutes ago," I muffled around his hand.

Brady shook his head, his eyes dancing in amusement, and like that, I didn't care what it took, I wanted to make it work.

"Come on. I made popcorn. We can watch a movie *after* you brush your teeth."

He led me to the front door, and we parted briefly so I could shower and clean up. When I was done, I wore lounge pants into the family room and found Brady in sweats and a T-shirt, munching on his bowl full of popcorn. The paused television screen showed Steve Carell's face.

I let his eyes rove over my bare chest unchallenged. "You're squishing my pillows," I said.

He rolled his eyes as he lifted his lower half to free the throw pillow trapped beneath him and tossed it across the room. "Reruns of *The Office* okay?"

I nodded and stepped between his open legs.

"C'mere." He yanked me down. I twisted until my back was against the end of the sofa and rested my legs on his lap. He took my bare feet in his hands and squeezed.

I moaned.

Brady smiled. "Feel good?"

"Yeah." I nodded.

"Good."

I reached toward the table for the remote, but Brady stopped me. "So I was thinking... We don't have to label this right now."

I tensed. "We don't?"

"No." Brady massaged my feet a little too firmly. "One thing this situation doesn't need is more pressure. So I think we should relax about it. Sort of let things happen naturally."

"Okay." I drew out the word. "But isn't that what *you* wanted?"

"Yeah. It is. But we said we wanted to go slow and it's not only for you. I'm scared too, Josh. I don't want to mess up our relationship by being selfish."

"You're not selfish."

"When is the last time you went to the gym?"

"Um..." The last time had been with Brady.

"Exactly. You're helping me workout and not taking care of your own needs. I know what to do now. I can take it from here."

"Brady—"

"Josh, did you or did you not get so stressed from our first attempt at dating that you ran until you puked?"

"I did."

"Okay, then that's settled. We're going to take whatever this is very slow and you're going back to the gym so you can be in a better headspace while we figure it out."

"So, you're ordering me to go back to the gym because I'm too much of a control freak?" I laughed. "When did you get bossy?"

"Maybe you bring it out in me."

I arched my eyebrow, slightly turned on by the possibility. "Oh, I do? Care to show me?"

Brady smirked, pushing my feet off his lap. He yanked my arms until I straddled his thighs. His eyes held me still, hovering over him until he cupped his hand behind my neck and guided me into a kiss.

I melted into him, content to let him touch me while I kept my hands on his shoulders. We'd been here a few times now, and I'd learned that if I wanted him to continue kissing me, I needed to let him set the pace. I could feel him grow hard, and it took everything in me not to rock against him.

Just when I figured Brady would stop, he moaned into my mouth and hauled me closer, deepening our kiss. The opening theme song to *The Office* started to play. We kept kissing leisurely, his tongue dancing with mine until my hands roamed down over his shoulders of their own free will.

I slid my hands lower, seeking the hem of his shirt, when a Texan accent blared in the background.

"Sorry." He fumbled blindly for the remote.

I was too busy focusing on the prominent tenting of Brady's crotch to process his apology. God Bless gray sweatpants. I dropped little kisses along his neck, but Brady was batting the couch cushion, still distracted. "What's wrong?"

"She's kind of a mood killer." He straightened his shirt before gesturing to the source of the voice.

Confused, I twisted to see the commercial on the screen. I recognized the woman with the accent but couldn't place her. "Who's that?"

Brady scowled. "That's Laura Anderson—conservative commentator. She ran for the House of Representatives in Texas a few years ago on her anti-trans bathroom bill and religious-right-to-discriminate platform. She didn't win thankfully. I heard she started a clothing line. This must be it." He gestured to the television where a woman was sliding her handgun into the side pocket of her blue camo-print yoga pants.

My stomach dropped.
"Freedom Athletics," Brady muttered. "What a stupid name."

Chapter Eleven
Brady

I stretched before turning left out of our front yard toward the park. My mission: run the mile to Stanwell Park, around the walking path that circled the entire perimeter, and back. Five miles according to my Fitbit. The longest I'd ever run.

My first attempt, I made it past the basketball courts before a few off-putting stares from other joggers left me unable to ignore the amount of jiggle going on in my midsection to keep going. I ended up cutting through the park and walking home. Wednesday, I'd started earlier, making it to the back end of the park without seeing a single soul, but was walking before I made it home.

Today was the day.

I started off at a good clip, headphones on, my inhaler bouncing against my left thigh, my sweatshirt providing some extra jiggle coverage, and my mind focused on the scale. Thirty-three pounds gone. Damn had it felt good to see that *one* in the tens column.

Not that I was in danger of looking like Josh anytime soon. Muscle definition and body fat percentages as low as Josh's required workouts dedicated to particular body parts. I could guarantee that in no version of my future would there be shirtless gym selfies captioned with things like #chestpump or #armday. No, thank you. At best, I could manage a couple of free weights and some sit-ups, call it a "don't be humiliated naked" day, and be done with it.

A zing of caution ran up my spine as I approached the blackness of the park. Motion lights flickered on, illuminating the path, as I ran by. My breath evened as my eyes adjusted.

When I reached the dimly lit backside of the expansive park, I kicked up the pace. I ran at full speed past the dark voids of the soccer fields until I reached the sign marking the south entrance to the park. *Don't stop.*

On strong legs, I neared the well-lit area of the park again, and my thoughts drifted to Josh. After our disastrous evening, Josh and I had talked about what had happened like old times. Only way better because all the affectionate, wanting looks I'd always assumed he'd given to everyone were just for me. I'd meant it when I said we didn't need a label right now. In a way, it'd taken the pressure off both of us.

His class analogy had really hit home for me. Josh had spent his college days completely overwhelmed. His schedule packed to the point that he barely slept. That experience was the first time I'd witnessed what happened when Josh's plans went drastically awry. When he reached that limit, there were only a few things that made it better—and I much preferred the running to the alternatives.

I needed to show him I could do this on my own. He didn't need to worry about me.

The sun cracked through the horizon. I checked my watch as I ended the park part of my run. Four miles down, one to go. Josh would be up soon, ready for the gym. If I pushed hard, I'd see him before he left. I took off, my head singularly focused on not collapsing on the street in exhaustion. I burst into the house, breathing hard from my efforts, but elated I'd made it.

"Josh. Guess what?" I knocked on his bedroom door and opened it. His spastic movement sent his phone flying to the floor. I took a minute to digest the image.

"Brady. Get out!"

"Oh shit." I tugged the door closed and cringed. "I'm sorry," I said and waited for the porn sounds and the buzzing from whatever toy he had in his ass to stop.

His drawer opened and closed, and his footsteps grew louder, then farther away. I turned to leave him alone, then thought better. We'd lived together long enough it wasn't the first time I'd caught him jerking off. He'd caught me too. Granted, this was the first I'd seen him use anything other than his hand, which wow . . . But still, why was this so different? If I didn't make a big deal about it, neither would he.

"Josh," I said. "Can I come in?"

His door flew open. He wore light-blue briefs, seemingly unconcerned by the prominent outline of his cock. He had a jockstrap in his hand and left me at the door to place it in his open gym bag.

My throat thickened, and I swallowed against it. I could do this. *Act casual.* "Hey, sorry about that." I walked into his room and sat on his bed. The scent of lube and sex clung to the air.

Josh shrugged. "What's up?"

Okay, we would pretend it hadn't happened. Josh excelled at that. I could do it too. Now, what had I meant to tell him? He stared at me expectantly, and I wet my lips.

"How was your run?"

Josh stood in front of me. Jesus. Was that a wet spot? Just below the waistband...

"Brady?" I glanced up to find him smirking.

"Huh?"

"Your run?"

Oh, yeah. "I made it around the park. Five miles."

"That's great." Josh leaned forward and kissed my cheek. His bare chest was right there. So smooth, and muscles...

I grabbed him and gathered him to me until he was sitting on my lap face forward, his knees on either side of my thighs. "That's all I get for five miles?"

Josh's eyes blazed down at me, his face still flushed from embarrassment or arousal, maybe both. Hands resting on my shoulders, he leaned in, meeting me in a passionate kiss. I rocked my hips toward him, hoping for some contact, but he sat back on my thighs. "Better?" he said, his tone reserved.

"Are you upset?"

"No." Josh wiggled out of my arms. "Of course not."

"Yeah," I said, shaking my head. "You are. Tell me why."

"Let it go." He averted his gaze and began pulling on clothes.

"No. Look at me, beautiful." That got his attention. I didn't know where it came from. I'd never used a pet name with him before, even after he started calling me baby.

He turned to face me. His lower lip dragged between his teeth, working through his options, debating if he would make me break out my decoder ring.

"I can't fix it if I don't know what I did."

Josh slumped on his bed. "You didn't *do* anything."

"Is it because I barged in? It's not a big deal. We've caught each other jerking off before."

He stood, retrieved a dress shirt from his closet, tossed it aside, pulled more things from his drawer and kept packing to avoid answering.

"Are you moving out? I'm pretty sure that's the third pair of pants you've crammed in there."

Josh sighed and pulled out the last wad of clothes and tossed them onto his bed. He pinched the bridge of his nose and searched me like I should be able to read his mind.

"Brady, please let it go. It's fine. I'm embarrassed is all."

"Why are you embarrassed? Come here." I took his hand and pulled him toward me. He straddled my lap again, and it took everything in my being not to haul him closer. "Look at me. What's the matter? This is a good test for us, something we'd handle differently now than before."

"It's been harder than I thought it would be."

I smirked, and Josh chucked me on the biceps.

"I'm trying to share my feelings with you, perv. Brace yourself."

I hauled him down for a brief kiss. "Sorry. I'll behave."

"Listen. Until now, I've always had a pretty clear roadmap for what was going to happen with a guy. You know? We'd exchange blowjobs, or sometimes we'd fuck, but I knew ahead of time where the lines were. I think I need to know when you said we'd go slow, what exactly does that mean?"

"Do you . . . I know we said no labels for right now, but did you want . . . um . . ."

"Brady, no! I meant what I said. I don't want anyone else. I just don't want to pressure you, and I'm trying to figure out what's okay. You know I hate not knowing what I'm doing. I guess I want to make sure you know I want you, without it sounding like I'm trying to push you before you're ready."

"You won't."

"So, I have to be honest and talk about my feelings and shit, but you get to play dumb?"

"Josh—"

"No, Brady. The moment things get heated, you pump the brakes, but then you also initiate things sometimes."

"What are you talking about?" *Shit. I was* totally playing dumb.

"Sex."

"I don't want to script our make-out sessions. We agreed to take things slow. That's what I'm trying to do."

"Okay, but I want to understand what you're comfortable with and not try to figure it out in the middle of things when we aren't thinking clearly. I'm terrified I'm going to screw this up, and every time I think I have your boundaries figured out, I'm wrong. I've been thinking about this for six years and—"

"No, you haven't." I huffed. In hindsight, I could see Josh's feelings for me had evolved. That Christmas when his parents made their big "pray the gay away" play had bonded us closer, and I was sure that was when Josh stopped commenting about other guys around me. But there was no way Josh's feeling went back that far.

Josh dug into the back of his closet and emerged with something red and white in his hands. The pattern seemed familiar, but I couldn't place it. "Do you remember the night you and Sid checked out that international students' party and came back to the room early because he thought it was dull?"

"Yeah, you were sick. You puked on my pillow."

Josh unfolded the pillowcase and tossed it to me. There were bleach stains all over it. "I lied. I thought I'd be alone long enough and took your pillow just to smell it . . . and well, let's say I misjudged both my control and how far I could shoot."

"You can't be serious." I didn't know if it turned me on or weirded me out. I looked at Josh, lost for words. He seemed so vulnerable, like he expected me to judge him and was bracing against it. His plump lips parted. The rhythmic rise and fall of his chest came faster.

Blood hummed in my veins. Was that the face Josh made when he . . .? *Okay. Yep. Definitely turned on.* I moved the pillowcase to my lap and gazed up at him. "You kept it?"

"I tried to wash it, but . . ." He gestured to it.

I chuckled. God, he was clueless about laundry that first semester. Every pair of his underwear was pale pink during freshman year. I loved him in pink, but he rarely wore pastels intentionally.

"I bought you a new pillow, so no harm, right? And you can't be mad because you told me I needed to talk to you and look at how honest I'm being. Now, your turn to be honest... Go..."

"You aren't pushing me, Josh."

Josh scoffed, and I thought he'd mention I'd recoiled when he'd gone for the button of my jeans last night. Which, fair point. But I'd been really bloated following dinner. "We haven't even been on a date yet."

"What are we going to learn about each other on a date that will make or break the decision if we have sex? What aren't you telling me? Is it because I slept around? I get checked every three months because I'm on PrEP but I can get tested sooner if you want me to."

I shook my head. "If I pump the brakes, it's because I'm getting too turned on and need to stop before I can't anymore. It's not because you did anything wrong, I swear."

"Are you sure that's all it is?"

"You're supposed to be conflict-avoidant."

Josh chuckled. "And you're supposed to be good at communication, but if you want to date, then let's do that. There's one problem, though."

I cocked an eyebrow at him.

"You forbid me from paying for you like a year ago, so that needs to be revoked. It's my turn to take you out."

"That was not a date, that was a self-defense justification for murder. I like the idea of taking turns planning and paying though. The point of going slow is so we're sure we both want this. I've done the sleep-together-too-soon thing, I can't do that with you, Josh, and not be sure. Where do you want to go?"

Josh frowned. "I'm screwing this up. I should probably have planned something before I asked you. That's what you do when you ask someone out for real."

"Hey, no pressure. You're doing fine."

"You want real dates, though, right? Like dinner and stuff. We eat together all the time, so I'm not sure that we should even count that as dating. I should plan something better. How many dates do you think people go on before they just are? Like if we did this normally."

I could hear Josh's gears turning, trying to find the perfect date to schedule. Mapping out our relationship until he could circle the day we'd call each other boyfriends. He was still putting so much pressure on himself to get this right. "I don't know. I've never had a boyfriend either. Probably three or four dates. And dinner is fine, you don't need to get stressed out over it."

"Does your work thing tonight count?"

I shook my head, fighting off my smile. Chester's was loud, and my coworkers would be around. "I doubt we'll have time to talk."

"Okay. Then let's go on a real first date after the party. I'll find a place to have dinner nearby. I'm going to get better at the dating thing, I swear. You'll see." He zipped up his bag and hoisted it over his shoulder, then leaned down to kiss me hard on the lips. "Good talk, babe. I see why you like this shit. I'm going to the gym. Have a good day."

I stared after him, stunned speechless.

The door to the garage opened, and Josh yelled, "So proud of you for those miles, babe," before it slammed shut. Alone on Josh's bed, the smell of sex in the air, I clutched an unraveled pillowcase. Six years. How high would his expectations be after six years?

My day passed by in a blur. Before I knew it, I was dropping my small cardboard box full of personal effects into my trunk and pulling out of the parking lot on the way to my farewell party. Josh texted he was leaving work, and I pulled into the parking lot of Chester's with Erica and a car full of underwriters behind me.

As soon as I walked through the front door, I regretted not asking more questions.

"Brady," Amelia called and flagged me to a row of joined tables. A bouquet of "Best Wishes" balloons floated above the table, and a cake sat in the center. My inner fat kid squealed. I loved cake enough I could almost overlook the stage and microphones and the binders full of songs on the tables.

A hand landed on my shoulder, and I turned to see Erica's devious grin. "Karaoke night?" I groaned.

"We have to send you off proper," she purred. "Don't worry, Raeni brought her secret sauce."

I eyed her suspiciously. Raeni was another processor. She was from Jamaica and the one and only time I'd sung karaoke with my coworkers, Raeni had failed to mention that the flask she used to spike my Diet Cokes contained some super potent Jamaican equivalent to moonshine. A brew they'd discovered turned self-deprecating, stage-fright-prone Brady into rock star Brady.

The table was full except for the spot I'd saved for Josh. A few people brought gifts, and there was a card on the table—presumably the contents of the manila folder I'd seen being circulated all week.

The entire office turned out, even Priya, who didn't drink and rarely participated in office social events. Amelia smiled at her when she walked in and, by Priya's response, I suspected she hadn't presented attendance as optional.

"Is Josh coming?" Erica asked.

I checked my watch. "Yeah. He left work about thirty minutes ago. Should be here soon." I considered texting him but was too busy fighting off people trying to put my name on little slips of paper. Then when Amelia and a few others sang "9 to 5" in my honor, I was too busy laughing to object when Raeni spiked my drink.

We were three songs and two shots in when Josh appeared in the entryway. My mouth watered. Not only had he gone home to shower, but he'd also changed into my absolute favorite outfit of his. Indigo jeans that molded to his body, and a black V-neck T-shirt that stretched across his chest. He grinned when he saw me and waved from across the bar.

"Oh, damn," Erica leaned in. "Your roommate is sex on a stick."

"Back off, bitch," I joked, but she cocked an eyebrow up at me. "He's mine," I said as Josh snaked his way through the bar to our table.

"What?" Erica gasped.

Had I told them? Should I tell them? We hadn't discussed announcements yet. Josh solved my dilemma by kissing me stupid. When he pulled back, fifteen sets of eyes were on us.

"Um . . . so . . . this is my Josh," I said to everyone and ran a hand over his chest. And I was sure Raeni had put more in my glass than I'd noticed because I added, "He's still my roommate, but now I get to suck his—"

"Face," Josh said as he clamped a hand over my mouth and turned bright red. Everyone laughed, and another group started singing, which drowned out the conversation. Josh tugged me down to my chair and smiled at me. Leaning in, he whispered, "Feeling pretty good there, baby?"

"Raeni has magic rum," I slurred.

Josh laughed and smiled at Raeni who offered him a taste. He declined and wrapped his arm around my shoulder.

"Josh," Erica said, "everyone is picking a song for Brady to sing." She pushed the book toward us.

His eyes snapped to me. "You're singing?"

"No," I said, the same time Erica said, "Yes."

Josh took the book with a conciliatory smile and studied it like it held the secrets to the universe.

"Give me that," I said and made a play for the book.

Josh leaned into my neck, his breath whispering past the shell of my ear. "Please, sing. I love to hear you. Please." He pulled my earlobe between his teeth before moving back. Oh, Jesus. I wanted him so bad my body throbbed for it.

"I can't sing with a hard-on," I whispered back. Or maybe I hadn't whispered because Priya looked scandalized.

After the entire table showed me the true meaning of the full-court press, I downed three shots and agreed to go up on stage for "Man! I Feel Like a Woman," stand in the back row, and sing as my coworkers giggled their way through the Shania Twain hit.

The bar was full, and our group whooped and cringed through several other performances and snacked on the trays of appetizers Amelia sprung for. A few of the parents in the group started to check their watches, and Amelia said, "Let's cut the cake and open gifts before everyone needs to head out."

I nodded and opened a few of the larger gifts. One was a fancy pen in a case that impressed Josh. The others were knickknacks and other small tokens of appreciation. When I opened the card, I was expecting just that, but a generous gift card came out too.

Josh caressed my shoulder. "That's so awesome."

"Thank you, everyone. So much."

"You can thank us by singing solo," Erica said. "One song, Brady. We all love your voice."

I opened my mouth to say hell no, but the anticipation in Josh's eyes made me reconsider. I sighed. Maybe I couldn't handle the exposure that came from getting naked, but I could give him this. "One song. Which ones have you already suggested?"

The group named about ten songs for me to sing, but I only knew one well enough to sing solo. I exchanged a smile with Josh, and I knew he'd been the one to pick it. He shrugged. "They didn't have any Troye."

A quick conversation with the host and I was next. My heart beat erratically, probably because of the Jamaican poison coursing through my veins or the memory of being laughed off the stage when an asthma attack interrupted my first junior high choir solo. Josh sat at our table, conversing with my coworkers, but his eyes tracked me. His face relaxed, and he winked at me as the poor girl on stage finished butchering "Sweet Caroline." Then the host called me up.

The first notes of the song played, and Josh stopped talking to give me his full attention. My eyelids fluttered closed to block out the audience. I'd heard this particular song a million times.

Thankful I didn't need the written prompts, I sang the first verse blind, but when I got to the chorus I opened my eyes, and immediately found Josh's, brimming with his usual affection mixed with something entirely new. Something I'd never change my mind about and would last until we were old men. Once again, I'd fallen hard for a friend, but this time I knew it was real. I poured my certainty into the lyrics of Josh's favorite song and sang it to him. Because we *had* found love right where we were, and I was drunk enough to think that out loud for an entire bar full of people.

I finished to rousing applause. I practically threw the microphone at the host and hurried off the stage. My coworkers surrounded me, expressing their best wishes and saying their farewells. Amelia suspended the open bar, and the party died off a little at a time until it was Josh and me.

"You ready?" Josh asked, his hand ruffling my hair.

"Yeah." I stood, and we gathered my gifts and walked toward his car.

"You hungry?" Josh checked the time on his phone.

"Not really," I said. "I had cake and a stack of wings." My stomach lurched with the thought. "Do you mind if we head home?"

Josh shoved my balloons and gifts into the back seat of his car, then he straightened and met my gaze. I had to be honest. "I have to tell you something," I admitted. "I'm sorry I keep giving you mixed signals. I can't seem to—" My voice broke with emotion.

Josh placed a finger over my lips. "Shh. I know." He smiled reassurance and put his hands on my waist, right below my love handles. I tried not to flinch, but Josh squeezed tight enough, I knew I had. He leaned into me, pressing his lips to mine and parting the seam with his tongue. Heat flared in my body. I wanted him so much.

"It's okay. Once you convinced me it wasn't about me, I sort of put the pattern together on my run this morning. I don't know if it helps for me to keep saying this, but I don't care that you're bigger than me; in fact, I like it."

"How can you want me?"

"Brady, I do. I promise you I do." He brushed his lips over mine.

"I need more time."

Josh nodded. "We'll wait as long as you need." He stroked my cheek and pressed another kiss to my lips. "I love hearing you sing, baby."

"It's the *only* reason I did."

Josh stared at me. The weight of his intense gaze was so heavy, my body sensed his next words before he said them.

"I'm . . . I love you."

"I love you too." Our collective exhales collided in the space between us.

Josh's lips parted in a teeth-baring grin. He brought his forehead to mine, rested his arms on my shoulders, and breathed into our shared air. "I think I love it when you say that."

"I think I love saying it," I said, then stepped back, laughing softly. "You realize we are so disgusting right now?"

His arm roped me toward him. "No, we're not. We're getting awesome at communication. We're gonna be good at other things too. When you're ready."

When *I'm* ready. I hated being the one to throw up a roadblock. "I can, um, take care of you if you want."

Josh shook his head. "It's fine, babe. I can wait for as long as you need, but let's stop pretending this doesn't have a label."

"You sure? We can keep going slow."

Josh huffed. "Six years, Brady. I'm not sure I know what I'm doing, but I'm sure what I want." I nodded, and he kissed me, pulling back with a lopsided grin. "In my favorite rom-coms, this is the moment where you'd use the b-word and ask me properly."

I half laughed. "Are you kidding me?"

"You know how I like things to be clear."

I rolled my eyes. "Josh Meyer, will you please be my boyfriend?"

"Took you long enough. Yes. Now can we please stop sleeping in separate rooms? You can wear whatever you want and there is no pressure, but knowing you're on the other side of the wall is driving me crazy."

Crazy didn't begin to describe a world where Josh looked at me like that.

Chapter Twelve
Josh

I closed the trunk, feeling pretty proud of myself for getting the car loaded while Brady was distracted. For our second official date (we'd agreed the Lotus dinner didn't count but karaoke had) I'd taken Brady to see the new Star Wars movie. For our third date, Brady had taken me to this adult arcade, then for Thai food. We had fun, but other than one of us paying for the other, our dates hadn't felt all that different than when we hung out as friends.

It was my turn again. I'd been obsessing over what might up the romance factor. All my ideas were pathetic, but we hadn't told anyone we were dating, so I couldn't exactly start calling people to crowdsource better ones without arousing suspicions.

After deciding to take Brady on a picnic, I called Joy to get the apple crisp recipe she'd made for Brady every time she visited, but our conversation about the best apple varieties for baking had led to a great suggestion.

I'd woken early, gone to the gym, then to the store, baked the apple crisp, packed a lunch, and checked the weather. My stomach already did weird flips when I thought of Brady, but today, it could give Simone Biles a run for her money. I'd never tried to be romantic before, and while there was still some low-level worry that something would go wrong, I couldn't wait to see the look on Brady's face.

"You driving?" Brady asked, standing at the front door, his keys in hand. He had on my favorite jeans and a zip-up hoodie.

I nodded. Brady shoved his keys into his pocket, ambled down the front steps, and met me at the driver's-side door. He grabbed onto my waist and kissed me. When he pulled back, his eyes drifted to the back seat, where his heavier jacket was lying. "I need a coat?"

"Maybe. Better safe than sorry."

"Where are we going?"

I rolled my eyes. "Just get in."

Stewart Orchard was about thirty miles from our house, but the signage became obnoxiously frequent as I pulled off the freeway. Still, Brady's excitement made it hard to be disappointed I hadn't fully pulled off the surprise.

"They have a pumpkin patch," Brady said, his eyes widening with childlike glee with each passing sign. "Want to get one for the porch?"

"Sure."

Brady jumped out of the car the second it was in park. I chuckled at his enthusiasm. "You're so cute."

A small crowd of folks walked by carrying blankets and picnic baskets. "Oh, look. There's some kind of symphony concert." He pointed to the large sloping field across from the orchard, where a stage was set up.

I pulled our coats out of the back and Brady froze. "You knew? Is that where we're going?"

"Yeah. But we have time if you want to get a pumpkin."

Brady glanced at the line to get into the orchard. "I don't want to derail your plans."

"My plan was for you to have a good time. I thought we'd pick apples, but we can get a pumpkin instead. We can drop it back at the car before we set up our picnic."

Brady and I rode on a hay-covered tractor to the pumpkin patch. We'd been pretty reserved with PDA so far, but I think we were both trying to get more comfortable about touching when we went out. He glanced at where my hand brushed over his jeans and covered my hand with his own. Our touch sent pulses of electricity through me.

"I don't think we've ever gotten a pumpkin before," I said

"I got one for our dorm freshman year."

"Oh, right." Brady and I had gone to plenty of parties to celebrate Halloween, but I hadn't realized he was into the day for more than candy and slutty costumes. My own parents had never let me observe it, so the traditions were a little lost on me. "What was your favorite costume growing up?"

"Probably the year I was a transformer. My mom loves Halloween. She had to work a lot of holidays, but she always managed to get off for trick-or-treating. She'd go all out for my costumes. We had this whole thing made out of cardboard, and when I crouched down it looked like a race car. There was this haunted hayride at the orchard near our house; we went every year. The owner was a regular customer of my mom's diner. She'd let me pick out the biggest pumpkin I could carry. When she married my stepdad, I told my mom I didn't want to do it anymore, but I always secretly missed it."

I nodded, marveling at him. When he said he wanted actual dates, I'd been pretty sure there wasn't anything new to discover about each other, but I'd never been so happy to be wrong.

When the tractor came to a stop, Brady and I walked back and forth through the rows. It took much longer than I'd expected to find one that met Brady's requirements—symmetrical, round, but not too round. I lifted up a few suggestions before I gave up and followed Brady on his quest for the perfect carving pumpkin.

When he found the one, his celebration dance had me smiling so big my cheeks hurt.

The tractor driver acknowledged Brady's joy with a little laugh. My mouth formed the sentence without thinking. "Isn't my boyfriend adorable?"

She nodded.

Brady had always been unguarded around me, but today felt different somehow, more intimate. Four dates had proven a reasonably accurate prediction. This was the new normal for us—we were no longer friends who were trying to date—we just were.

I followed Brady back to the tractor, and we rode together to the entrance. I pulled my card out to pay, but Brady grabbed my wrist. "I'll get it," he offered.

"It's my date, babe. I get to pay."

Brady let go of my wrist, thanked me, and let me carry the pumpkin to the car for him. As we neared the parking lot, my eyes were still focused on his smile when his face fell.

"Oh no," Brady said, stopping short.

I looked up to see the field overrun with people. We'd be lucky to find a place to put a postage stamp, let alone a place to set up my full picnic.

I lowered the pumpkin into the trunk, fighting off the onslaught of distress calls coming from my brain. *It's okay*, I reminded myself. *It isn't the end of the world.*

Brady's face was full of guilt. "I'm so sorry."

"Don't be." I grabbed the blanket and picnic basket and took a deep breath, determined to keep my bullshit issues from tanking this perfect day. "Grab our coats and follow me."

Face to face in Brady's bed the next morning, I knew I'd made the right decision. Even if the only area left to sit had been behind a small hill, where there was no view of the stage and no trees to buffer the wind, our date had been a success in upping the romance. The cold had only forced us to snuggle closer, and we still had heard the music perfectly.

I brushed my fingers over the scruff that'd sprouted on his chin over the last two days. I babbled, attempting to answer his question about how I'd spent the summer before college without getting too explicit.

The only upside side of being outed by Anna was supposed to be having the freedom to find LGBT friends who'd accept me. There were none in Hobart, but away at college I knew it'd be a different story. I was so determined to leave Hobart and discover this radical acceptance I'd been desperate for. Instead, I found being around other gay men was a little like moving to a new country where you didn't speak the language. I might have been eager to explore, but I'd spent most of my time lost and confused. "I signed up for that summer intensive for incoming freshman," I reminded Brady.

He nodded. "I remember, but I always wondered why you didn't have like a boatload of friends when I showed up. People are naturally drawn to you. Wasn't the point of the summer intensive to meet people before school started?"

I sighed. "I didn't exactly try to make friends." Instead, I joined all the hookup and dating apps and tried to figure out how to be gay. I said the wrong things. Did the wrong things. Sent the wrong messages. A smile wasn't always a smile. If I rejected someone, I must be self-loathing. If I agreed, I had to navigate a foreign language to figure out how to communicate what I craved without getting something more than I bargained for. I resigned myself to never escaping the cycle of constant humiliation. Until Brady. Being around Brady had been the most right I'd ever felt in my skin.

I kissed Brady, partly to change the subject and partly because I loved that I could. He moaned into my mouth, and the hum vibrated through me, making my cock twitch. When he pulled away, he stroked my cheek with his thumb.

The combination of talking and making out a little, then talking more was blowing my mind. "I love this."

"Pillow talk?"

"Yeah. I'm so happy we're doing this."

"Me too." Brady kissed me and once again, we lost ourselves until one of us needed air. Neither of us had seen a toothbrush in over twenty-four hours, but I'd given up being worried about morning breath hours ago. When we separated, Brady kissed my nose and continued our conversation. "Tell me something else," Brady whispered.

I hid my smile in the crook of his arm before peering up at him. My heart fluttered. I'd tell him anything he asked as long as he looked at me like that. Well, almost anything. Brady kissed me, lips only this time. I ran my hand over his sweatpants to the curve of his hip. When he didn't flinch, I used it for leverage and scooted closer. "It's your turn."

"What do you want to know?" Brady asked. "Unlike you, my life is an open book."

He nuzzled against the hand I used to stroke his cheek. "Not everything." I gave him a mischievous smile he greeted with an eye roll. Adam spoke only in generalities, while Cade, Sid, and I had no reservations about dishing details, but Brady . . . he could be notoriously vague about his sex life.

"You probably know more than you think." Brady kissed my open palm. "There is sadly little to tell, but ask away."

I rubbed my foot over his calf and tucked my leg between his. "How many guys have you fucked?"

Brady laughed. "Wow. Okay. Not gonna ease into this, huh?"

I shook my head.

"Three."

"You still okay with us not using condoms? You know, when we're ready."

Brady blushed, but nodded. "What about you?"

"Oh. I'm very okay with it." I didn't try to hide my enthusiasm.

"Oh. I know you are. You practically ran out of the house to get tested the second I agreed."

"I can't help it. I love that we'll get to have a least one of our firsts together."

"Me too, but that wasn't what I meant. I wanted to know how many guys you fucked?"

"Topped?" I wasn't sure I even knew the number otherwise.

"Sure."

I buried my face in his armpit and mumbled, "Less than you."

Brady gave a gentle shove to my shoulder. "What was that?"

I rolled onto my back and stared at the ceiling. "Once to try it. I'm not... you know." I covered my face with my hands.

Brady laughed, pulled my hands away, and coaxed my chin toward him. "Now you're shy? It's not a secret you're a bottom." He tugged me back on my side and into his arms. His hand landed on my ass and squeezed.

"And you're a top," I said. The soundtrack between Matt and Brady I'd been forced to listen to pretty well confirmed my long-held suspicions.

"Meh. Not really." I tensed in his arms, and his laugh assuaged my alarm. "Don't worry. I'm well aware of what you expect of me."

"I can be verse if it's important to you." *Please don't let it be important to you.*

Chuckling, Brady shook his head. "Aren't we getting ahead of ourselves? Forget the sex talk. Ask me something that matters."

"Fine. I want to know what your deal is with Tom, then."

My heart thumped harder when Brady beamed at me. "You go from sex to my stepfather. Are you trying to give me whiplash?"

"Brady, c'mon. You vented about him all the time, but now you act like he doesn't exist."

"Nothing to say. My mom loves him. I love my mom."

"But did he do something? I know he can be an asshole to you." Not that I'd ever met the man. Money was tight for Brady's family. They lived in Ohio. I assumed Tom never visited because of finances, and Brady had never corrected me.

"Not really. Tom never had kids and married my mom when I was thirteen, so you know, his first parenting attempt was with a teen whose absentee dad dropped dead from a heart attack a month before and who was questioning his sexuality. He went all-in trying to bond over things he enjoyed, like football and fishing. I guess he thought it should thrill a fatherless kid to have someone who gave a shit, but he always ended up ranting about how I didn't listen or respect him. We tolerate each other for my mom's sake. Honestly, I didn't make it easy. I'd have hated anyone she dated at that time."

"So why are you all cagey when I ask about him now?"

Brady swallowed hard, his face tense. "After that Christmas when you came home early... It just... Tom would never do something like that to me. I guess I realized there are worse things than a stepdad who wants to spend time with me."

I cringed, thinking of all the support Brady had given me when I finally cut ties with my parents. But I'd come a long way since then, and I wanted Brady to know he could talk to me about anything on his mind. "I want you to be able to vent about him if you need to. I can handle it."

Brady shrugged, and I had to work hard not to see that as disagreement.

"He's gotten way better since I moved out. He's pretty woke about the gay-son thing now."

I chuckled, then sobered. Joy had been such a PFLAG mom, I'd never considered Brady might have had a less than ideal coming out story too. "How did Tom handle your coming out?"

Brady rolled his eyes. "Bought me a pack of condoms and told me to not get AIDS."

I gasped, but his bemused expression told me it wasn't as bad as it sounded. "You're kidding."

"No. But he thought of it as supportive. He was trying to say, 'I'm cool with you being gay, but I want you to be safe.'" He did the little shrug–eye roll combination he used when he was trying to seem indifferent, but I could tell he was still low-key hurt by his stepfather's reaction. "We worked it out in therapy."

I startled. "You never told me you had therapy."

Brady's eyebrows drew together, as if trying to remember, then relaxed. "It wasn't for very long. My mom wanted me to go, so you know... I saw someone after my dad died too."

"Did it help?"

"I guess." Another shrug. "I used to worry it was a betrayal to grieve for him. Here I had this amazing single mom who worked three jobs to raise me. My dad wasn't around much, and when he died, I missed him. The therapist helped me figure out it was okay."

"I can't imagine your mom working like that."

Brady nodded, and a nostalgic visage swept over his face. "My dad's social security money was a windfall for her compared to having to beg for his child support over the years. At least Tom has a steady job and made her life better. Why do you think I love living with you so much? I was such a latchkey kid. Never had home-cooked meals growing up. I ate fast food or from the diner my mom waitressed at every night. I remember when you and Sid complained about the cafeteria food and the lack of privacy living in the dorms. But for me, it was heaven."

I nodded, but my thoughts were stuck on Brady admitting to having seen a therapist like it was no big deal. "I, uh, talked to someone the other day."

"Really?"

"Yeah. Kind of unofficially I guess."

"Unofficial therapy? That sounds like something Cade came up with." Brady's brows knitted together.

"We talked and he was a therapist, but I guess it wasn't the real thing. We were in a bar. He goes to my gym."

Brady nodded with a wry smile. "That doesn't sound like it counts."

"Probably not. He gave me his card in case I wanted to talk for real." I peeked at him. Surely, Brady had an opinion about his boyfriend seeing a psychologist. His face was stubbornly unreadable.

"Are you gonna go?" he asked, with no hint to his position.

"Do you think I should?"

Brady snorted. "You must be crazy if you think I'm dumb enough to answer that."

"Brady, I'm serious." My words lost some oomph when I couldn't keep a straight face. Not with Brady's amusement on full display.

"Yeah, me too. Let's talk about sex again. Don't you want to hear about the first time I gave a blowjob?"

I chortled. "Shut up." I shoved him playfully until he rolled on his back, then I climbed on top of him. His hands rose to my hips. I bit my lip as I gazed down on him. "I'm serious," I tried again.

Brady quit laughing and tugged me down. "I think—" he kissed my nose "—you should do—" another kiss to my chin "—whatever you need to do—" another kiss on my lips "—to be as happy as you can."

"You're perfect."

Brady turned his head, averting my eye contact.

"Hey." I sat up to free my hands, then used a finger on the side of his chin to pull his gaze back to me. "Don't do that. It wasn't flippant. I meant it."

"Josh, don't say things like that."

"Why not?"

"Because I won't live up to your expectations."

"I didn't mean you actually have to be perfect. When you say things... You always know what to say to me. That's perfect."

Brady opened his mouth to protest but snapped it shut. Which further proved how well he understood me. "What time is it, anyway?"

I leaned over him until I could see the clock on his bedside table. My cock hardened as it pressed against Brady's thigh, and after a full night of starting and stopping, I couldn't resist the sweet pressure. "Almost eleven."

He gripped my shoulder. "Shit. We need to get up."

I rolled back onto my side and pinched the bridge of my nose. I had to stop pushing. "Why?" I asked and willed my erection to go away.

His eyes flicked down at the tent in my pants and traced back up. "Because we have groceries and laundry and things to do. I wanted to get some stuff for this week."

I laughed, but let his explanation go unchallenged. "You want me to make you a special lunch?"

"Shush," Brady said, sitting up. "Did you want to shower first?"

"You think our shower is big enough for two?"

With a terrified expression, Brady stood and ran his hand through his hair, tugging at the ends. Welp. That was a hard no. "Um..."

I beat back my disappointment. "Relax, baby. I'm teasing."

"Oh, okay." In a flash, Brady's shoulders dropped, and he pressed his lips together, then adjusted his T-shirt over his pronounced bulge.

"Unless..." I swallowed. Did Brady want me to push him? I kept straddling the line between expressing my interest and reassuring him I was okay to go at his pace. I sensed Brady needed frequent reminders of how sexy I thought he was, how turned-on I was by him, but pushing him definitely fell into bad-boyfriend territory. "Do you maybe want to watch me shower?"

The corner of his mouth quirked. "Really?"

I sat upright and gathered a handful of the sheet by my side. "If you want. I've got no problems putting on a show for you. I could really stand to . . . relieve the pressure."

Brady ran his hands through his hair again. "That's, um . . . Yeah." He cleared his throat. "That would be good."

"Okay." My tongue ran over my front teeth as I attempted to combat my dry mouth. I hadn't expected him to agree, but my body reacted to the fact that he had.

"If it's okay with you."

I stood, walked around the bed to him, and wrapped my arms around his shoulders. I rubbed along the nape of his neck. "That sounds perfect."

I kissed him, desperate to remove any doubt from his mind. My hand crept up, combing my fingers through his hair, gripping it at times to keep from touching him in a way that would cause him to stop. I pushed deeper, sliding my tongue over his and whimpering as his arms collapsed around me. His hardening length pressed against me, and I popped my knee out to give him my thigh to rub against. Brady's fingertips dug into my skin, hauling me as close as possible to him. He moaned, and I wanted to touch him, feel the heat of his hard cock.

His grip loosened on my waist, and we laced our fingers together. "Follow me," I said.

In the bathroom, I lowered the seat to the toilet and encouraged him to sit while I turned on the water. I stripped off my tank, lifting it slowly. Brady loved my chest, and I would be lying if I said I hadn't enjoyed showing it off to him for years.

Brady licked his lips. His all-consuming stare sent a chill through me. The bathroom filled with steam, moisture settling over my naked skin, but it was the heady way Brady looked at me that sent a shiver up my spine.

"Are you cold?" Brady asked.

"You want to warm me up?"

For once, Brady's nod lacked tentativeness. We weren't testing the waters, we were jumping in.

Brady clenched his hands by his sides, a determined expression on his face. I couldn't tell if he was fighting his desire to touch himself or me.

"It's okay." I jutted my chin toward his crotch.

Brady shook his head, and I pulled the shower curtain open to test the temperature. All that was left to do was lower my boxer briefs. I dragged my lower lip between my teeth, enjoying his attention. With a single glance, he could push away all my uncertainties. "You want to do the honors?" I was only a step away, but I crossed the gap with a strut.

Brady peered up at me, his dilated eyes framed by long lashes. His hands caressed my sides until his thumbs rested inside the elastic band. He paused, breaths coming a little faster, and inched his hands lower, pulling the thin cotton along with it. Brady bit his lip as my cock popped free. He smiled, seemingly content to look but not touch, the flesh begging for his attention.

"You're . . ." Brady swallowed and released an incredulous sigh as he stroked a hand over my abs. "You're so fucking hot."

His response was so perfectly Brady, I laughed. "Thought I was beautiful?"

"That too," Brady said. "Does it bother you?"

I shook my head. There was a time when I would have considered his pet name for me too effeminate, but I honestly loved when he called me beautiful. Brady had used a lot of words to describe attractive people to me over the years—hot, sexy, gorgeous—but he'd never used that word. It felt special. "I like it." I leaned down to kiss him, and he stiffened.

His head turned toward the door. "Did you hear that?"

While we were straining to listen, the doorbell rang. "Probably a delivery."

A loud bang, then another ring. "On a Sunday?" Brady kissed me. "Hold that thought. I'll be right back."

I sighed and watched Brady leave, taking the steam and the mood along with him. When he didn't return right away, I kicked off the underwear Brady had left around my ankles and climbed into the shower. Was it too fast? Did I scare him away? No, he was into it, I decided, confident in the progress we'd made.

I'd rinsed the shampoo from my hair when the door opened and snapped closed. I pulled back the curtain, and Brady, a little pale and poised to speak, froze and gawped.

"Change your mind?" I teased and moved my hand over my cock. "I could use some—"

Brady blinked hard and shook his head as if doing the human equivalent of a reboot. "Don't freak out."

"What?"

"Did you maybe mention having brunch today? Cade, Sid, and Adam are here."

"What?" I said louder. A vague memory of my conversation with Cade floated back to me. "Oh, shit. But we didn't even talk all week. I confirmed nothing. Why would he show up?"

Brady rolled his eyes. "Cade? You know how he is, and it's not like we don't always meet at eleven. We both have messages from them. I let them in and said we were running late."

"But I have nothing prepped."

Brady shook his head. "It's fine. I told them we decided to go out."

"But . . ."

"It's fine. Just get dressed."

I sat next to Brady at our favorite brunch spot and listened as Cade pumped Sid for details about his new job. Brady cast glances in my direction, but we'd reached a stalemate in our silent communication. Should we tell them, or shouldn't we? The longer the conversation went on without Brady saying anything, the more I thought he'd seen reason. They didn't need to know anything quite yet.

A round of Bloody Marys later, Cade turned his focus on me. "Hey, Josh, I meant to tell you I saw you at the gym on Wednesday. Who was that man you were talking to? Looked intense."

Brady stirred next to me, and I gripped his thigh to reassure him. "No one. Just someone I met a few weeks ago. We've run into each other at the gym a few times. Interesting guy." I searched Brady for understanding. "He's the one I mentioned. The therapist."

Brady's syrupy smile melted me. *Maybe we should tell them.*

Cade raised his empty Bloody Mary to his mouth slowly. He slurped air through his stirrer, eyes narrowed as he scrutinized us. Then he turned to search Adam. Then back to us. "Are you two—"

"Cade..." Adam warned and shook his head.

Cade's glass hit the table with a clatter, and he gestured with his usual animated flair. "Adam, Josh's face looks like he rubbed sandpaper on it. Brady has a hickey the size of Texas. And as soon as I mentioned that guy, Josh started stroking Brady's leg under the table and Brady literally swooned. I'm supposed to ignore this? Do you even know me at all?"

Brady choked on his drink and shot me a horrified expression. I pulled down his collar and checked his neck. *It's tiny*, I mouthed, and returned my attention to Cade.

Completely flummoxed, Cade stammered and gesticulated like he'd watched Miss Shangela get shut out of the final lip sync in *RuPaul's Drag Race All Stars* all over again. "I knew it," Cade declared, his eyes bouncing back and forth between Adam and Sid. "Why are you two all calm? This is huge."

Sid and Adam stiffened, and Cade unleashed another round of outrage. "If you two kept this from me, so help me..." He slapped any arm or chest in his reach in a less-than-playful way.

Sid rubbed his assaulted biceps. "I didn't know anything."

Adam cringed and leaned into my lap to stay out of Cade's reach. "I may have already known."

"You did?" I asked. "How?"

"He may have given me a nudge," Brady admitted. Patting Adam's head, he shoved him up and back into his own chair.

Adam's chest puffed out, and Brady laughed. "Settle down, Cupid," he said before clarifying to me. "Adam's the one that told me to help you in the kitchen and to pick romantic comedies."

Okay, well that explained so much. I burst into laughter. "Adam, don't help Brady anymore."

Adam's face fell. "Hey. That was solid romantic advice."

Cade comforted Adam with a pat to his hand. To Brady and me, he said, "You don't have to be great at romance when your dick is big."

Adam smiled his appreciation, then frowned when all the words processed. Cade batted his eyes. "I'm kidding." But there was an edge to his voice that seemed intentional.

Thankfully, Sid pulled a... I didn't know what to call it. Sid pulled a Sid. He was always our tension diffuser. "So, I'm not surprised, but I am confused. What happened to you and Brady were only friends? I asked you at Lotus if you were on a date."

Brady fixed his gaze on me.

"What? Don't look at me like that. It stopped being a date as soon as I saw Matt at our table."

"True," Brady said and jokingly scowled at Sid, who laughed; then Brady grew serious and took my hand on top of the table. "Okay. Josh and I are dating, and as much as we love you guys, we're gonna leave it at that for now, okay?"

Adam and Sid nodded, but Cade wasn't going down without a fight.

"Uh, no. Not okay. You guys got to hear every detail about Adam and me."

"That's because you have no filter," I said. "We didn't actually need to hear everything if you wanted it kept private."

"Some of us didn't have a choice of hearing it. Cade moans like he's being possessed by the dick," Sid deadpanned. Cade gasped but started laughing when he noticed Adam beaming.

After we all composed ourselves, Adam placed his hand over Cade's arm, I wasn't sure if it was to calm him down or to keep it from flailing dangerously close to his glass again, but the mood shifted. Our friends all melded into a pool of acceptance and happiness. They were good like that.

"Josh, Brady, we're all thrilled for you," Cade said, offering a toast. Brady and I marked the milestone by clinking our glasses with everyone else's. We were doing this. Our friends knew about it. And that meant they would know if we failed. The stakes felt instantly higher, but Brady didn't appear nervous, so I ignored my racing heart and forced out a smile before downing the remainder of my Bloody Mary.

After our big reveal, the conversation moved on to mundane gossip and catching up. Despite Cade's persistence, Sid guarded his relationship progress with Matt, except to say they were still talking. Adam had a new project coming up at work and was debating if he wanted to make his long-avoided trip home to Atlanta for Christmas or wait until after the New Year. Cade's baby sister was graduating from college in early December and talking about moving to Boston.

When the meal was over, we lingered to sober up, then parted with hugs and kisses. Brady grabbed my hand as we stepped outside. There was no hesitation. No tentative looks. He grabbed it like he hadn't taken one moment to think it over beforehand. A warmth spread through my chest, and a sensation swept over me, igniting desires I'd long ago given up on. When I left Hobart to live my out-and-proud life, this was the moment I'd dreamed of.

Brady slowed as we approached his car, and he spun me until my backside rested against the trunk. His hands rose to my cheeks. "You still drunk? You seem a little floaty."

I shook my head.

"That went better than I thought."

"Me too." I yanked him toward me.

Brady nuzzled his lips against the spot below my ear. "I'm sorry they interrupted our morning." He nibbled on my earlobe, and I clenched the back collar of his shirt. "No more hickeys," he whispered before pulling away.

I gave him a sappy smile and nodded. "I'm sorry."

"It's okay, but not my thing. Bad look for a new job."

"I get it. But it is tiny."

Brady dropped his forehead to mine. The sweetness of strawberries he'd eaten on his breath. "This is crazy," he said. "I can't stop thinking about this morning. I want you so much, Josh."

"You can have me. Anytime. I want you too."

"I know. That's what's so crazy."

"Hey." I lifted my head to focus on his eyes. "It's not crazy." I cut off Brady's retort with a kiss. Wolf whistles from men leaving the restaurant interrupted us.

Brady laughed against my mouth and pulled back. "Good thing we're in the gayborhood. Let's continue this discussion at home." Brady moved to open the passenger side door. He kissed the protest off my lips. "I'm showing you I care. That's it, okay?"

"I don't mind," I said, which wasn't true. I cared, but I wanted not to care, which was progress.

The ride home was full of smiles and touches. I sensed Brady was still trying to reconcile what he wanted with his earlier decision that we should wait. I spent most of the ride trying to decide if I should push him like I had this morning or let him lead the way. The energy between us was so charged I wasn't sure I could resist much longer, but if we ran Brady's errands first, I could get a hold on my desire.

Brady started drumming the wheel as he turned into our neighborhood. Wait. I needed more time. "Didn't you need to stop?"

Brady glanced at me. "For what?"

I shrugged. "You mentioned wanting to get some things for the week."

"Oh." Brady's jaw tightened. "It can wait. Unless you need to."

"No." I nodded. "So, um, you want to start laundry, then?"

"Were you going to the store? We're out of fabric softener."

"Oh . . . can that wait? I can stop after work tomorrow."

"Um, yeah. We can chill. If that's what you want, I mean."

His comment was so loaded, I blushed. "I think it's more about what you want."

Brady pulled into the driveway and put the car in park. He stared straight-ahead, and after a few seconds, I placed a hand on the lever to open the door. No sense making it a big conversation. It would happen when it happened. I glanced back at Brady, who wasn't moving. "You okay?" I asked and pulled the handle. The car door clicked open, and Brady grabbed my leg.

"I should stop stopping," Brady said in a single breath.

"Huh?"

"Um, I don't want to go at it now cause, well, that was a lot of food we ate. But, like, tonight... we can try, and if I freak out, I'll blow you at least because your balls have got to be hurting as much as mine." Brady face-palmed in the most adorable way. "I can't even tell you I'm not usually this awkward because you know me so well. I don't know what is wrong with me?"

I pulled his hand away from his face and kept it in mine. "It's kind of nice to not be the neurotic one for a change."

Brady sighed, and I couldn't resist the small smirk that crept over my face.

"You know what I was thinking about today?"

Brady's gaze heated, and the corner of his lips quirked, like he was working hard to keep some sarcastic comment locked down.

I rolled my eyes. "Okay, fair. You know what *else* I was thinking about?"

"No."

"I left Hobart almost seven years ago. I was so messed up. Anna had destroyed me, and I'd been so incredibly stupid. My parents... I'd worked so hard to not be a disappointment to them, but it didn't matter. Nothing I did mattered if I couldn't be straight. I wasn't sure what I wanted to do or who I wanted to be. It was such a dark time, but I always had this vision in my head of what life could be like. Of how I would feel when I didn't have to carry around the weight of their disapproval and shame all the time. My shame, really. I used to search for movies or read books about gay men who had partners who loved them and successful jobs and seemed well-adjusted and happy. I wanted it so freaking bad, it kept me going, you know?"

"Josh—"

"No. Wait. I know you're going to say this is setting my expectations too high, but today, for the first time, I feel I'm living that vision. I love you, Brady. I've loved you for a long damn time, but it's more than that. It's having lunch with old friends. Being good at my job. Having my house. It's holding hands in public and not feeling like I'm doing something wrong. It's you too. And the way you look at me like you want me for more than an orgasm."

"Of course, it's more—"

"I know. That's my point, babe. I'm happy. Like really, truly happy. And I almost feel like I deserve to be this happy, which is such a big deal. So, as much as I would love to rip your clothes off the second we walk through that door, I'm not going to. Because when we do have sex, I don't want our hang-ups to be the focus. I love to bottom and being pretty freaking vocal about that during sex is a major turn-on for me. And I know that doesn't make me less of a man, but it's hard for me not to censor it because I'm embarrassed about how I sound. You're a big guy, and I know you're not confident about your body. But it doesn't make you unattractive, and it doesn't make me want you any less."

"Fuck," Brady exhaled.

"What?"

"Don't censor. Ever. With me."

"Really?" I raised an eyebrow. "So, if I begged for you to fill me up..."

"Yeah. Don't ever censor that. I'm..." Brady swallowed. "Wow. I want that. I'm awful at dirty talk, so I don't, but I... Yeah, say all the words."

"I will, if you promise when you're ready, you'll let me see you completely naked."

"Done."

"With the lights on."

"Wait—"

"If you do, I'll tell you what I was thinking of when you caught me jerking off the other day."

"Damn. Hard bargain. Fine. Lights on. But it better be worth it."

"It will be."

Chapter Thirteen
Brady

Monday morning, I woke up, ran my five miles, and returned to find a reusable lunch box on the table. There was a note from Josh wishing me a good first day. I peeked inside the bag and found all my favorites and another note that said he loved me. His sweet gesture overwhelmed me with a big-time case of the "awes," but simultaneously left me self-conscious by how much I enjoyed it. Giddiness before coffee was new freaking territory.

I undressed, wishing I'd made it back in time to kiss Josh before he left for the gym. After seeing Josh naked, the bathroom had a whole new ambiance. I took my time shaving as I waited for the water to warm, hummed "Lucky Strike" to myself, and wondered about all the ways I could show Josh I loved him because—well, it wasn't a competition, but if it were, he would be winning.

Josh's love of romantic comedies had translated into a very distinct perspective on what made someone a good boyfriend. I was massively benefiting from his perfectionist tendencies. It was all a little overwhelming.

I stepped on the scale and my good mood came crashing down to the tile floor.

I jumped off, went to pee, and delicately stepped back, shifting all my weight to my right leg. I had gained three pounds. "Fuck."

One more time. I tapped the scale to zero it out and wiped my feet off because they were sweaty and clearly that was fucking with the instrumentation. *One point four pounds.* Better, but still up.

Instead of thinking about how hot Josh was naked, I spent my shower reviewing my entire weekend. Josh and I had spent over seventy percent of it horizontal, either in bed or watching movies on the couch. I ate normally except . . . fuck, for brunch. What had I eaten? Two Bloody Marys, fresh fruit, egg white omelet with tomato and spinach and *damn it*—a basket full of cinnamon bread. *How many pieces?* After Josh and I made our announcement, I'd stopped counting. At least three before our meals came. *Was anyone else eating it?* Sid had at least one. Adam rarely ate gluten. Cade rarely ate anything. Josh didn't eat refined sugars. But the basket had been empty. Or did Josh move the basket away? *Had he?* He must have.

I finished my shower, dressed, and was halfway to work before I realized I'd left my lunch on the table.

Weston Security occupied the top two floors in a ten-story business building downtown. Floor nine, where my office was, included human resources, sales, marketing, accounting, and the help desk. Floor ten was divided into two areas. The west side was the executive suites. The east side was so top secret I didn't have access to it. That was where the engineers and computer programmers worked. There were also two off-site data centers, one on each coast.

The human resources staff was seven people. Angela, our manager, was a short woman with spiky hair and a stocky build. I frantically took down notes as Angela reviewed the team and my responsibilities.

"Your position is new"—Angela smiled over her desk—"so you're either going to get overwhelmed by everyone giving you things to work on or have nothing to do because they all think you're too busy."

I peered up from my notes. "Do I have tasks that are mine or will I be getting work from others?"

"All in good time. We don't want you to get too overloaded, but we've discussed your role in our staffing meeting. Carter and Robert would like you to own job posting and Hannah would like you to assist in the open-enrollment process. Anything that requires a system setup in HRworks, we want you to own. Trey has a long list of items for you to take on, and he'll coordinate those tasks with you. He'll be your primary trainer. Unfortunately, you'll need to do some of that learning on your own."

"No problem. I have a few manuals from my internship, I already started reviewing them to refresh my memory. Trey is the tall guy in the yellow shirt, right?"

"Yes. Good. So today will be training modules and paperwork. Trey organized our new-employee orientation, so give him feedback on what you like or didn't like. He's rather proud of it, but honestly, the feedback has been mixed. He's not the most technically savvy person, and since we employ technical staff, I think people find it lacking."

"Okay. I'll take notes as I go through them, then."

On her way out, Angela paused in the doorway. "I almost forgot. Mr. Weston mentioned he wanted to meet with you for lunch today."

I stiffened. "Oh. Does Ma— um, Mr. Weston . . . Is that a normal thing he does?"

"No," Angela said matter-of-factly. "You should head up about a quarter till noon. Check in with Tessa, his executive assistant. He's sort of a stickler for promptness, so don't be late."

I grinned because Matt was the opposite of Josh in that regard. "Okay. Will do."

I checked my phone and organized my desk and computer. I had some corporate policies to read through, and Carter dropped by to give me some info on their open positions and recruitment channels.

At about twenty till, I made my way up to the tenth floor and found Tessa. After introducing myself, she told me to take a seat in the small waiting area outside Matt's office. A few minutes later, Matt appeared. It had only been a few weeks since I'd last seen him, but he looked better—less fatigued, healthier skin.

"Hey, you ready?" I asked, checking my watch. At Stanford, we all pretty much ate as quickly as we could at our desks. I wasn't sure what Weston Security culture was for lunch breaks, so I made a mental note to add it to my running list of potential onboarding topics. I didn't want to take special privileges, but I figured dining with the boss gave me a pass.

Matt nodded. "We have reservations at a little bistro I like."

"Oh. Okay," I said slowly. *Reservations? For lunch?*

I followed Matt to his car and attempted to ease the tension with jokes. None of which earned me more than a half-hearted smile. Man, tough crowd.

After valet parking at a bistro I'd never heard of, I sat across from Matt at a too-small table overloaded with empty dishes and glasses and nothing to say.

"So," Matt began. "I wanted to talk about the other day at Lotus."

"Oh?" Wow, did my voice go that high? I cleared my throat. "What about it?"

"I may have been out of line."

"We don't need to—"

"Yes, I think I do. Sid was quite angry with me."

"Well, I'll tell him we're cool if you think it will help." It wouldn't unless Josh was also willing to give Matt a pass. Frankly, I had a better chance of winning Miss America.

Matt grimaced. "I'd appreciate that, but it's not exactly my motive here. I realized I may have applied some of my own experiences to Josh."

"We're dating now. Josh and me," I blurted loudly.

Matt flinched then gaped at me. "I know, hence the reason for my apology. Listen, Brady, I think you should know that I'm a very loyal person and I set high standards for integrity. I like you, and I enjoy your friendship. But you weren't exactly forthcoming about you and Josh merely celebrating your job that night; in retrospect and with Sid's help, I understand why you may have positioned it that way to me. I didn't really have friends growing up or even in college, and I enjoyed attending your dinner; inviting myself and Sid to join you and Josh was an incredibly clumsy way of trying to reciprocate."

"Why go after Josh?"

Matt straightened his knife and fork and slid them until they were even with the top of his napkin. "I didn't go after Josh. I . . . Look, he reminds me of someone I'd like to forget about."

"But you barely know him."

"I know. I didn't say it was fair. There was this guy once. My own Josh, I guess. We grew up together. We didn't run in the same circles, but our fathers worked together and so it would force us into social situations. When we were away from school, things were different. He made me think I should be grateful for every crumb of attention he gave me. It's a long story, but suffice it to say I ended up here because of him and some very empty promises. The stress eating was a big cause of my weight problem . . . Anyway, he made it clear I embarrassed him. It's not an excuse, but I wanted you to understand, it's not really about Josh."

"Josh doesn't think like that."

"Then I'm happy for you."

"No, Matt, you need to understand. It's not the same for Josh and me. He doesn't see me as fat. I mean I am, but he doesn't care."

"That's great, Brady. It's not been my experience with men like Josh."

Mine either. "But you think he should care?"

Matt squinted at me and shook his head. "Um, I'm not sure. That wasn't the point of my story. I'm not saying it's right, but—and again this is only in my experience—really fit guys seem to place a lot of importance on physical appearance."

"It's not only your experience. I've been there. I've gotten the 'you're a great guy, but' speech. And I know Josh is way out of my league." So, why was I making him wait for sex? I didn't even want to make him wait, I was just neurotic about my body. It was the dumbest thing ever.

"Brady, I think you're misunderstanding me . . ."

"No. I think this is helping. I'm having an epiphany, stay with me," I said, then remembered who I was talking to. "I'm sorry, this isn't . . . Are we in personal territory or professional, because I know you said not to mix, but this is pretty personal, and we're in the middle of the workday?"

Matt took a long sip of his water and beads of perspiration broke out on his forehead. "Let's make this an exception. But I want it on the record that I am not trying to tell you what to do about Josh."

"No. This is good because you get it. You know what it's like to be overweight and feel unsexy. No offense." Matt lifted his arms and gestured as if to say no offense taken. "I've slept with guys who I knew were not going to want me beyond the night. Even if I was hoping for more, there was no doubt. I knew the rejection was inevitable, so I wasn't all that worried about impressing the guy. With Josh, I've been worried about that a little. What if after we have sex, he realizes that he isn't attracted to me? But my head knows he'd never do that. So how do you let it go? Say 'fuck it' and be in the moment?"

"I don't. It's always there. Even now, with my new body, it's still there."

"So, what you're saying is that I could lose all the weight and it won't matter. I won't ever feel good about myself? Fuck, man. That is discouraging."

"No. That's not what I meant. I like the progress I've made, and I'm happy with the way I look mostly. What I meant is that the mindset doesn't magically change with the scale."

I stared at him, expecting a more thorough explanation. Our server greeted us and, likely sensing the tension, quickly took our orders and left.

Matt's brow raised in question. "A double cheeseburger?"

"According to you, it doesn't matter. I'm up a few pounds today, so I'm taking a cheat day to wallow."

"Okay, listen. It doesn't matter what you weigh as long as you feel good about it and you're not in an unhealthy relationship with food. I had the gastric bypass surgery for my health. What hasn't changed for me—and remember I am a single person; this isn't a scientific study or anything—is that I still see food as more than it is."

"What?"

"Food. People like Josh, they see food as nutrients and energy, right? Fuel for the body. They eat to live, or whatever they call it. For me, food is how I comfort myself. The lower I am, the more calories I need to bring myself back to normal. Unfortunately, the more calories I eat, the lower I sink. And so on, and so on. Food has always been that way for me. Now I can't eat like that. So it broke the cycle, but basically, I'm a toddler figuring out how to self-soothe without their binky."

"What does that have to do with sex?"

"Nothing. I'm explaining the mindset. For me, I always blamed the weight, right? I didn't like myself because I was fat, but the thing is, if you take away the fat, I still don't like myself. Sex is the same, and I don't have any words of wisdom here. I'm trying to help you set the right expectations."

"But I like myself. I mean, I want to be thinner, but I don't think food is the same for me as it is for you."

"I hope that's true."

"But you don't think it is?"

"You're the one that ordered a double cheeseburger because you gained weight." Matt smiled to soften the blow, but still. God, I hated that he was right.

"Fuck, man. This sucks so much."

"It's not too late to change your order." Matt raised his hand, and the server made her way toward us.

"Can I help you, Mr. Weston?"

Matt gestured toward me.

"Do you mind if I change my order to the grilled chicken? And can you sub out the fries for a garden salad, please?"

"Certainly, sir." She nodded and flitted away.

Matt smiled at me, and I scrunched my face at him. "Happy?"

"I don't care what you eat, Brady, or what you weigh. If Josh is worthy of you, then he won't either. But you care, so I guess my advice is to get real with yourself about why. What do you want from the weight loss?"

"I want to feel better about how I look."

"Okay, now be specific."

"I don't want to be out of breath when I climb the stairs."

"And..."

"I want to buy clothes in a normal store."

"Good. Go on."

"I don't want to disappoint Josh."

"See, now we have a problem."

"What. Why?"

"Because you're tying your weight loss to how Josh feels about something. That's not realistic or even remotely correlated. I learned the hard way not to lose weight to please someone else. They'll never be satisfied, and you'll never feel successful."

"I meant in bed. If I get winded and can't, you know, satisfy him."

"I assure you from personal experience, you're good on that front." I blushed furiously, and Matt laughed. "If you get tired, tell him you want him to ride you. Worked with me."

"Oh my god," I groaned.

Matt smirked. "Listen, my point is these are not insurmountable problems. Tell him you're too close and suck him off if you need a break."

"We are not having this conversation."

Matt shrugged. "You're right. I'm sorry. I told you we should keep things separate and I'm totally failing here. If you say you forgive me for being a total bitch to Josh, I will change the subject. I'm happy to continue this conversation off hours. I would like it if we can stay friends."

"I forgive you, but Josh might be another story."

"I will clear things up with Josh, too, if you wish."

"Well, it's more a question of how much you like Sid."

"Yeah?"

"I'd say Josh could torpedo that situation pretty easily."

"Duly noted."

"And thanks, Matt. For the advice."

"Anytime."

"As long as it's after five or on the weekend?"

"Touché," he said as our food arrived.

I dug into my salad, my spine straighter because of it. Matt was right about Josh. Josh couldn't have been clearer he didn't care what I weighed. That issue was mine. But he cared what I ate. Food was how he took care of me. He never outright made my food choices for me, but there was always a lot of talk about what would make me feel good or what was best for me, and I let Josh make those decisions because I loved that he wanted to. Despite my cheeseburger slip, I was pretty sure food wasn't my comfort, but maybe Josh making me the food was. It was how he showed me he loved me, and it was something I'd lacked in my childhood. Not that my mom didn't do her best, but she was too busy worrying that I had food to eat to care how good it was for me.

If Matt was right, waiting to be a little thinner was futile. I was stocky, big-boned, and my face was too round. I wanted to look like Josh, who had four percent body fat and a Superman jawline. No amount of dieting and working out would fix that. There would always be something I didn't love about my body. Maybe my expectations were the ones that needed to be adjusted? If Matt's predictions were correct, I needed to love the body I had. Or better still, let Josh love my body, because I was pretty much over self-loving.

We ate in comfortable silence before Matt turned the conversation to work. When we'd finished, I pulled out my wallet and protested when Matt waved me off. "My treat," he said. "As an apology."

I smiled. "Thank you."

"Thank you for hearing me out."

"I didn't really have a choice, seeing you're my boss's boss and my boss told me to meet you."

Matt frowned. "You're right. I should have asked you directly. It won't happen again." His lip stiffened, and I sort of felt guilty for making it seem like I cared when I hadn't. He seemed sincere, and I was happy to get rid of any potential source of friction.

"Does this keeping our personal and professional lives separate mean we can't game anymore?"

Matt's eyes widened. "You still want to play?"

"Well, you do have a pretty kick-ass setup, and if you're searching for new ways to comfort yourself, I find shooting aliens to be a semi-satisfying alternative to McDonald's."

"Would Josh mind?"

"Fuck, yes. He absolutely will." No sense sugarcoating the truth when Matt couldn't eat sugar. "But you're gonna stop being an asshole to him, and I'll stop pretending I'm some blushing virgin, and that combination should put it back in the realm of possibility that Josh will change his mind about you being a complete dickhead."

"My odds don't sound great."

"Your odds are terrible. So, we'll need Sid on board too."

Matt's ears perked up. "Josh listens to Sid more than you?"

"Not really. If you at all need glasses, it would be an excellent time to pull them out."

"Wait, so what are you saying?"

"I'm saying Sid is way into the professor type and we need him to bring you to Sunday brunch."

Chapter Fourteen
Josh

The prevailing material in my office building was glass, which in addition to keeping a small army of window washers, squeegee makers, and janitorial staff employed, gave everyone the experience of working in a giant fishbowl.

When Mike Kennedy got off the elevator two floors shy of the executive suites, the entire fifteenth floor resembled a giant field of meerkats, all peeking up to see where he was headed. He stopped short of the section of glass-enclosed coffins reserved for junior account managers that worked with our data analytics tool and cleared his throat.

"Josh Meyer," he called out loudly. I froze, sure I'd heard him wrong.

"Which one of you is Josh Meyer?" he repeated. A few people pointed toward my office, and I stood. He lifted his chin in recognition and stepped toward my door, meeting me on the other side as I placed my hand on the handle and pulled.

"Mr. Kennedy, can I help you, sir?"

He pushed his way into my office and took a seat at the lonely visitor chair. As soon as his butt met with the hard plastic, he frowned and motioned me to sit down like he didn't want to be in my presence, or in that chair, one second longer than necessary. I took my seat and cracked my knuckles, but before I could ask what he needed, he told me.

"You did a nice job on the Freedom Athletics analysis. Ken informs me you're from Texas."

I nodded. "Yes, sir."

"Jennifer Burgess, you know her?"

I shook my head slowly, and the hairs on the back of my neck stood at attention. Surely he didn't expect me to know someone because they were from Texas. "No, sir."

"She's a senior account manager on my team focused on business expansion support. She's . . . pregnant." He said the word like it offended him.

"Oh," I said, trying hard to keep my face unreadable and my spine straight. I'd heard plenty of rumors about Mike Kennedy's side of the office, but they couldn't all be true.

"Yes, I know. It's only her second year here and she plans to take three months' leave. Ken tells me you don't take much time off. Is that true?"

"I take a day here and there when work is slower. Did you need help with coverage or something?" I guessed, although that didn't seem likely because Kennedy had a team of junior account managers.

"It's a three-million-dollar account now, but Laura Anderson is attempting to expand her footprint—shoes, jewelry, handbags. This could easily be forty million if this pitch goes well. Jennifer is from Dallas and this client . . . Let's say she is Texan through and through. Jennifer made an impression, but it seems Laura thinks being from San Francisco makes me all horse and no cattle."

"All hat and no cattle," I corrected.

"See." He gestured as though I proved his point. "All the other senior managers on my team are Ivy Leaguers or 'coastal elites.'" He used air quotes, which did sort of validate the legitimacy of his need. "It's unusual, but because of Jennifer's situation, we want to assign a co-account manager. I need someone Laura can relate to, show some authenticity in Jennifer's absence, and flatter her. Ken says you're the perfect man for the job and single too, which will be good for this particular client."

I shifted suddenly, and Mike must have noticed because he smirked.

"Settle down, tiger. We're not running that kind of operation. Strictly hands-off. I don't need your dick complicating my deal. Laura loves attention, just charm her. You're a team player. You can do that, right?"

Team Player. The magic freaking words used by my father and every coach I'd ever had. The small flutter of nerves took hold at being given the opportunity. *He'll think I don't want my job. That I'm not committed. That . . .*

I gulped. *If I turn this down, he'll know about me.*

With the amount of social and networking events we were expected to attend and how friendly some wives were with each other, being single was a disadvantage. Being the single *gay* guy wasn't exactly going to make my career path any easier. Sharing personal information, in general, was viewed as a sign of weakness; sharing *that* personal information was a sign of insanity.

This wasn't a simple "don't ask, don't tell" type omission; this was an intentional lie. The first one I'd told since Brady and I began dating, so not only was I hiding my sexuality, I was also pretending to be single. Two little words would clear the entire thing right up, but when I opened my mouth to tell him I was gay, he added, "Jennifer will be there for the pitch. If she wants to work here, she can keep the baby in for a forty-million-dollar account. I'll have my admin send you an invite to the internal strategy meeting this afternoon. I just need a few evenings from you when she's in town. Take her out. Show her a good time. I want you to get familiar with the file for when we need you. Jennifer left early for some medical appointment but call her on her cell to get caught up."

After Mike left my office, I replayed the conversation a million times before the strategy meeting. I wasn't happy about it, but what choice did I have? If he would fire Jennifer for giving birth, then I didn't stand a chance of keeping my job if I came out.

That afternoon, I took a seat in the large conference room. Mike's administrative assistant was setting out packets of PowerPoint slides that contained some of the graphs I'd put together. The pitch was still in storyboard format, with placeholders for key data points. I bit my tongue to keep from pointing out there were a perfectly good projector and large screen television for us to review a practically blank slide deck.

"Meyer," Larry's voice called in greeting as he entered the room.

I didn't say anything, but my sour face couldn't have read anything other than "What are you doing here?"

"Relax, Meyer," Larry said while taking a seat. "Ken asked me to come because I worked on the data analysis too."

He hadn't, he really hadn't, but before I could protest, a woman I assumed to be Jennifer filed in with Mike. I stood, but she gave me a "not necessary" gesture and eased her very pregnant body into a chair.

I had barely introduced myself, when Ken entered, took the seat at the head of the table, and launched into the agenda. I took furious notes, listening more than talking. We were deep into the weeds of the proposal when Jennifer spoke up to counter one of Ken's ideas.

"That won't fly with Laura. She won't be receptive to expansion into Latin markets."

Ken scoffed. "You've seen the numbers, Jennifer." I glanced at the projections, which basically made Ken's case.

"There is a huge opportunity in Mexico alone," I concurred.

Jennifer stayed firm. "I'm telling you what she'll respond to, not what makes sense. You make the wrong comment with her, we'll be down so many anti-immigrant rabbit holes, you might as well have given the entire pitch in Spanish."

"Seriously?" Ken's eyes narrowed at Mike. "Do we want our firm associated with this?"

Mike grinned broadly. "Ken, flip to slide twelve."

All of us shuffled our pages until we arrived at the final graph I'd prepared, the one that showed how heavily Laura leveraged firms like ours and her growth potential. Knowing I had contributed to highlighting how lucrative the account could be turned my stomach. Ken sighed. "Okay, Josh, work with Jennifer to cut the Latin market figures and recalculate based on the North American and Asian markets alone."

The meeting adjourned, leaving Jennifer and me alone in the conference room. I stood, then began walking around the table to gather the leftover handouts to recycle. She shifted away from me and adjusted her clothing, exhaling relief as she lowered some kind of elastic band that was covering her bump.

"I've never seen Ken cave like that," I said. "I'm impressed."

"I don't need a co-account manager."

I held my hands up, palms toward her. "Hey, I don't think you need one either, but I wasn't given a choice. I want the experience, and if I can learn some things along the way, even better."

Jennifer's dubious glare instantly sent me into charm mode.

"I swear. I'm not trying to take over. I'm looking forward to working for you. I expect to learn a ton."

"Okay, Meyer," she said, her mouth turning up at the corners. "As long as you and I are on the same page. You're the backup."

I nodded. "Sounds like a plan. Can I ask when?" I gestured to her stomach.

"A couple more weeks, but it's my first baby, so probably longer."

"Good. Then I'll get to watch how you impress the hell out of the Freedom Athletics team."

Jennifer broke into a broad grin, shaking her head in amusement. "Oh, you're good. I can see why Ken likes you. Now sit down and cut the shit. We have work to do."

Jennifer relaxed as we worked. By the end of the hour, I'd made more progress winning Jennifer over than retooling the data for the pitch. It was apparent Jennifer had grown uncomfortable sitting for so long, so I suggested we adjourn.

Jennifer's hazel eyes softened a little and she nodded.

"When do you want to meet again?" I asked, knowing she'd prefer to control the schedule.

"Early tomorrow, okay? My husband is on me to take it easy. I want to leave by six without my laptop for a change."

"Works for me." I gathered my belongings as she continued to type away on her laptop. "Hey, Jennifer, can I ask you something?"

"Sure." She rubbed her stomach. "As long as it isn't related to this guy." She smiled, which wasn't relaxed but was in the ballpark. "You'd be surprised how many people have opinions about pregnancy and childbirth."

I shuddered. "No, you *definitely* don't need a comanager for that. I was curious: is Laura as bad as she sounds?"

She smirked. "Ahh, don't worry. You're perfect for this. She'll love you."

The emphasis on *love* made me feel like a shiny trinket being dangled for bait. I wasn't so sure I liked being considered perfect to handle a homophobic, xenophobic client. Bile rose in my throat and the hairs on the back of my neck stood at attention. "Any tips?"

"Laura likes to push boundaries. She wants to be seen as the woman in charge, it's her brand. She'll say controversial things to get a rise out of you. She loves putting men in their place, making sure they know she's in control."

"Now I see why Ken is involved."

"Yeah. Mike has to work really hard to keep his mouth shut. Laura loathes him, but don't tell him I said that. You seem sweet, so you'll be fine. Don't be an asshole. Take her out for beer. Can you two-step? She loves to dance."

"It's been a long time."

Jennifer laughed, leveraging the arms of her chair to push out of her seat. She clamped her hand over my shoulder. "Well, dust off your boots and pull out your Stetson, Meyer."

I walked with her to the elevator and then returned to my office, continually reminding myself how this was part of the job. No question Laura Anderson was awful. The woman had written entire books on how the gay agenda was eroding our country, but all I was doing was running financial data and helping out a colleague about to go on maternity leave. That wasn't so bad.

No matter how much I tried to keep my focus on my career, I kept hearing Jennifer's words. *"She'll love you."* They were meant to be reassuring, but what I was doing for that love kept infecting my thoughts. Even though I hadn't come out at work, I thought I was past pretending to be someone I wasn't. Past standing by quietly because I didn't dare give anyone a reason to suspect I was like *that*. Was I really willing to do it again?

My misgivings about Laura marinated in a stew of bad memories. All the times I'd bitten my tongue or, worse, laughed along when Anna, my friends, or my parents said ignorant things or used cruel, hateful words about anyone who was even slightly different.

I wished I could talk to Brady about it. He'd been the first to tell me I couldn't blame myself for staying closeted when it wasn't safe for me to come out. But what was my excuse this time? To keep my job. That wasn't remotely on par with being a scared kid with nowhere to go, but it wasn't like I could do anything about the toxic corporate culture either.

I knew how far I'd let Anna push me to keep my secret, but what about Laura? Where would I draw the line?

The what-ifs took hold and by the time I pulled into my drive, my skin was starting to feel too small for body.

I sat in the car for a few minutes trying to calm down enough to go inside, but there was no way Brady wouldn't take one look at me and force me to talk it out. I just couldn't face him. I backed out of the drive and headed to the gym.

Anna's arrival at the Freedom Athletics pitch should have been a clue that I was having a nightmare, but I made it through an entire presentation of slide after slide of my Grindr profile screenshots before awaking with a jolt. It took a few disorienting seconds for my brain to realize what had happened. I rarely remembered my dreams, but this one had felt so real. My heart was still pounding.

Eyes closed, I released a long breath.

It was only a dream.

I stretched, feeling every minute of the previous day in the tight knots behind my shoulders. My legs were sore. And the part of me that knew Brady was going to have questions this morning was making it really hard to get out of bed.

With a quick check of the clock, I blew out a breath and followed the sound of running water and the smell of coffee to the kitchen.

Brady was up earlier than usual. His back was to me, and I took every second to admire him before he noticed me.

"Hey," Brady said over his shoulder. "I made coffee."

"Thanks." I shuffled forward and pulled my favorite mug down from the cabinet to his left. Brady watched me without comment as I poured my coffee. He held his own mug with both hands while leaning back against the sink, his head tilted slightly.

I took a sip, searching out something to do. The kitchen was spotless. Not one dish to be washed.

"You okay?" Brady asked, setting his mug down on the counter.

I turned on my heel, attempting to erase the rough night from my face. "Sure. Fine. Why?"

"You were at the gym pretty late, and then you slept in your own bed."

"Crazy day at work. I didn't want to wake you. You're up early this morning."

Brady used my hip to haul me toward him and pressed a kiss to my lips. "Actually, I'm going to the gym." He feigned a horrified face and I relaxed a little.

"The gym?"

"Yesterday, I mentioned to Matt that I'd plateaued, and he suggested I check out his gym. They had a special through work. It was sort of an impulsive decision to join."

Inordinate amounts of insecurity crashed over me like a wave. I could blame it on the lingering resentment I hadn't shaken for his ruining our first date, but nope—this was jealousy, plain and simple. Brady didn't want *me* to work out with him, didn't want to go to *my* gym, but Matt comes along and suddenly it's clear where I stood in this picture. "Great," I grumbled, pulling away. "Have fun."

"Josh—" Brady sighed.

"What?"

"There's no reason to be jealous of Matt."

"I'm not."

Brady eyed me skeptically.

"Fine. I don't *love* that you're working out with Matt. Why not come to Canal Street with me?"

"I know you love it there, but that gym isn't right for me. I need something with less pressure, and this place has more people like me. I don't feel like anyone is staring at me there. It's mostly middle-aged straight men and suburban moms."

"And Matt."

"He just made the suggestion, and I can bring a guest anytime. I'd much prefer to go with you, beautiful. Do you want to join us?"

In my head, I knew it was irrational, but as much as I didn't trust Matt, I trusted Brady. It wasn't like Brady could refuse the invitation from his boss. Lord knew I didn't have room to judge after what I was doing to appease mine. I sighed. "There's a lot going on with work right now and I have to get in early."

"New project?"

"Yeah. I'm working with this senior account manager—Jennifer. She's great. I think I'll learn a lot from her, but I kind of need to bring my A game. It's going to be a long few weeks."

Brady laughed. "Do you even have a B game?"

I held back my sigh. My overachiever tendencies were a common source of ribbing by all my friends. Some days I handled it better than others. After little sleep, not so much. "Probably not. Thanks for the coffee, but I need to get moving."

He leaned in and pressed a kiss to my lips. When I pulled back, I could see Brady's renewed concern. "You sure you're okay?"

I forced a big smile. "I'm fine. I love you. Have a good day."

Chapter Fifteen
Brady

H*ome late tonight. There's a leftover turkey burger in the fridge. Salad mixes in the crisper.*

"What's wrong?" Matt asked as we stepped off the elevator together.

"Josh is working late again," I said, thumbing a response to Josh as I spoke. *Nooo. Come home and cuddle with me.*

The response came quickly. *I wish. Can't. Sorry.*

I sighed, and Matt patted my shoulder sympathetically. "Want to grab a drink?" he offered. "Or you can come over and we can play MtM again."

That was what I'd done the last two times Josh had worked late. Josh said he'd be busy with his new project, but this was getting ridiculous. I missed him, and it was different than before. The house felt lonely when we weren't together now.

"Nah," I said as we neared Matt's reserved parking spot. "I think I'm just going to head home. I want to be there when he gets back."

I wondered if he'd be at the office working or if he had a dinner. At least with the dinner, we could go to bed together. In addition to the rich food late at night, which he hated, Josh always complained about the people he felt forced to socialize with. I typed out an offer to join him or bring him food, but deleted it. *He's busy. Don't nag him.*

Matt nodded and clicked his car fob. "All right. See you tomorrow, Brady."

I said my goodbyes and drove home, then used my night alone to game and relax.

About eleven, Josh came in through the garage, tiptoeing as though he expected me to be asleep, cowboy boots in his hand.

"Hey," I said, removed my gaming headset, and switched off the console. "Take up country line dancing lately?"

"What?" He flinched.

I jutted my chin toward his boots.

"Oh. No. I had a client dinner." He tossed the boots in the corner and cracked his knuckles.

I tipped my head, searching him for a clue. He still seemed off. "Go okay?"

He dropped to the sofa next to me, lifted my hand, and clasped it to his chest. "Yeah, fine." I cringed at the word that'd been in heavy rotation.

"Long day?"

Josh yawned. "Yeah. I'm beat. Gonna head to bed."

I stood and yanked him to his feet and into a hug. He did look tired, and his eyes were bloodshot. I ran a hand up his back, and he dropped his head onto my shoulder. "Glad you're home. You sure you're okay?"

Josh straightened with a small smile. "Yeah. Of course. I'm just tired. You coming to bed?"

I nodded, and Josh squeezed my hand, then shuffled past me toward his bedroom. He tossed and turned all night.

A few days later, I arrived home excited to see Josh's car in my spot. I hauled the trash to the curb before bounding into the kitchen. I took a deep breath, assailed by heavenly aromas. "Is that Cincinnati chili?"

Josh beamed at me and shrugged. "Sort of. I called Joy for the recipe. I made whole wheat spaghetti, substituted leaner ground sirloin for ground beef, and it's the low-fat cheese. I've been so busy, I wanted to make it up to you. I'm over this account, trust me."

Relieved to find him in a more relaxed mood, I sidled up behind him and kissed his neck as he rinsed kidney beans. "This work project has you busy, huh? I've missed you."

He leaned his head back on my shoulder and kissed my cheek. "I've missed you too."

I kneaded his neck while he cooked, but he didn't really respond. "You're tense."

"Yeah. You want to run after dinner?"

"You already ran this morning."

"I can go again. It was ab day. I only ran for a little warm-up."

I laughed. "Your warm-up is double my whole workout."

"Not today. You can do six miles now."

"What's so special about six miles again?"

"That's the sweet spot. For me, at least. I want to find yours."

Laughing, I slid my hand into the back of his shorts and squeezed his bare ass. God bless jockstraps. "But I'd have so much more fun finding yours."

"Stop teasing." Josh pulled free from my grip. "I need to get this done."

"You know, I can go with you now to these work events. Keep you company."

Josh twisted and his face tossed a bucket of ice water on that idea. When the timer beeped, he turned away from me. "Awe, thanks, babe. I wouldn't do that to you. They're awful. I got this, go change."

My chest tightened at his words, sending my optimism for the night plunging. He moved around the kitchen like a man possessed. He had a smile on his face, but it wasn't his real smile. It was his *I'm fine* smile. I'd seen it plenty of times before, but it was the first time I wondered if I was contributing to it.

When it was clear I was just in his way, I retreated to my bedroom to regroup and change my clothes. I rubbed over my torso down to my belly; the squishy, moist blob of fat-lined, sweat-slicked flesh soured my mood. I sucked in my stomach, but not much changed.

With a heaviness in my chest, I dressed, then made my way back to the kitchen. Josh had given up on waiting for me to set the table and was scooping the spaghetti into a bowl.

We situated ourselves in front of the television, and Josh turned on a sitcom for background noise.

Biting my lip, I watched him and considered my approach to elicit something real about what was going on with him. I wanted him to talk to me, but for the first time, my reasons for getting him to talk were more about reassuring me than helping him. "So, how's your project going?"

Josh muted the television. "Fine. Larry screwed up by leaving some files at his house and his wife had to bail him out. You should've seen Mike's face when his wife and their two-year-old twins showed up in the conference room to drop them off. Poor woman. She talked my ear off at the Fourth of July picnic. He's such a tool."

Josh's phone rang and he excused himself, saying it was work. When he didn't return, I played Mission to Mars for a while until I got frustrated and turned it off. I tried to remember Josh's job often went through these crazy periods, but it didn't make me feel any better.

I seized our dishes from the coffee table and cleaned up the kitchen. Josh was a meticulous cook, so there wasn't much to do but put the food away and load the dishwasher. There were two servings of pasta left, and a couple of cups of the chili sauce. I used Josh's stirring spoon to take another bite.

I pinched a few pieces of spaghetti between my fingers, before loading the pasta tongs into the dishwasher. I remembered that Fourth of July thing: It was the summer after graduation. Josh and I had made plans to go to the lake with Adam and Cade when Josh realized his company social events weren't really optional. I'd offered to go with him, but he insisted I go to the lake without him. In fact, he did that every year, always making sure to explain the events included spouses and significant others. So much so, I'd stopped offering. It made sense when we were only friends, but now . . . I couldn't shake off the feeling that our relationship was somehow a liability for Josh. I took another, larger bite of the chili.

Once I had the kitchen cleaned and most the dishes loaded, I pulled down the containers to store the leftovers and froze at the nearly empty pots. I'd eaten several cups of plain whole wheat pasta and nearly all the remaining chili without even noticing.

Who did that?

My stomach gurgled, and with a groan, I shoved the pot into the sink, washed it, and took my frustrations out on more Martians. My overfull stomach clenched with guilt. Sluggishness settled into my muscles, and I couldn't find the energy to get off my ass. Josh would have run without making excuses, but it was always so easy for me to find a reason not to. I was hungry when I got off work, but now I was well-fed. It had been a long day, but I would feel better afterward. Josh was working, but nothing stopped me from going alone. *Why was I so lazy?* No wonder Josh didn't invite me to his work dinners; his career was all about image, and I wasn't anyone's idea of a trophy wife.

I made my way to the bathroom and stepped on the scale, unsurprised when I read the numbers. It was always up at the end of the day, and I had eaten three servings at dinner. *Why did I do this to myself?*

I peeked in on Josh. His earbuds were in and his laptop open. He waved and made a vague motion to his screen and mouthed the name *Jennifer*, so I figured it was important.

I went to bed feeling like something was missing inside me. Some gene or hormone. Something that made me incapable of following through on my plans.

A week later, the gym bag on my passenger seat started to mock me every time I got in the car. I'd packed it Tuesday morning planning to go with Josh, but he'd had to cancel abruptly. Something about Larry trying to weasel his way into another meeting.

Matt was on the elliptical when I trudged into the gym. I waved and detoured to the circuit system that promised an all-over workout in thirty minutes. I did a round, knowing I wasn't using enough weight but unable to find the fucks to give.

I lifted my arms above my head in a press. The wings of flab where my triceps should be stole my focus. *Where the hell had that come from?* Losing the weight slowly was supposed to save me from that fate. *Why do I even bother?*

The weights made a loud *clank* that drew the ire of the gym attendant. Matt wiped down his machine with a concerned smile and strolled up to me. "You want to talk about it?"

"I need to get my run in," I said.

"Warm up first?" Matt glanced at the clock above the check-in desk. "I have time."

I nodded. My warm-up became another side-by-side emotional purge about my diet failings and exercise avoidance with Matt on the adjacent treadmill.

"Sounds like you've been really struggling this week, did something happen?"

"Not really. I guess I've been worried about Josh."

"Oh? What's up with him?"

"I don't actually know. Josh, he's always struggled with— I don't know what you call it. When he gets stressed about something, he does this thing where he's so focused on pretending that he's okay and controlling his emotions, he gets a little obsessive trying to keep all the balls in the air sometimes."

Matt frowned. "Can't you talk to him about it?"

"I would normally, except the boyfriend version of the 'Hey, I think your overdoing it' conversation sounds too much like 'Stop working and pay attention to me.' The last thing I want to do is add pressure when he's like this."

"Well, can't you find *other* ways to relieve the pressure?" Matt laughed with his thinly veiled innuendo, but I'm sure my expression didn't hide much. "Are you two still not . . ." Matt's face was already flushed from the exercise, but I read his embarrassment easily enough. "Sorry. Not my business."

"No, it's okay. I kind of need to talk it out anyway, if it's not too weird."

"It's fine. Go ahead."

"So we haven't . . . yet." I confirmed, my cheeks heating with the reality of admitting that.

Matt arched an eyebrow. "I thought you were ready?"

"Oh, I'm ready. *So* ready. It's just been timing. He's stressed out and I've been pretty bummed about my lack of progress. I guess neither of us are really focused on it. The sad thing is, I thought I was starting to like the way I looked."

"You're looking good if I'm allowed to say that. How much are you down?"

I shrugged. "I'm sort of hovering at the forty-pound mark. Can't seem to break through. I had a few weeks of nothing, two weeks ago a big loss. Now I'm up a few."

"The weights should help. At some point, cardio doesn't get the job done."

"Yeah, that's what Josh keeps telling me. That's another reason I was hoping he would come work out with me. He pushes me. Fuck, I'm so pathetic."

"Hey. Don't say that."

"Why is it so easy for some people? I glance around, and all these people seem to love it. It's like I'm bombarded with fit people all the time, and I want to lose weight, but I get all in my head about people judging me, then I can't make myself get here. Josh gets anxious if he doesn't work out; he claims some magical euphoria exists at mile six. When will I start to love it?"

"You don't," Matt said glibly. "You hope you love the results enough to keep it up, but I'm convinced you don't learn to love it. Learn to accept it as necessary, like taking medication. Lower your expectations."

"You sound like me to Josh." I huffed. "Maybe I should take a break for a while."

"Why?"

"Because I have to weigh myself before I know if I feel good. That can't be healthy."

"How about you quit weighing yourself but don't quit exercising and eating well?"

"Without Josh, the only thing that keeps me motivated is the scale."

Matt scowled at me. "Okay. That's it. Enough pity. Do you remember when I asked you what you wanted to accomplish with the weight loss? What did you say?"

"I want to feel better about my appearance and buy clothes at a normal store."

"Yeah. So how are you doing with those goals?"

"Good, I guess. I'm down to a size forty."

"And you take the stairs up to my office."

"One flight. Big deal."

"It is a big deal. A year ago, would you have taken the stairs?"

"Probably not."

"How's your asthma?"

"It's good. I haven't used an inhaler in weeks. I don't even carry one with me anymore unless I'm running."

"Okay, then. Sounds like you met those goals. Now set some new ones and get rid of the fucking scale."

"I don't know," I hedged.

"Think about it. You need to weigh less frequently at the very least."

I made a disagreeable noise.

"I get it. When I was first starting, I weighed multiple times a day. Trust me, I understand how hard it is, but try to cut back to once a week, and you have to do this for you, Brady. *No one* else."

I nodded more for a conversation change than in agreement. "What's going on with you? Things with Sid good?"

Matt smiled. "Things with Sid are great so far. He's brilliant, we can talk for hours about anything, but he's also so good with people. You don't get that combination often. I work with some technical geniuses, but they have no interpersonal skills."

"Yeah, I know. Good friend, remember?"

"Yes. Sorry. I'm just crazy into him. Plus, he's the most attractive guy I've ever fu—" Matt flashed a guilty expression my direction.

I chuckled. "You can say it."

Matt checked his watch. "I need to get going, but don't be so hard on yourself—trust me, I had no complaints. Have a good rest of your workout." He stepped off the treadmill, but when he walked in front of mine, he paused, a deep line of worry across his forehead. "I seem to remember you had one other goal in mind the last time we spoke. I hope you're not still waiting because you're afraid of disappointing Josh, Brady. Because that's not good for either of you. If he doesn't want you the way you look now..."

"He does," I assured Matt. "That's not it."

Matt nodded, but the seed he planted sprouted on my run. I hadn't hesitated with Matt for a reason. I trusted that Josh wanted me and I *definitely* wanted him, so why did it feel like we were stuck?

In the past, Josh *had* used sex for stress relief, and now I had an entire new arsenal of stress-relieving tools at my disposal. I'd been more than the usual amount of discouraged about my weight loss, so maybe I'd been giving off a not-interested vibe, and now we were both just giving each other space we didn't really want. I understood what Matt was getting at now—there was always going to be some level of fear in me that I wasn't attractive enough for Josh, but that worry might not ever go away, so waiting for it to was pointless.

I loved Josh and, yeah, sex wasn't everything, but it was something. It would make us both feel better. More importantly, it was a new way to connect with him and take our relationship to a deeper place.

A place where maybe Josh could let go of pretending to be fine all the time.

The next morning, I woke to a nearly naked Josh blanketed against me. I blinked hard until my eyes could focus on the long planes of his muscular back and arms. His soft lips parted as he breathed into the space between my underarm and shoulder. So *tempting. So, so tempting.*

He hadn't been sleeping much, so there was no way I dared wake him.

The alarm sounded, music flowing through the speaker on the bedside table, and I glanced at the window. There was no light streaming through the blinds.

"Good morning," he said while yawning. He nuzzled closer, moving his chin into the space between my scruff and the pillow, and pressed his lips to my cheek.

"Morning." I slid a hand over his back until I reached his ass. When he was pressed against me, his sleepy eyes focused and his hand resting on my face like he couldn't believe he was next to me, I wanted so badly to see what he saw. "What time is it?"

Josh didn't move. He kissed me again and mumbled, "Five," against my lips.

I groaned. "Why?"

"I want to run with you this morning or we can go to your gym. Your choice."

My brain formed a protest. "My gym is out of your way."

Josh chuckled. "Baby, don't you know there isn't anywhere I wouldn't go for you?"

"Ugh. Stop," I groaned. "You can't say things like that to me."

Josh blushed, but his eyes were earnest.

Any temptation I had to say no melted away. I needed to exercise, but after nearly two weeks of "I'm fine," what really motivated me to get out of bed was the chance of seeing Josh's real smile when he worked out. "Okay. Let's go run, beautiful."

The streetlights flickered as Josh and I approached the park. The early-morning chill should have been a relief, but my knees ached, and my stomach clenched with nerves. The second we started, Josh would realize I hadn't done more than a short half-hearted run all week.

Josh bounced up and down and shook out his limbs before bending into a stretch. I wasted most of my warm-up admiring his. When he finally turned his attention to me, he put his hands on his hips and laughed. "Did you stretch at all?"

"Part of my body has stretched, yes."

Josh's smile broke into a laugh. Fuck, I'd missed that sound. "Brady . . ." he chastised. "You have to stretch."

"Yeah, yeah." Since the grass was wet, I sat on the sidewalk and went through a few stretches. When I was done, I stood and kissed Josh. "Happy?"

"Very. Let's go."

Josh started off at a pace I couldn't maintain and still speak, but he seemed more relaxed than I'd seen him in weeks, so I kept with him stride for stride the first mile. When I slowed, he did as well. His indulgence much appreciated by my knees. Rather than quit, I eyed the bleachers near the basketball court. "Hey, can you come up with some exercises to do between miles? Like for core and strengthening?"

Josh's grin was bright enough to illuminate a small country. "Absolutely." He took off for the bleachers and had me run up and down a few times until I was begging for water. He gave me a "rest" as he called it, which was long enough for the burn in my lungs to subside, before he led me through some inverted push-ups and triceps dips that weren't awful. Josh was so vivacious when he was working out, and always pushing for something a little closer to perfection.

It was an impossible standard, but each time I was about to give up, he remotivated me with encouragement and his endless energy. After we'd finished, we were short on time, so we headed toward home.

"You should do this," I said.

"What?"

"Train people. You're good at it. I love your face when you're working out."

Josh shrugged. "When would I have the time?"

"I mean as a job. You'd make a great personal trainer or coach."

"Meh. They don't make much."

"Yeah. But is money really that important to you? I can cover more of the expenses now."

Josh shot an annoyed scowl at my question. I understood, having grown up without much money, but at the same time, I didn't think he should intentionally rule out a career he loved either.

"I've been worried about you. You seem kind of disenchanted with your job lately. Like these dinners you say are so awful."

"If you can talk, we can go faster." Josh pushed ahead and jogged backward briefly to scrutinize my form. "You're dropping your elbows in the backswing. Try to keep it at ninety degrees."

I adjusted my form to keep my position like Josh had taught me. "Better?" I asked, deciding this might be a good morning to try one of the other tools in the boyfriend tool chest.

He nodded but motioned me to pick up the pace.

I sped up, struggling to maintain my form. After a quarter mile, the increased speed had me breathless, but I managed to stay within a stride of Josh the rest of the way home. Running with him had been a good thing. It was the most time we'd spent together in weeks.

We entered the house, and Josh handed me a glass of water and a sheet of paper. "Here," he said. "That was a great workout. I wrote down some things for you to try in case you want to go to the gym in the mornings without me. You seem to do better if you work out early. I don't mind getting up and going with you if you want, though."

I glanced at the torture—er, exercises—that Josh had outlined. My legs were shaking, which I rarely achieved when I ran by myself. I kind of did need Josh with me, if he were willing, but that could wait, because we had a tight timetable and I had an idea.

"Do you maybe want to try to shower together?"

"Really?" He chugged down some water.

"You know, for efficiency."

"Uh-huh," Josh said, a bemused smile playing out on his face.

"That would give us time for a proper cool down." I studied the paper he'd handed me.

"Cool down?" Josh said laughing. "Is that what you call it?"

"Lay down. I want to 'hip circle with lunge' you."

Josh rolled his eyes and walked toward the bathroom. "You're ridiculous. I've warned you about teasing me. I can't be late today."

I trailed him, still checking out his detailed instructions while he adjusted the water temperature. "Who says I'm teasing?"

Josh shot me a curious glance over his shoulder, stripped off his clothes, and stepped into the spray, almost daring me to play along. I bit my lip. This was a do-or-do-not kind of moment. I'd be naked. In full light. I looked down at the paper, trying to buy myself some time and find my nerve. I wanted to do this. We needed it.

I glanced up, sucking in a breath at Josh in cascading water. It definitely trumped making fun of his exercise descriptions. I stared at him moving under the stream, marveling at his unreal body. He wasn't just beautiful. He was thoughtful and caring and always willing to help me out. I was so damn lucky...

"Brady, quit ogling my ass and get in the shower. I'm running late."

Fuck it. I needed to rip this Band-Aid off. I was going in.

I lifted my shirt, grateful that Josh closed his eyes and stuck his head under the water to give me some privacy. I didn't know if he was doing it intentionally, but it helped.

My heart raced as I stripped quickly out of my clothes and stepped into the tub, grabbing his hips and pulling his back against my chest so I could wrap my arms around him. My hands slid over his soapy torso, and he sighed as I worked up the courage to roam.

I made it to his navel, when his hand came to cover mine. He leaned his head back on my shoulder, face tilted away from the spray, and met my lips in a kiss. "I'm going to turn around now."

I took a deep breath as he pivoted. His eyes stayed locked on mine and my heart pounded harder than during the first mile we'd run. He cupped a hand behind my neck and pulled me toward him in a sweet gentle kiss. His body pressed against mine, and I couldn't help feeling disappointed by his lack of erection, but then again, he didn't have quite the same inspirational view that I had.

His hands came to rest at my waist, and he smiled proudly when I didn't flinch. "I love you," he whispered, eyes still closed, as we parted.

"I want you" slipped from my lips on a breath.

Josh groaned.

My eyes opened as I realized what I said. "I mean, I love you too," I said sheepishly.

"Now? You tell me this now? You know I have to be at work in like twenty minutes, and I'll probably be late tonight."

"It's okay. You waited plenty long for me."

"I suppose you want me to live up to my end of the deal now?"

"Huh?"

"We agreed: you naked in the daylight, and I tell you what you walked in on the other day."

"Oh shit. I forgot about that."

"Well, if you don't—"

"Josh." I said his name like a curse. "I'm dying here."

"I recorded it."

"What?"

"On my phone after our conversation that day. I took a video of me using that toy and talking about what I was thinking."

"Oh my god." I reached down to touch myself and found Josh's approving smile more than enough to start stroking.

"It's really graphic. I'm not sure you're ready for it."

"Jesus Christ, Josh."

"No, definitely was *not* thinking about him. I have to go, babe, but maybe check your phone *before* you get dressed for work."

Chapter Sixteen
Josh

My great morning sent my mood soaring. I deserved a damn medal for making it to work on time. If Jennifer wasn't counting on me to do the last-minute prep for her, I didn't think I could have resisted. I'd learned a ton from her, and when it came down to it, she didn't feel the need to hog the kudos like most of the others I worked with. We made a good team, and I was a little sad her work on this account meant it was unlikely we'd work together like this again.

Regardless, I could not wait for this fucking pitch to be behind me. Client dinners with Laura reminded me of my first few dates with Anna, where she was on her best behavior. She still made me want to scrub my skin raw, but at least there hadn't been any overtly upsetting things said, and we'd found common ground in our appreciation of the Dallas Cowboys. Thank God for football—the great unifier. When I turned on the charm and steered clear of any controversial topics, I could pretend to enjoy it. Thankfully, the purely social nature of my dinners with Laura meant the only control struggle we'd encountered was a brief moment on the dance floor, probably the only place she'd allow someone else to lead her.

Mike Kennedy stood at the head of the conference room, nodding approvingly as I wrapped up the last run through of the presentation. "Nice job, Meyer. I love that you included the virtual prototyping solution for this client. You're really coming up to speed on our side of the house."

"Thank you, sir." I gestured to Jennifer's empty conference chair. "It was all Jennifer's idea. She really knocked this out of the park."

"I think I can sharpen some of the visuals in the slide deck," Larry added because of course he was there. It was Jennifer who finally figured out the pattern. Larry would book the conference room before our meetings and then make up an excuse to lurk around, pretend to be helpful, and wait for everyone to forget he hadn't been invited to our meeting.

"The visuals are fine. Jennifer's approved them already," I said sharply.

"Where is Jennifer?" Ken asked. He at least sounded concerned, which was more than Mike had mustered.

"She had an appointment and unfortunately this is the only time before the pitch when yours and Mike's schedules aligned."

"*Another* one?"

I glared at Larry. I knew nothing about that particular topic, but whatever tools or tricks women had at their disposal to keep babies inside, I was pretty sure Jennifer was doing it more than she should. She was two days before her due date and determined to make it to the pitch. "Jennifer and I have it covered. Don't let us keep you, Larry. I know that Peterson Furniture account is demanding."

"Ken, what do you think about Josh doing the pitch?"

My head whipped to Mike. "Jennifer's prepared to do the pitch. I helped with the data, but this is her baby."

"Apparently, she has another baby that needs her attention. I want someone who can focus solely on *this* baby, Meyer."

I snapped my jaw closed while Ken seemed to mull over Mike's suggestion.

Larry's eyes narrowed at me, and his whole body tensed. His hands balled into tight fists at his sides. There was a savageness to his expression. I didn't want to give the pitch, but I'd be damned if Larry was going to get it instead.

"Mike, let's talk about that offline."

"The pitch is Monday, Ken. If Jennifer isn't here the business day before the pitch to hear our feedback, I'm not sure—"

"We're meeting Sunday," I blurted.

"What?" Ken asked.

"Jennifer and me. Since she couldn't move her appointment, she asked me to meet Sunday to ensure she was up to speed."

"Oh," Ken said. "Well, there you go. Jennifer seems on top of it. Josh and I will be there for backup."

"I can attend as well," Larry offered.

Ken smirked as he briefly turned his attention from Larry to me. I hated when he blatantly enjoyed our rivalry. "How many attending from Freedom Athletics?"

"Three," I answered quickly, scanning my notes for attendees. "Laura plus her CIO and CFO."

"I don't think we need you, Larry. You never want more consultants in the room than clients."

"Of course. I didn't realize they weren't sending a bigger group."

My own confidence benefited from the dip in Larry's. "According to Jennifer, Laura doesn't like a lot of folks weighing in on big decisions. She keeps everything need-to-know and if she's impressed, she'll move right away."

"Good. You met with her, right? What were your impressions?" Ken asked.

"Yes." I swallowed hard. "She's abrasive and goes off on random rants at the slightest provocation. I think Jennifer is the best person to read her and adjust the messaging on the fly if something isn't landing like we hoped."

"Very good. Send me any changes after you speak to Jennifer," Ken announced, standing tall with a supportive clamp to Larry's shoulder as he turned toward the door. "Mike, why don't we go finish up in my office?"

Larry hadn't moved. His clenched jaw worked as he glared at me while I disconnected my laptop and packed up my belongings. He could sit there and fume all day for all I cared. I had work to do, and it wasn't like when the tables were turned, I sat around stewing in anger. I was steps from the door, when his chair rolled back from the table. "Do you *actually* have a plan here, Meyer? You think they're going to make you a senior if you turn down an opportunity to make the pitch?"

I pivoted on my heel to face him. It was the knowing smirk that turned my confusion to anger. "Fuck off, Larry."

But back at my desk, the reality of the situation hit me. Jennifer was on borrowed time. What if she had the baby before Monday?

Turning it down wouldn't raise the same eyebrows as refusing to work with the client at all. All I had to do was explain to Mike and

Ken that I didn't feel ready for such a high-stakes pitch, but Larry was right: it would tank any promotion potential, and he'd be more than eager to step in. I didn't know if Ken would go for it, but still. Just Larry's willingness and my reluctance would say something. I'd been justifying my participation as a necessary but unpleasant requirement of my job. But giving the pitch to keep Larry from getting ahead? This wasn't that.

My hands shook as I pulled on my running shoes, my mind still reeling from waking up in the middle of Anna and Laura hog-tying me in a rodeo arena full of my coworkers, who kept trying to put hands on me to pray.

I didn't need a psychologist to tell me I felt trapped.

"Where are you going?" Brady's sleepy voice called to me in the darkness.

I leaned over to kiss him. "To work for a few hours. I have to meet Jennifer." Then catch up on all the work I hadn't been doing for my own projects, and please, God, let me squeeze in a run.

"But we have brunch with the guys today."

Shit! Okay, no run.

Brady yawned, stretching so wide that his shirt rode up and exposed his belly. Watching him scratch his stomach should not turn me on, but it did. Or at least the fact that he took the time to scratch bare skin before covering it with his shirt did.

Brady gazed up at me, smirking as he wrapped a hand around the back of my thigh and pulled me forward. I went willingly, falling over him, and settled my legs between his.

"You practically worked all day yesterday. What you really need to do is get back into this bed with me." He rolled me onto my back and paused briefly before leaning down to kiss me, letting some of his weight fall on me and hooking his leg over mine. "That video you sent me isn't going to get me through another twenty-four hours." He scooped up my wrist and pinned it to the bed above my head.

A thickness formed in my throat, becoming more and more uncomfortable as Brady started pressing against me and my movement became restricted. I closed my eyes, willing it to pass, letting Brady kiss up and down my neck. *Relax, already. You want this.* This was Brady, not some random guy from an app. *Not Anna.* Then, Brady shifted on top of me, and my brain responded with an internal scream that shook through me so hard I had no choice but to struggle free. *Nope. Nope. No. Don't like that.*

Brady rolled off me or I shoved him, I couldn't be sure, but the way he came alive with panic as he scrambled to sit told me it didn't matter what I'd done. "You okay? Was I— Oh my god, was I crushing you?"

I shot up from the bed and cringed at the embarrassment on Brady's face—he was mortified. So was I. Why couldn't I relax already? Jesus. Fuck. I straightened my clothes, trying to stop the bleeding with a reassuring smile. "Sorry. I'm fine. I have to get to work is all, and you're not making it easy to leave."

"You're not fine. I need you to talk to me." I hated myself when he pulled the blanket over his body. "I'm worried about you. Talk to me."

I waved him off. "It's fine." I gestured to the clock. "I really have to get going."

Brady stabbed his fingers through his messy hair, which didn't do much other than change the direction the hairs pointed. "Josh—"

"Babe, please. I'll be late. I need to go."

Brady sighed, and I knew I'd been granted a temporary reprieve. "I think you're working too much. It's . . . You're worrying me."

"I've got bills to pay, and Larry is breathing down my neck. It is what it is; I can't take my foot off the gas now."

"I can help. We never talked about the bills, but I'm doing much better. Let me pay my fair share. You don't have to do this alone."

"No," I said shortly. "I have it under control. I don't need you to pay my bills." Brady sucked in a tight breath. And that was the exact wrong thing to say. "Shit—"

His nostrils flared. "You mean like me, right? Why is it okay for you to help me out and not for me to help you?"

"That's not what I . . . I make plenty of money. I don't need your help with paying my bills. I don't even know how we started talking about this. I need to go. I'm fine. Should I meet you at Busy Bee or pick you up so we can ride together?" I leaned in to kiss him, but the damage was done. He barely responded. "I'll make it up to you tonight. I promise. We'll have all night, so we don't have to rush."

"I can... meet you there. I think I'll try to get to the gym."

I nodded in approval, ignoring the blister of anger in his voice. That was exactly what Brady needed—feel-good endorphins. "That's great, babe. So proud of you."

I swore as yet another parking spot was snatched before I could get to it. The parking lot of the Busy Bee Café was as packed as expected on a Sunday morning.

"*This* is why we don't come here," I muttered under my breath. The popular restaurant had great food, plus ample options for Sid, but it was right next to a large Methodist Church so the crowds were ridiculous, and they didn't seat incomplete parties, which meant everyone would be irritated with me that I was running late. I'd also gotten an earful from Jennifer about my tardiness and again during the final dry-run when I freaked out after Jennifer suddenly clutched her belly. How was I supposed to know about Braxton-Hicks contractions?

When I planned our regular brunches, I made sure to make a reservation and move the time to ten, so we didn't fall right in between the church's service schedule. I know I resigned my planner duties, but honestly why couldn't they stick to my recommendations?

At last, a family emerged from the front entrance, and I turned on my blinker and texted Brady while I waited for them to strap some kids into seat belts and pull out.

Easing my foot off the break, I rolled forward and started to turn into the spot. A text from Jennifer lit up my phone that rested on the passenger seat, and I glanced at it briefly.

"Fuck," I shouted.

Ken texted me, wants to add Larry to the meeting. Sorry.

I heard my father's voice loud and clear. *No son of mine is going to allow himself to be pushed around. Stand up for yourself. Be a man. What is your goddamn problem?*

My jaw started to quiver, and I pounded my dash with my fist as a tidal wave of frustrations crashed down on me. "Fuck. Fuck. Fuck."

I didn't care what it cost me, the next time I saw that guy, I was going to win. I fantasized about the scenario. Larry was a big guy, so he wouldn't expect it. I could knock him on his ass with one punch. Climb on top of him and unload. A laugh rang out as my mind's eye pictured him bleeding on the ground.

Dropping my head, I brought my hands up to cup my face. If only I had the balls to do something like that. I didn't and he knew it, and that was *my goddamn problem.*

"Fuck." I exhaled a long breath and chastised myself. If I didn't get a grip soon, I wouldn't be able to distinguish my father's voice from my own.

My phone rang—*Brady*, shit. No wonder he was worried. I'd been sitting in my car indulging in revenge plots for ten minutes. I hurried to gather myself and reached for the door handle, wincing as a familiar pain shot up my arm.

"Finally," Cade said, as I opened the door.

"Sorry," I said sheepishly, leaning down to hug him. Adam and Sid were fighting their way through the crowd toward us. "Where's Brady?"

"Oh, he went out to the patio with Matt. I think it was too crowded in here for them."

Matt? Matt was fucking here? Fantastic.

My eyes narrowed at Sid for an explanation. "Hey, Josh." He leaned in to kiss my cheek. "There they are."

I knew the second I locked eyes with Brady there was something wrong. His mouth was flattened, his shoulders tensed, and that furrow between his eyebrows was never a good sign. There were a few steps where I deluded myself into thinking he was upset Matt was there as well, but as he drew closer, I knew it was me he was angry with.

"Hey," I said cheerfully. Ignoring Matt, I wrapped an arm around Brady's waist and hugged him to my side. His cursory response hurt. "Sorry I'm late."

"Our table is ready," Adam chimed in, motioning to the hostess who was holding a stack of menus. The group filed in line behind her, first Cade, then Adam, followed by Sid and Brady. Matt gestured ahead like he was giving me permission to walk behind my own boyfriend. *This fucking guy.*

We settled at a round table, big enough for six only if no one required much personal space. The multiple conversations around me were lively, but my thoughts were centered on Matt. My lip curled. I was so onto this bastard. Of course he showed up the second Brady and I had our first fight. He was like Larry, always inserting himself into places where he didn't belong. These were my friends, my boyfriend. Why was he fucking here? The sharp jab of Brady's elbow landed in my ribs.

Knock it off, he mouthed.

It took me a minute to realize I must have been giving Matt one hell of a glare. I sighed. Brady wanted to drop it, so I tried.

I reached under the table to squeeze Brady's thigh, which earned me a weak smile. Sid, thankfully, sent the conversation in another direction. First about Sid's work, then an update on Cade's older sister, who was in the midst of some health issues, followed by Adam's detailed review of a new drag club that had opened near his place. Our group ate, drank, and laughed, sharing stories and cracking jokes.

Brady was more reserved than usual, and his plate went virtually untouched. I leaned in, whispering, "Hey, you okay?"

"Yep. Fine," he said flatly.

"What are you two lovers talking about?" Cade asked, fluttering his long eyelashes.

I zeroed in on that word. *Lovers.* We weren't. Not really. And if our friends didn't know it before, they probably did by the way Brady physically winced at the word. The remaining chatter stopped as the conversation came to an uncomfortable halt.

"Cade—" Adam warned.

"What? I asked what they were talking about?" He gestured to us. "What's going on with you two? You're not fighting already, are you? You hear about that, you know. People will, like, live together blissfully for years and then get married and all of a sudden divorce out of the blue."

"Nothing. We're talking about our meal." Brady immediately launched a question to Adam and Cade about their plans for Thanksgiving.

The conversation moved on without me. I resumed my slouch and stirred the ice in my glass with the straw, listening but mostly focused on Brady's icy demeanor. I sat up to drink my remaining Bloody Mary, only to catch sight of a man across the bar staring my direction. He looked familiar—dark skin and pouty lips that definitely qualified as attractive—but not someone I recognized. He smiled at me and, reflexively, I smiled back, realizing my mistake only when the man patted the stool next to him.

I turned my attention back to the conversation when Matt heaved a disgusted sigh, and the table conversation stopped again as Brady twisted to follow Matt's line of sight to the man at the bar. Then he raised an eyebrow at me.

"What?" I asked, confused as to why the whole table seemed to have decided I was an asshole because I smiled at someone. I smiled at everyone. I occasionally even smiled at Larry and I hated that guy. Not like there was anything special about my smile that screamed *hit on me* when I was clearly with my boyfriend.

Matt opened his mouth, poised to speak, when Brady's attention snapped to Matt. Matt got the message and closed his mouth. I did a double take at the exchange. *Since when did Brady and Matt have silent communications?*

Tension sliced through the table until Adam tossed out what I'm sure he thought was a lifeline. "Josh, Brady was telling us you've been swamped lately. How's work?"

I flashed a regretful smile at Brady, trying to convey my apologies again for the rough morning. "It's been kicking my ass, but it's almost over."

"Are you up for another promotion?" Sid asked.

I nodded sharply, unable to explain that my chances largely depended on whether a baby could hold off another twenty-four hours.

"That's great," Adam said. "More money is never a bad thing. What about you, Brady, job is good?"

"Um . . ." Brady hedged, gazing at Matt with a little too much admiration. "Yeah. It's been great so far."

"I'm so happy for you guys," Sid joined in. "Tell us more about the promotion."

I swallowed the burn of acid reflux and tried to explain it as dispassionately as I could. "It's just a senior account manager. It's similar to what I do now, but I would handle bigger, high-profile accounts and have more autonomy."

"So you'll have more control over your schedule," Brady said.

"Well, sort of. I mean, I'll have more demands on my time, but yeah."

"*If* that's what you want, then I hope you get it."

If he was going for supportive, it left me cold. Irritation lanced through me. I tried to force an awkward smile, but then Brady stole another look toward Matt, who smiled sympathetically. I knew that look. That was the same look the women at church gave my mother after Anna outed me. The *I'm sorry you have to deal with him* look.

I started could feel myself filling with rage. The corner of Matt's mouth twitched like he was suppressing a smirk. Brady touched my fisted hand, and I yelped, yanking it back and shaking it.

"What did you do to your hand? It's so swollen."

"Nothing. It's fine."

"It's not fine!" Brady yelled and slapped the table. "Stop fucking saying it's fine."

Matt placed a hand on Brady's shoulder to calm him, and I wanted to murder him.

"Don't fucking touch him. What are you even doing here? I mean, it's super obvious you want to fuck my boyfriend, but using Sid to do it is pretty fucking low."

Matt failed to fight a smile that read *I already fucked your boyfriend*, and I lurched at him, knocking over glasses and plates, as he pushed back from the table out of my reach. *Just one punch*. For Larry. For my dad. For Anna. Just once.

"Josh." Adam shot up and grabbed hold of me, restraining me in a way that had my body reacting on instinct alone. One second, I was in a crowded café, the next I was seventeen again, in Anna's bedroom. I swung wildly, connecting with something that unleashed shockwaves of pain.

Adam rocked back, holding his jaw. The look of pure horror that washed over Sid's face was closely matched by Cade's. But nothing quite delivered the skin-shriveling punch of Brady's pissed-off expression as he stood protectively in front of Matt.

I wasn't oblivious to the fact that my insecurities had spewed out in the most embarrassing way possible, but fuck.

"It's okay," Matt said. "You warned me Josh had to be in control. Maybe we should have asked his permission before I came. Sid, I think we should go."

Sid nodded and threw some money on the table before following Matt out of the door.

As if waiting for an opening, a man approached. "I think you should all go, gentlemen."

Cade and Adam nodded, joining in the effort to straighten the mess and get the hell out of there, equally disgusted by my behavior as the throngs of Christians enjoying their Sunday brunch.

I stayed engaged in a silent standoff with Brady, holding my now-throbbing hand with the other. "I'm—" I didn't know what to say. Anger and jealousy still coursed through me. But my need for Brady to tell me it was all right; to chase away all the thoughts that were telling me he couldn't love me, that I wasn't good enough for him; to say I wasn't wrong or dirty or sinful was like a pulsating drum. "Please," I begged. *Please tell me I didn't lose you.*

And in less than a heartbeat, Brady deflated. "I can't," he said with a small shake of his head, and walked away.

I made it fourteen miles before I knew nothing was going to make the dark thoughts go away. The only thing found at mile six was the realization that in one afternoon I'd managed to blow up every relationship in my life and break my hand in the process—again.

I'd punched Adam and insulted Sid, which pretty much guaranteed Cade would never speak to me again. But Brady . . . I felt the stabbing pain of rejection as vividly as the day my father told me I was dead to him.

"I can't."

I heard it over and over again in my head.

And why should he?

I knew going in he wanted more than what I could give him.

Mile after mile, no matter how hard or how fast I went, I couldn't escape the fact that I had only myself to blame—for everything.

Memories lit up my brain like flashbulbs.

That first message had been so out of the blue.

Aren't you tired of pretending to be someone you're not?

I'd ignored it for weeks, doubling down on football, friends, and Anna until some days I could fool myself into believing I was who I claimed to be. I wasn't gay. I couldn't be. No, I was the good kid—the only son of a pillar of the community and his happily married, stay-at-home wife. A talented quarterback and straight A student dating the most popular girl in school. We were shoo-ins for Homecoming King and Queen for chrissakes.

It was after a football game. We'd won, but barely, against a team we should have blown away. I'd thrown two interceptions and bungled a snap. My mind had been on that message, of who knew about me and how, when I'd been so, so careful.

My dad would not let up, and my mother stood there, saying nothing. My dad didn't only scream at me, no—that wasn't enough. He raged. He berated. He wasn't satisfied until he'd gotten me to break, and then kept going because I dared to cry.

I told myself I needed to know who it was. For my own sanity. One of the many lies I told myself back then. There was something about the possibility of someone knowing and not rejecting me for it that I couldn't resist it. So, I wrote back.

Every fucking day.

And I kept doing it, until she had me. And everything that came after—Anna's demands and my acquiescence to them, reluctant as I might have been—*I'd* given her that control.

It was my mistake and I'd paid the price.

But now, I didn't have an answer for why I kept making that same mistake. I let my father—a man who'd spent years breaking me down for being weak, then tossed me aside when I dared to stand up for myself—still control my actions. I didn't even like my job, but I was tying myself in knots over it. I was far from fine, but I was determined to hide that from the person who loved me more than anyone ever had.

Why was I still fucking pretending every day?

I didn't know, but if I had any hope of giving Brady a future he deserved, I needed to deal with my past—and my hand—because both were slowly killing me.

Chapter Seventeen
Brady

"You okay?" Adam asked me for the millionth time and handed me some water. He tossed the overnight bag I'd packed on the floor and took a seat next to me. His couch was new, still didn't quite give when you sat on it, and the print a little out there—which I suspected was selected by Cade, because it didn't match his taste.

"I don't think I've ever been here before without everyone else."

He shrugged, staring expectantly.

"You like this?" I asked, hugging the throw pillow to my stomach.

"Cade picked it out. I'm hoping he'll move in with me, so whatever helps, right?"

"He seemed pretty upset."

"I'm not worried about Cade right now. I'm worried about you and Josh. What's going on? Talk to me."

I wish I knew. "Did you talk to him?"

Adam shook his head and adjusted his ice pack. "He texted me an apology about the jaw. He, um, don't freak out, but he broke his hand. He was in the ER getting a cast."

"What?" I yelled. "How could you not tell me?" I stood and started looking around for my keys. If Josh was hurt, I couldn't leave him alone.

"Brady. C'mon stop." I turned to face him, and the remorse on his face was enough of an explanation.

"He asked you not to, didn't he?" I slumped back to the couch and drew my legs up to my chest. It was all coming apart.

Adam cocked his head to the side. "I hate to ask this, but is there something going on with you and Matt?"

I rubbed my temples, irritated that Josh could make such an insane accusation, let alone that anyone would believe it. "No. Jesus. Why would you think that?"

"Listen, I know Josh. He can't be easy to... I've been there okay? I'm crazy in love with Cade, but in college, he—I'm not saying it's his fault or anything—but sometimes when the person you love is difficult... I'm just saying I've been in that place where a relationship is hard and then something comes along that's easy."

"No offense, Adam, but don't compare your cheating on Cade to anything happening with Josh and me."

Adam recoiled and fuck...

"I'm sorry. But I'm not cheating on Josh and never would. Matt is my boss."

"So what's his deal, then? He was intentionally provoking Josh."

"He was standing up for me. You saw how Josh flirted with that guy."

"Oh, please." Adam rolled his eyes. "If that was Josh flirting, then he flirts with my mother and yours and all of Loman Hall. That's Josh."

I frowned because I knew Adam was right; it wouldn't have even bothered me if Matt hadn't given me an earful about his ex. "I told Matt about some shit that happened with Josh this morning, and he gave me some things to think about."

"I bet he did," Adam huffed. When I glared at him, he laughed. "C'mon Brady. You fucked him and he clearly doesn't like Josh. He may be a decent guy, but you can't say he doesn't have an agenda, and what's all this 'he's my boss' nonsense? You're clearly closer than that."

"Matt's only agenda is to help me."

"Okay, but with Josh? You know Josh better than anyone. What did Matt say to you?"

"I... It's personal."

"Oh fuck, you talked to Matt about your sex life with Josh, didn't you?"

"So—"

"You're so getting off on two guys competing over you."

"What? No, I'm not."

"You—who does not share any details about your sex life even with your closest friends—are talking to your boss and former lover about your current lover, who he doesn't like. Do I really need to spell this out for you?"

"Josh isn't my current lover."

"What?"

"Josh, he isn't my *lover*."

"I don't understand."

Dear sweet Adam. "We haven't had sex."

"Like," he paused, clearly befuddled. "So you're talking anal, right?"

"No, I mean nothing. No handjobs, blowjobs, no nothing."

"What? How? I mean, why?"

"I don't know," I cried, exasperated. "I mean, at first it was because of me, then he was busy, and then this morning—I tried to start something and he—he saw me naked and now I think he's revolted by me and he basically admitted that he doesn't want an equal partnership. It's just, what if we made a terrible mistake?"

Adam stared at me with his mouth gaped for a long minute. "Not this shit again. Are you out of your mind? Or blind? Josh practically drools over you; there is no way he isn't attracted to you, Brady."

"You didn't see him this morning. He couldn't get away from me fast enough."

Adam patted my thigh sympathetically. "I don't know what happened this morning or what's going on with Josh, but you need to look in the mirror."

"What?"

"Come here." Adam tugged my hand until we were in his bedroom in front of a full-length mirror and pointed at my reflection. "See?"

"Adam," I protested. He latched on to my chin and pulled it until I could see myself.

"You're gorgeous, Brady."

"Stop."

"Your chest and arms are sexy. You have a great head of hair, pretty eyes, soft lips, smooth skin. You dress well."

"Stop it, Adam." I spun on my heels, but he kept going.

"You're also smart, generous, hardworking, and have a great sense of humor. Josh wants you, Brady. He so fucking does. Just take that to the bank. If anything is wrong, it's not that, okay? It's not the way you look."

"Then why doesn't he want me? I've tried, Adam. I've tried to take things to the next level, and he keeps running away. He keeps saying he's fine."

"Josh always runs away. Like always. It's sort of his thing. He evades and avoids and pretends he's okay. You know Josh better than any of us, why are you acting like this is news?"

"Matt said—"

"Fuck, Matt. What do you say?"

"I'd say..." I sighed, recalling the long minutes I'd seen Josh sit in his car. He was so angry—wait, not angry—upset. Matt had witnessed it too, but instead of concern he started asking me questions like why was Josh so angry? And I'd gone along, not wanting to get into a protracted explanation of Josh's background that I didn't understand completely. I did exactly what Josh asked me not to do. I'd involved Matt without telling Josh, and then I'd taken his side. I'd forgotten to be his friend first. "I'd say I'm being an idiot."

"And Matt?"

"What about him?"

"I'm not saying you need to cut him off, okay? But you talk about work, television, bullshit you read in the news. You don't involve him in your relationship. If you need a friend to talk to about Josh, come to me or the guys; we know him, and we love you both."

"Matt doesn't think about me like that."

"Well, forgive me for doubting you, but your track record of knowing when guys are into you is really spotty."

"It's not the same, but you're right. I shouldn't have let Matt make me doubt Josh."

"It's not too late. You can fix it, but Brady, you know Josh. You don't need anyone to explain his behavior to you." Adam patted my leg and left me to my thoughts.

I relived the entire day. The fact that our physical relationship hadn't taken off felt like a sign. We loved each other, but part of me couldn't stop thinking it shouldn't be this difficult. I reexamined Josh's behavior, looking for signs of what I was missing. What had caused him to lash out like that?

I made it to the end, all the way until I walked away from him in the café without an answer.

Shit. The one thing he was afraid of was losing me and I abandoned him. He would come home to find out I wasn't there. I had to fix this. I took out my phone.

Are you okay?

The little dots appeared soon after. *Adam told you.*

Is it broken?

My hand?

Yes. What else did you hurt?

The dots appeared and disappeared a few times before a broken heart emoji appeared, followed by *I'm sorry, Brady. So sorry. And embarrassed. Are you coming home? Can we fix this?*

I'm sorry too. I need a little time to think, but it's going to be okay. You haven't lost me.

Tuesday night, then? Dinner?

Yeah. I'll be home.

We'll figure it out, right?

Yeah. It's going to be all right.

I exhaled as I set the phone down. For the first time, I worried my assurance wouldn't be enough to calm the dark thoughts in Josh's mind.

Chapter Eighteen
Josh

Bare's office was not at all what I expected. The décor was homier, less clinical. There was no couch, only two large brown leather chairs facing each other on a blue and orange circular rug in the middle of the room, a table-size ottoman between them, and off to the side, a plain desk. His degrees hung on the wall, and I smiled when I saw the doctorate.

"Do I have to call you Dr. Bare?" I laughed, my nerves getting the better of me now that I was here.

"Have a seat." He gestured, slipping off his shoes and plopping his feet on the ottoman, then invited me to do the same.

I sunk into the chair, keeping my shoes on and feet firmly on the ground. I held my cast protectively. It still throbbed. I should have taken more ibuprofen.

"So," I began, "how does this work?"

"How was your day? When we spoke this morning, you said you had an important meeting."

I nodded, still relieved Jennifer had showed up. "Fine. We probably got the account."

"Congratulations. You don't seem happy about it?"

"The pitch was for Freedom Athletics, heard of it?"

"Should I have?"

"Do you know Laura Anderson?"

Bare's eyes widen. "The political commentator?"

"Yep. It's her company. We're going to make her the next Ivanka Trump."

"I see. How do you feel about that?"

"Fine... Actually, no. I sort of hate myself."

Bare cocked his head. "That's a strong word."

"Yeah, it is. But I keep asking myself why a person who gave up his entire family to be openly gay would hide in the closet to help someone like that?"

"Did you come up with any answers?"

"Nope. Just more self-loathing."

"You mentioned before that your dad selected your career path. What did you want to do?"

"I don't know."

"Nothing comes to mind?"

"No. I mean, I played football; my dad thought it would get me to college. Then I'd be in business, like him. I guess when I first started college, I took an intro class in nutrition—sort of got me thinking about nursing or maybe something like physical therapy."

"What drew you to those fields?"

"I don't know. I like health and fitness and taking care of people. The science part was hard, but it was interesting."

"Why didn't you pursue it?"

"'Cause my dad wouldn't let me have my college fund if I didn't do what he wanted."

"Even after he cut you off emotionally, he still paid for school. Why?"

"So I would still do what he wanted," I deadpanned. Wasn't it obvious?

"How did you feel about that?"

"Weak. I always felt weak around my dad. Always."

"But you stood up to him. You walked away."

"Not completely. As you pointed out, he controlled my career choices."

"When your dad made you feel weak, how did you react?"

"What do you mean?"

"I mean, what did you do? How did you cope? Did you cry? Scream? Punch things?" He gestured to my arm.

"When I was with my dad?"

"Yeah."

"No. I cried in front of him twice, but he used it against me, so I never did it again. I don't even know what would have happened if

I screamed at or punched him. Nothing I wanted to find out, that's for sure."

"How do you cope with other stressors?"

Jesus. Did I have to say it? He'd seen how I tried to deal with it in that parking lot. "Other than the ways you already know?"

Bare fought a smile. "Yes, other than sex."

"Well, clearly, I don't. Exercise helps, but mostly I just pretend I'm fine as long as I can."

"Okay, looks like we have our first rule of therapy."

"Rule?"

"You, young man, are forbidden from using the word 'fine.'"

"Fine— Okay." I smiled nervously. I was unprepared for rules. Particularly that one. There were no rules given during bar therapy.

"Now, you want to talk about what happened on Sunday?"

I nodded. That was why I was here, after all. "I fucked up and Brady left me, exactly like I told you would happen."

Bare's lip quirked. "How about you start at the beginning: what happened when you woke up yesterday morning?"

"Brady wanted to mess around, but I had to work."

"Is that common?"

"No. I mean, yes. Wait? Which part?"

Bare laughed gently. "This isn't an exam, Josh. You don't have to check the right answer. Relax and explain."

I took a deep breath. Therapy was going to be hell on my overachiever side. "No, it isn't common that Brady wanted to mess around. Yes, I work a lot."

"How would you describe your sex life with Brady?"

"I wouldn't. I love him and I think he's sexy as hell, but we haven't really gotten there yet."

"Hmmm. How long have you been together?"

"Six years. Oh, you mean dating?"

Bare nodded.

"A few months."

"But no sex. Any reason why?"

"Because Brady wanted to wait. He's got some hang-ups about his weight."

"I see. Does he still?"

"He still doesn't believe that I think he's hot, but he says he's ready."

"Do you not believe him?"

"I guess."

"Was he aroused?"

I closed my eyes, remembering how it felt lying on top of him. "Yes."

"Were you?"

I swallowed hard, the memory coming back to me. "At first."

"Did you lose your erection?"

Jesus. What kind of questions were these? I stirred. "Isn't that kind of inappropriate?"

"I assure you my interest in your erection was entirely therapeutic, but I get the picture. What happened when things changed?"

"He rolled me over on my back and kind of pinned me under him."

"How did you feel when Brady did that?"

"Restrained," I deadpanned.

Bare didn't seem amused. "Did you panic?"

"I flailed a bit, and he moved off me."

"What were you thinking about when Brady restrained your arms?"

I shrugged, but I don't think Bare bought it.

"Did you tell Brady that you don't enjoy that?"

"No. I went to work."

"You don't think he'll understand?"

"I didn't say that."

"So why didn't you tell him?"

I tilted my head back and sighed. How many of these questions was he going to ask me? "Why do you think? What kind of a man—particularly one who likes to be fucked—freaks out over something like that?"

"Someone who's been through trauma."

I rolled my eyes. "Jesus, 'trauma'? My dad was a bastard and my ex outed me. Don't make it sound like I'm a victim."

"I didn't say you were."

But he was. Fuck all this poor-Josh nonsense. This was why I didn't like to talk to people about shit. This was why I hadn't told

Brady what happened with Anna—not all of it, anyway. This was why it fucking hurt that Brady was talking to Matt about my issues. I hated when people thought I couldn't handle my shit.

"This was a mistake." I stood, angling for the door.

"Josh, give me one more minute. Please."

"Fine," I said, knowing full well I'd broken the only rule he'd given me. Good. Maybe that would get me kicked out of therapy. I clutched the back of the chair with my good hand, giving him my attention.

"What I'm hearing from you is that when you get upset or overwhelmed, you pretend you've got everything all under control, because you've been taught men shouldn't feel those things. When you can't ignore it, when you can't pretend, you try to fuck or run or punch something to feel better, because you've been taught that that is a man's way of dealing with emotions. But that panic you get when you feel weak or out of control—like you did this morning and like I suspect you did again now—you'll have to learn to lean into that. You'll need to acknowledge it and talk about it—if not with me, then with someone you trust. You need to feel it, Josh, because dealing with emotions, processing trauma, crying when you're sad, admitting you're overwhelmed—*that* is what real men do."

"I don't—"

"It won't be easy, but I promise you that if you give this a chance, if you try to work on changing these behaviors, it will have a profound impact on you and your relationships."

"I just want to fix things with Brady, not be told I'm not a man."

"No one is saying you're not a man. But if you want to be a man in a functional relationship, these are skills you are going to need, so get comfy."

I curled my fingers inward and Jesus. Fuck. My cast stopped me from forming a fist. I closed my eyes. I was so tired of feeling this way. Feeling like I couldn't control my emotions, like I couldn't make decisions without hearing my father's voice. In my head, I knew Bare was right. This was what I needed to be the man Brady deserved. I'd told him once I'd go anywhere for him, and it was time to make good on that promise.

Bare watched me slink back into his oversized chair. His eyebrow arched, which served as a demand that I remove my shoes and take up more real estate than the edge of my seat. I sighed, but what the hell, if it helped me get rid of my father's fucking voice, it'd be worth it.

"So do you want to tell me about what was going through your mind when Brady restrained your arms?"

"Anna," I admitted and turned my face to avoid his judgment. "She did that after she blackmailed me into having sex with her."

Chapter Nineteen
Brady

Tuesday night, I arrived home and hauled the trash to the curb. The last few days had been tough. Josh and I texted back and forth, but there was still a lot left unsaid. The best friend side wanted to force the conversation I knew Josh would struggle to have even if that meant admitting we'd made a mistake. But the boyfriend side desperately wanted us to restore our connection in other, more physical ways. I hadn't slept much deciding which one would be better.

I sidled up behind Josh and kissed his neck as he sprinkled a light layer of cheese onto the peppers. He startled and glanced back over his shoulder. "More?" he asked, with a relieved smile, but I shook my head.

Josh pressed his lips to mine and dipped his long fingers into my waistband. I nearly cried in relief, I'd missed his touch so much, but the best friend side took over.

"Not yet." I stilled his hands. "We need to talk. Now or after dinner if you need more time to prepare yourself, but sometime tonight."

"I know." His lips were fuller than normal, and my gaze settled on the small tooth-size cut on his lower lip. I ran my thumb over it, and Josh flinched.

He would rather break his hand and chew his lip off than talk to me. I heaved a sigh. This was out of control.

"Let's eat, okay. I made your favorite. Then we can talk. I promise," Josh said.

We settled down on cushions in front of the couch, siting side by side quietly for a few bites, but I couldn't eat.

"You're not hungry?" Josh asked.

"The last two days have been—"

"For me too. I've missed you. I'm sorry again."

"I saw you in the car at the Bee. You . . . you looked really upset, even before."

"I was. Larry had weaseled his way into my pitch."

I continued to pick at my plate while Josh finished his food. He seemed calmer, more in control, and I feared that was lulling me into a false sense of complacency. He'd answered my question about what happened with a nice little bow; I still had no idea what to make of his behavior inside the restaurant.

After we cleaned up the kitchen, he tugged my hand toward my room. "You stained your shirt," he said quietly.

I sighed. Of course I did. I yanked it off and bent to pull another out of my drawer.

"Don't," Josh said. "Come here."

I climbed into my bed and let Josh tug me closer. We settled in and I closed my arms around him. My heart hurt for him, for us. We both wanted it so badly, I knew it. So why wasn't it working?

"Your room is always so clean," he said, glancing over his shoulder.

I shrugged. "When you grow up poor and fat, people expect you to be a slob. I don't like to give them any ammo. Plus, the trailer was smaller than our first apartment."

His hand traced over my chest, combing his fingers through the thick patch of dark hair over my pecs and torso. When he reached my belly, I sucked in my gut.

"Just breathe normally." His eyes lifted to me. "You're so sexy."

I leaned in to kiss him, the press of my weight slowly rolling him onto his back. I'd missed him so much, my hands started to move on their own volition. Just touching him enough to allay my doubts. Nothing had ever felt more natural than having Josh in my arms.

"Brady," Josh said firmly, and pressed me back until there was space between us. Laughing softly, he kissed me, pulled my hand off his crotch, and interlaced our fingers. "We need to talk first."

Josh's fingers unhooked from mine and trailed over my squishy parts, light enough to tickle. I grabbed his hand to stop him. "If you want me to keep my shirt off, no tickling. Laughing does not do good things to fat rolls."

"I wish you believed me when I said I don't care that you have a belly. It suits you. I love the way you look. Do you understand that?"

I nodded and let go of his hand. He stopped what he was doing to lift my arm and cuddled closer to me, nuzzling his chin into the crook between my arm and chest, and rested his head on my shoulder, tilted toward me, and sighed. "You deserve an explanation."

"I don't understand what's going on with you. Do you think we made a mistake?"

"No, babe. The only mistake made was me thinking I couldn't talk to you. About Anna." He pushed out a shaky exhale, and I stiffened at the vulnerability conveyed in his breath. He spoke softly, but clearly. "Before Anna outed me, she came over to my house and confronted me."

I jerked in surprise. I'd heard the story of his ex-girlfriend's catfish scheme, but he'd always made it seem like she blindsided him. My body tensed, and Josh ran a hand over my hip to calm me. If I started getting angry, he wouldn't get it out.

"I didn't want to let her in, but my parents were home, and she started making accusations on the front porch, so I agreed to meet her at her place. When I did, she gave me a choice. Either we kept it between us and continued to be boyfriend and girlfriend, or she would out me."

My breath hitched, and he didn't have to say more. I'd already put the bigger pieces together.

"I knew what would happen if she outed me, so I agreed to keep pretending. But she said we'd been going out long enough and that if we were going to stay together, we should have sex." He stopped for a second, his lips quivering as our eyes met. "There was no way I could face my father."

"I know. Josh, you were a kid. It wasn't your fault."

Josh nodded, but I wasn't sure how much he believed me. "I'll spare you the details. It didn't go well, and Anna thought my dick was not, um, cooperating on purpose. She got really angry and was taking it so personally, like it meant I thought she was ugly or something When I tried explaining it wasn't about her, she pushed me down and climbed on top of me. She kept shoving her boobs in my face and telling me how I needed to try it the right way. I didn't know what to do. If it was a guy I would fight, but a girl? I kind of froze and let her do some stuff to me, because part of me kept thinking maybe . . . you know, maybe that would be easier. Even after she let go of my wrists, I still felt trapped, and I don't know if it was a panic attack or something else, but there was so much pressure in my chest, kind of like I was being suffocated. That's when I realized it would never work, that I couldn't pretend with any girl, but especially not with her. I shoved her off my lap and bolted toward the door, but she'd locked us in. I panicked and tried to bust it down to get away."

"Oh, Josh. Why didn't you ever tell me?"

"I'm not done," he said, his voice wet. "Eventually, I started to punch the door, and Anna finally unlocked it." Josh took a stuttering breath, and I stroked a hand through his hair. "Later, my hand swelled up, but I kept playing football until my dad noticed."

My heart ached knowing the lengths Josh would have gone to hide what had happened from his father. His dad had ridden him constantly about any perceived lack of masculinity—he had to be the best, the strongest, have the hottest girlfriend. To Josh's father, a woman attempting to rape a man would have been incomprehensible. "What did you tell him?"

"I told him I'd gotten in a fight. Said I was fine. Kept playing. My father kept telling me how proud he was that I played through the pain. What a man it made me. It was the first time he'd ever been proud of me, but it was all this big lie.

"Then Anna got pissed that I wouldn't talk to her or meet her again, and I've told you the rest of it. She told everyone what happened and sent out the letters as proof. My father quit speaking to me. I was an outcast. Football was gone. I lost everything."

"I'm so sorry." My sympathy felt so inadequate, but it was all I had.

"It's okay. Care to revise your non-opinion on my need to see a psychologist?" He huffed out a laugh, but I couldn't indulge him.

"My opinion remains you should do it if you think it will help." I kissed him, then pulled back to see his eyes, but his gaze dropped to the mattress. "Beautiful, look at me. You have nothing to be ashamed of."

"I do think it's going to help. I'm seeing someone—the guy I told you about. His name is Bare. I don't want to run from you, Brady. From us. I don't want to pretend I'm okay, because I'm not.

"Because of what happened to me, I need you to understand. My head can be a dark place sometimes. There are some things I've done and said . . . and thought. I can't always tell you about them. My dad, he's still in here." He tapped his temple. "Running helps when his voice gets too loud. I promise you when I run, it won't be to get away from you. I'm going to work on finding better ways to cope, but I can't promise you I'll always handle things the best way. But I know that I have a hard time if I feel restrained—like when you were on top of me Sunday morning and pinned my arms or when Adam grabbed me—I'm not sure I can do that."

"So it wasn't about me . . . my weight."

"No. I— I'm not sure if you want to know this or not, but you should probably know. Before you, I told you I always knew what was going to happen."

I nodded.

"Well, one of the things I made clear beforehand was that restraining my arms was never okay."

"You could have told me."

"I should have. But I always thought with you—someone I loved and trusted—it would be okay. Trust me, Bare is all over that one. There are a lot of things about what Anna did I'm realizing are impacting me more than I thought."

I flashed back to the café and Adam holding Josh back, the almost animallike response to being held. "So you didn't try to punch Adam."

"I don't even remember punching him; I was trying to get away."

"But you *were* trying to punch Matt?"

Josh groaned. "Honestly, I don't know what I was going to do. I've never hit someone before, only objects. I'd like to say I wasn't going to hit him, but it scares me that I'm not certain. That my emotions were controlling me and not the other way around. I can't be like my father, Brady. That's not me. At least, I'm going to do whatever it takes for it to not be. I promise to work on my jealousy. In my heart, I know I have nothing to worry about. I know you love me. I'm so sorry I did that."

"I do know you. I know that's not who you are. And as far as you being jealous of Matt, I may have downplayed how close we've gotten . . . as friends, I swear only as friends. In the interest of full disclosure, I've been talking to Matt a lot about my body issues."

Josh challenged me with a pointed look. "You've been talking to Matt about a lot more than your body issues."

"I'm not interested in him like that."

"I know that, but I'm not sure he can say the same."

"I'm sorry. Sometimes our conversations delved into other items and I overshared some of our issues."

"Did you tell him about Anna?"

"No, I would never. I was so confused about what was happening with you."

"Did he help?"

"I thought so, until Adam sort of laid into me about it. I didn't mean to take his side over yours. I'm so sorry about that."

He caressed my bare chest and smiled. "Do I have Matt to thank for this change?"

"Sort of," I said. "I like my job. I want to be friends with him, but I promise to set better boundaries. I want you to be good with that, but if it's a deal breaker, say so."

"I don't get to pick your friends. No matter how much I struggle with control issues, I never want you to think that it'd be okay for me to dictate who you spend time with. But maybe we need to talk about what aspects of our relationship we share with our friends, and what we keep private."

"When I've talked to him about you, it's mostly about my confidence issues." I paused, realizing that without telling him the truth, there was no way for him to truly understand. "I can talk to him about my weight without feeling like a loser." He eyed me suspiciously, so I said, "Matt had gastric bypass surgery."

"Oh," he said succinctly, apparently processing that news. "Can't you talk to me about it? I want you to feel like you can talk to me too. About anything."

I shook my head. When he frowned, I caressed his arm with a contrite smile. "It's not that I can't talk to you exactly, but you've never struggled with weight so there are some things you might not be able to relate to as well."

"Okay," he said, clearly disappointed. "I get it."

"I'm not trying to keep it a secret from you, though. I will tell you what I've learned about myself if that helps."

"It couldn't hurt."

"I don't like my body—"

"Brady—"

"Just listen, beautiful." I kissed his nose. "I know in my head you like my body, but I don't. What I've figured out is that isn't going to change with some weight loss. I'm down to my lowest adult weight. I'll keep working at it, but I need to figure out how to be happy with what I have because there is only so much diet and exercise can do. I also need to watch how much attention I give my weight loss, because I can't need the scale to tell me if it's going to be a good day or a bad day. It's not only about weight. It's about growing up with less than everyone else. Bullies I can handle. I know how to react when people make jokes at my expense. When people like you look at me like you do, I don't know how to react. Sometimes, I'll start thinking that we haven't bridged this gap between friends and lovers because we're not supposed to. Like maybe there is a reason guys like me don't end up with guys like you."

"God, please don't say that. I know I have work to do and we need to communicate better, but please don't give up on this. I love you, and I'm so attracted to you."

"And I believe that. Which is why my shirt is off. But just like there isn't some number of dates in my head that make us official, there isn't a number on the scale that's gonna magically make me confident. And sex can be terrible when you're hung up on things like that, and that's not my self-esteem talking either. I've been told my weight was a turnoff. While still wearing a condom."

He growled. "Ma—"

I rolled my eyes and put a finger to his lips. "I'm not talking about Matt. You've been with a lot more guys than I have, Josh. I want it to be good."

"It will be," he said confidently. "There is no way it won't be amazing."

"See. That's what I'm talking about. Your expectations . . . I can't live up to that."

"Can I suggest something that might solve both of our problems?"

"Sure."

"There is something I like to do to clear my head besides run. You trust me?"

"Yes," I said unequivocally.

He climbed out of bed and grabbed my hand. When I put on a T-shirt, Josh didn't stop me. "Follow me."

Chapter Twenty
Josh

I led Brady to the couch and handed him a controller. "Start it," I said. His eyes clouded in confusion, but he turned on his console. "Sit down on the couch, relax."

Brady sat, and I took the seat next to him. As soon as his avatar was on the screen, his eyes narrowed in concentration. I waited until he was engrossed in the game before I slid into position.

Brady eyed me. "Josh," he whined as I found the button of his pants and pulled it free from the slot. "Are you . . ." Brady groaned as I pushed my left hand inside his pants and palmed him. "Fuck."

"Pay attention to your game," I reminded him as I fumbled, trying to do everything with the wrong hand. "Wait until I can use this one." I lifted my casted hand.

"Let me." Brady reached down, but I swatted his hand away and pulled his cock free. He was still soft, and when I peeked up at him, I could see he was nervous.

"I used to fantasize about doing this in our dorm room. The first time I asked you to teach me to play, this is what I really had in mind, but I lost my nerve."

I drew him into my mouth with a soft slurp. Licking up his shaft until the vein there pulsed with new life. I loved every whimper and keening whine and how he let me touch him, even if he was mostly clothed. When the game noises confirmed he was still playing, I let loose. He wasn't watching me so he couldn't see how into it I was. I let my mind and mouth off its leash, moaning my pleasure. Stupidly turned-on, the ache of my cock had my hips humping forward searching for relief, but I found none.

When the video game warned about critically low oxygen levels, I peered up, to see Brady's eyes shut, his face blissfully relaxed. He cursed softly as I eased up and down his thick cock. With a flick of my tongue, he gasped, his eyes blazing down at me, eyelids heavy with lust. He slid his fingers into my hair, massaging his fingertips into my scalp. "Josh," he moaned, thrusting a little, like he couldn't hold back, and it was so perfect, I shattered.

His hands fisted in my hair, drawing me closer, and my name fell in a rhythmic chant from his lips. I gazed up at him again, not wanting to miss a second of his reaction. Blown pupils, parted lips, fast breaths. His euphoric expression exactly matched my fantasy. That was all it took. I hollowed my cheeks and accepted him as deep as I could handle until he throbbed and flooded my mouth with his release.

"Holy fuck." Brady's breathless praise gave me power. I stayed still, my cheek resting on his thigh as he recovered and stroked my hair.

"C'mere." Brady tucked himself inside his underwear and tugged me until I was on his lap. "Let me see you."

He yanked my T-shirt over my head and pulled me to him, sucking on my nipple and kneading at my ass while I tried to finish removing my shirt. I exhaled pleasure as his tongue flicked over my hard, sensitive nub. "Fuck, baby."

He continued to tease me, licking and giving me gentle bites that made me gasp. When my shirt caught on my cast, I squirmed, and Brady instantly retreated.

"Wait. No. Don't stop. Cast," I said, and launched back into where we were.

"Sorry," he murmured, and kissed me. "You okay?"

I nodded, and Brady scooped his arm around my waist and tipped me sideways until I was on my back.

Shirt dangling from my arm, I caressed his back one-handed as he kissed me and struggled to keep his weight off me. The soul-touching dance of tongues tapped into a reservoir of emotion, and we were in free fall.

He slipped lower, and I used the time he worked my pants off to free me of my shirt. And at last, I was naked.

He wasted no time returning the favor. Spread out, half on and half off the couch, he buried his face between my legs and extended a hand to tweak my nipple. I lifted my hips and Brady encouraged me with a moan that sent electricity up my spine. My eyes closed, and I found my voice. "Yeah, suck me." When I expressed my pleasure, Brady took me deeper, more aggressively. "Fuck, baby. I want you so much."

Brady looked up in question, and I laced my fingers behind my head and curled to meet his admiring gaze, shamelessly flexing my abs and biceps for his benefit. Brady's expression sent a wave of pride through me. I loved turning him on. Every minute I spent at the gym was now dedicated to that reaction. "I want you inside me. Are you ready?"

"Fuck. Yes." Brady scrambled to his feet and undressed in the low pinkish light of the television screen. He lifted off his shirt in one fluid movement, then dropped his unbuttoned pants and boxers soaked with my saliva. He gave himself a few hard strokes until his length was again mouth-wateringly rigid, then glanced around. "Here?"

I gazed at him and blatantly admired his unclothed body. I wanted to climb him like a tree. Instead, I rose to my knees on the couch and touched him, exploring his solid, imposing chest. Brady's nipples were flat dark circles against creamy skin with dark hairs poking out. I flicked them as an experiment and bit my lip as he responded with a breathy curse.

I stroked along his arms, squeezing his broad shoulders and running down the curve of his biceps, which flexed under my palms. "These arms . . ." I purred but didn't finish my thought. It was too damsel-in-distress for the mood, but he understood. I told him with my caress and I kissed his hands. His arms made it safe to be me, and I wanted nothing to hold us back from expressing our desire for each other.

When I brought my chest to his, his rounded stomach flattened against mine, and he tilted his pelvis until his length slid along my shaft. I kissed him, and he dropped his hands to my ass, then hauled me even closer.

I lost myself, drawing breath from Brady's mouth and dizzy with anticipation. He clutched my left buttock and squeezed. I gasped with the near pain, until the fingers of his other hand reached their destination and started their intimate massage.

Too quickly, the pleasure was withdrawn, and I groaned as Brady brought his fingers to his mouth to wet them. He swallowed and licked his lips, visibly concerned when his dry mouth couldn't comply.

Finally, I understood what Brady had been trying to ask me earlier. *Here?* As in are we doing this in the family room where we lacked certain necessary supplies? I kissed him, dry lips and all, and pulled back, smiling.

"Bedroom," I said, my needy, sex-drenched voice barely recognizable to my own ears. "Only if you're ready."

He nodded and helped me to my feet. Our bodies aligned perfectly. His longer legs meant endless possibilities. Standing against a wall. In the shower. Bent over a table. But that could wait. I grabbed his hand and led him to his bedroom.

His eyebrow raised as I slid open the top drawer of his dresser and retrieved his lube. I'd discovered it while putting his clothes away forever ago and had never said anything. I poured some in my hand and worked it over his length, kissing him passionately as he returned to rock hardness with my touch.

He walked me backward, kissing my neck, until my knees hit the mattress, and he kept moving so I was on my back, and he was covering me, his arms locked by my head to keep his full weight from me. I sighed and worked my hand free to tug him down. "Lay on me."

Brady's elbow buckled, but he rolled off to my side in the same movement. He nudged my hip in a silent request for me to turn over.

I turned to meet him, his skin flushed and breaths heavy. "I want you on top of me, face to face."

Brady shook his head. "I don't want you to feel restrained."

I'd had six years to imagine it, and I was too close. I wanted it the way I'd always pictured it. "Yes, I need to know. Please. Just don't hold my arms."

Silently, he shifted until he hovered over me, one arm locked stubbornly straight by my head and his knees wedged under my thighs. He opened me with lubed fingers and aligned our bodies. I lifted my legs and wrapped them around his waist, straining to give

him the best angle. When he slid in, I cried out and collapsed my legs around him to draw him deeper. "Yes," I moaned. "Baby, it's so good."
Brady cursed, tipped his hips forward, and collapsed on me. Then things got moving. He rocked into me, grunting with exertion, giving me just the sweet bit of pressure and friction on my cock I needed. I closed my eyes and let my thoughts die on my tongue, my pleasure escaping in soft moans and sighs until I remembered, I didn't have to do that anymore.
"Yeah, fuck me," I moaned in Brady's ear. "Open me up with your thick cock, baby."
Brady pulled back, his mouth gaped, face strained like he was seconds away from losing control. "Oh, hell." His eyes rolled back in his head.
"Good?" I asked.
He pushed into me hard. "Say all the words." Brady laughed, pure joy and pleasure on his red face. Definite "confident Brady feeling himself" energy in his movements.
Brady dropped his forehead to my shoulder and thrust deep, groaning as I clenched around him. "So tight." Brady's growly voice vibrated on my skin.
"Yeah. You feel so good inside me. Need you. Wanted this for so long. Give it to me, Brady. Fill me up."
It was everything I'd imagined. His smell. His sweat. His breath in my ear. The way he loved me. A perfect blend of animalistic desire and gentle touches. I spewed all the words that came into my consciousness. I begged unabashedly for what I wanted—for more, for deeper, for harder—until he thrust into me so forcefully, pleasure sparked throughout my entire body. Our lips met. We kissed until the need to draw breath was too strong to ignore. His body lurched, a desperate rut and an ecstatic roar signaling his climax. I gripped him closer. Anchored to him and my innermost desires. Gifted with a fuller understanding of my sexuality, of what had been missing. I cried out as the heat of his orgasm flooded my insides and quickly followed him over the edge.
He rolled off me, smiling and stroking a heavy hand over my chest. I stretched my legs, enjoying the soreness of my well-used body and turned toward him. Exhaustion mixed with unadulterated elation.

There was no hanging back and waiting to see if Brady was okay with it, even with my cast, I needed to touch him. I needed as much of my skin in contact with his as possible.

He kissed me and reached down between us, brushing his hand over my spent cock, triggering a convulsion that slithered through me so fast I recoiled. "Gaw. I'm so sensitive right now."

"So, you're good?" he asked with a laugh.

I sighed contentedly. "Very. Why? You want to go for a third round?"

"I need a few minutes, but if you want."

I peered up at him to assess if he was serious. He was. Damn, Brady had stamina. "I was kidding."

"Oh, okay," Brady said. "I just want to make sure you're, um, good."

"I'm amazing. Do you not know how amazing that was?"

Brady lifted his arms and rested them behind his head. His chest puffed out, and for a minute, I thought he might fish for more compliments. Not that I wasn't willing to give them, but no. It actually worried him. He didn't know.

"Brady," I said to get his attention. When he wouldn't meet my eyes, I lifted to straddle his hips. With me on top of him, he couldn't avoid my gaze. Our eyes met, and the uncertainty in his made my heart ache. I leaned over to kiss him. "That was the best sex I've ever had."

He huffed and I regretted every time I'd given him a throwaway compliment.

"Brady, I need you to hear me." I poured everything into a kiss. When I sat back on his thighs, he smiled at me, slightly more relaxed. There was no shortage of words to describe what we'd done, but Brady needed to hear one thing in particular. "I'm completely satisfied."

"Really?" Brady asked, voice ticking up in optimism. "I can go again if you need it."

"I'm sort of a one-and-done kind of guy. I promise I'm good. Just cuddle me now."

Brady exhaled and tugged me down, waiting for me to situate myself before he closed his arms around me. I yawned as Brady kissed the patch of skin below my ear.

"So, we're lovers now," Brady said, imitating Cade's deep voice with the word *lovers*. He laughed into my ear and the warmth of his breath sent new shivers down my spine.

"Do you feel differently?"

"Kind of. Like there's more at stake, I guess."

"I want you to know I'm going to do everything I can to be the man you deserve."

"You already are," Brady whispered as he kissed along my neck. "Don't put pressure on yourself to change for me, Josh. Okay? I'm proud of you for getting help, but I love you as you are now. Remember that, please."

I kept my adoration inside, choosing instead to wiggle my back against his chest and sigh in utter satisfaction. I exhaled as he relaxed his arms and tossed a leg over my calf, surrounding me more fully.

"This okay?" he asked.

I nodded. Like a weighted blanket, it calmed me, and my eyelids grew heavy. I slept deeply wrapped in Brady's arms.

Chapter Twenty-One
Brady

"You ready for this?" I cast a nervous glance at Josh, but we were already sitting in Sid's driveway and Adam had pulled in behind us, so it seemed a little late to back out.

"Yeah." Josh sighed. "I need to get the apology tour over with. Matt just brings out the same bullshit testosterone-fueled, competitiveness I felt with Larry, but Sid likes the guy and he's been really supportive to you, so he must have good points. I need to make the effort."

I rested my hand over his cast and squeezed his fingers lightly. We'd never had a true Friendsgiving before, but when Sid had proposed the idea, I think we were both grateful for the chance to talk to everyone together.

"Okay, then." I pulled the door handle, and Josh flinched at the *click*.

"I'm going to talk to Adam first. Alone if that's okay."

"Of course." I nodded and retrieved the laundry basket full of apology side dishes Josh had made. When he exited the car, I cast a reassuring smile at him. *You got this, babe*, I mouthed as he made his way to Adam's car.

At the front door, Sid greeted me with a smile. "Hey. Happy Thanksgiving. Where's Josh?"

"He's talking to Adam."

Sid nodded and waved me inside. "Good. Let me help with that." He took the basket and made a face as he realized how heavy it was.

"Oh my." He chuckled. "He does realize there are only six of us, right?"

I smiled, remembering how I'd said the same thing that morning before he tossed me out of his kitchen for trying to help again. "Josh finds cooking therapeutic."

"I see. Well, take your coat off. Get comfy. Cade's running late. Matt's finishing up a call with his family. He might be done if you want to talk to him alone."

"Um..." I smiled weakly. "No, I think I'll wait for Josh."

"Okay. Want a drink, then?" Sid offered.

"Yes, please." I laughed and followed him toward the kitchen.

We chatted a bit, before Adam and Josh entered the room, conversing easily enough that I knew they had cleared the air. I'd expected nothing less, since Adam had texted me multiple times to check in on how we were doing.

"Hi, Brady." Adam smiled, going in for a hug without hesitation. "Happy Thanksgiving."

"You too."

"Man, the food smells amazing in here," Adam said, grinning as Matt entered the room.

"Hey," I said with a wave as Matt's gaze settled on where Josh was holding my hand, and smiled. Sid offered Matt and Adam a drink, and we stood around, shifting uncomfortably for a few minutes while he fixed them.

"So..." Adam broke the deafening silence with a nervous laugh. "Anyone want to watch the game?"

"Yes," I said, a little too enthusiastic about an excuse to get us out of the weird kitchen standoff. Josh and Sid both turned to me with outraged faces that quickly dissolved into hysterics.

"What's so funny?" Matt asked.

Shaking his head, Josh kissed my cheek. "All right, well if Brady here is desperate enough to watch football, I might as well put us out of our misery. Matt, I already apologized to Adam, but I'm sorry about the other day. I said and did a lot of things I'm not proud of. It won't happen again, and I hope you won't hold my behavior against Brady." Josh extended his hand, and Matt, after glancing briefly at Sid, who gave a quick nod, accepted it.

"I think we both could have behaved better. I also apologize. I didn't intend to upset you."

Josh nodded, curtly, but he wasn't trying to force a smile, and that was a step in the right direction. "Why don't you go watch the game? I just want to put the potatoes in the oven to keep them warm."

"So who's playing?" I said to Adam, anxious to move us anywhere else, but also to give Josh a moment alone. Apologizing to Matt wasn't easy for him, but he'd been determined to do it. I grabbed the beer Sid had given me and followed Adam to the family room. Matt took the chair, which left Adam, Sid, and me on the couch.

When Josh returned, the lines across his forehead had relaxed. "C'mere." I motioned for Josh to sit on my lap since all the other seats were occupied and I needed him close. He flashed a grateful smile and slowly lowered himself onto my leg, knees tucked between my thighs.

"Proud of you, beautiful," I whispered next to his ear. He turned and met my lips in a kiss that spoke to his relief. I wasn't naïve enough to think Josh was going to address all his problems in such a short time, but knowing he hadn't done any lasting damage to his friendships seemed to make a huge difference in his anxiety about today.

"So which color are the Rangers?" I asked.

Josh laughed in my arms, shaking his head. "The Rangers are a baseball team. These are the Cowboys and the Falcons. You are cheering for the Cowboys."

"Because you like losing." Adam fake scowled, then checked his phone and smiled. "Cade's on his way."

"Oh, good. I'll start getting the food out." Sid rose. "Matt, will you help?"

Matt nodded and followed Sid into the kitchen, while Adam kept his eyes glued to the game.

I held Josh, kissing his neck and enjoying his reactions to the game until the vibration of his pocket made him frown. He shifted on my lap to retrieve his phone, keeping one eye on the game as he navigated to his email.

"Offsides," Adam screamed.

"Fuck," Josh swore.

"Is that bad?"

"Not for the Falcons," Adam explained. "They get five yards because the Cowboys jumped the snap."

I was about to ask Josh what *jumping the snap* meant, but his concentration was still on his phone, and I quickly realized he'd not been reacting to the game. "Everything okay?"

"Yeah," he said, a little less convincing than I needed it to be. But that was good. I liked that he wasn't trying to pretend.

He sighed, shifting off my lap into the seat Sid had occupied, then looked at me. "There's a dinner to celebrate the Freedom Athletic team. Ken messaged to ask Jennifer and me if we had any concerns about adding Larry and his wife to the invite."

"So he's giving you an out?"

"Maybe. It's a holiday. He probably thought I wasn't going to be checking email." He slid his phone back into his pocket and leaned against me, pulling my arm around him.

"So you're not going to object to Larry attending?"

Josh shook his head. "Nope."

"Can I ask why?"

"Because it's a bunch of macho bullshit and I don't want to play that game anymore. If Larry goes to the dinner, who cares. *I* don't even want to go to the dinner. If he gets promoted and I don't, so be it. I'm done fighting for shit I don't even want."

"Cade's here. Let's eat," Sid announced. Josh stood, and we joined our friends at the table. Conversation was fun and light as we enjoyed our meal, but the entire time I kept wondering why I hadn't been invited to the celebration dinner.

Chapter Twenty-Two
Josh

On the night of the Freedom Athletics dinner, I decided not to go.

I thought about making excuses—feigning illness of some sort, but in the end, after a very productive session with Bare, I declined the invite without explanation. Brady had been a little off since our Friendsgiving and more than patient through the zillion hours I'd spent catching up my regular accounts. I wanted to be with him, not Mike or Larry and their toxic bullshit. Besides, I was one hundred percent over Laura Anderson and her company. The last thing I wanted to do was celebrate it.

I jumped out of my car and jogged into the house. "Brady!"

"Josh. You're home?" I followed the sound of paper being crumbled to the living room, arriving as Brady tried to shove something under the couch. His eyes caught mine like a deer in the headlights. I could smell the grease in the air, and the ketchup stain on his shirt confirmed the rest. The guilt hit me hard. Brady only turned to junk food when he was feeling terrible about himself. I opened my mouth to apologize when Brady beat me to it, "I'm sorry."

Wait. What? I recoiled.

"I was gonna work out, but I had a rough day and you weren't gonna be home tonight."

I sank next to him and pulled the bag from beneath the sofa and tossed it on the table. I sighed. How did I keep messing this up? "Got any fries left?"

His eyes wide, he pulled the remnants of a super-sized French fry container from the bag and handed me the carton.

I picked up the Styrofoam drink from the table and took a sip of his chocolate milkshake. "Strawberry is better. Want to kill some Martians?"

"Josh, your celebration dinner is tonight. Why are you home? Did Larry do something?"

I shook my head, nervous, but more than ready to come clean about my recent therapeutic breakthrough. "We used to have some good talks in the dorms over video games. Try not to be too disappointed in me, but I need to tell you some stuff, okay?"

"Um, sure." Brady reached for the controllers and tossed me mine as he set up the game. "What I remember was you trying to talk my ear off without making eye contact."

"You know you should eat what you want to. There isn't a reason to sneak food into the house and eat it in a dark room like you're doing something wrong. I hope you don't think I'm trying to control what you eat."

Brady frowned. "I know that, and I like that you care about what I eat. Shit! Switch to your shrink ray."

The game paused as we changed our weapons out. "I like to take care of you, but that doesn't mean I expect a vow of food fidelity. I love you regardless of what you want to eat." An alarm sounded as my avatar veered into dangerous territory.

"Upgrade your heat shield," Brady instructed, and I scrambled to remember the combinations of buttons to execute on his command. When the alarm stopped, I followed Brady in the game to a mission room, when he paused it. His eyes searched me.

"I need you to push me a little. I know I give you shit when you tell me you're proud of me—"

"I am."

"I know, but I want you to be proud to be *with me* too." His eyes flicked up to me, full of vulnerability and doubts. In that instant, I recognized what had led to his dinner choices. Brady thought me excluding him from my work dinners had to do with him.

"I'm proud to be with you. Always."

"I thought... because you talk about the trophy wives. Maybe..."

"No. Not even a little because of that. I promise. The Christmas party is coming up. Come with me."

Brady chuckled. "I would love to. Now stop procrastinating and tell me why you think I'll be disappointed in you."

"I'm not out at work," I confessed. "And I realized I want to be. I need to be the type of man who isn't afraid of that. I can't keep pretending. I don't want to."

Realization dawned on Brady's expression, then he slouched back into the couch and sighed. "I mean, I guess I understand why you stayed closeted, but why didn't you think you could tell me?"

I leaned against him and lifted his arm so it was around my shoulder, then tilted my chin up and smiled. "I want you to know that it wasn't that simple, okay? I didn't actively set out to be in the closet and lie to you about it." Brady eyed me skeptically, but it was the truth. A truth he deserved to hear. "During my internship, I didn't really think about it as staying closeted. I wanted the job so much that I kept my head down and worked. Larry didn't have any personal conversation with coworkers, so I followed his lead. No one asked me basic stuff like where I was from or what I liked to do, so it didn't feel like lying because it never came up."

Brady nodded for me to continue.

"So that was how things went for a while. There was work and there was you and my personal life, everything stayed separate. Until I went up for that first promotion. I mentioned we were planning to buy a house, and Ken gave me this look, like he was surprised, then in the next breath he told me I would be expected to attend a lot of social events and asked me if that were going to be a problem. It messed with my head, so I stressed that we were only friends."

"At that time, that was true."

I appreciated that Brady was trying to give me a soft landing, but I didn't need it. My lies of omission had already put me in a dark hole, I wasn't about to keep digging. Besides, I trusted what we had; he might be disappointed, but I knew he'd understand. "Yeah, it was, and when I first said it, that might have been the way I justified it to myself. But, Brady, I kept saying it and a lot of other stuff too, and it wasn't to set the record straight. It was to keep my coworkers from knowing I was gay. But by that time, you'd assumed I was out, and I didn't know how to admit that I wasn't, especially not after all you did to help me accept myself. I was worried you'd think *I* was weak if you knew. It never occurred to me, not once, that you'd think it was about you. If it had, I would have told you."

"You and me, we got to get, like, a 'take a number' situation going on our insecurities. Maybe I should see Bare."

"I've spent a lot of time with Bare on this. I rationalized a lot of it. I'd never brought a beard to a social event or pretended to have a girlfriend, so I wasn't really lying, you know? My coworkers thought I was a perpetually single guy, which I was. But things are different now. Not bringing you to this dinner tonight felt all kinds of wrong. Pretending to be straight was one thing, but I told Bare I didn't want to pretend to be single."

"What did he say?"

"He reassured me that I didn't owe anyone an explanation of my sexuality, but when we dug into it deeper to find the real crux of the problem, all I came up with is that I don't like my job that much and I'm afraid coming out will make me hate it even more."

Brady nodded. "I don't think you've been happy there for a while."

"Bare gave me some insights into high-functioning anxiety disorders that basically described me to a T. All the things I do—like my routines and never saying no—it all kind of fits."

"Do you think you want to look for the same kind of job somewhere else? Is it the work or the company you don't like?"

I shrugged. "Would you believe that I don't know? Bare gave me some homework to research options. I liked my job okay until this account I've been working on—it's for Freedom Athletics."

"Oh, Josh. That must have been hell. So you're coming out at the Christmas party? If you need some time to talk to your HR, I can wait."

"No. That's part of the problem, actually. The culture there is toxic, and HR doesn't seem able to do anything about it. I want to bring you because I love you, Brady. If they don't like it, fuck 'em. We're a two-income couple. I got a man who can support me if I need it, right?"

Brady huffed. "Like you'd let me."

"Is there something wrong with letting you help me financially?"

"No." Brady beamed. "Not that I can think of."

"Okay. Good. Because if they fire Jennifer to give me this account, I'm going to resign. It wouldn't be right for me to stay if they did that to her, and I can't work for Laura. That's a red line for me. But I need to figure out if it's the job I don't like or the company, or maybe it's just feeling like I can't be myself."

"You can quit now if you want to. We'd be okay."

"I want to know I came out intending to stay."

"Are you sure?"

I nodded. "Yes. At least until I have a plan for myself. I'll keep working with Bare to figure out what that is, and I don't think it'll be easier to do with the pressure of looking for a job. I don't want to be tempted to take something just so I have a paycheck." I paused, recalling other insights from my session with Bare. I deserved to do something that made me happy. "I might go back to school. I need to take my time and make sure I'm doing what I want to do and that it has nothing to do with my father."

"That sounds like a great plan, but what if they fire you? They can't fire you for being gay, but if you refused to work on a specific account, they could use that against you, or they could retaliate in other ways. Are you going to be able to handle that?"

"Yeah. Bare and I talked about how it's important that I react to what is actually happening and not what I fear might happen. So, I'll come out and we'll see what they do. I doubt they'll let me anywhere near Freedom Athletics afterward, but if so, I'll resign."

"You know you have my full support whatever you need."

"I know that. You'll come with me to the Christmas party and I'll introduce my partner to the partners."

"So we're partners now?"

"Boyfriends?" I offered.

"Fiancés?" Brady shot back.

My breath stuttered erratically. Brady was the one for me. I'd never regret making him mine, even if I wasn't sure about my job situation and I still had a lot of issues to work out with Bare. Maybe he'd be okay with a long engagement so I could go back to school and figure out what the hell I wanted to do with my life and how to be a better husband.

I didn't know what I was doing, and this was anything but planned, but what the hell? I took his hand, cleared my throat, and tried to calm my heart before it escaped my chest. But before I found the right words to tell him we should absolutely take the next step, he hauled me to the couch, pushed me onto my back, and crashed his lips to mine so hard our teeth clanked. His weight sank against me and we kissed until my lips felt bruised.

"Brady," I mumbled against him. "I haven't even asked you yet."

Brady rolled off of me, gasping from laughing so hard. His belly shook as he tried to get things under control. "We're not getting engaged tonight."

"But if you—"

"For the record, I was kidding. And I do want to, eventually, but I'm not in any hurry and, beautiful, we both have some serious baggage to offload. I'll tell you what—when the thought doesn't terrify you, let me know and we'll try this again." He tittered some more and hauled me up until I straddled his lap. He clasped his hands on my cheeks and kissed me again, gently. "God, I love that you were willing to do that for me."

My body stiffened when I realized I wasn't freaked out, I was excited, and a little disappointed he hadn't let me follow through on a romantic whim.

Concern swept over Brady's face. "What's wrong?"

"I'm not terrified of it. You're the one for me. I was thinking about figuring out what my next steps were and didn't know how soon you wanted to get married, but I want that with you."

Brady guffawed with a wild-eyed look of dismay. "Are you for real?"

"But you know, now that *you're* the one that freaked out, the next proposal is on you."

"Seriously," Brady choked on the word, turning his head to cough.

I delighted with the tables turned. "Are you going to have an asthma attack for each of our big moments?" I smirked.

Brady playfully flipped me off as he finished his coughing fit and composed himself.

"I want flowers and super-romantic, surprise me. And whatever you do, don't ask Adam for suggestions."

Brady chuckled, and I reached down to peel his shirt off him, smiling as he lifted his arms without hesitation. I was so rocking this boyfriend thing. I'd nailed that conversation.

"I'm getting so good at this. You better keep up." I combed my fingers over his chest before gripping his hips to pull myself closer and melded my mouth to his.

"It's not a competition," Brady deadpanned. "But for a one-and-done kind of guy, you're awfully cocky."

"Race you to the bedroom?" I asked, running my hands through his silky hair. There was an undeniable appeal in the way he let me freely touch him now, how he strained his neck to deepen the pressure, pulled me that much closer.

"Nah." Brady smiled, his full lips seeming eager to claim every inch of my skin. "We've got all night, let's pace ourselves."

Chapter Twenty-Three
Brady

"I want to stop at one more place," Josh said as he yanked me by the hand through the mall. He ducked into the store and beelined for the men's section before I could object. My shopping stamina had worn out an hour ago, but Josh still wasn't happy with his Christmas party outfit.

He held up two shirts over his chest. "Pale pink or red?" He bit his lip and openly admired the lighter one.

"Definitely the pink," I answered. "It will work nicely with your gray slacks. Plus, it coordinates better with me, I'm wearing my lavender shirt."

He fluttered from one rack to the next, picking up a fitted evergreen shirt with a small floral pattern. "This will be fantastic on you." He passed it to me, and I checked the price tag. "Josh, I have plenty of shirts." With his uncertain job situation, my brain had gone into savings mode.

"Please. Just try it on."

"Fine. Get me an extra-large though. This place runs small."

"And these." Josh flipped through some brown slim-fit chinos marked fifty percent off. "What size?"

"Not the brown."

When he challenged me with a questioning eyebrow, I explained, "I'll look like a tree."

He laughed and kept combing through the clearance rack, but I was all about getting what we needed and getting out of the store as quick as possible. "Fine. Hand me the black in a forty."

Josh beamed, and I let him have his triumph.

"Try the thirty-eights," he countered, slapping both pairs against my chest.

I rolled my eyes but took them. My work pants were growing a little looser. Josh's recent surge of optimism must be contagious.

I followed Josh around for another half hour as he loaded up his arms with his clothes and mine.

"Josh, enough. Let's try these on, please." I gripped his waist and steered him toward the dressing area.

My face went stoic at the sight of a busty blonde dressing room attendant. I muttered, "Unbelievable," and shook my head, snickering.

"Hi. How many pieces?"

I flipped through the hangers in Josh's arms. "Fifteen."

"Oh, sorry, the limit is six each," she said.

Josh stole a look at the name tag hanging off her shirt. "Misty, we have an important dinner tomorrow. Do you think you can—"

"Here." I handed over three of the dark-blue shirts he'd picked out for me. "Now we have six apiece."

"Good. I'll hold these shirts right here for you." She grabbed two tags with the number six and held them out with a smile.

I snatched the tags out of Misty's hands and hauled Josh into the handicap stall. "Get undressed," I said, but then began removing his clothes for him.

"Brady," he moaned as I pushed him against the wall with my palm and kissed him, my other hand yanking at his belt buckle. "What are you doing?"

"Shh. You don't want Misty to hear us." I sunk to my knees and worked his long cock free of its confines. Bracing my hands on his thighs, I licked along the flesh jutting up between Josh's muscular legs. Let's hear it for leg day.

Josh gasped and balled the sleeve of the evergreen shirt into his mouth as the back of my throat closed around him. I swallowed a few times and slid the tip of my finger into his ass. A mumbled cry accompanied a pulse in the vein flattened against my tongue. Josh's hand flew to my hair, pulling me toward him and holding me there. Strong fingertips pressed on my scalp while his release flooded my mouth.

After, I stood, wiped my mouth with the back of my hands, and dropped my jeans. Tugging the black pants from the pile, I purposefully did not check to see if I'd snagged the size thirty-eight or forty before sliding them on.

"Well," I exclaimed. "They're a little snug in the thighs, but they fit." I picked up the other pair and checked the tag. "Guess I'm in a thirty-eight now." I glanced at Josh, who, with his spent cock still out, was sitting on the small triangle wedge that served as a seat, looking a satisfying degree of relaxed. I leaned down to kiss the top of his head and quickly changed. "You ready to leave yet?"

My smirk shined a spotlight on my plan, and Josh guffawed. "No fair. You know I require a nap after coming," he whispered.

"Not my problem you have no stamina."

"But I need something for tomorrow. I have nothing to wear."

"Here." I tugged the pink shirt off the hanger and passed it to him. "I'm sure it's perfect." After helping him to his feet, I dragged off his shirt and helped him pull the pink one on. "It looks great."

He turned to the mirror. "I like it."

"Good. Give it to me, and I'll go pay while you get dressed."

When he went to undo the buttons, I kissed him again, and we were both laughing as he tried to focus on both tasks at the same time. I rocked back and swatted Josh's hand aside. "Let me do it. You take forever." When we finished, I freed the hanger from the pile and replaced the shirt, grabbed my pants, snuck out of the dressing room, and . . . ran straight into Misty.

"Oh, I was just coming to check on your friend. Where did he go?" Misty bent down, checking for feet under the adjacent stalls.

"Thanks, but he's been taken care of."

Josh choked on his laughter. I tried my best to move over and pretend that she hadn't heard him, but Misty's eyes went every bit as wide as I remembered, and her jaw dropped. "Were you in there with him?" She pointed.

I nodded, with a stupidly proud smile, I'm sure.

She moved beside me and rapped her knuckles on the dressing room door. "Let me know if you need anything, handsome."

"Thanks, Misty. I'm gay," Josh's voice shouted over the dressing room wall. "I mean great. I'm doing great."

Josh made a bunch of noise as he scrambled to get dressed. Finally, the door opened, and Misty took a step back. "And I have a boyfriend." Josh gestured to me.

I tucked my hand flat under my chin and batted my eyes at her.

"Will that be all?" She turned back to Josh, bad-ass sales bitch back in action.

Josh removed the clothes from my hands. "Yes. Just these." We followed her to the cash register, eyes straight ahead, afraid even a glance would cause us to surrender the tenuous hold we had on our laughter.

"Thanks, baby." Josh laid it on a little thick as I pulled the debit card out to pay. Once we merged accounts, we'd recognized that I'd be better at managing the household finances—Josh was a whiz with spreadsheets, but saving, budgeting, and couponing . . . not so much. Other than the day I calculated what he'd been spending a month in groceries, it'd been an uneventful transition. For a self-described control freak, Josh had surprisingly few issues with me taking over our finances. In fact, I thought he liked it, particularly once he decided he needed a total career change that had nothing to do with business and I'd showed him how my plan made it possible for him to go back to school.

We left the store, giggling as we walked hand and hand toward my car. Freshly washed as usual. I popped the trunk, and he slipped the bag into it before joining me.

"You nervous about tonight?" I asked. "I have visions of you storming out of this thing in a dramatic fashion."

"No, I'm good. Jennifer will be there, and she totally has my back. Bare and I worked out a whole strategy at my last session," Josh said. "It might get rough, but I want to give people time to adjust before assuming the worst. I'm not going to punt on the first down. Besides, I think I decided about school. I love training and motivating, but if I could help someone walk again or get rid of their pain, I think that would make me feel really good, you know?" I smiled and Josh gave a definitive nod, like all he needed to be sure was my approval. "I'm going to apply to the physical therapy program, and I can only start it in the fall, so hopefully I can stick it out six more months, but whatever. It's going to work out however it's supposed to work out."

I chuckled, shaking my head. "Fucking sports metaphors."

"It means—"

"I know what it means. I think you should hold the line, but I'm totally prepared to run interference for you. See, I can do it too."

Josh rolled his eyes. "You watch one football game and suddenly you're an expert."

"Nah, beautiful. I just want to impress your coworkers with my masc. sports lingo."

"If you stop now, I might let you score in my end zone when we get home," Josh said, laughing.

"Jokes on you, because that was all I had," I said and pulled out of the mall. Josh turned on the radio, and I sang along. I wasn't about to perform a striptease or serenade him anytime soon, but after our talk, letting go of my insecurities was a top priority. I was hopeful there was some "mile six" out there waiting for me in that regard, and at some point, it would become easier to keep going than to stop, but in the meantime, Josh's approving smile was the only motivation I needed.

Josh had resumed his role as my biggest cheerleader and personal trainer. He even canceled his membership at Canal Street and joined my gym so we could exercise together.

The list of things I didn't know was daunting. Would my weight loss journey end with a bang or a whimper? How would Josh's coworkers react? Would Josh like his career change? Would I continue working for Matt? When would I feel ready to propose? Would we have kids someday?

In some ways, my future seemed as unwritten as the day I first walked into Room 230 at Loman Hall.

The only thing I knew was that whatever the future had in store for us, Josh and I would be carrying a fuck-ton less baggage as we traveled that road together.

Dear Reader,

Thank you for reading Logan Meredith's *The Weight We Carry*!

We know your time is precious and you have many, many entertainment options, so it means a lot that you've chosen to spend your time reading. We really hope you enjoyed it.

We'd be honored if you'd consider posting a review—good or bad—on sites like **Amazon, Barnes & Noble, Kobo, Goodreads, Twitter, Facebook, Tumblr,** and your blog or website. We'd also be honored if you told your friends and family about this book. Word of mouth is a book's lifeblood!

For more information on upcoming releases, author interviews, blog tours, contests, giveaways, and more, please sign up for our weekly, spam-free newsletter and visit us around the web:

Newsletter: riptidepublishing.com/newsletter
Twitter: twitter.com/RiptideBooks
Facebook: facebook.com/RiptidePublishing
Goodreads: tinyurl.com/RiptideOnGoodreads
Tumblr: riptidepublishing.tumblr.com

Thank you so much for Reading the Rainbow!

RiptidePublishing.com

RIPTIDE PUBLISHING

Acknowledgments

Thanks to Jenn S. for her early encouragement and thoughtful suggestions in the writing of this book. I hope you keep writing Cor and Mandy's story.

Also by Logan Meredith

Heartland series
Healed Hearts, Heartland Book 1
Expanded Hearts, Heartland Book 2
Open Hearts, Heartland Book 3

Stand-alones
Crossroads
The Story of Us

About the Author

Logan Meredith began writing as a teenager when beautiful boys started keeping her company at night. Unfortunately, the voices she heard were imaginary, and their conversations resulted in horrible insomnia. They only let her sleep when she started typing their words down. Thankfully, being awkward as hell and a head taller than anyone else in school afforded plenty of spare time for writing.

At first, she tried to make them play with characters from her favorite television series or books. She found her lost tribe with a ravenous, crazy group of fan fiction lovers online and started sharing her stories. Then something amazing happened: new characters arrived and demanded their own stories. Only they wanted their own world to play in, and they wanted to find their true loves. So between her day job and making time for her family, she tries to keep up with the requirements of her beautiful men for their happily-ever-afters.

A native of San Antonio, Texas, and a graduate of the University of Texas at San Antonio, Logan is an accomplished cross-country mover having honed her skills bouncing between five states. She currently resides in Houston, Texas. In addition to writing, she spends her time reading and rereading her favorite books, cheering for the San Antonio Spurs, playing Words with Friends, and procrastinating pretty much everything else.

She is a proud member of the LGBTQA community and vocal advocate for mental health awareness, suicide prevention, and equality campaigns.

Logan welcomes the chance to interact with readers.
Twitter: @ll_meredith

Enjoy more stories like *The Weight We Carry* at RiptidePublishing.com!

Hard Truths

He can't have the family he wants, but he may get the love he deserves.

ISBN: 978-1-62649-847-1

Relationship Material

It's not always possible to meet in the middle.

ISBN: 978-1-62649-902-7

Made in the USA
Columbia, SC
09 November 2023